I0675437

ROMULUS

Innerworld Affairs Series

Book One

Marilyn Campbell

Without limiting the rights under copyright(s) reserved below, no part of this publication may be reproduced, stored in or introduced into a retrieval system, or transmitted, in any form, or by any means (electronic, mechanical, photocopying, recording, or otherwise) without the prior permission of the publisher and the copyright owner.

This is a work of fiction. Names, characters, places, and incidents either are the product of the author's imagination or are used fictitiously, and any resemblance to actual persons, living or dead, business establishments, events or locales is entirely coincidental.

The scanning, uploading, and distributing of this book via the internet or via any other means without the permission of the publisher and copyright owner is illegal and punishable by law. Please purchase only authorized copies, and do not participate in or encourage piracy of copyrighted materials. Your support of the author's rights is appreciated.

Copyright © 2014 by Marilyn Campbell. All rights reserved.

Cover and Book design by eBook Prep
www.ebookprep.com

September, 2014
ISBN: 978-1-61417-627-5

ePublishing Works!
www.epublishingworks.com

REVIEWS & ACCOLADES

"First of a landmark series…provocative…will fascinate and charm romance fans."
~*Romantic Times*

"The fiery passion will singe your heart…You will be mesmerized by this exceptional reading adventure!"
~*Rendezvous*

"Beautifully written, wonderfully imaginative…a guaranteed page turner!"
~*Margaret Chittendon*

PART I

Innerworld

CHAPTER 1

Dan Halsey considered himself a successful young man. He valued his freedom and loved the ocean, good food and pretty women, and as first mate on The Baronette, he had it all. No expense had been spared when they built this honey, he thought as he briefly scanned the state-of-the-art equipment on the bridge. The NAVSTAR global positioning system was a virtual guarantee against getting lost at sea.

Working this particular charter had only taken him from Fort Lauderdale, the private fishing charter's point of origin, to Walker's Cay in the Bahamas. But two hot babes were along for the ride which meant, for once, he might not have to compete with Nick.

The balmy October night added to the perfection that was his life. The only thing missing was a cold beer. He headed for the spacious lounge to fix that, toasted his suntanned face in the mirror behind the bar then headed downstairs. Strolling the length of the polished teakwood deck, he noticed only one light on inside the marina's small clubhouse. Even the Customs Office of this isolated port was closed by the time they had tied up.

At the end of the dock, two men reeled in their lines and packed up their tackle box. Real fishermen didn't sleep if the fish were biting, Dan thought, smiling as he watched the guys casually make their way back along the wooden pier that ran in front of The Baronette.

Dan leaned over the brass railing. "Catch anything tonight?" The men halted in front of the gangway, but the ship's shadow kept Dan from seeing them clearly.

The taller man set down the ice chest he was carrying and called back in a voice laced with a Spanish accent. "Got several good-sized snapper using live shrimp. We did a little better last night." As he talked, he leaned over and raised the lid on the chest. "Take a look at these last two we hauled in." Both fishermen reached in to prove his claim.

The men's arms raised. Expecting to see fish, Dan's mind refused to register what his eyes actually perceived. In a heartbeat, the imagined fish took the form of two automatic weapons. Dan knew he should run, knew he should drop for cover, but he froze.

Victor Rodriguez opened his mouth to order the man on duty to cooperate, but the short bark of José's silenced gun cut Victor off. A deadly missile instantly pierced the mate's forehead, hurling his body backward onto the deck.

Victor's shocked expression turned to fury as he turned on José. "*Te dije que no! Pendijo.*" Jerking his head, he quickly surveyed the dock area, assured himself that no one was about then stormed the gangway, leaving José to struggle with their fishing gear.

Victor's anger was not aroused because of the messy murder but because his order to keep everyone on board alive had been ignored. He had intended to force the captain's assistance by threatening the lives of the others on board. He knew from Pete that the captain's wife was on board as the cook. Besides, the crew and the guests would be needed for the upcoming manual labor.

As soon as José joined him on deck, Victor spat out his orders in a Spanish slang he knew the man would understand. "First, stash the body in the cargo hold. We'll dump it after we're out to sea. Second, clean up the mess you made. I can't afford to have anybody slipping and breaking their neck. Third, plant the explosives exactly like on the picture I gave you. Every trace of this yacht and the people on it has to disappear. And then, stand guard at the end of the companionway, just in case any of our *guests* decide to leave their cabins before morning."

Victor spun away from José and took the stairs to the bridge two at a time. Pressing the button labeled Engine Room, he spoke one word into the intercom. "Pete."

A moment later, a sleepy voice responded, "Yeah?"

"It's a go."

Victor's background in seamanship had prepared him for this score. Once he'd recruited Pete, learned the layout of the yacht and obtained the list of passengers and crew, he was ready to put his grand plan into action. Finally, all his patience and hard work would be rewarded.

Although he could feel the engines start to purr, he was confident none of the others on board would detect any change over the steady hum of the generators. They were all in a deep sleep by now, helped along by alcohol or sheer exhaustion.

He eased The Baronette out of the slip and headed for the open sea. No one had seen the yacht pull in, nor now witnessed her smooth departure. Since Pete had destroyed the float plan, Victor also knew that no one at the marina had ever expected them.

Lady Luck was riding with Victor…as usual.

The stateroom door crashed against the wall and Aster Mackenzie bolted upright in bed. Through sleep-blurred eyes, she saw a Neanderthal of a man enter her room. His hooded black eyes narrowed as he appraised her. She scooted to the corner of the bed against the wall but the man's hand roughly grabbed her ankle and yanked her toward him. He jerked her up, nearly dislocating her shoulder, and pressed the cold metal of a gun to her head.

Aster whimpered in a mixture of pain and fright. "What do you want?"

The silent man pushed her toward the door and, as Aster stumbled into the hall, the door to the adjacent stateroom opened.

"What the fuck…" Dressed in an oversized t-shirt with Minnie Mouse on the front and knuckling her eyes, Cherry Cochran looked like a little girl.

"Harold!" Cherry yelled and turned to dash back into her room. But the cave man pointed his weapon at her and grunted. A moment later her elderly companion joined them in his robe and slippers. He kept silent and obeyed the man's pantomimed orders to head for the bridge.

The three were prodded into the lounge where the other guests and the crew were already gathered. A tall, lanky stranger swaggered toward them and Aster thought he looked Latin, like the man who had dragged her from her cabin, only more evolved. In fact, he looked quite civilized. He grinned, displaying a diamond inset in his upper right incisor. The thin black line of hair over his lip curved upward as his smile broadened.

"Well, well, what have we here?"

Aster held her breath as the man circled her and Cherry with a lascivious leer that cut through the surface civility.

"My name is Victor and your escort is José. He speaks no English but his comprehension of body language is excellent."

Victor's body responded to the pleasant surprise of the two women before him. He had been under the impression that the entire group was senior citizens, like the man footing the bill for the charter. His eyes scanned the petite brunette clinging to the arm of one of the old guys. He wondered if the boyish haircut and freckles on her nose were indicative of her innocence or if she had a bonfire hidden under that childish t-shirt. The fearless sparkle in her big brown eyes gave her true nature away.

But it was the tall one who made his blood sing. The wild tangle of long, silver hair topped off the body of a real woman. She met his stare, her dark eyes only inches below his. Ah, this one was afraid but she was also cold as ice. He would see her thaw before this trip ended. He purposely ogled her full breasts trembling beneath her satiny pajamas.

"Now, I have introduced myself to you. I would appreciate a like courtesy."

"Courtesy?" Aster demanded, suddenly finding her voice. "You're holding a gun on us! What's this all about? Drugs?" she sneered at the man but his husky laugh swept through her like a freezing wind.

Victor stepped back and smiled at Cherry. "Perhaps you have better manners. Your names?"

Cherry frowned then nodded at her escort. "This is Harold Leonard, I'm Cherry Cochran and the *lady* you're drooling over is Aster Mackenzie."

Victor's eyes flashed when he heard the last name

and looked at Aster again, this time as though something tugged at his memory. He gave José a lengthy order in Spanish and a moment later Cherry and Aster were nudged onto two bar stools and tied together back to back. Harold was lashed to a separate stool next to Cherry.

The young ship's steward, Nick Valentino, and the host of this quiet fishing holiday, Paul Feinstein, were secured a few feet away in the same manner as the two women. When Aster looked directly at Nick, he lowered his eyes, clearly embarrassed by his helplessness. She could see he realized this was one situation where his handsome face and tight butt weren't going to earn him any special consideration.

So what useful assets did she possess to help them out of this situation? A genius IQ, a highly developed sense of organization and a healthy dose of intuition, all of which enabled her to critique a situation and to make an accurate judgment call faster than most of her colleagues. She just needed to calm down enough to think.

"*Senora?*" Victor's polite voice broke into the silent tension of the room as he addressed Betty Basiglio, Captain Johnny's wife. "José will accompany you and Mrs. Feinstein to the galley to prepare breakfast. Keep it simple, if you please."

Like the two older women, the captain had not been tied up but was well-guarded nonetheless.

Victor stationed himself to one side of the bridge, where he could watch Captain Johnny at the helm and keep an eye on all the captives. He reached into his jacket pocket and pulled out a plastic bag filled with white powder. He tucked his gun securely under the arm holding the bag and used his free hand to extract a stiletto from the inside of his calf-high cowboy boot. With an efficiency borne of a long-time habit, he dipped the knife's tip into the bag and brought out a bit of the substance. Carefully, he lifted it to his nose and, with the index finger of his hand holding the bag, he closed off one nostril and snorted the powder deeply into the other. His features relaxed almost immediately and his eyes closed for a second as he enjoyed his self-induced euphoria.

Aster cringed. Victor had appeared quite self-assured when he had first introduced himself, now he might believe he was invincible. She knew what he was feeling, not that she had ever tried it. But her fiancé, Dennis Waverly, had told her in great detail how cocaine affected a user.

Dennis had been an undercover narcotics detective for the San Francisco Police Department long before Aster had met him. When they got engaged a year after they started dating, he promised he would transfer to a safer department. A month later he was dead—shot in the back of the head at close range. Her heart contracted at the memory of that day, six months ago, when she got the call. If Dennis were here, he'd know what to do to save them. He certainly wouldn't sit here reminiscing or feeling sorry for himself.

Victor returned his stash to his pocket but continued to play with his knife in his left hand after he transferred his gun back to his other hand. As if he had heard Aster's thoughts about him, he strode across the room and confronted her. "I know you. I don't remember why yet, but I will." He studied her face intently then slipped the stiletto beneath her hair.

Aster felt the blade touch her throat as he lifted her hair away from her neck. As a fear-inducing technique, it was quite effective. "What do you intend to do with us?" she dared in a voice just above a whisper.

Victor snorted at her attempt to sound courageous.

"I had that worked out before I saw you, *lady*. Now I wonder what you'd do to save your pretty neck."

Aster stared at him, unblinking. Years of practice at masking her fears took control.

"I don't frighten you? Then perhaps watching someone else suffer would be more persuasive?" His gun hand whipped up to press against Cherry's cheek.

"Stop it!" Aster shouted. She took a deep breath as he returned his attention to her and lowered both his weapons. "I'll…cooperate. Just leave everyone else alone."

"Is that so?" Victor's sneer was solidly in place. "But I can't even see what I'm bargaining for."

Aster bit her lower lip and turned her head away from him, only to be faced with their reflection in the mirror behind the bar. With the edge of his knife, he slowly sliced through the threads that held the top three buttons on her pajama top.

"Leave her alone, you bastard!" Nick demanded.

Victor's hand swung through the short space between Aster and Nick. Blood trickled down Nick's throat from the tiny puncture the knife pricked in his chin.

In a heartbeat, the captain pushed his heavy-set form between Nick and Victor. "Is this the way you honor your promises? You said no one else would be hurt if I assisted you with the navigating. Either you keep your hands off my passengers and crew," he gritted out between clenched teeth, "or you can make it the rest of the way by yourself."

The seconds ticked by as Victor and Captain Johnny glared at each other. Victor backed off with a shrug.

"You are quite right, *Capitan*. I'm afraid the sight of this beautiful flower caused me to forget myself. I promised no one would be harmed and I intend to keep that promise, as long as you continue to provide me with your services." He paused and straightened his shoulders. "However, all of you should be warned. I will not tolerate any insolence or attempts at mutiny. If you cooperate, you will survive our departure from this vessel when our business transaction is completed."

Reluctantly, the captain returned to the helm as Victor resumed his previous post and slid the knife back into his boot.

Aster let out a ragged breath. Now she knew why they were still alive. Victor needed the captain's abilities. Her intuition said there was more to it but for now, that was enough. Suddenly in her mind she heard a replay of the captain's words, "No one else would be hurt." Who had been hurt already? Who was missing?

All the guests were accounted for so that left only the crew, two of whom were missing—the first mate and the engineer. The tragic answer popped into her head—Dan, the nice-looking man she'd met when they boarded. The first mate had the night watch. The engineer had surfaced only briefly yesterday and she was fairly certain his vital responsibilities were enough to keep him alive. But Victor had separated him from the others. There would be no help from the engineer. Besides, when she had seen him, he had looked rather sickly, with very pasty skin and long, stringy hair.

She glanced at the captain. He and his wife could be counted on. Both were in their fifties and somewhat overweight, but they seemed strong, energetic and levelheaded. Their mutual contentment was evident to anyone with eyes. Johnny would be fiercely protective if Betty were in danger.

Nick could be useful, if he kept his temper under control. She just hoped there was a brain inside that pretty Italian head.

The Feinsteins were kindhearted sweeties and lavishly generous with their wealth, but those qualities weren't enough to counter their advanced years or the precarious state of Sheila's health.

Harold's age was not as detrimental as his mouth. If he started griping, Victor might be tempted to shoot them all to shut him up. She never understood how Cherry could tolerate his company. A cruise around the world couldn't entice Aster to sleep in the same bed with that man. But, in all fairness, Aster had always been able to afford the kind of things Cherry desired. If only she could have purchased the kind of things Cherry already had.

There was no uncertainty about her and Cherry's abilities. The two of them would do whatever they had to do to help the others survive.

Betty and Sheila returned carrying large trays laden with coffee-service items. José followed them with his pistol in one hand and a large, napkin-covered basket in the other. In spite of the circumstances, Aster's senses responded to the smell of warm bread and fresh coffee.

Victor inspected the fare as the two women arranged it on a table. "To show you I regret my momentary lapse of chivalry, I will have José untie all of you to enjoy your breakfast." His words were apologetic but his stony gaze held a clear warning that they would be watched closely.

While José loosened their bonds, Victor spoke into the intercom. "Pete." When there was no response after a few minutes, he tried again. "Pete, are you there? Pick up." Still no answer.

Victor slammed his fist against the speaker and barked at José. Aster listened intently to his instructions. Her Spanish lessons hadn't prepared her for their lightning-fast, garbled communication but she deduced that the engineer was an accomplice and José was to find him. A few minutes later, José's gravelly voice babbled excitedly through the intercom.

It was not necessary to understand the language to see that Victor was hearing disturbing news. Aster turned her head and pretended to be fixing her coffee, her ears alerted to the conversation. Victor might reveal something important if he thought no one understood what they were saying.

"Slow down. I cannot understand you. Where is Pete?"

"Dead…cold…needle…arm…What…"

"Stow his body with the other one and get back here. Now I will have to do his job too."

While they ate, Aster told Betty and Cherry as much of the conversation as she had understood and Betty confirmed Dan's death. Apparently, Victor was too macho to think three women could be plotting and allowed them to chat. They knew they might not get out of this alive unless they did something. Overpowering the two remaining hijackers was out of the question as long as they were awake and holding weapons.

A loud splash in the water outside diverted the women's attention. Victor rushed to an open window and leaned out. The others followed his lead.

Aster spotted Harold who had managed to sneak out of the lounge and get a raft into the water. But he apparently landed in the water himself when he tried to jump from the deck. His hands now clawed desperately at the sides of the small craft as he tried to climb in. Just as he managed to heave his upper body over the edge, heavy footsteps pounded along the deck below and Aster saw José. Taking only a split second to get his balance, José extended his machine pistol and released a long series of pops.

Everyone stared in horrified silence as Harold's bullet-riddled body collapsed over the edge of the life raft. Again José fired his weapon and the small rubber boat deflated. The surrounding water took on a murky reddish film as Harold's body sunk into the ocean.

She spotted one pointed fin which was joined by several more as sharks appeared from the deep. Agitated by the bloodied water, they ripped Harold's body to shreds in a frenzy of activity. Only a few scraps of rubber remained floating to attest to the macabre scene.

With both fists raised in the air, Cherry let out an anguished wail and threw herself at Victor. His eyes revealed his momentary panic in the face of a rebellion. He jerked his gun up and caught Cherry's shoulder and upper arm with a three-round blast. She gaped at the wounded limb hanging by her side then slumped to the floor.

Aster rushed to Cherry's side. The sight of blood and splintered bone meshed with mutilated flesh made her gag on the bile rising in her throat but the pain visible in Cherry's eyes brought her to her senses. Aster looked around frantically for something she could use as a tourniquet and settled for the length of rough rope that had previously bound them. As she tightened the knot above the wound, a hard tap on the back of her head made her turn to face Victor's gun. It was so close she felt the heat from its barrel. She should have been terrified into speechlessness but revulsion overcame her fear.

"What kind of animal are you?"

"Watch your mouth, bitch. You can easily be next. Get over there so José can tie you up with the others."

Aster's body vibrated with fury. "I'm not leaving

Cherry. If you want me to move, you'll have to shoot me too."

Victor squeezed her cheeks in his hand and pushed his face close to hers. "Listen to me, bitch. You and I have some business of our own to attend to before this is over and if you think that will keep you from getting what she got, you better think again. I don't particularly care what condition you're in when I take what I want from you. Keep that in mind the next time you want to smart-mouth me."

He released her face with a shove and Aster quickly turned her back on him. She grasped Cherry's good wrist and located a weak pulse. The brunette's eyes were closed now and her face somewhat relaxed in unconsciousness. Aster could see Cherry's chest rising and falling very faintly but knew she was losing too much blood to hold on without medical attention. Time passed, but Aster refused to move. She stroked the other woman's hair, counted to three, stroked again then counted to three. Her body rocked back and forth in time with her counting until she blotted out everything but the numbers and the rocking. It had been some time since she had needed her mental escape routine.

The reduction in the boat's speed roused Aster from where she had fallen asleep next to Cherry, and she noticed that night had fallen.

"What did you slow down for?" Victor demanded of the captain.

"Look around us. We'll tear up the engines if we try to race through that. Anyway we're almost at your coordinates."

A full moon and a clear, star-filled sky dimly lit the interior of the lounge. Slowly, sleeping forms moved and stretched, perhaps awakened by the same thing Aster had sensed. Cherry's limp hand felt cold in hers, but it was not yet rigid. Reassuring herself that her friend was still alive, she rose. Her legs throbbed as the blood pumped feeling back into them.

"How is she?" Betty asked.

"Alive. But I don't think she's been conscious for a while." Aster gave Cherry another glance before turning to Betty. "What's going on now?"

"Come take a look outside."

They had cruised right into a solid green mass of seaweed. The breeze had completely disappeared and the air had changed as well, heavy now, so that it was impossible to take a deep breath. She looked questioningly at Betty.

"We're in the Sargasso Sea. People often include it as part of the Bermuda Triangle mystery but it's only very thick seaweed. Johnny and I usually try to avoid the area if possible." Betty lowered her voice to a whisper. "I overheard Victor talking to someone called Madre Uno over the radio. He told Johnny packages had been dropped for us to pick up."

The ship plowed slowly through the dark green field then José's shout announced the end of the trail. Thousands of brown plastic bags tied to blocks of wood floated on top of the plants.

Victor ordered everyone to go below as Captain Johnny reduced speed and the ship drifted to a stop.

After a quick glimpse at Cherry's still features, Aster went down onto the deck with the others. José hauled in one of the packages with a fishing net while Victor kept his gun pointed at them and issued his directions.

"José and you three men will bring the packages in using the nets. The women will start stacking them along the companionway. Now, move it! We want to be out of here before dawn."

Victor's eyes were bleary and the gun shook slightly

in his grip. Aster imagined him passing out. With all of them moving around freely, surely it would be possible to push José overboard before he could shoot anyone. With renewed hope, she whispered her plan to Betty and found her companions had been thinking the same thing.

The task of loading the boat was monumental. Aster watched as the men's arms strained under the effort of lifting the packages out of the tangle of seaweed. As she placed one of the packages on top of another, perspiration trickled down her face and made her pajamas cling to her body. Package after package was carried from the nets to the growing stacks on deck and Aster realized that breathing itself had become hard labor.

Sheila sank down on the deck and pressed her hands to her temples. Paul slid down onto the deck where he had been working, too weak to move to Sheila's side.

Victor lifted his gun to threaten them again, but his arm drooped back down. The effort seemed to have drained him even more and he leaned heavily against the railing.

Aster hesitated, waiting for him to fall. A surge of adrenaline filled her with renewed energy. Betty stood in readiness as well.

Victor must have sensed the sudden tension around him and recovered slightly. "Okay, you two take a few minutes break and then start separating all the bags from the wood. That shouldn't be too strenuous for you."

Aster noted that they were close to completion when the first hints of dawn appeared. But by this time, even the younger members of the group were barely moving. She hadn't noticed anything unusual about the ship until Victor called it to Johnny's attention.

"Captain, I think the engine has stalled. I can't hear

the generator, either. Go up to the bridge and get her started again. No funny business or you know what will happen to your wife."

The captain grunted with disgust as he hauled in his last package and dragged himself up to the bridge. A few minutes later he reappeared, breathing hard.

"There's no...power. Everything's...dead. I tried...to warn you..."

"What the fuck do you mean, no power? This craft is in excellent condition and has all sorts of backup systems."

Aster groaned. She was not worried about the power, only that the problem had jolted Victor into wakefulness again.

Johnny drew in a shallow breath. "If you don't believe me, go check yourself!"

Victor put José in charge and hurried to the engine room. When he finally returned, his confusion was evident. "There didn't seem to be anything wrong in the engine room, so I went back up to the bridge. I don't understand it. The compass is spinning around, crazy-like, first in one direction then the other. NAVSTAR shows no reading at all, as if this ship isn't even here. It must be some kind of magnetic field. It'll pass. Just finish up and be ready to take off as soon as we get power back."

By now the sun should have risen. The sky should have had at least a tinge of pink and baby-blue but a dark cloud blocked it out. It *was* getting lighter, but not from the sky. Gradually, Aster realized the rapidly brightening light was coming from around and beneath them, up through the seaweed. It was eerie and fascinating at the same time.

To her further bewilderment, a bluish-green fog began rolling in on them. Suddenly an odd tingling sensation raced through her body, as if she had been plugged into an electrical socket. She spun around and discovered the entire ship was now enveloped by the peculiar haze.

Johnny's temper finally erupted. "Victor, you stupid son-of-a-bitch! Now you and your precious cargo can go to hell together!"

With a savage growl, the captain lunged at Victor, but he had given him too much warning. Victor fired into the other man's chest before he could close the distance between them. Blood gushed from the captain's heart. Red matter exploded out of his back where the bullet exited. Aster was so close her face stung where Johnny's blood pelted her. The captain remained upright for several seconds beating then collapsed on the deck.

Captain Johnny's murder pushed the others into action. Nick and Paul jumped José, knocking his gun into the water. Aster and Betty flew at Victor before he could fire again. The attack succeeded in momentarily stunning him but he maintained a grip on his weapon. The women struggled futilely against his greater strength. Just as he managed to turn the gun toward Aster's head, a deafening roar of rushing water distracted him.

The next instant a powerful gust of wind knocked Aster off her feet and blew her across the deck. Struggling against the force of the wind, she crawled back to Betty, huddled beneath the side rail.

Anything not permanently secured took flight around them. A small skiff was ripped from its mooring cables and flung into the fog, as if by some enormous, unseen hand. The loose bundles they had labored so hard to stack simply vanished in the swirling mist. Was it a hurricane? A sea tornado? A deck chair soared by and struck Victor in the head. As his body slid across the deck leaving a trail of blood,

Aster hoped he was dead. In a flash, his body and the captain's levitated inside a ferocious wind tunnel and disappeared.

Aster could no longer see any of her companions and prayed they had found better shelter than she and Betty had.

The roar grew louder and louder, but the wind suddenly died down. Using the railing as a lever, Aster pulled herself up to peer over the side. An unbroken wall of blue-white frothing water completely surrounded the ship. It had no beginning and no end. The gigantic fountain extended as far as she could see in every direction, shooting straight up to the darkened sky. She slumped back down and accepted Betty's embrace.

She mumbled desperate prayers but was convinced they would go unanswered. The ship began to move, to turn. She was overcome by nausea and a wretched vertigo. The yacht spun faster and faster within the circle of wild water, like a Tilt-a-Whirl at a carnival, pulling her out of Betty's arms. Then the centrifugal force pinned her firmly against the side of the ship.

With superhuman effort Aster managed to move her head. She cried in horror as Betty's face was pulled back tighter and tighter until it resembled a skeleton mask. Blood oozed from her flared nostrils and her eyeballs collapsed under their lids.

Aster lost her sight but not her hearing. Metal screeched against metal. Some unspeakable power was wrenching the ship in half. Soundlessly, she screamed in pain and terror as the ear-splitting noise obliterated her sanity.

CHAPTER 2

Romulus touched the screen of the vidcom embedded in the desktop and the monitor shifted to an upright position. "Operation Palomar, confidential data file, text only." A flicker of light scanned his retina for authorization and the requested material appeared on the monitor.

As with everything that had crossed his desk in the past week, he was looking for a flaw, an oversight, something to explain this nagging feeling. His nerves were on edge, a highly unusual state for him, and he was certain it was because he had missed an important fact that only his subconscious had picked up. He reviewed the facts on Operation Palomar.

Reports from Innerworld's Stellar Monitor Control were normally repetitious observations of the positions and conditions of the planets in and around Earth's solar system. But two weeks ago, an SMC technician had recorded a shift in Jupiter's gravitational pull against the sun. It had caused a realignment of bodies in the asteroid belt between Jupiter and Mars and several asteroids had altered their individual orbits entirely.

Many asteroids' orbits were normally irregular and might occasionally cross Earth's path but were rarely a matter of concern. This time, however, one particular asteroid—actually a planetoid since it measured almost two hundred miles across—was heading directly toward Earth. From its current position and speed, its collision with Earth would occur in just over a year.

As a respected member of Earth's scientific community, Innerworld's Emissary K66's assignment was to make sure his Terran colleagues picked up the shift and were proceeding properly with all due haste. K66 was in a position to help the Terrans prevent global destruction without any overt assistance from Innerworld or their home planet, Norona. The Ruling Tribunal's directive of noninterference would not be disobeyed.

But the Terrans definitely needed that assistance, Romulus thought grimly to himself. Earth's own experts disagreed on whether to explode or attempt to deflect the planetoid. If they decided to destroy it, a fragment might ricochet at an even greater speed and still hit Earth. If that fragment were as big as ten miles in diameter, the resulting earthquakes, tidal waves and pollutants could destroy all life on the surface and Innerworld could be sealed off. If the planetoid was not deflected at all, it would knock Earth out of its orbit and destroy Innerworld as well. They would have no choice but to evacuate.

The most efficient method would be to implant rockets in strategic locations on the planetoid. When detonated, the blast would change the planetoid's orbit again, redirecting it into the sun, where it would burn up.

The problem was the timing. It was essential that the planetoid be diverted within a precise area of space. If several of Earth's governments pooled their resources, they would have a sufficient number of space shuttles and firepower to do the job. Given the limited speed of their ships, however, even if they launched tomorrow, they would not make the rendezvous point in time.

Emissary K66 was responsible for handling that problem also. He would have to feed the knowledge of how to achieve the necessary speed to the right Terran scientist.

But Romulus knew there was no reason for concern. The solution was simple and the situation would not become critical for another six weeks.

He requested an intermediate update then called for his assistant, Tarla. He needed a powerful energy drainer.

Tarla leisurely chose a seat in the empty gallery. When word got out that Romulus was playing, the Arena benches would be jammed. He was respected as Chief Administrator of Car-Tem Province, but his outstanding skill in the games was what roused the fans.

To her right, at the far end of the field, a giant black stallion pawed the dirt as its rider mounted. What fantastic luck! An hour ago when Tarla had called the Arena for an appointment for Rom, she had used his name to insist on a human opponent for the games, but she had never expected it would be the infamous Black Knight. Rumor had it the mystery man was actually a trainer who only accepted the most adept students and refused to play in the games for fear his superior skill might result in injury to his opponent.

She could imagine Rom's immense pleasure when he discovered who he would be fighting. She knew better than anyone how badly he needed to burn off some excess energy. For the last several weeks he had been uncharacteristically nervous and impatient.

Thank the heavens, the official notification of his nomination had arrived today. In spite of being half the age of the current Governor of the Innerworld colony, Rom was obviously the best qualified of all the candidates nominated for the governorship. Tarla had expected the news to delight as well as calm him. Instead, he had gotten worse.

The Arena games excited her as much as they did her boss. After a millennium of social and cultural refinement, the primitive man still lingered deep inside Innerworld's occupants. Since their laws prohibited violence, they had been forced to create outlets for their unreleased aggression.

Rom appeared from the left, nodding slightly when the crowd applauded enthusiastically. Tarla smirked when she glanced around at the number of people filling the stands.

Even covered from head to toe, Romulus presented a formidable figure. His paper-thin silver armor, helm, boots and gauntlets fit his tall, muscular frame like a second skin. A navy-blue tunic hung from his broad shoulders to just below the protective codpiece. He was the Blue Knight.

Rom swung his body onto a white Arabian as large and anxious as the black. Modern technology had created the men's armor but the lances were replicas from ancient times.

When the first game began, the men ran their horses at full gallop toward the center of the field where they lanced a ring balanced on a post.

In the second contest the knights hurled their lances at a small target while flying by on their well-trained steeds. The scoreboard confirmed that neither game had offered the men much of a challenge. Black and

Blue each had twelve, the maximum points possible.

Tarla's excited cheers blended in with the noise of the crowd, as the time for real battle arrived. The warriors exchanged their pointed lances for blunt-ended ones and shields while the referees lined up the railings for tilting. The contestants had to attempt to unseat their opponent as they raced past each other in separate lists. If both men were still mounted after three passes, the fight would continue on foot with swords and shields.

The trumpet sounded and the mighty four-legged creatures performed as they had been trained. The breakneck speed alone would have upset an amateur rider, but neither of these men fell into that category. With their bodies pressing forward, they managed their horses with straining legs as they bore their weapons in front of them.

With a thunder of hooves, the figures came together. Metal clashed as shield struck against shield then parted again.

On the second try as the noble steeds charged ahead, both men brandished their lances threateningly. Romulus directed his toward his enemy's helm, above the shield. The Black Knight aimed straight for the center of his opponent's shield.

The Black Knight managed to swerve just in time to avoid the attack on him but still achieved his own goal of hitting Rom's shield. Upon impact, the wooden post of The Black Knight's lance splintered into pieces. The force of the blow was so powerful that Rom's horse reared dangerously backward and it took all his strength to right the animal again.

When both men managed to remain seated through a third pass, they dismounted and the fight continued. The game would end only when one man contacted the other's heart area.

The combatants circled each other with swords and shields raised. Somewhat shorter and leaner than the Blue Knight, Black had the advantage of greater agility. The two knights put on a show that Tarla was convinced the fans would be talking about for months.

Unexpectedly, Blue used his shield as a discus and flung it at Black's knees. Black succeeded in leaping high enough to avoid the twirling metal but lost his footing and fell backward into the dirt.

Seizing the opportunity, Blue whirled his sword toward Black's heart. The final trumpet blared, signaling that the sensor device in the armor had detected a direct hit. The score had been twenty to eighteen, in favor of the Black Knight. But the win went to the Blue Knight.

Wild cheering filled the Arena as the Black Knight knelt before the victor. Without revealing his identity, the defeated knight remounted his waiting black stallion and rode off the field.

The Blue Knight trotted his white mount around the playing area, waving to the crowd then headed for the locker room.

Tarla waited patiently in the lobby for her champion. She supposed more than a hot shower occupied him. Undoubtedly, there was a throng of backslappers hanging around and, being all male, and a political creature at that, Rom could not resist their attentions. A night like this could add a little more sparkle to his campaign, not that his image needed it, Tarla thought.

Rom exited the locker room between two laughing men and Tarla greeted him across the room with an understanding smile.

She couldn't help thinking how very handsome he was. His hair, damp from the shower, looked jet-black and she knew his changeable eyes would be dark green in his happiness. When she had first met him, his potently masculine appearance had knocked her off balance. After that, however, the attraction had fizzled. Though she liked him as a special friend and admired him as her boss, she had accepted that there simply was no spark to their relationship.

She admitted to herself that she had done everything she could to create some heat between them. The times she had maneuvered him into coupling with her lacked something she thought should be there. Not that there was anything really wrong with him. His sexual skills were perfect and he had easily brought her to a satisfying release, but she could do that much without him. She had realized his emotions were not involved in the physical activity and that had left her feeling very unsettled. He had even seemed surprised when she had encouraged their becoming physically intimate.

Tarla had quickly discovered her competition and knew there was no contesting it. His work was his mistress and his political aspirations the only future to which he gave any lingering thought. Rom was never rude or inconsiderate but at times she thought she was working for an android. Only on rare occasions, like tonight, did he relax enough to have any fun.

"Sorry it took me so long," he said when he finally extricated himself from the two men.

"That's okay. I figured you were fighting off your fans in the locker room."

"Actually those guys were only part of it. I also took a few minutes in the whirlpool. My body already feels like I was run over by a marsh bull."

"And you loved every minute of it. Listen, why not come back to my place? We could have dinner and if you're real nice, you might get a massage."

Romulus laughed and put an arm around her

shoulders. "You don't have to ask me twice. I don't think I could keep up this charade much longer."

Being pulled to his side as they walked made Tarla aware of the other thing that nagged at her when she was with Rom. She knew she was slender but she was hardly a stick, and at five foot three she had never thought of herself as a dwarf. Rom towered over her by a full twelve inches, making her feel like a miniature person. Some women liked feeling that way but, it only made her feel invisible.

By the time they entered her apartment, he had already recounted each detail of the game at least twice. "I cannot believe how great that guy was. He played the part of the Black Knight better than anyone I've ever seen, dirty tricks and all. I asked around but no one admitted to knowing which trainer he was. I guess it adds to the mystique of the game. One of these days I'll figure it out, though, and I'll take him on again. I think I should be ready in about two years." They both laughed heartily as he collapsed on the couch with an enormous groan.

Tarla gave her facilities manager their dinner instructions and, a few minutes later, set a platter of appetizers in front of her guest. "I heard from my father, the bigot, today."

"Shame on you, Tarla, talking about your esteemed parent that way!" Rom was teasing her. He knew well the extent of the man's prejudice.

"Oh, you know I love him, but he won't listen to reason where Terrans are concerned."

Rom winced automatically. Although the term literally referred to humans born on Earth's surface, it was too often used in a derogatory manner.

Tarla shrugged. "It seems a family of *them* moved in next door to him and he's absolutely beside himself. It might turn out to be the best thing that could have happened. If he would only take the time to get to know them, he might have to admit the fact that our colony is quite safe in spite of those *creatures* running around loose.

"I remember how shocked I was the first time one was pointed out to me. I had expected them to walk on all fours and have fangs that could tear my throat out if I crossed their path. I certainly never thought they would look the same as us. When I realized what nonsense he had spouted all those years, I was so angry I was ready to go out and join with one just to shake him up. I didn't care that it was against the law."

Shaking his head, Rom recalled how furious her father had been when Tarla went to work for him. That man still blamed him personally for the Terrans in Innerworld being integrated into society over twenty years ago.

Through the years Rom had worked closely with Governor Elissa in her efforts to grant equal rights to Terrans and they had been highly successful. Only a few restrictions now remained on the books. The prohibition against joining with a Terran had originally been passed to maintain the purity of Innerworld's superior race, but it was also a safeguard for the Earthlings. No one was certain a Terran could survive the joining ceremony.

"Sometimes I really feel sorry for them," Tarla continued. "No matter how hard they work to blend in, there are still a few people like my father who won't let them forget they're an inferior breed. Hey, how'd we manage to get so serious? You must be ready for that massage, my brave knight! I have a unit in my bed or you can have the good old manual method." She wiggled her fingers at him.

"You know I prefer the human touch. You don't

really have to do this, you know. However, I'll probably be eternally grateful if you do."

"As my lord wishes," Tarla said, curtsying.

Rom quickly shed his clothing before she could rescind her offer. Letting out a long moan, he lay stomach down on the soft carpeting. He stretched his muscles to their full length and relaxed.

Tarla admired his well-proportioned physique. His leisure activities of horseback riding and wielding broadswords definitely countered his penchant for vegetating behind a desk.

"L-four," she instructed the facilities manager and the lighting in the walls dimmed to a soft rosy glow. After warming a container of kolmander oil, she knelt beside her willing victim. Her straight, black, waist-length hair lightly brushed his bottom as she situated herself.

"Hey! That tickles," Rom jokingly complained. "Did you say this was mercy or mayhem?"

Tarla poured some of the soothing oil into her hands and began to work her magic, kneading his aching muscles.

"By drek, that's good. You could be a masseuse at the Indulgence Center."

She continued, working up one arm then moving around to concentrate on the other, purposely letting her hair tease him as she leaned over his vulnerable form.

"Seriously, Tarla, have you given any thought to what you want to do if I do get the governorship? I mean, you could come with me or stay and work for the new chief of this province. If you're interested in trying something different, though, I'd certainly be glad to help you in any way I can. You've been a good assistant, but you've never given me the impression that administrative work was your heart's desire!"

Tarla giggled. "You're right about that, of course. The problem is, I don't know what my 'heart's desire' really is. I keep thinking one day it will come up and hit me between the eyes and I'll run around screaming, This is it! I finally figured out what I've been waiting for! Until then I'll just stick by you, I guess."

"Hmmm, honest but a mite unflattering." Rom groaned again as her thumb found a particularly tender spot in his shoulder.

"Why don't you just be quiet and try to relax?" Tarla vigorously rubbed the oil into his back and pushed and pulled his muscles with greater strength than she appeared to have. She circled his buttocks with the palms of her hands and found his muscles no less developed there.

She kneaded his legs from his ankles up and back down, each time coming tantalizingly closer to the soft flesh slightly exposed between his thighs. With one long fingernail, she accidentally scraped that tender skin and smiled when he flinched. The power he had placed in her hands was too heady to resist teasing him. She knew he was becoming increasingly uncomfortable lying on his stomach.

"Turn over," she commanded softly.

His obedience revealed the full evidence of his discomfort. Although most of his body had relaxed under her skilled ministrations, he sported a glorious erection. Tenderly rolling his swollen sacs in one hand, she firmly grasped the shaft with the other, her fingers barely meeting around his width.

When she lowered her mouth to him and flicked her tongue over the tip, he gasped his acceptance of her offering. "Yes, please." And Tarla granted him an efficient, quick release.

Afterward, he stroked her hair and whispered, "Thank you."

Tarla sat still for a moment, feeling suddenly drained. It didn't take much thought to realize it wasn't due to the physical energy her efforts had required. It was his response. *Please. Thank you.* Those were appropriate words relating to a full-body massage. She knew what she had done was merely a physical service performed for a friend but he might have offered to return the favor. Since all she had to do was ask, his unintended neglect should not have annoyed her...but it did.

"Rom," she said as she got up and gathered his clothing for him. "I need you to go home now."

He was clearly confused.

She put her fingers to his lips. "I'm just tired. I'll see you in the morning." Tarla said no more while he dressed and walked to her door. Placing a light kiss on her forehead, he bade her good night.

She had told him she didn't know her heart's desire. That was not entirely true. She knew she wanted to be loved by a man whose hatred of another race did not blind him to her love, a man who would put her before everything else, including his work, a man who needed her touch as desperately as she needed his.

Once upon a time, that was not such an odd goal for a Noronian female.

Once upon a time, Noronians were as uncivilized as Terrans. But going back to that less complicated, more interesting era was not an option.

On his way home, Romulus analyzed the evening's events. The game had been his best ever, as well as the most strenuous. And without requesting a favor, Tarla had treated him very well and that took care of the other item on his agenda for getting rid of his frustration. So why didn't he feel better?

He could tell something was bothering Tarla also, but he had no idea what it might be and she didn't seem anxious to reveal it.

He should have been ready to drop into an exhausted sleep. Instead, he felt as though his nerve endings were on the outside of his skin. Maybe it was the knowledge that he was truly in the running for the governorship, that it was no longer wishful thinking. After all, he had devoted his entire life toward that goal and now it was within his grasp. He had every reason to be excited. After a moment, however, he rejected that explanation. He knew intimately the feeling of having achieved hard-sought goals and this was not quite it.

He suddenly recalled that he had felt like this once before.

When he was ten years old, for a week or more, he had roamed around aimlessly, scratching his oversensitive skin, agitated by every little thing. An old woman with white hair hanging to her ankles had arrived at his parents' farm. Her name was Mem, eldest of the Ruling Tribunal of Norona. She had stayed for two days, talking, questioning and debating with him. By the time she had left, he knew a future of leadership awaited him and his path had been neatly planned. His case of nerves had departed with her.

Though he was not precognizant, the answer hit him like a thunderclap. He had never put much effort into developing any of his extrasensory powers to their fullest potential but this message came through in spite of his limited abilities.

Something important was about to happen again.

The second he acknowledged that probability, a dream from the night before came back to him. He had been tangled in a silvery spider web and the more he struggled to get away, the more he was entrapped. He was aware that the web held danger, maybe even death, and yet it also had a seductive quality that made him want to burrow deeper into the snare. When he finally pushed the silver strands away, he was gazing into a clear midnight blue sky.

Rom tried to analyze the symbols of the dream but if they held a clue about what was coming, he had no idea what it was.

As he entered his residence, his facilities manager announced that a confidential transmission awaited his attention. Romulus sat down at his desk and opened the vidcom. A coded message appeared on the monitor for a brief moment before it unscrambled.

> *TO: Chief Administrator Romulus*
>
> *FROM: Outerworld Monitor Control*
>
> *RE: Operation Palomar Update*
>
> > *Neither Emissary K66 nor his mate have reported in for forty-eight hours. A tracker has been dispatched to locate them.*

He ran his hand through his hair. Drek! As OMC was responsible for keeping tabs on everyone and everything on Earth's surface, they had been instructed to notify Romulus immediately of any development concerning Operation Palomar. He had hoped their next communique would contain good news. Instead, the tracker assigned to the case would be the only one to welcome this advisory. As special enforcers with highly developed extrasensory powers, trackers rarely had the opportunity to use their abilities for anything more interesting than finding lost items.

Rom feared he now had the reason for his restless condition. Determined to get some sleep, he ordered himself to go to bed and put everything out of his mind until the morning. It seemed he had barely nodded off when he was jolted awake by the signal from his vidcom.

"Romulus here."

"This is Berrix at OMC. I'm afraid there was another accident in the Sargasso Sea this morning, sir."

"How many this time?"

"Five males, four females."

"I'll be there in an hour."

"Uh, sir, there's one other thing. There is clear evidence of violent personalities in two of the Terran males."

"Drek!" Romulus muttered, now certain that whatever surprise was coming his way, it wasn't going to make his life easier.

CHAPTER 3

What a nightmare, Aster thought, half-awake. She had never had one quite so vivid or so violent. As she moved her head, she felt as though cymbals were clashing inside her skull, but the heat of the sun on her body soothed her aching muscles. She really felt awful. Maybe she was coming down with something.

As tempted as she was to go back to sleep, something nagged at her, something about the sun. She forced her eyes open to see how the sun could be shining so brightly and so warmly inside her bedroom. The blinding light above her forced her eyes shut again and brought her completely awake. Okay, she told herself, open your eyes more slowly this time.

Through narrowed eyes, she looked at the wall beyond her feet. On a tall antique chest sat a delicately etched lead-crystal vase filled with lilac orchids. Not only were they her favorite flower, but her favorite color of that flower. She was certain neither the chest nor the flowers had been there when she went to bed last night.

Aster sat up and was nearly overcome with dizziness. Gradually, she absorbed the rest of her surroundings. Where was she? The high narrow bed was similar to a doctor's examining table and the warm sunshine was actually an enormous heat lamp in the ceiling.

Her mind reeled. Perhaps she was still dreaming. No, her surroundings were real! What was going on?

"I see you are awakening. That is very good. Please remain on the bed until you are fully recovered."

The words were barely a whisper behind her. Aster spun around too abruptly and almost fell off the narrow bed. In the corner of the room a small, middle-aged, Oriental woman sat very straight with her hands folded on her lap. She wore turquoise slacks and a matching short-sleeved turtleneck with the letters OONA sewn above her left breast.

"Where did you come from? Or better yet, where am I? How did I get here? You said *recovered*. Was I in an accident? Why don't I remember it?" Aster willed herself not to give in to the horrendous headache and queasiness. Then she realized what else was wrong. She wasn't wearing a stitch. Crossing her arms over her breasts, she demanded, "Where are my clothes?"

"All of your questions will be answered very soon," the woman said in her hushed voice. "My name is Oona. I have been assigned as your caretaker. I do not have the authority to explain your situation. You must remain in bed awhile longer. It is necessary for you to complete your treatment under the healing beam before you can be released."

Aster would have been incensed if she had merely listened to the woman's words, but she was thrown off by what she saw while she heard them.

"How do you do that?"

"I beg your pardon, miss?"

"Your lips move at a different speed than I hear

your words." It was like watching an old foreign movie where the voice-dubbing is slightly out of sync with the picture.

"I understand. I suppose it would not hurt if I explain that." She pulled the front of the turtleneck down to her collarbone and revealed a very thin gold choker. "This is a universal translator. Although I am fluent in several languages, yours is not one of them. In order for us to communicate, I must rely on the external translator. It is programmed with my voice. As I speak in one tongue, it is automatically converted to your language, and vice-versa. There is barely a second's delay in the translation. Very few Terrans notice it."

"Uh-huh. Okay...listen, uh..." Aster hesitated a moment as she looked at the name again. "Oona, right? I don't know what's going on here, but I want some answers—now!" She slammed her hand on the bed and jumped off for emphasis. The extreme movement proved to be more than her body was ready to handle and she collapsed on the floor.

In the hectic receiving area, Romulus doled out orders in a tone of voice that permitted no questions. His attention was abruptly diverted as the new caretaker, Oona, hurried toward him. He hoped nothing had gone wrong with her assignment.

"Chief Romulus, please excuse the interruption. The woman in room five awoke and became very upset. She fell. It happened so quickly. There was nothing I could do. I was looking for the doctor when I saw you."

"All right, Oona. I'll check on her now." He strode away, annoyed that Oona had not been able to handle the woman. With all the paperwork required to integrate the new arrivals, he did not have time to calm one frightened female.

But the sight of that female crumpled on the floor halted Romulus's unkind thoughts. He knelt down and gathered her into his arms. When he tried to lift her, however, he misjudged his burden. Attempting to shift her weight, he lost his balance and ended up sitting on the floor with her cozily on his lap.

The sudden jolt interrupted Aster's dark oblivion. She opened her eyes and tried to focus on his face. Groggily, she murmured, "Much better. I know you. You've been in my dreams before." Closing her eyes, she nestled her head against his chest. From the contented look on her face, Romulus concluded it must be a very pleasant dream.

Romulus tried to pull his eyes away from the soft smile and dreamy expression on the woman's face. For a moment he wished he was the man she imagined him to be. His hand disobeyed his disciplined mind and brushed the hair away from her brow. The woman turned her cheek into his palm, and her mass of silver hair spilled over his arm. It was a very appealing feature but nothing like her eyes. When she looked up at him a moment ago, he was shaken by their blue-black color. It reminded him of the midnight sky on his home planet. That thought seemed to bear analyzing but now was not the time.

Just then a deep sigh caused her breasts to rise and lower and the peaks noticeably puckered, betraying the direction her dream had taken. It was enough to jar him back to the situation at hand. Remembering Oona standing expectantly behind him, he realized how unofficial he must look sitting on the floor holding this female. With effort, he stood up and placed the female gently on the bed, feeling oddly reluctant to release her.

"Oona, what's the medical on this one?" There, he

was all business again.

"Cerebral hemorrhage, multiple bruises, fractures and contusions. She did not remain under the beam long enough for a complete recovery and may have reinjured herself from that fall. Sir, I am afraid I provoked her unintentionally. I understood I was not to offer explanations, but she was very agitated and when she detected the difference between my voice and lip movement, I told her about the universal translator."

Chief Romulus considered the extraordinary pronouncement that the new arrival had been able to discern the translator's miniscule lapse. Apparently, besides her striking exterior, a definite possibility of higher intelligence existed as well.

"What is her name?"

"Aster Mackenzie. She prefers to be called Miss Mackenzie."

"Go find the doctor. I'll stay with her until you return." His motives for remaining with the patient were unclear. A backlog of work beckoned to him but he ignored its plaintive call. Something stronger held him back.

It seemed to him that this woman possessed some invisible characteristic that lured him to her. After Oona exited, he tried to appease his curiosity with a visual examination.

Her physical beauty did not stop with her face. Every inch of her was impressive. Her breasts were full but firm, her abdomen muscles taut, her waist narrow compared to her hips. Her limbs revealed additional proof of attentive conditioning.

Whatever was he doing? Here he was, in the midst of turmoil, ogling a nude woman like some adolescent boy. She was only a female, and a new arrival at that. What was taking that caretaker so long?

By the time Oona returned with the doctor, Rom had exiled himself to the hall outside the patient's room. "Good, you're back. I must return to my office. I've spent too much time here already. Orientation is scheduled for eighteen hundred hours in Conference Room B." Before he finished his last sentence, he was already heading back to a more rational domain.

"Rom? Is something out of order?" Tarla's voice filled with concern as the chief administrator stalked past her to his office.

"What? Oh, no. A new caretaker waylaid me. She had a problem with one of the arrivals and now I'm behind schedule. This is the third time this month. The more polluted Outerworld becomes, the harder it is to prevent these accidents. Something is going to have to be done about it soon, whether the Tribunal is ready or not." He planted himself behind his desk, intending to immerse himself in his work and forget the interruption.

Romulus stared at the large vidcom monitor on the wall next to his desk, but he could not read the report displayed there. Instead, he saw those blue-black eyes seducing him. What madness was this? He assured himself that his imagination running amok must be an aftereffect from trying to analyze his strange dream.

He concentrated on preparing for the upcoming orientation. From his earliest days in Administration, he had taken on the responsibility of the new arrivals and had always enjoyed it. It would go smoothly, as usual...if he could just stop his hands from shaking.

"Miss Mackenzie, do you hear me? Please open your eyes now."

Aster felt a pressure against her temples then it was gone. She blinked a few times and found herself staring into a strange woman's face.

"If you do not rise so quickly this time, you should feel much better," the soft voice warned.

The excruciating headache had eased. But when she tried to sort out the jumble of confusing scenes in her mind, the pain came back with a fury.

"My name is Oona, Miss Mackenzie. Do you remember? I am your caretaker. The doctor said you may get up now, if you promise to remain calm."

Aster gave her a slight nod.

"You were involved in an accident and suffered many injuries, the worst of which was a cerebral hemorrhage. You are completely recovered now but if you feel the need to rest a little longer, that is not a problem. I have brought clothing. When you are ready, I will escort you to orientation."

Aster started to speak, trying to focus on asking the right questions. "I'm very confused. What kind of accident? How long have I been unconscious? Apparently I'm in a hospital but where? And what was that about orientation?"

Oona spoke haltingly, selecting her words with great care. "At orientation the accident and all information about your whereabouts will be explained to you. You have been unconscious about ten hours."

"Hold on. How could I have suffered a cerebral hemorrhage, slept ten hours then be fully recovered? Either the doctor's a quack or you're lying."

"I do not lie. Nor do I comprehend why you are criticizing the doctor. Do you not remember the healing beam? It was shining in your eyes when you awoke for a few minutes earlier today. It repaired your body while you slept. The beam also serves as a sanitizing device for new arrivals."

Aster did not doubt that she had a head injury. That would explain her headache and her earlier bout of nausea and dizziness. Perhaps she suffered from a form of amnesia as well. As hard as she tried, she remembered nothing beyond leaving her office yesterday to go home. It occurred to her that maybe her brain was not yet working to capacity and she misunderstood what Oona had said to her. She would begin again...with an easy question.

"Oona, what day is this?"

"Saturday, Miss Mackenzie."

"Saturday?" Her voice took on an edge of hysteria. She had left the office on Wednesday and had planned to go...to go somewhere...somewhere with Cherry. The pain behind her eyes returned as she attempted to fill in the lost days. For some reason, the thought of Cherry agitated her further. What was it about Cherry that bothered her?

"Do you feel pain? Perhaps I should get the doctor again," Oona offered.

"No. It's better now. I would like to get dressed though."

"I hope you like the color. It was as close to the unusual shade of your eyes as I could duplicate."

Aster looked at the dark blue, two-piece outfit on the chair. Oona was trying her best to be helpful and it would serve no purpose to harangue her further. She may as well wait for this *orientation* thing and get all the answers at once.

"Thank you for the thought, Oona. By the way, those orchids are lovely." Aster realized her head stopped hurting once she relaxed.

Oona smiled happily. "They are from us. I am glad to see that they please you."

"They're my favorite."

"Yes, I know. The nurse had to touch your mind to learn your name and the condition of your mental health. While she was in contact, I requested your floral preference. It seemed logical that seeing them when you awoke might make you feel better."

Touched my mind? While she was in contact? What in heaven's name was this woman talking about? She recalled some other nonsense about a translator...This kind, soft-spoken woman, who thought of matching borrowed clothes to her eye color and providing favorite flowers to cheer her up, had to be deranged.

The slacks and jersey fit perfectly but Aster could not identify the material. Although it felt a little like cashmere, it was very thin and there was no visible weave. She tried to ask about it, but her caretaker had stopped talking.

When they reached Conference Room B, Oona placed her palm over a light in the wall and the door slid into the adjacent wall.

"Aster!" Cherry squealed as she rushed forward and hugged her. "Thank God you're all right. Everyone else was here ages ago. You look wonderful, damn you. How did you manage to get a custom wardrobe? The rest of us must have been outfitted in identical drab grays just to help you shine!"

White-hot lightning pierced Aster's head. She closed her eyes and leaned back against the wall. It had all come back to her—not the nightmare she had had when she first awoke, but the unspeakable reality of the last two days.

With feverish eyes, she stared at the group surrounding her—Cherry, Nick, the Feinsteins and the Basiglios." Cherry! You're alive! But your arm— How?"

Cherry flexed the fingers on her right hand. "Amazing, isn't it? I'm a regular bionic woman now. Johnny's our resident miracle though." She cocked her head in his direction.

Aster gaped. "How can this be? You were killed. I saw it. You couldn't have survived!"

"You're telling me!" he replied with a loud guffaw. "We've had some time to compare notes before you got here, so you have some catching up to do. We've already figured out that none of us has the entire picture but we know for certain, we're not in Kansas anymore. The doc explained that I was technically dead, but he put me back together with an artificial heart and something that looked like a penlight. The weirdest part was I actually saw the doctor working on me. You know, like an out-of-body experience. Take a look at this." He lifted his shirt to expose a hairline scar on his chest. "They tell me even this line will fade in a few weeks."

Aster listened to each of her fellow travelers' stories and saw the confirmation in Cherry's new arm and Johnny's scar. Everyone was laughing and excited about this incredible adventure they had stepped into. It was completely illogical, yet she was positive she was no longer dreaming. Somehow they had been rescued, but by whom and how?

They were sharing speculations when Aster suddenly felt the hair rise on the back of her neck. Cherry's eyes widened to the size of half-dollars as she stared beyond Aster.

"Miss Mackenzie?"

At the sound of the deep-timbred masculine voice, the shiver at the back of Aster's neck slid straight down to the base of her spine. Where had she heard that voice before?

"I hope you are somewhat recovered from your ordeal."

She turned and felt her heart stop and start anew with a tremor. *Him!* There was no mistaking those hypnotic hazel eyes. She had seen his handsome face so many times in her dreams, she had stopped questioning who he might be and had simply accepted him as a very well-developed figment of her imagination. But the man standing before her didn't seem like a figment. Was he real or was she caught up in yet another dream? As always happened when she dreamed of him, she tried to say his name, a name she felt she should know, but again, it eluded her.

Rom's hand reached out as if it were a separate entity, needing to touch her face again. He had been so certain that his powerful emotional reaction to this woman had been a result of too much stress and an overactive imagination. But here it was, happening again, this time in a room full of witnesses. *Witnesses!*

He pulled his hand back and ran his fingers through the side of his hair. Drawing himself up to his full height, he cleared his throat along with his thoughts.

"Good evening, ladies and gentlemen. Would you please take a seat as quickly as possible? We have a lot of information to cover." They responded to his request and he was satisfied that they had noticed nothing peculiar. Positioning himself at one end of the oval table, he began.

"I'm sure you have many questions that you're anxious to pose. However, due to the complex nature of the situation, it will be considerably more expedient if I speak first without interruption. When I finish, if I have left any of your questions unanswered, I will deal with them individually."

Although Romulus had been momentarily distracted by those midnight-blue eyes, he was now back on firm ground and proceeded to deliver his familiar presentation. To avoid being distracted though, he limited his line of vision to the other people around the table. He had heard of Umerian women who could turn human males into slaves by staring at them, but this woman was definitely a Terran and they had no such powers as far as he knew.

"There is no way to ease into what I am about to tell you. Some of what I say may shock you, yet in time you will not only accept what we have to offer but will enjoy it."

Aster squirmed in her seat and rocked her crossed leg back and forth beneath the table. She glanced at the others. Each sat forward in his chair, staring at this man as if he were a savior. Cherry had not managed to close her mouth since he walked into the room.

"My name is Romulus. I am the chief administrator of the Car-Tem Province." He pressed several icons on a panel located in the table in front of him. The lights in the room dimmed and a rotating three-dimensional globe appeared suspended over the center of the table. "As you can see, this is Earth, as you know it." He touched another icon and twelve bright red spots on the holographic picture lit up. "These are magnetic fields that your scientists are aware of but these areas also represent doorways to our world.

"Here is the area where you were earlier today." The image of Earth transformed into a map of the United States' eastern seaboard. A blue arrow flashed on a location in the Sargasso Sea. "Depending on several variables, such as the Earth's orbit and the position of its moon, we use different doorways at different times of your calendar year. This morning we were using this particular opening when your accident occurred."

He continued his scientific explanation, seemingly oblivious to the dismayed looks passing back and forth around the table. "We take every possible precaution but occasionally, for various reasons, the presence of a small vessel in the area at the time we are opening a door goes undetected. In such a case, the vessel is pulled downward into the core of the

Earth."

They now viewed a tiny ship spinning down within a tunnel toward the heart of the sphere. The fluorescent vision changed shape again. A yellow illuminated arrow blinked on one spot of another map. The outline was not recognizable.

The group of castaways sat mesmerized by the play of lights performing in mid-air as the chief administrator continued. "This is where we are at this moment, in the city of Car-Tem One, Car-Tem Province. This entire map constitutes the Noronian colony of Innerworld, as opposed to Outerworld, where you previously resided. It is approximately half the size of the United States and has a population of almost twenty-five million.

"We are completely self-sufficient but we do communicate with and travel to and from our home planet, Norona, on a regular basis. We provide our people there with a valuable commodity that is found in Earth's core. Thus the need for our colony and the doorways."

At this point, Romulus paused to switch off the image and to bring the lights back to normal but Aster continued to stare at the spot where the holograph had been. Completely baffled by everything she had seen and heard so far, she hoped the punch line to this joke was near at hand. Romulus's voice drew her gaze back to him.

"Not everyone has an avid interest in history or scientific achievements. Therefore, rather than dwell on either of those aspects, I suggest you visit our library. Information is available both electronically and in the physical form. Who we are, how we came to be here and all our knowledge has been recorded in detail.

"The most vital piece of information you need to

absorb today is that you cannot go back." He hurried on as their heads popped up and they turned to one another in panic. "Now that you know of our existence, we cannot return you to Outerworld. The temptation to share your unusual experience with others would be too great. Therefore, it is now necessary for me to introduce you briefly to our laws and the general structure of our society."

Aster's headache returned in full force. He could not have said what she thought she heard. Never go back? This did not sound much like a joke. He had sounded dead serious.

"We will help you adapt to our world as quickly and smoothly as possible. A caretaker has been assigned to each of you to assist with your acclimation.

"Our laws are not so different from yours. You will receive written guidelines before you leave this room. There are a few restrictions you must abide by but they mainly involve travel and politics. The primary requirements of each individual in Innerworld are to work at something productive, to enjoy the work one chooses and to maintain a healthy body. Violence or abuse of any kind will not be tolerated.

"We have more leisure time than you may be accustomed to. You will be expected to make good use of that time as well. I am sure you will be pleasantly surprised by the variety of games and energy outlets available to you."

The chief administrator hesitated, taking a moment to look at each person directly…except *her*. All through his speech, he had pointedly avoided meeting her eyes.

The faces on each side of Aster revealed a combination of bewilderment and tension. Fidgeting in her chair, Aster felt she might burst if she did not speak her mind soon, but she had no idea what to say.

"You may work in whatever field appeals to you. Each of you will have the opportunity to discuss what might be suitable with a career counselor. If training or education is required, that will be provided.

"To begin with, you will receive a supply of food and clothing, free of charge, and an entry-level apartment will be made available to you, prepaid for two months. You should adjust to our system of economics without much difficulty."

Rom's earlier resolve not to look at her disintegrated instantly when Aster ceased her nervous movement and sat forward in her chair. Her expression changed from pure defiance to mild curiosity. It occurred to him that he may have discovered Miss Mackenzie's touchstone.

"The main difference between our systems is that we do not use hard currency. An accounting file will be opened for each of you. You receive credits to your account for working or attending school and debits when you make a purchase. You cannot spend more than you have. Ten percent of your credits is automatically transferred to the Car-Tem Provincial Account. In return, you are provided with education, medical care, utilities and public facilities. If you have any questions about how all this works, I will be glad to discuss it further at a later time."

Romulus risked one more glance at Aster to make sure she had heard his offer but she was intently studying a spot on the table in front of her. Opening his mouth to continue, he received a shock. He could not remember where he had left off. This had never happened to him before. What was it about that woman? Rather than reveal his problem, he skipped to the question-and-answer segment of his presentation.

"I will now try to answer some of your questions. I would appreciate your introducing yourselves first."

He nodded to the man seated at his left. "Go ahead, please."

"I'm Johnny Basiglio. This is my wife, Betty. I was the captain on The Baronette. I'm just so glad to be alive, I don't know what to ask about first. How about those three guys—the pirates—what happened to them?"

"After you arrived, we reviewed a replay of the incidents that had occurred on your ship during the previous twenty-four hours." When several sets of eyebrows shot up questioningly, he explained, "The process involves picking up images left behind on matter before they dissipate. At any rate, one of the criminals was dead long before the accident. His body and that of another crew member had been...previously removed from the ship. The other two were dispatched to the Rehabilitation Clinic in a distant province. They will be dealt with according to our laws."

Paul Feinstein broke in. "I certainly don't want to be accused of being a wet blanket but it seems like you're taking our acceptance a little too much for granted. We have three grandchildren back home whom you're telling us we'll never see again. It's easy for these younger people here to start a new life but we don't want to finish our days in a strange place."

"Please forgive my husband's blustering, Mister Romulus. We're Sheila and Paul Feinstein and we really are grateful that you came to our rescue. But, you see, I have terminal cancer. Paul was upset at the thought of living without me in our own world, among our family. Isn't there some way he could get back...after I'm gone maybe? He would never tell a soul where he's been."

"First, we do not use the title *Mister* here. You may

call me Romulus, or if you prefer something more formal, Chief Romulus, but it's not necessary. Next, we will not send anyone back for any reason. That is not negotiable." He recalled the report on Sheila Feinstein. "I gather you are unaware that the disease was eliminated from your body while you were under the beam. Not only are you not dying but you both have many years left to enjoy life. You're barely middle-aged by our standards. A few visits to our medical facilities and you'll be feeling like youngsters again."

Sheila and Paul hugged each other tightly, tears of joy flowing freely down their weathered cheeks.

Romulus permitted a smile to soften his purposefully stern expression for a moment. "I hope we will eventually discover something that will please the rest of you just as much, or at least make up for what you left behind."

He looked at Aster but the brunette spoke up.

"Hi, I'm Cherry Cochran, and I want to know something a little more personal. I mean, are you human or is that some kind of super bodysuit?"

The unexpected question caused snickers around the table and Romulus had to struggle not to join in. Clearing his throat, he quickly regained control. "Occasionally I monitor Outerworld media, so I have a fair idea where you would get such an idea. Let me assure you, we are humanoids. The differences between us are mostly technological."

Aster struggled with a problem of her own and it was far from Cherry's silly concerns. Anxiety overwhelmed her. She felt her heart constrict and her head was woozy. Her lungs strained for air in a room that had become a vacuum.

Too many times in her life, events beyond her control had turned her upside down. After Dennis's death, she had prayed for a little peace, for everything to remain stagnant for a while. But this time the change was beyond her imagination. She had to do something and she employed the relaxation technique she used many times before. Calm down, breathe deeply, count to three. Repeat.

Feeling some relief, she had exchanged her panic for anger. "Excuse me for interrupting," Aster cut in impatiently. "It seems to me there are more than *technological* differences between us. The woman who was with me said the nurse 'touched' my mind and learned things about me. Are you all able to read our minds? How are we supposed to deal with that? And what other secrets haven't you told us about?"

Unable to stay seated another minute, Aster stood up and paced restlessly behind the chairs. The frown on Romulus's face told her she had brought up one of the subjects that he would rather have avoided but his tone of voice remained amiable.

"I can see how that might have upset you but it's not as frightening as it sounds. Yes, we have expanded mental capabilities, some more than others. However, you will learn that we put great store in individual privacy, not that we have anything to hide from each other or from you.

"In certain situations, such as an emergency, we have the right to *touch* or read your mind but only to the extent to provide help. Otherwise, it is required that you give the other person your permission. We are bound by a code of honesty and I am sure you will come to trust us eventually."

"*Trust you*? I not only do not *trust* you, Chief Romulus, I don't even believe in you. This could be some sort of group hallucination. And if not, if what you've told us is real, then that's even worse. I mean, who do you think you are anyway? Snatching people out of their world, rearranging their whole lives to fit yours and aren't we lucky that we're here! I have responsibilities and a job that I love out there. Besides, the whole premise of our being in the center of the Earth is ludicrous. Everyone knows the inner core of our planet is a ball of fire.

"And what about the rest of you? Sitting there nodding and smiling like this man has the right to do what he's done!" Aster was picking up momentum. She would have continued venting her anger and frustration except when she looked at the rest of the group, they turned their eyes away from her.

Betty walked over to Aster and took her hand. "Aster, dear, you must face certain facts. There is no question we would have all been dead at the hands of those pirates. That's usually the way it ends. We've been offered a very rare opportunity to begin our lives all over again, in a new and unusual way. Try to look on the positive side of this, for your own sake."

"How do you know we would have been dead? Maybe they would have let us go like they promised." Aster didn't even believe that herself but she wasn't ready to give in.

"I'm afraid Betty is correct. Miss Mackenzie," Romulus answered before Betty could. "Explosives had been planted in the bulkhead of the ship. Upon reading the thoughts of the two men, we learned of their intention to kill you and detonate the explosives by remote control once they removed themselves and their cargo. I would be most happy to show you the proof in the wreckage before it is recycled if that would help convince you."

Aster knew they were right. It was just so hard to accept that she could never go home. She met the chief administrator's gaze and allowed it to touch her for an instant. "No, thank you. That won't be necessary." Lowering her eyes, she returned to her seat.

She could not decide what disturbed her more—the situation she found herself in or the fact that the man from her dreams had dared come to life and talk to her as if he were real. Somehow she was sure she could rationalize this whole thing if she could only get away from him and his tempting mouth that had almost kissed her so many times, but never quite— No, that was the dream again.

"In answer to your other questions," Romulus continued, "I am certain you will find as much satisfaction with your employment here as you once enjoyed in Outerworld. With regard to the inner core, we created our own protective shield, along with our environment, as you will witness when you leave here. As was our intention, Outerworld scientists cannot detect anything extraordinary."

Nick then spoke up. "Sir, I'm Nick Valentino. To tell you the truth, and, uh, Aster, I'm sorry you don't agree with me but I can't help being excited about all this. I didn't have that much back there that I'd miss anyway. I would like to know though, hasn't anyone ever gone back before? You know, like escaped?"

"Actually, Nick, Outerworlders who have acquired knowledge of our civilization have no interest in returning to their world. I believe you will feel the same way soon." He pressed an icon on the panel and murmured a few words.

A heavy-set man entered the room, carrying a small stack of notebooks. Aster noted that he wore the same shade of uniform as the rest of her group. She suspected that the color of one's clothing might correlate to position or rank and wondered what her dark blue might mean. Allowing herself a glimpse at the administrator, she decided the deep forest-green jersey he wore indicated a high level of management. Regardless of its meaning, it did do wonderful things for his hazel eyes. What a ridiculous thing to be thinking of!

Romulus took the bundle from the man. "Tha—" The word froze in the air as the man pointed a small black box directly at the chief's forehead.

"Don't y'all even think about touchin' that alarm, you snotty sumbitch," the man growled in a thick Southern accent. "Git up and stand over by the door, and don' try nothin' cute."

Romulus maintained a semblance of control as he speculated about what was happening. Imperceptibly, he nodded toward the monitor concealed in the far wall, hoping that the runner, Karl, was unaware of its existence. Something was very wrong with the normally mild-mannered man. His eyes were wide, his pupils dilated, as he stole glimpses of the others in the room. But his hand was steady on the paralyzer, his thumb poised precariously over its firing button.

"Karl, what's the problem? What do you want?" Rom's voice remained quietly concerned as he obeyed Karl's command.

Karl blinked, hesitating for a fraction of a second during which the glazed look in his eyes almost cleared. Then it returned. "What do ah want? Ah want to git out of this damned place. Back to the good ol' U. S. of A. Ah'm sick and tired of bein' treated lahk a slave. Sick and tired of you and all the other sumbitches 'round heah lookin' down on me. Ah want to go back to the greatest country in the world, mah world, where ah can come and go as ah please, where ah get to vote for the assholes who run the damn country, where a man can smoke a pack of cigarettes and drink a quart of bourbon whenever he hankers fer it!" He was shouting now as he turned toward the group of new arrivals.

"Fifteen yeahs ah bin heah. Fifteen goddamned yeahs without a cigarette or a real drink. For our own good they told us. Hah! Well, no more. Ah know the way out and y'all are comin' with me, befo' they brainwash you lahk they did all mah friends. Git up, all of you, line up behind the chief heah. He's the magic ticket that'll git us home."

So, no one had any interest in returning, Aster thought as she cautiously stood up. She and the others moved behind Romulus, hoping the demented man did not turn his anger on them. The box in his hand had to be a weapon of some sort, considering the respect it elicited from the chief administrator. Why did he look so calm? Why was he just standing there, letting the man rant on?

Her answer came the next moment when the conference room door slid open. Five black-uniformed men and women surged in. A flash of light streaked from one of them to the man named Karl. Again his eyes seemed to focus for an instant before they closed and he collapsed to the floor. The invasion force picked Karl up and exited.

Romulus blocked the doorway. "Please remain here for a few minutes," he ordered tersely, then quickly followed his people. The entire episode was over in less than two minutes.

Nick rushed to the opening but not fast enough. He slammed his fist against the metal closure. Hurriedly, he passed his hand around the smooth edges but the door remained closed. "Damn! I know I saw it open this way. Hell! Something's not right here. We should have run while we had the chance."

"And get a taste of that light?" Johnny answered sarcastically.

"What do you think?"

"Why would…"

"What if…"

Everyone spoke at once and Aster held her palms over her ears and took a deep breath. She could not stand another minute of this chaos. "Stop it! This isn't getting us anywhere. Besides, I'm sure we're being watched. I saw the administrator nod at a spot somewhere behind me before he responded to Karl's command. Then a security team instantly turned up to eliminate the threat. Who knows what the truth is? The only thing we do know is the pretty Garden-of-Eden picture Chief Romulus painted must also have the proverbial serpent in it."

"But, Aster," Sheila interrupted. "You can't simply discount everything because of the ravings of an obviously disturbed man."

Betty put her arm around her husband's ample waist. "Johnny's alive. That's good enough for me."

"So am I," Cherry added softly.

Aster looked from one worried face to another. "It seems you've outnumbered me again but the jury's still out as far as I'm concerned. Our alien host swears to a code of honesty but I'm positive we didn't hear the whole truth about this place."

"Holy stars, Rom. I just heard about it." Tarla jumped up from behind her desk and followed him into his office. "What could have possessed Karl to do that?"

"The only thing that's been verified so far is that he was acting under a post mind-link suggestion. He has no idea where the thoughts came from. The paralyzer appeared in his mail cart and triggered his actions. The fact that he was so easily stopped indicates that his puppeteer was either unaware the meeting was being monitored or didn't care if Karl was caught. It's possible the plan was thrown together too hastily."

"Oh, my. The governorship...You just got the announcement of your nomination. Could there be a connection?"

"I guess that's a possibility but it doesn't make much sense. I'm the only candidate residing in Innerworld and personally involved with the Outerworlders here. I have the backing of Governor Elissa and she's fairly certain two-thirds of the Tribunal have already decided in my favor.

"No, the only thing Karl's actions accomplished was to let the new arrivals know there are some restrictions on their activities. New arrivals usually discern their full status within a few weeks anyway but, by that time, they don't find the restrictions too objectionable. They simply have to learn to avoid those Innerworlders who would rather not associate with them. Orientation is difficult enough without introducing every negative aspect of our society."

"Had you finished your lecture?"

"Pretty much." Rom decided not to mention the odd effect that one Terran female had on him.

"Will regular procedures be followed now?"

"Not immediately. For tonight the new arrivals will reside in the dormitory upstairs. We've called in a tracker to follow Karl's movements over the last twenty-four hours and see if we can get any more clues about who was behind this. If the tracker doesn't come up with anything, we'll let the arrivals settle in tomorrow. We'll keep close tabs on them for a while, in case our criminal is serious about helping them get back to Outerworld.

"By the way, if anything comes in from OMC, find me immediately."

"Problem?"

"I sincerely hope not."

CHAPTER 4

Victor stared at the screen on the wall opposite his cot for several seconds after it went blank. It had to be a hoax of some kind, that much was certain. The group of people from the ship seemed to have been taken in by what they had heard but Victor was smarter than that.

The man in charge, Romulus, was damned good, with his magic light show and arrogant speech. His people, whoever or whatever they really were, had rescued all of them from the grave. Okay, he could buy that much but what was the purpose of that fiasco at the end?

The small room Victor had awakened in revealed no clues as to his whereabouts. It had no windows or clock, only a cot, sink and toilet. The screen had lit up when Chief Romulus's 3-D show started, so he had watched.

But what if this was not a hoax? Doubt filled his mind for the first time since he'd awakened. He shuddered as he thought of being trapped in the type of society the chief had described. Being a dishonest person among a population of sheep that lived by a code of honesty had a certain appeal. But the fact that they could read minds, as they apparently had already done to him, and could see events long after they had happened put an end to his optimism. The truth was that it would be pure hell and that crazy man, Karl, obviously felt the same way.

First he had to get out of this jail. But Victor was confident that Lady Luck would help him find a way. Escaping Innerworld, however, sounded a bit more difficult. Karl had said he needed Romulus to do it. That was the first piece of information Victor had filed away. But before he departed, he would pay a visit to the silver-haired bitch. She would undoubtedly be very grateful to the man who helped her get back home.

There was one other person he needed to find, too. Although he hadn't seen José, he assumed his associate was nearby and hoped he would not be too hard to locate. As annoying as José was at times, Victor couldn't just leave his amigo behind.

Doctor Xerpa's fingers danced over the icons, keys and dials on the control panel. From her position on the raised platform, she observed her technician and the Outerworld patient, José, immobile on the aluminum bed. Large metal clamps held him and all hair had been removed from his head and face, making his rolling eyeballs appear even wilder. His mouth had been taped to shut off the constant stream of obscenities.

Her attempts to converse with him had failed, in spite of her using his own dialect, and she felt that the Board's decision to fully reprogram this one was justified. He was more animal than human.

Doctor Xerpa had been in medical school a century ago when this method of conversion was used on any new arrival who showed the slightest reluctance to behave in a civilized manner. Now the drastic measure was only approved for the most incorrigible cases.

The tech opened a drawer located in the pedestal workstation next to the man's head. Selecting a small needle with a green bubble on one end, he smoothly inserted it behind the man's left ear. José's eyelids drooped a second later. While the green liquid dripped from the bubble, the technician made several adjustments on the viewing screen until it clearly displayed the patient's brain.

As the doctor stepped down from her station, the tech removed the tape from the man's mouth then turned to her. "The patient has reached the necessary level of unconsciousness, Doctor Xerpa. Everything is ready for you."

Xerpa immediately replaced him at José's head and chose twelve six-inch needles from the rows of implements. She connected each needle to a different colored wire. Instantly, the tips flared brightly.

With steady hands, she expertly punctured the bald head with the first needle, effortlessly pressing the white-hot point through the skull. She stared intently at the screen as she concentrated on the needle's route deep into the brain. Only when she was satisfied that it had reached the precise target did she release her firm hold and switch off the light in that needle. She carefully repeated the process eleven more times in separate areas of the brain before she relaxed.

"You are truly an artist, Doctor," the technician offered with an unmistakable note of awe in his voice. "I've never had the privilege of observing a stage three before. Plenty of ones and twos, but not a three."

Stage one proved very effective in correcting minor personality deviations and neuroses without seriously interfering with intelligence or memory. The more powerful stage two eliminated certain negative memories found to be at the root of a person's antisocial behavior. But Xerpa knew that one of the unfortunate side effects with stage two was irreparable damage to the subject's innate intelligence.

Doctor Xerpa invited the tech to observe the final steps of the conversion process. He happily followed her back to the control panel as she briefly described the data that would soon be streaming into the man's brain.

"A completely new identity has been developed for this man, including a history of his life to date. Though small pieces of memory are taken away in stage two, in this procedure, all existing thought is wiped out and replaced with the personality and memory we have created for him. When he awakens, he will have no recollection of his former life. This reprogrammed man will step into our world believing he was born here, ready to take his place as a productive citizen in our society."

"What are the Board's plans for the other one?"

"You know the Board members were all hand-picked by the governor and most of them share her liberal sympathies about the rights of the transplanted Outerworlders. In spite of the evidence, they hesitated in making the decision to reprogram this man. They were even more reluctant to use this procedure on the other man as he possesses an unusually high level of intelligence. Therefore, they have decided to discount his criminal background and violent tendencies. We will be working with him using stage one and counseling. If he cannot be rehabilitated with a few sessions, the Board will reconsider their recommendation. If he responds positively, he will be given the opportunity to enter our society. At any rate, we'll know by the end of the week."

Doctor Xerpa touched a button then stood back. The only visual proof that something was happening to the body on the table was a spastic twitching of the fingers and toes. Five minutes later, it ceased.

After removing the needles from José's skull, she gave her tech a final instruction. "Call the cosmetic surgeon. The patient is ready for him."

CHAPTER 5

After everything they'd been told and witnessed in the last hour, the top floor of the five-story Administration Building provided a much needed dose of simplicity for Aster. The large room had pale yellow walls and was minimally furnished with several rows of neatly made-up cots with yellow, green and blue plaid blankets. Each cot had a small nightstand and lamp on one side.

But it was the scene outside one of the many windows that captivated her attention. How could it be sundown if they were in the center of the Earth? A lovely garden filled with flowers fronted the building. Tiny twinkling lights illuminated the trees and lilac bushes that lined the walkway leading to a street. A fiery orange sun with a surrounding white ring had begun to set on the horizon of a lavender-blue sky.

Oona joined her and explained that the plants were from all over the universe and that the sun and sky had been simulated to help the transplanted Noronians feel at home. She added that the design of the buildings and the layout of the city of Car-Tem emulated the great cities of their home planet as well.

Aster watched the sun's last rays create iridescent rainbows on the nearby buildings, which appeared to be constructed of clusters of crystal prisms. Across the street a group of children were playing. One boy threw a ball into the air and the others aimed lights at it. When a light hit the target, the ball lit up like a sparkler. A little dog chased the lights back and forth. Two girls whizzed by, balanced on small boards that seemed to be a blend of a surfboard and a magic carpet.

Aster could not help but appreciate the view and be somewhat comforted by the happy children. She had always longed for such a carefree existence. But was life here as peaceful as the scene implied? Karl had not seemed very pleased with his lot in life. Had she and the others only traded the terrors of the hijacking for this confinement—a room from which she could look at the world around her but not touch?

"Pretty, isn't it?" Cherry said as she came up to Aster. For once, her natural exuberance seemed subdued.

"Very. But I can't help wonder if it's only a three-dimensional picture put there to deceive us."

Cherry shivered. "I can always count on you to point out the gloomy side of things. C'mon. I made dinner."

Aster raised an eyebrow. "You? You don't even cook in your own apartment."

"Yeah, I know, but this was fun." She directed Aster to the kitchen where the others were already enjoying a variety of meals. Johnny was twirling strands of spaghetti covered in red sauce, Nick was cutting a thick steak and Sheila was savoring a bite of breaded fish.

At Aster's place sat a juicy cheeseburger, baked beans and an iced tea. Cherry knew Aster preferred that to a gourmet meal. She bit into the meat and tasted hickory smoke and the baked beans were flavored with molasses.

"Mmm. This is great. How did you do it?"

Cherry winked at her. "While you were being antisocial, we were learning about the facilities manager. It controls everything in your environment and provides whatever you need, just by your talking to it. And it can talk back too. Plus, it knows all about Outerworld foods. You just tell it what you're hungry for and a few minutes later, *zap*. Your order appears in one of those steel cabinets on the wall they call the supply station. Or you can choose from a menu of about a zillion choices. By the way, that's not real meat you're eating."

Aster choked and stopped chewing. Cherry had done it to her again.

"Oh, don't worry, kid. It's not ground bugs or anything gross like that. These people are vegetarians, that's all. But what's the difference, as long as it tastes like you expect it to? You get clothes the same way, by picking from pictures on the screen. And everything gets thrown away, recycled actually, when you're done. Can you imagine? No more cooking, dirty dishes and, best of all, no more laundry! What's more, if I earn enough credits, I can even buy an android like Perd over there to pick up after me! It's real hard not to get excited about a society that can give me all that!"

"What did you just say about Perd?"

Cherry tilted her head. "Didn't Oona tell you anything? While you were studying the landscape, Perd told us about them." She purposely chewed another bite of her salad slowly to keep Aster on the hook. "They're all androids, the caretakers I mean. But I distinctly recall Romulus saying he was definitely human."

Aster choked again. *Damn*. Even the mention of his name was upsetting. She could feel the heat in her cheeks and hoped no one else noticed it. One look at Cherry's smug expression told her she had not been that fortunate. Thankfully, Sheila misunderstood her embarrassment and attempted to explain.

"It's not so terrible if you think of them as highly sophisticated machines. Our caretaker told us they are used for dangerous situations as well as dealing with new arrivals."

Johnny cut in. "That man, Karl, must have been telling a few truths. It seems some people here might not treat us as kindly as our caretakers have. On the other hand, some new arrivals are not as calm as we are. Using robots, er androids, to break us in is their answer to the problem."

Aster was stunned. Oona, that sweet, thoughtful lady, not human? She felt the old anxiety creeping over her again. Was there nothing she could depend on? She fought her fear and allowed the conversation to flow around her until she could politely seek out the limited privacy of her cot.

It was not to be. Cherry immediately joined her, making herself comfortable on the narrow bed. She handed Aster a notebook. "This was the manual you were supposed to get in the meeting. Perd said it'll tell us a little bit about everything we need to know. There're more detailed manuals on everything over there on the bookshelf. Everything can be accessed on something they call a vidcom, which sounds a lot like a computer only more advanced, but they don't provide one in here. My guess is they don't want us to know too much all at once."

Aster opened the thin book and scanned the pages. The Table of Contents looked like an outline an anthropologist might use to study an ancient civilization—Career Selection, Clothing, Economics, Education…Reproduction. She felt herself blush and wondered why her well-disciplined mind had taken a leave of absence.

"How do you think they do it?" Cherry pounced on Aster's very thought.

"Cherry! Is that really the big question here?"

"Me?" she asked innocently. "And, pray tell, how did you know what I was referring to? And while I'm at it, how did you manage to come through the same shipwreck I did and still have time to bewitch the most gorgeous hunk of beefcake this side of heaven?"

"I have no idea what you're talking about." Aster tried to keep her roiling emotions out of her voice.

"Okay. Have it your way. But it's a wonder any of us got out of that room without being electrocuted by the sparks that were flying between the two of you."

Aster opened her mouth to deny the accusation but had to chuckle at the picture Cherry described. What was the sense of arguing about something so ridiculous?

"I'm going to try my hand at designing clothes with the supply station. Care to join me?" Cherry asked.

"All right. Just for a little while. They tell me I slept all day, but I'm worn out."

Besides, there were times when a little of Cherry went a long way. At twenty-nine, Cherry was six years younger than Aster, but in the ways of the world in general, and men in particular, she was decades older.

In spite of or because of their differences, they became friends the first day they met at The Mackenzie Foundation in San Francisco. Aster's grandmother had set up the organization as an endowment fund to keep her money circulating.

Cherry had just been hired there as a receptionist when Aster started as a prospectus analyst. At that time Aster's job was to review applications for grants and determine whether the agency or individual was worthy of receiving funds for their project. Now, ten years later, she was the director of the board of trustees and Cherry was her unorthodox, but efficient, executive assistant.

Her stomach clenched at the thought of what would happen to the foundation now. Aster had never gotten around to writing a will after her grandmother's death, nor had she left proxy instructions for her vote in the event of her absence. She had had no intention of ever being absent. She had battled to turn the foundation away from advancing technology and certain private interests and toward environmental and humanitarian concerns. Now, without her presence, her opponents on the board had a better than fifty percent chance of swinging it back again. There had to be something she could do to prevent that from happening.

When she returned to her cot, Aster reopened the notebook. The words on the inside front cover jumped out at her—"Compiled by Romulus Locke". Her heart did a little double step. She wished it would quit doing that. At least now she knew Romulus was his first name.

The first page was an itinerary covering the next several days, but Karl had apparently changed the schedule. She wondered how long they would be kept here.

A quick read through the Clothing section did not answer her question about the different colored uniforms. So Aster went to the bookshelf Cherry had mentioned and found a manual entitled Clothing. It was well-organized, like the notebook and it was easy to verify her assumptions. Turquoise denoted a caretaker, gray was assigned to low-level functionaries and dark green was reserved for top administrative positions. There was no category for dark blue. Oona had indeed made up a uniform to match Aster's eye color.

She started to close the book when the same four words on the inside cover caught her attention. Aster returned the book to the shelf and opened the covers on several more. The name Romulus Locke shouted at her from the pages. Obviously, Outerworlders were his personal domain. *That* had to be the reason he had observed her so closely. Some sparks! In his eyes, she was just a specimen or more likely, as Karl had suggested, a lower life form.

Aster shoved the books back on the shelf and returned to the bed. Her eyes closed but her mind would not go to sleep. She was tired and irritable and she was angry with Cherry for talking her into the cruise and angry with herself for accepting the invitation.

Cherry had decided it was her duty to break Aster's mundane routine of working, eating and sleeping. The little nag had fretted about her being a workaholic, had harassed her about being devoted to a dead man and had threatened her with the dangers of celibacy. Aster had declined every social invitation Cherry had issued. Recently, Cherry had gotten desperate enough to resort to deceit and trickery by setting Aster up with several *coincidental* meetings with nice, eligible men.

To put an end to Cherry's good-intentioned harassment, Aster had finally agreed to go along on the Feinsteins' four-day fishing trip. She had even tolerated the flight from San Francisco to Fort Lauderdale. Between battling her own fear of flying and tolerating Cherry's garrulous companion, Harold,

Aster had started regretting her decision before they ever boarded the ill-fated yacht.

How ironic that she had made Cherry swear that the long, quiet weekend was not another elaborate ploy to introduce her to yet another perfect playmate. Aster had thought being stuck on a private yacht with a strange man was the most unwelcome thing that could happen. If only it had been that simple.

She had not wanted to get out and socialize. Her life had been fine just the way it was.

Her relationship with Dennis hadn't been based on the kind of intense physical attraction that was glorified in romance novels, but she had loved him— as much as she was capable. The important thing was that she had felt safe and comfortable with him, not frightened as she was now. None of this would have happened if Dennis had not gotten himself killed.

Ah, Dennis, how could you abandon me too? She cried inwardly and for the thousandth time she repeated that she could count on no one but herself. If Aster had been alone in that room, she might have given in to the urge to have a good sob session. Instead, she pictured Dennis's face and willed herself to dream of him.

Several hours of deep sleep passed before her will was manifested but no sooner was she dreaming of her lost love than the other dream took over. Dennis's crooked grin straightened. The face was no longer Dennis's but the *other* man's. She could feel his strong arms encircling her, as they had so many times before in this dream world. Her heart beat faster, knowing that she would awaken in another moment, unfulfilled and confused because it always ended abruptly before his lips touched hers. His body heat scorched her as he lowered his head. For the first time in this recurring dream, Aster slid her arms around his neck and rose up on her tiptoes to accept his caress. And for the first time, she whispered the name she had waited a lifetime to learn. *"Romulus."*

Aster's body jerked awake, damp with perspiration. Frantically, her gaze searched the darkened room. Everyone was asleep.

Feeling disoriented, she glanced at her wrist to see the time before remembering she no longer owned a watch. She wasn't even sure time had any relevance in this place with a fake sun.

Deciding to freshen up before anyone else stirred, she thought she'd try out the facilities manager and supply station in the kitchen. She knew there must be instructions in one of the manuals but didn't want to disturb anyone by turning on a light in the main room. Though it wasn't like her to simply take a stab at something, the circumstances she found herself in were hardly normal.

She stood in the kitchen, took a calming breath and did what Cherry had done earlier. "Hello?"

"How may I help you?" a friendly voice responded.

"I'd like a dress."

"Specify style."

Aster thought of one of the outfits she'd packed for the cruise. "A sundress. Do you know what that is?"

"Translating. Ready. Touch the image when you see the preferred style."

Instantly, the front of one cabinet became a monitor and a dozen sundresses flashed on the screen.

Aster touched one with a fitted bodice, wide straps and slightly flared skirt. "Can you take that one and make the neckline higher and rounded instead of a vee?"

"Complying." The modified design appeared the next moment. "Advise color and material."

Aster was almost enjoying herself. "Turquoise and

polished cotton."

"Translating. Scanning for size." A light strobe shot out from the screen and outlined Aster's body from head to toe then vanished. About a minute later, the manager spoke again. "Completed. Your apparel is in bin three."

When Aster held the dress out in front of her, she had to admit, the process was pretty cool. She requested panties and low-heeled sandals. She learned jewelry of any kind had to be purchased.

The bathroom was as well-equipped as any of the better hotels she had stayed in, including grooming supplies and a selection of makeup. Telling herself she would feel even better if she pretended she was getting ready to go to work, she put on a little lipstick and mascara.

She could not find any hairpins, so she let her unruly waves hang loose. Just like her grandmother, her hair was thick and had gone completely gray when she was twenty. When she tucked it into a tight bun, she looked older and much less conspicuous. At five foot ten with silver hair, that was no small accomplishment.

By the time she was finished, the rest of the group was awake, getting cleaned up or having breakfast. Feeling more appropriately attired, she managed to smile and greet the others pleasantly. Everyone gave a sigh of relief when three of the caretakers appeared and announced they would be taken on a tour of the city and moved into their new residences without further delay.

Nick's caretaker addressed Aster and Cherry. "Oona and Perd have been delayed. It is requested that you stay here awhile longer." The android did not wait for a reply before leaving to catch up with the departing group.

The two women shrugged their shoulders and sat back down, neither caring to speculate what the delay meant.

"Good morning, ladies," Romulus said pleasantly as he entered the room. He managed to smile, but his insides were in turmoil. One look at Aster negated a night of convincing himself she was nothing special.

"Good morning, Chief Romulus," Aster finally said in a strained voice. "We were told to wait here."

"Yes, I know. Your caretakers were needed for other duties. I'll be taking the two of you on your tour and they will meet you at your apartments later." It was not a lie. He had given them another assignment. He had considered testing his responses by being alone with Aster but, from his experience with other new arrivals, guessed she might be more comfortable if her friend accompanied them.

Cherry jumped to her feet. "Hey, now that's what I call getting the royal treatment, huh, Aster!"

Rom saw Aster narrow her eyes at her friend and wondered what it meant...until she spoke directly to him.

"Thank you for stepping in, Chief Romulus, but I would have thought you would be much too busy writing manuals about Outerworlders and manipulating the lives of us wretchedly inferior beings. Certainly there must be another android you could assign to us."

Cherry's eyes widened. "Aster Mackenzie! He has offered us his personal hospitality and we're going to accept...*gratefully*."

Romulus shook his head. "After what happened last evening, I'm sure you're wondering who to believe." He caught Aster's telltale gasp. "No, I have not been reading your mind. But that's what I would have been thinking. I want the chance to show you that our colony is quite safe for you to enter and enjoy. Karl worked for me for years. Someone put him up to his actions yesterday and we have not yet determined who it was or the reason for it. We are convinced, though, that no one means to do you any harm.

"There are Innerworlders who have not yet accepted Terrans, er Outerworlders, as equals. They still remember another time and the violence Terrans are prone to. To put it into perspective, remember the Italian or Irish immigrants who entered your America in the late 1800s. They were treated unfairly, even hated by some, but they persevered and eventually blended into the population.

"In a relatively short time we have made great progress in integrating your people into our society and most of my people have accepted them as their friends and neighbors. I was not trying to hide any of this from you yesterday. I just believe it's too much information to bring up on a new arrival's first day."

Cherry punched Aster's arm. "See? Isn't that what I said?"

Aster was only giving his explanation one ear. Her mind was busy formulating a plan in which he would be a key player. But she would have to be cordial to him to make it work. "And how do *you* feel about *Terrans*?"

She saw a flash of heat in his eyes but he quickly quashed whatever his first reply would have been. Instead, he simply said, "We are all human beings, Miss Mackenzie. Now, if you will accept my company, I will endeavor not to *manipulate* you."

The look he was giving her was not that of a superior being looking down on a lesser one. If anything, his eyes were…pleading with her. She nodded and rose. The smile returned to his face as he showed them the way.

On the ground floor they approached a moving walkway and Romulus explained, "My commuter is in the rear of the building. This mover runs through the entire complex."

When Aster saw him support Cherry's elbow to assist her onto the track, she tried to avoid his touch by stepping on before he had a chance to help her. The walkway moved fairly slowly, but in her rush she lost her balance. Before she could grab the handrail to right herself, he stepped on behind her, supporting each of her elbows with a firm grasp.

The effect of the sudden contact shocked Aster into immobility. His supportive hold became a caress as his palms eased along her forearms. The flexed muscles of his chest pressed against her back and the warmth of his arms around her made tiny hairline fractures in her shield of ice.

Aster's subconscious quickly sent out the alert that her defenses had been breached and she abruptly jerked out of his hold. "Thank you for your help but I can manage on my own if you don't mind."

She was appalled by her momentary weakness but worse, she knew Cherry had witnessed the incident by the way her shoulders shook with silent laughter. Cherry, the little matchmaker, would make the most of this situation.

Romulus coughed, cleared his throat and took a step backward. He had only meant to be of assistance, but the feel of her in his arms again had been intoxicating. His palms burned from the contact. His entire being responded to her presence, shattering his innocent intentions. It was almost as if—

No! It could not be time.

He began doubting his good sense at wanting to spend the morning with her. He had no business becoming personally acquainted with new arrivals as the complications were sometimes insurmountable. That's why android caretakers were used.

Romulus cleared his throat again and dove into his role as their escort. "This complex contains medical, financial and counseling offices for employment, housing and education. I believe you'll both be visiting career counselors tomorrow morning. Here's where we get off." This time Aster accepted his assistance without a fuss.

There was only one vehicle in the small lot as they exited and Cherry ran ahead to get a closer look.

"Damn! Would you look at this car!" She stroked the shiny red finish with her fingers as she circled the vehicle. It was long and lean, like a convertible Lamborghini, except it had no wheels. The body sat flush with the ground.

Romulus touched something behind the driver's seat and a section in the rear of the car slid open to reveal a small seat.

"Well, what d'ya know—a rumble seat!" Cherry climbed in, not waiting for him to open the door.

Romulus grinned at the young woman's exuberance as he held the door open for Aster then folded himself in behind the steering bar. The reports had noted that the two were very close and yet, their reactions to his world were nearly direct opposites. He was certain there was much more to discover about Aster than Cherry but it would take a lot more than a superficial mind-touch performed by an indifferent nurse. Such a discovery would take time and a more in-depth study, perhaps a hands-on approach.

He slammed the door on that thought. *What the drek was wrong with him?*

With a whisper of air, the car rose off the ground and glided above the roadway. "This next cluster of buildings is the Cultural Center. Here you will find the museum, art gallery and, my personal favorite, the main library. Despite our technological advancements, most Noronians have a fondness for physical art, including books."

"Chief Romulus…" Aster began.

"Please, call me Romulus or better yet, Rom."

"And you call us Cherry and Aster," Cherry quickly countered and received a warning glare from Aster.

"All right…Romulus," Aster conceded, "you mentioned the library yesterday also. Would I find books like we have or just more manuals?"

He winced at her repeated sarcasm about his manuals. "We have a great number of novels and non-fiction works from both our worlds as well as many others."

On another street they passed a park filled with people of all ages and a sparkling blue-green lake on which several sailboats floated and around which three bicyclists raced.

Cherry leaned forward. "Why, it looks like Sausalito. If it wasn't for this car, I'd think we were still in California. Hey, kid, remember the first time we tried sailing and ended up in the Bay?" The two of them laughed out loud at the memory.

Rom's heart tripped at the harmonic sound of Aster's husky laughter combined with Cherry's little-girl giggle. The way his body responded to everything the silver-haired female did was putting him on edge.

"Not exactly Sausalito, Cherry," Aster corrected. "There's no trash in the streets and no smog in the air. In fact, it smells cleaner than a mountaintop in Colorado."

Rom smiled at her observation. "Everything here is recycled, so there is no trash and the air is continuously filtered."

"Filtered?" Aster asked. "Do you have a problem with pollution too?"

He shook his head with a laugh. "Hardly. The air is filtered for the dust. That's the commodity we provide to our home planet, Norona." He stopped himself from delivering another lecture.

"You collect dust?" Cherry giggled again. "Man, have I got a vacuum cleaner bag for you! Hey, ya know, we could sure use some of those filters back home. Aster could even provide the money to install them."

Aster saw her opening and grabbed it. "My Foundation endows funds to protect and clean up the environment but so much of it is guesswork. We could work miracles overnight if we brought back just a little of your knowledge. Planet Earth is—"

"No," Romulus interrupted firmly.

"No? Just like that?"

"No one may return to Outerworld and we are not permitted to interfere with the natural progression of your civilization."

"But it wouldn't be interfering. You'd be helping."

"There is nothing we can do."

His curt words were obviously meant to officially terminate her thoughts of his aiding her world. Aster had no such intention of course, but she knew when to quit pushing and to wait for another opportunity.

Cherry changed the subject. "Where's the mall, Rom? And the beauty salons and restaurants?"

"The Indulgence Center has every conceivable method of pampering or entertaining yourself, including a number of interesting restaurants based on cultures beyond this galaxy. I don't know what that other word is—a mall? I try to keep up with Outerworld news but I rarely have time to absorb much more than the highlights."

"A mall—you know, *stores*, places to buy things."

"Oh, I understand now. The Indulgence Center has some physical stores, but most ordinary shopping is done through your vidcom. Your caretaker can explain it to you."

"No more all-day mall trips hunting for the perfect pair of shoes? This is not paradise after all!" Cherry buried her head on her knees to dramatize her sorrow.

"Don't give up on us yet, Cherry. I think you'll enjoy the Indulgence Center."

As they passed through another residential area, Romulus noted, "These are an example of our more expensive, free-standing residences."

The construction here contrasted severely with the uniformity they had seen elsewhere. One house was made of the crystal prisms, next to it was a ranch-style. There was a gingerbread house and a structure that resembled a miniature Acropolis, even one that looked like a flying saucer.

Aster stared at the peculiar menagerie. "What a conglomeration! Oh, dear." Her eyes opened wide in concern. "Do you live in one of these?"

"Drek, no! This area is a zone where all design controls have been lifted. I do have a free-standing residence but it's on the other side of the province in a zone that maintains strict rules on appearance."

"Hey, ya' know, it's not my thing, but Aster's always been into architecture and design. Like, why dontcha show her your digs one of these days, Rom?"

"Of course, Aster, if that's one of your interests, I'd be proud to show you my home."

She kept her eyes on the road ahead but she felt him looking at her a bit too intensely for the matter at hand. Aster's thoughts leapt at the possibilities his invitation suggested. She needed to spend time with him to work on her plan but she also needed to keep it on a strictly business level. "Oh, I don't know. I gather I'll be kept pretty busy for a while." She expected him to have a follow-up comment to that, especially since he was the one in charge of everything that would be keeping her busy, but he let it drop. The level of disappointment she felt was incomprehensible.

Rom slowed the commuter in front of a magnificent palatial estate that seemed to go on forever. "That's the Indulgence Center and the stone castle next to it is the Arena. If you recall your history about the Middle Ages, you might find the Arena games interesting."

Aster, the perpetual student, came alert. "Middle Ages? You mean knights and jousting and fair maidens?"

"Exactly! As a matter of fact, the other night I had my best match ever. I defeated the Black Knight, which…"

As they drove on, he went on about the games but Aster found it nearly impossible to concentrate on his words. His hazel eyes had changed to a sparkling green and combined with the deepening of his dimple when he smiled, the effect was devastating to her senses. Perhaps her plan wouldn't be so difficult after all. She just had to bide her time.

She asked him several inane questions just to keep him talking and discovered his laughter was a wonderful rumbling sound that she felt as much as heard.

"There's the last thing I'd like to show you today." Romulus pointed to a huge red barn. "Car-Tem Province is made up of four cities which are laid out very much like what you've seen today. However, only here in Car-Tem One will you find the Administration Building and that—our Dance Hall."

"Your what?" Cherry asked incredulously.

"Dance Hall," he replied with a broad grin. "We adopted the name and structure from your culture. It's the largest social gathering anywhere in the Province, every Saturday night. People even come in from some of the far provinces."

"I don't believe this," Cherry mumbled with a groan. "First no mall and now I find out the biggest excitement in this world is a Saturday-night dance. I'm going to wither up and die here."

A short while later, he brought the car to a stop in front of a building similar to the Administration Building, only a fraction of the size. "This is where you'll both be staying. I see Oona and Perd are already here. Good. Make sure they explain the transport system."

Aster swallowed her dismay. Their time with him was over and she hadn't made any progress with her plan. She supposed it was just as well. She had started to enjoy herself and that certainly would never do.

She surveyed her new neighborhood. Trees with red flowers that looked similar to roses lined the street, and the buildings were all made of the same glistening prisms she had noticed last night.

By the time Romulus came around to the passenger side, Aster and Cherry had both stepped out of the commuter on their own.

Cherry held out her hand. "Thank you for the tour, Rom."

"Cherry, my reward was getting to know you a little better. You are a delightful young woman. I'll be anxious to hear from you after you've visited the Indulgence Center."

"Okay, but only if you promise to let us know the next time you'll be playing that game of yours."

Rom congratulated himself on piquing the interest of at least one of his guests. Hoping for a similar response from the other, he turned to Aster and offered his hand. "Aster, it's been—" As their hands touched, a coil of white heat swirled up his arm. When her midnight-blue eyes met his, the desire to pull her closer was overpowering, but the bewilderment he saw there restrained him. She swiftly lowered her gaze, but at least she didn't try to escape his touch this time. For as long as he could protract his sentence he held on to her hand. "...a pleasure."

Aster mumbled something that didn't sound anything like thank you. Pulling her hand away from his, she hurried to catch up with Cherry.

Romulus watched her disappear from view then slowly got back into his vehicle. He still wasn't clear why he had felt such a need to see her again this morning. It was illogical and impulsive. Any relationship with a new arrival was discouraged and destined for disaster. Yet he had been unable to resist.

It was not in Rom's nature to be dishonest, particularly with himself, and he readily admitted this was no simple infatuation. He was inextricably drawn to this woman, logic and ethics be drekked.

His mating time was not due for at least another ten years and just because his father's mating time had come early did not mean his would also. He needed every day of the next ten years to secure his political future before giving in to the distraction and responsibilities of a mate. The premature burning inside him was unexpected and annoying. The fact that the cause of the fever appeared to be an Outerworlder—an alien to be precise—made his response to her entirely improper as well.

Perhaps it was only a false alarm, too much work and not enough play. The asteroid threat alone was causing him enough stress to play havoc with his nervous system. He had heard of such things happening. But there was only one way to find out. Couple with the woman as soon as possible. If the desperate yearning did not go away afterward…Well, there was no need to worry about that ahead of time.

Some people would find fault with him for fraternizing with an Outerworlder for one night but he had to believe his reputation was solid enough to withstand a little gossip.

The immediate problem was the woman herself. Most of the time she seemed to be repelled by him, but he had seen a few glimpses of interest. He could tell she had felt the coil of heat when they'd touched, yet she hadn't seemed to understand what it meant. Surely male-female relationships weren't *that* different for Terrans.

Faced with an unknown, Rom set out to do what any intelligent Noronian would do—research the sexual customs of Terran females.

CHAPTER 6

Aster and Cherry followed their caretakers into the apartment building. Inside, the pleasing design brought a smile back to Aster's face. A fountain bubbled in the center of a lushly landscaped courtyard and the reflective crystalline walls gave the illusion of an enormous park. An indented doorway could be discerned on each of the four sides of the garden on the first floor. On the upper floors, silver latticework-trimmed balconies extended out in front of each of the doors. Nothing about it suggested an alien world but Aster felt quite sure that was completely intentional.

Cherry's apartment was on the ground floor. "I'll come see you when Perd's done showing me around."

Oona led Aster to a waist-high crystal column with vertical silver striations on each of its six sides. "Stand behind the podium and say 'forty-two'. You might want to hold onto it for balance."

Aster did as she was told and was immediately glad for the warning. The second she spoke her apartment number, the entire section of stone beneath them rose straight up in the air, made a smooth left turn and abruptly stopped in front of a balcony on the fourth level. A section of the latticework slid aside and Oona guided Aster through the opening. Instantly, the lift returned to its original location. So, Aster thought with a shake of her head, the place did have a bit of alien world to it after all.

"This button on your gate will call it back up when you need it," Oona advised.

"I think I'd better go back down and get my stomach." Seeing Oona's blank expression, Aster waved her comment away. "Never mind. It was supposed to be a joke."

"I am programmed with an understanding of humor but not the ability to interpret it. Please place your right palm over this sensor then state your name and the words bumblebee, fascinating, house, nowhere, permanent, quick and zoology."

Aster did so and felt a tiny shock.

"Your handprint, voice sample and DNA have now been registered as belonging to the resident of this apartment. From now on, yours is the only hand or voice to which this unit and its facilities manager will respond."

Like the courtyard of the complex, the efficiency-style apartment felt familiar to Aster. The one room was furnished with a dark green sofa and chair, a light wood coffee table and a small dinette set. A Murphy-style bed was concealed in one wall with closet space on each side. A cream-colored carpet covered the floor and soft light emanated from the walls.

Opposite the bed wall were the reflective chrome panels of the supply station and a small desk and chair with a monitor in the wall behind it.

It took Oona very little time to fill Aster in on the capabilities of the facilities manager, as she had received a fair introduction the previous night. The residence came equipped with a full set of manuals anyway, in case she preferred a hard copy.

A soft bell chimed from the desk. "Your vidcom," Oona said, pointing to the monitor. "Touch the screen to accept the call."

Aster smiled when she saw the name *Cherry Cochran* on the monitor and actually chuckled when the instant she touched the screen she saw Cherry's face. "Hey, you. Miss me already?"

"Wait. I hear you but I can't see you. You need to allow the video transmission. Slide your hand down the right side of the monitor to get a menu. Once you do that it's pretty much like the computers we're used to. I think it's just a matter of learning the terminology. Then we can just talk to it instead of choosing from menus."

Aster thought she had no problem figuring it out until Cherry shrieked.

"Whoa! This is definitely too cool! Tell me what you did so I can do it too."

"I chose the full image option. But I don't know what you're so excited about. We've Skyped before."

"Step back a couple feet and you'll see."

Aster did as requested then let out a startled gasp when a three-dimensional image of her friend popped in front of her.

Cherry laughed out loud. "You should see your face. It's a hologram, like we saw in the meeting yesterday. I'm on my way up. Bye!"

A few minutes later Aster opened her door and Cherry burst into the apartment. "Wow! Don't you love that crazy excuse for an elevator! My apartment looks like yours, except it's done in burgundy and grays. I'm hungry. How do you turn on your magic maker?"

"Hello, Josephine," Aster prompted.

"Hello, Aster," the lifelike computer voice replied.

Cherry frowned. "You are so disgustingly predictable. You named your facilities manager after your housekeeper? Oh, well, order me something with a lot of calories and some of that fake wine. Even if they don't allow alcohol, I can pretend."

Before Aster could reply, Oona interrupted. "Excuse me, Miss Mackenzie, now that you have company, I will return to my post in the lobby. But I have one more thing to show you." Oona picked up a box next to the vidcom and handed it to her.

Inside, Aster found what looked like a cross between a watch and an ID bracelet.

"It is your portable vidcom. You can wear it on your wrist or simply attach the bar without the band to your clothing. It is automatically synchronized with your primary vidcom and your facilities manager. I can demonstrate it after your company departs."

Cherry waved a hand at her. "It's okay, Oona. I got this."

"Very well. Miss Mackenzie, just call if you require something." She bowed her head and left them alone.

"Did I hear her say she has a *post* in the lobby?" Aster repeated.

"Yeah. Rom may have said they don't believe anyone means us any harm but they also aren't leaving us unguarded."

"I can't help but wonder if they're protecting us or protecting others from us."

"Ooh, what a spooky thought. Let's talk about Rom instead."

Aster made a face and ordered lasagna and salad for lunch. Throughout their meal, Aster flitted from one topic to another without Cherry interrupting. By the time they were cleaning up, Cherry had had enough.

"C'mon, kid. Lower the shields and talk to me."

Aster sighed. "I left so much undone. I keep

thinking about the Greener Oceans research project. We were finally starting to get some sizable donations. These people could probably save us years of research just by advising us of how to do what needs to be done. We have a golden opportunity to make some real progress out there.

"But that's not the worst of it. If I'm declared dead, the whole Foundation is in jeopardy. I need to get back. I've decided that Romulus seems very rational. I'm going to have to convince him how important my work is. I've faced tough audiences before."

"And had them eating out of your hand in an hour. So what's the problem?"

"I'm confused. He makes me so damned nervous. He touched my hand and I practically fell apart."

"Well, hell. Your hormones finally woke up, that's all. And what a man it took! You want him to help you. From what I saw today, you've got something he wants too. Why not just go with it? Don't tell me you're still being loyal to a dead man."

Aster sat in silence, hugging her knees close to her body. "It's not because of Dennis. Well, not exactly. I just don't have what it takes to seduce a man into giving me something I want."

Cherry stared pointedly at Aster's full breasts. "*Au contraire* from where I'm sitting, sweetie."

Aster sighed and shook her head. "There's something I've never told you, but now, well, maybe it'll help you understand. There's something very wrong with me. As a woman. It's the reason I never wanted you fixing me up with men." She took a slow, ragged breath. "I'm frigid."

Cherry burst out laughing.

"It's not funny." Aster's eyes teared up and Cherry quieted. "I'm a pitiful lover. Dennis always said it didn't matter. He was gentle and didn't force me to do it every time we were together, but I still felt nothing but revulsion when he touched me. I tried to fake a response to please him, but I couldn't even do that right."

"Why would you get engaged to someone so repulsive?" Nothing Aster said about Dennis would alter Cherry's opinion of him. She had always thought he was a phony and he had known it.

"You don't understand. He made me feel more loved than anyone ever had. As far as sex goes, I felt the same way about every man who came near me since I was fourteen."

"You never told me that whole story."

Aster now saw no reason to continue keeping it a secret. "My next-door neighbor was nineteen and had just come home from college. I always had a little crush on him. One afternoon, we were alone in my grandmother's house. When he teased me into a kiss, I liked it. I was more than willing to kiss some more.

"Then he started groping at me. I tried to push him away but he slapped me and told me to lay still or he'd hit me again." Her voice remained flat, unfeeling. "He called me a tease. Said I'd been begging for it. He raped me. Twice. It hurt so much afterward I could hardly walk."

"Did you tell your grandmother?"

Aster grimaced. "She would only have said what she did every time I behaved improperly—'like mother, like daughter'. She would have thrown me out and I had nowhere to go. Anyway, for a long time after that I would get physically ill if anyone touched me at all. To this day, I still have a problem if someone comes too close to me without warning or happens to be wearing the cologne he wore that day. I dated after that but I never let anyone get beyond a good-night kiss, so they didn't stick around long."

"So now you feel it was your fault Dennis couldn't turn you on. I'm sorry about what happened to you, kid, but you're wrong. Your reaction to Romulus proves it."

"It doesn't prove anything except that he's outrageously attractive. I don't want to lead another man on only to have him find out I'm ice cold inside. This time there's more at stake than my shame."

Cherry realized what Aster needed was to be shown, not told, she was wrong. "Listen to me, kid, *doing it* is not the same as making love. There've even been a few men who couldn't get my fire started!" She wiggled her eyebrows. "Will you make me a promise?"

Aster gave a noncommittal shrug.

"The next time you're with Romulus and your body starts acting weird, I mean weird for you, stop thinking and let your gut take over instead. Then tell me all about it!" With that, she gave Aster a playful punch on the arm.

"I wish I could be more like you. Doesn't any of what's happened to us upset you? You have family out there."

"I haven't seen any of them since I left Georgia. You know that. It's too late to think about it now." She had hitchhiked to California the day after graduation and never looked back. Home had been a dirt farm where she slept in the same room with nine sisters and brothers, a place where nobody ever laughed or played or listened to music for fear the devil would possess them. She abruptly changed the subject. "Hey, Josephine, what's the Indulgence Center?"

When there was no response, Aster instructed the manager to respond to Cherry whenever she was in the apartment.

"It is a private enterprise catering to human pleasures."

"Like what?" Cherry prompted.

"I will run the directory of services for your perusal."

The beginning of the list consisted of items any full-service beauty salon and spa would offer, plus cosmetic facial and body alterations. The next section listed restaurants, shops, a variety of entertainments including some they had never heard of and theaters.

The third area, called Fantasy World, had a slogan—*If it's allowed by law and the price is right, any wish can be granted for a day or a night.* Both women groaned at the awful rhyme. Any wish, indeed! That was unbelievable but not as incredible as the services offered in Fantasy World.

"Oh my," Aster whispered.

"No kidding. Coupling, human or android, one-to-one or group. Look at that crazy list of *standard* fantasy enactments. Romulus was right. I'm going to have to check that place out!"

"Cherry!"

"You're such a prude. I didn't mean *everything*. Although it would be different."

"Different? Obviously their morals are a lot different than ours. I could never adjust that much."

"But just imagine pretending to be anybody or anything you ever dreamed of. Wow. Hmmm, I wonder. Josephine, is there any way we could find out if Chief Romulus visits the Indulgence Center?"

"Cherry!" Aster shook her arm.

"Scanning. Chief Romulus has a regular appointment on the first Thursday of each month for hair-trimming and one half-hour coupling with a single female."

Cherry ignored Aster's gasp. "Well, there you go,

kid, a real sex fiend. You better watch out for him. He's due to have his clock cleaned in another week."

"I cannot believe you did that. Anyway he's probably married or keeps company with a nonprofessional."

"Okay, Josephine, is Chief Romulus married?"

"That is an Outerworld term. The closest Noronian term would be joining. It is not equivalent."

"All right, then is the chief joined with anyone."

"No."

Aster tried to stop Cherry. "That's enough."

"Look, he's the one who said they have nothing to hide. I'm only reviewing public information."

"It seems pretty private to me."

"Oh, be quiet. I've only got one more question and then I'll stop. Josephine, would you have any way of knowing if Chief Romulus visits the home of any female or vice-versa?"

"I am able to scan the log of his message center and cross-check with addresses of females. Please define area and time frame."

Aster tried to cover Cherry's mouth but failed. "How about the city of Car-Tem One in the last two months?"

"Scanning." A few seconds passed. "In the last two months, on three occasions, he spent time at the residence of a female named Tarla Yan. No other entries correlate."

"That will be all, Josephine. Power down," Aster demanded.

Cherry pouted. "Sometimes you're no fun at all."

Aster's thoughts ran to safer ground. "This place is made up of such a strange mixture of cultures— jousting, dance halls, mechanical sex. I wonder how it all came together."

"For once in your life, kid, stop studying and try living. From the look on your face, I just overstepped my nagging limit for today. Okay, let's go walk off that lasagna. I'm sure Perd and Oona will keep us protected from any villains on our block."

Later that evening, when Aster snuggled up with her new pillow, she was prepared to see Romulus in her dreams and willed herself to let the sequence run its course. Sleep came quickly but instead of the dream she had intended to welcome, gruesome memories possessed her.

Blood! Oh, Lord, there's so much blood. The sharks are waiting. Harold was not enough. They want Cherry. Isn't she dead anyway? I've got to stop the bleeding. Something sharp stabbed her throat. She turned. Thin lips beneath a narrow black moustache opened into a cruel smile and a white diamond blinded her.

Once more she awoke gasping for breath, searching her room for the nightmarish threat. Remembering that Victor was incarcerated did nothing to calm her fears.

CHAPTER 7

Aster arose Monday morning with the realization that people on the planet's surface were probably searching for The Baronette's passengers. Out there, only four days had passed since she and her friends had boarded the yacht. Here it seemed like an eternity.

To keep from dwelling on that unhappy thought, she purposely shifted her attention to her morning's appointment. She created an outfit to impress an employment agent—a white linen skirt, tailored black silk blouse, and a pair of black-and-white snakeskin heels. All that was missing were earrings and the phony spectacles she usually donned as part of her dowdy, intellectual image. She had added the glasses when she noticed how people, especially men, kept staring at her eyes. Using a long, black ribbon, she secured her hair at the base of her neck.

As she reached the lobby, two women came out of another apartment. Aster smiled and introduced herself but the women stared back at her, looking shocked, as though she had insulted them in some way. They hurried away from her, whispering behind their hands.

* * *

"I am your career counselor, Edward. Please sit down."

Aster shook his limp hand, offered him her best smile and crushed the urge to gawk. He was shorter than she, pudgy around the middle, sallow-complexioned and completely bald. With his yellow uniform, he looked like a large lemon. When she tried to look him in the eyes, she was distracted by his lip movements. He used a translator.

"As you were told in orientation, it is required that you be productive and enjoy what you do for a living. It is imperative that you integrate into society as quickly as possible. Therefore, today I will present the guidelines and choices available to you."

His high nasal voice grated on her already-taut nerves but she folded her hands on her lap and forced another smile.

"Each job has an assigned entry-level income. Trainees, students and positions that require the least amount of education, skill or natural talent earn the lowest incomes. The highest pay goes to those people who perform services that are vital to our existence, such as farmers and miners. You are free to move from one field to another."

Although Edward went on in great detail, he sounded bored and spoke rapidly, as if in a hurry to be rid of her. He asked her to tell him about her education and career experience.

"I graduated magna cum laude from the University of California at Berkeley and received my PhD in economics at Harvard. Those are excellent schools in the United States," she added as an afterthought. She briefly explained her position as director of The Mackenzie Foundation. "My primary interest was in research projects involving the protection and restoration of the environment."

Edward squinted across his desk at the self-centered young female. Why, she not only acted as if she were his equal, her eyes betrayed the fact that she considered herself superior to him. He had opposed the movement to integrate these beings into Innerworld society. The fact that she possessed a degree of intelligence and an exceptionally attractive physical form added fuel to his annoyance. He hated beautiful people, even if they were his own kind. When he spoke again, he did not attempt to hide his distaste.

"We have nothing like that here but with your economics background, perhaps you would fit in at the Economics Center. They are always asking for help but it is much too dull for most Noronians. You would begin with an overall training period, after which you and your supervisor would determine where you would be of the most use. From the notations in your file, I assume it would not prove too difficult for someone of your potential."

"I don't understand. You mean someone has made *notations* about me?"

"Of course," he stated in a tone that implied she was a simpleton. "Your file was created when you arrived and your test results and responses to various stimuli since then have been recorded." He did not need to feed her ego by telling her she ranked in the highest percentile of all Terran humanoids ever tested. However, he was very curious about something in her file.

"The most significant notation was made by Chief Romulus. He normally only submits the briefest of impressions on a new arrival. His comment on you was, and I quote, 'a shining star added to our world'. I do not remember him ever waxing poetic before. You apparently managed to gain his notice for some reason. Perhaps he was carried away by your name." Edward snickered at his own little joke, highly satisfied with the blush coloring her cheeks. Could it be the esteemed chief's head had been turned by a bit of forbidden fruit? What an interesting turn of events that could cause!

"I'm pleased he believes I will be an asset but I truly don't see what his opinion has to do with my getting a job."

Edward gave her a look of pure disdain. Surely she was not as naive as she pretended. "The chief is a very influential man. Some people believe he could walk on water. Sooner or later you will hear how he singlehandedly prevented a rebellion and put an end to the chaos created by new arrivals. There were undoubtedly many others who were capable of instituting such systems but he was fortunate enough to be in the right place at the right time…as usual. It got him where he is today and some people say he might be appointed the next governor of Innerworld. Personally, I have always found him just a little too perfect."

Prevented a rebellion? Aster thought. Good heavens, the man was a hero on top of everything else. The next governor? She had already learned that was the highest authority in Innerworld. And Edward was none too pleased about it. Aster couldn't miss the sarcasm in just about everything Edward had said since she walked in. Why was he sneering at her that way? Jealousy?

The counselor pushed himself back on track and shifted into overdrive. "Would a position at the Economics Center interest you?"

"Yes, that would be fine."

"Such positions fall under the administrative

category and therefore you will make a very good income. When will you be ready to commence?"

Aster could not fathom why Edward should sound so jealous of her prospects but he clearly did. "I'd like to start right away, tomorrow morning if possible."

"Fine. I will inform them to expect you at 0900 tomorrow. Feel free to return to me if you need additional assistance." Edward's words were kind but lacked any sincerity or warmth.

Aster thanked him and offered her hand. His sweaty palm pressed against hers. It was all she could do not to wipe her hand on her skirt as she left his office.

Edward's rudeness reminded her of the two women in her apartment building. In spite of Karl's angry complaints and Romulus's warning, she had not been prepared for any real hostility. She tried to remember what Romulus had said about the American immigrants but it did little to soothe her discomfort.

Edward's comments about the file compiled on her was agitating as well. It made her feel like Big Brother was watching. It didn't matter that one of the Big Brothers had *waxed poetic* over her.

Immersed in her ponderings, she missed the turn to the lobby and tried to reverse her steps, but only managed to get completely lost. Stepping into the first open door to ask for directions, Aster froze. The nameplate on the woman's desk in front of her read *Tarla Yan*—the name from Cherry's little investigation. She stole a glance at the words on the door and almost groaned aloud—*Romulus Locke, Chief Administrator*. Of the thousands of offices in this enormous complex, how could she possibly have ended up here?

"May I help you?" Tarla asked politely. When Aster didn't answer, she tried again. "Are you looking for someone?"

Tarla was gorgeous, dark and petite, with an air of mystery about her. Everything she was not. No wonder Romulus was attracted to her. Aster's heart tightened in her chest.

"I'm sorry. I've lost my way. Could you direct me to the lobby?" She glanced toward the open door behind Tarla, hoping that if the chief administrator was in the rear office, he would not choose this moment to come out.

"You must be one of the new arrivals." Tarla came around her desk to offer Aster her hand. "I'm Tarla, assistant to the chief administrator. I believe you met Chief Romulus already."

"Yes. He…spoke at the orientation." Aster quickly returned Tarla's solid handshake. "Excuse my manners. I'm Aster Mackenzie and, as you might guess, a bit disoriented."

"Come, I'll walk you out."

They didn't get far. Romulus entered the doorway at that moment and his pleasure at seeing her was unconcealed. "Aster! How nice of you to stop by."

"Oh, no," she said too emphatically. "I got lost and ended up here. Tarla was about to lead me back to the lobby."

"That's okay, Tarla, I'll take care of Miss Mackenzie."

Aster started to object but he had already taken her firmly by the arm and was propelling her down the corridor.

Tarla remained in the doorway after the well-dressed stranger had been whisked away by her boss. She didn't need a meteor to fall on her to know that she had just met the reason for Rom's recent peculiar behavior. Aster was gorgeous, blonde and voluptuous, with an air of innocence about her. Everything she was not. No wonder he was attracted to Aster. Oh, Rom. You of all people should know better, Tarla thought miserably. The problems such a liaison could cause her friend were unthinkable.

"I can walk quite well without your support." Meeting Tarla had dealt a serious blow to Aster's already shaky ego.

"Only trying to be helpful." Rom released her arm without moving away from her side. "I was about to get an early lunch. Please accompany me. I'd like to hear how your counseling session went."

Aster's arm still felt warm where he had held it. She started to decline but recalled her plan and Cherry's orders. "All right. Is there someplace here?"

"Yes. It's nothing special but it is convenient."

Once situated in the dining room, Aster related the events of the morning, omitting the antipathy she had encountered.

"You raised my curiosity yesterday when you mentioned your foundation, so I did a little research. It looks like we've added a celebrity to our population."

"Hah! Some celebrity. My work has generated as many enemies as fans."

"That's not what the magazine article I read stated. You've certainly received an impressive collection of awards for your contributions."

She knew he referred to the issue of *Fortune* magazine, in which she was listed as one of the wealthiest women in the world and one of the most aggressive environmentalists.

"Tell me about The Mackenzie Foundation."

This was her opportunity to influence his thinking, and she found herself conversing easily once she ignored the way he made her feel.

"The Mackenzies made their first million during the

California Gold Rush. My grandmother discovered she enjoyed controlling people as much as money. By setting up the endowment fund, she could do both. When I went to work for the foundation, a good deal of money was being donated from business and industry and being directed toward technology. As far as I could see, they had too much to say about who received the grants. I badgered my grandmother incessantly about how much better the money could be used.

"It was my belief that since the Mackenzies got their wealth from Mother Earth, we should find ways to pay her back. I wanted to donate the bulk of our funds to agencies and individuals who wanted to work toward rehabilitating our environment. Eventually, I got my way.

"Our planet is dying and not enough people care enough to make it a priority. Sometimes I would get so frustrated, I wanted to chuck the whole thing. Then I would read about another once-beautiful lake being destroyed or another animal facing extinction and I'd be ready to spit fire again."

Watching the woman as she spoke, Rom could certainly believe that. He was overwhelmed by the glow that lit her eyes now that she was on familiar ground. Under that cool exterior beat a passionate heart. He hadn't analyzed his reasons yet but it was essential that she feel just as passionate about his world.

"Did you know we've created enough garbage to bury ourselves? Mountain-high landfills of trash spoil the countryside. Our tropical rain forests are being destroyed. Our oceans and rivers are being polluted so badly that our descendants may never see fish in their natural habitat. And the ozone layer— Oh my, it seems I never leave my soapbox far behind. I realize you're not very interested in all this, but I—"

"Hold on there. You couldn't be more wrong. The condition of Outerworld and the planet's atmosphere is of vital importance to me, to all of us."

"But yesterday you said you couldn't help with those problems."

"We can't. But that doesn't mean we're indifferent. You see, we must be able to pass through the doorways to conduct our business with Norona. At one time accidents such as you had on the boat were rare. The contaminants in Outerworld's air and water have a direct effect on Earth's magnetic fields. The worse the pollution gets, the more often vessels and aircraft in those fields go undetected. But that's not the only problem. In some places, the contamination is seeping below the ocean floor, into the crust. We have begun to find signs of deterioration in our tunnels. If the conditions in Outerworld aren't corrected, we could eventually end up being sealed off from the rest of the universe."

Aster's eyes widened in clear surprise. "But if cleaning up the planet is so important to your world, why haven't you made yourselves known? With your technology and knowledge, you could probably restore everything—even the ozone layer—and instruct everyone on how to keep it that way."

He was rapidly losing his patience in spite of his attraction to her. "I already told you, it's against our laws to interfere with Outerworld civilization unless the planet is facing imminent destruction. If you ever get around to researching our history, you'll understand better. It has been our hope that the people of Earth will learn how to take care of their home without our stepping in." His thoughts flew to the oncoming asteroid and realized that, if the emissary was not found soon, they may have no choice about interfering.

Aster huffed. "That's a ridiculous law. You could do so much good."

"And it could be construed as some sort of alien invasion bent on taking over your planet. We could also start a worldwide panic. Imagine how the people on the surface would react to our presence."

She pondered that for a moment. "Some would welcome you. But you're right about the fear factor. Way too many movies done on that theme."

"Exactly. Terrans were never as trusting after the Trojan horse incident."

She grimaced and took another moment before replying. "All right. I'll concede your point for the moment. Aliens making themselves known and telling us what to do might be a problem. So, why not pass the information on secretly, say…to a well-known environmentalist, who—"

"No!" The sharpness of his voice even stunned himself and he continued in a quieter tone. "You don't understand what's involved."

"*I* don't understand? You're the thickheaded one at this table. You say you were impressed with my work. If I don't get back there, all my efforts could go down the drain. I left half a dozen viable research applications on my desk that might be rejected now. If you can't see your way clear to revealing any secrets, at least let me go back to continue my work. There are several trustees on the Board who will jump on my absence to put a stop to the grants I was establishing."

He clenched his fists to keep from reaching across the table and shaking her.

"I would never tell anyone about your world."

How was she able to scramble his brain so badly that he couldn't even repeat the standard responses. What the drek was wrong with him?

"Damn it! This is important!" She paused and took a slow, calming breath. "Okay, look, let me go back, say for one month, long enough to secure the future of the foundation and ensure that the focus remains on saving the planet. Then you can bring me back. You could send Oona with me. What do you say?"

Romulus struggled against the unreasonable urge to give her whatever she wanted, just to make her smile again. Her emotional begging caused the most peculiar wrenching in his chest. Ordering his mind to get control of his body, he found his voice again. "Let me ask you a question. Why doesn't your government enforce more clean-up programs?"

"Which government? In the United States, the businesses that cause the majority of the pollution have much stronger lobbies than the people trying to save the planet. In other countries, sometimes mere survival is more than they can handle. I have always thought the only way Earth will be spared is with a worldwide environmental police force, but that's a dream that stands very little chance of happening in my lifetime."

"What about your United Nations?"

"The U. N. actively concerns itself with military aggression of one country against another, but environmental issues have pretty much gotten *outsourced* to other global organizations or committees, such as the U. N. Environmental Programme which has made great strides in research and analysis, but basically have no power. There was one group created with enforcement in mind, but they couldn't even convince the United States or China to join them."

It would be easier for Rom to disagree with her if she made no sense but her reasoning was valid, her conclusions irrefutable. A unified effort by all the governments of Outerworld was the only answer and she had worked long and hard to create a plan that might go a long way to get such a unification off the ground. And yet, Rom had no choice but to refuse her request to go back, no matter how important her work was. "Tell me about your family."

Aster blinked in surprise. She had at least expected a response to her comments so that she could continue the debate. But perhaps he lacked the conviction of his earlier words. Perhaps she was making progress with his rational mind. As if his changing the subject was acceptable, she responded to his question. "Cherry's like a sister to me and she's here. I was an only child but I don't remember my parents. My grandmother raised me and she died last year."

The arrival of their dessert spared her from explaining a source of embarrassment. Her childhood melted into a haze. She knew she was born in a commune in Oregon and that the teenage boy who had fathered her had taken off for Canada before she was born and never returned as far as anyone could determine. Her grandmother was his mother but he had rejected her and her vast fortune. Aster had no recollection of ever taking a bath or owning a pair of shoes for the first eight years of her life.

One day, her grandmother took her away. Her mother, far off on a hallucinogenic trip, never objected, then or afterward. Aster was immediately scrubbed to within an inch of her life and forced to wear frilly dresses and polished shoes that hurt her toes. A private tutor badgered her all day long. The only people to talk to in the huge mansion were the servants and they weren't permitted to play with her. The loneliness was worse than the unfamiliar rules and severe discipline. She learned quickly that if she obeyed each command, or better, if she could anticipate the order, she rarely experienced the weight of her grandmother's hand or the sting of her teacher's paddle. So she strove to be perfect enough to please everyone.

Upon her grandmother's death, she had inherited everything. The real irony was now that Aster would be presumed dead it would all go to the woman her grandmother had hated so much—Aster's mother. If she was alive. And if they could track her down. If not, where would all that money go?

When she set her fork on her empty plate, Romulus asked quietly, "Was there a man in your life?"

"I was engaged to be married. He was murdered six months ago." She looked away.

Warning bells clanged in Rom's brain. No wonder she was as skittish as a newborn colt. During her extended silence, he had clearly felt that she was remembering another tragedy. It didn't bode well for him that he was experiencing such strong empathy with her. Although he knew all the reasons not to spend time with a new arrival, the reasons why he needed to get to know this one were piling up.

The logical part of his mind demanded he return to his office and leave her and her grief to someone more capable, to run from her convincing arguments that tempted him—a chief administrator—to break a primary law. His emotional side argued that all she needed was tender loving care, something he suddenly felt very capable of offering. He could help her overcome her losses, make her understand his point of view. But it would take time, his mind told him, something he could not afford as a nominee for the governorship. By concentrating on his high hopes for his political future, his logical side won the brief skirmish.

From the frown on Romulus's face, Aster surmised

either her persistence had seriously annoyed him or her gloominess had depressed him as well. She decided to help him escape from her. "It was very kind of you to spend so much time with me but I know I'm keeping you from your work."

"I'm afraid you're right. I do need to get back to my office. I'll walk you out to the lobby first." This time he kept a good distance between them as they walked.

When they reached the front entrance, Romulus wished her good luck in her new job and walked away without so much as a parting handshake.

Faced with a free afternoon, Aster took a stroll down the lilac-edged sidewalk to the library. Romulus's comments about Innerworld's stand on noninterference convinced her to learn a little more about this world, so she settled in at an available vidcom.

To find the origins of Innerworld, Aster had to go back about twelve thousand years to the planet of Norona. She quickly learned that a fuel shortage had threatened to undermine their entire civilization. For centuries, expeditions had searched the galaxies for a new source of the energy needed to keep their planet from returning to a primitive age, but to no avail.

When the rare, dust-like substance, volterrin, was discovered inside the planet Earth in unlimited quantities, the people had rejoiced. It was estimated that the amount of Earth's volterrin was sufficient to power Norona indefinitely without affecting the donor planet. The fact that Earth was populated with *homo sapiens*, like themselves, was an unexpected dividend.

Fascinated, Aster read on. At the same time the Noronian energy crisis had peaked, a revolt sprang up, mounted by a small group of malcontents who wanted to return to the simpler ways of life, before technology and volterrin. It was decided that since that was their wish, the rebels would be sent to Earth where civilization was extremely primitive and would be scattered among the humans on the surface. Thus, when Noronian spaceships were outfitted to carry several thousand people to colonize the center of the valuable planet, the rebels were on board.

No one could have foreseen the catastrophe the Noronians had unleashed. During the long years the Innerworlders occupied themselves constructing a world to duplicate their own, the rebels in Outerworld thrived uncontrolled. With their superior mental abilities and knowledge, they allowed Earth's simplistic people to believe they were gods and the budding civilization regressed to barbarism and depravity.

The mythological gods of Greece and Rome were as human as their lowly subjects, but with their advanced mental abilities, they had no trouble inspiring awe in the Terrans. One of the cruelest Egyptian leaders was an extraterrestrial rebel who was mad with power and considered his subjects mere beasts of burdens. Without restraints, evil grew until it could no longer be reversed.

Something had to be done and the decision of the ruling Tribunal on Norona was extreme but successful. Earthquakes, volcanic eruptions and catastrophic floods were purposefully triggered and civilization had to begin again with hand-picked survivors, but without hindrance from the Noronian intruders. Earth's peasants who were saved did not comprehend the truth and so the memories of those gods and their temples lived on through the surviving worshipers.

Aster devoured the information as fast as it appeared on the screen. The inflexible part of her mind voiced doubts, but proof of the truth of what she had read was that she was here, in Innerworld, and the world she knew was no longer accessible to her.

She scrolled to the next paragraph and read on. After the "natural" disasters, the Tribunal had dictated that the future of the planet Earth must be carefully monitored so that such corrective measures would never again be necessary and that Norona's stability would be insured. As Outerworld civilization developed, it became essential to place Noronian emissaries in strategic locations on Earth, living quietly, but prepared to intervene subtly if their host planet or its natives appeared to be threatened.

Alien spies, Aster interpreted with a queasy feeling, until she read a little further. There were only a few events in recent history when emissaries had been used. One was the sabotage of Germany's atomic bomb research during World War II. No one would ever know how close the Terrans had come to doomsday. Aster shuddered to think of what her world might have been like without Innerworld's selective interference.

There was so much more she wanted to know but decided on just two more subjects for today. The first was the air filtration Romulus mentioned. When she got back home, and somehow she would, she wanted to take a treasure with her.

Ping. The faint sound caught Romulus's attention and he noted the blue flashing dot on his monitor, notifying him that someone had just accessed a Code II file containing Innerworld's most sensitive information accessible to the public. Code I was strictly confidential, like Operation Palomar, and could only be accessed by a few authorities. Out of curiosity more than concern, he pulled up the visual of the inquirer and the researched information.

When Aster's studious face appeared, he didn't wait to read the bio running across the bottom of the screen. He stormed out of his office and headed for the library. He had no doubt her questions about the filters went beyond casual interest. She didn't seem to comprehend the meaning of the word no.

For the first time in her life, Aster wished her background had been in science instead of economics. It was going to take more than a quick read to understand the construction of the filters. She would have to learn how to access the library files from her apartment where she could take extensive notes in private.

Now to find out about Edward's remarks. Since she knew so little about the near-rebellion he had referred to, it seemed to Aster the most expedient route to the information was through the man involved. She activated a keyboard and typed *Romulus Locke*. As though typing the letters generated the power to conjure up the subject, she heard his voice behind her.

"Hello. Learn anything interesting?"

Her fingers quickly switched off the screen. When the ripple stopped at the bottom of her spine, Aster stood and turned to find herself within inches of Romulus's imposing form. She could not back up and he seemed intent on crowding her.

"How long have you been standing there?" she asked, hoping he could not sense her momentary panic.

Romulus blocked her escape. "What were you reading?"

"History." It was suddenly so stuffy she could barely breathe. "Do you have the time?"

"About 1800 hours. Do you have another appointment?"

"No. I just wondered. I was so involved with what I was learning, I lost track of time. Let's see, that would be six o'clock, right?"

"Right. May I give you a lift home then?"

Aster paused only a moment before accepting his offer. It would be easier to let him take her home than trying to find her way on the shuttle.

En route, Romulus encouraged her to share what she had learned.

"As a matter of fact, I covered about twelve thousand years of history. That was plenty for starters."

"And?"

"I was fascinated. I always thought there were too many holes and myths in our early history."

"What did you want to know about me?" He kept his eyes on the road.

Aster cringed. He had seen his name. Compose yourself, she thought. "I heard you prevented a rebellion but it wasn't mentioned in the history I read. Will you tell me about it?"

"It wasn't much." Wasn't much? Just the most important event of my life. He had planned to question her about her interest in the filters when he walked up behind her. Then she typed his name on the screen and his stomach had done a somersault.

"For many years the handful of Outerworlders who got trapped here were easy to deal with. Unfortunately, as their numbers grew, some reacted violently to their circumstances. Terrans were considered too dangerous to be allowed to live among Innerworlders. They were contained in camps, taken care of and...studied.

"About twenty years ago, one group refused to live out their lives under such controls. They escaped their encampment and took over the central mine and Car-

Tem's Administration Building. I was a junior administrator at the time and they held me as one of the hostages. To make a long story short, I convinced their leader and Governor Elissa to meet and work out some compromises. She had the tougher job. She had to convince the Tribunal on Norona that we needed to update the laws concerning Outerworlders."

They pulled up in front of her building and Aster regretted that they had arrived so quickly. She had so much more to ask him. "Would you like to come in for dinner? It's the least I can do for a living legend. I really would like to hear more." Wouldn't Cherry be pleased she had taken the initiative?

"Great." What happened to his good resolutions of only hours ago to stay away from her? He rationalized that he still had to discuss the matter of her curiosity about the filters.

Throughout their meal, Aster pumped him for details of his exploits. She couldn't help but notice how his eyes turned greener the more she showed interest in his accomplishments. "I apologize for the snide comments I made about your work, Romulus. You've earned the right to be proud."

His stomach did another flip. She had called him Romulus *and* praised his work, all in one breath. In the case of this female, he considered it real progress. Suddenly he knew why he had accepted her dinner invitation. It was his curiosity, not hers, that had to be dealt with.

Aster watched his green eyes soften to a warm brown as his gaze drifted over her and settled on her mouth. He rose from his dinette chair and came toward her with an expression on his face that seemed to be desire. *Had Cherry been right about his being interested in her personally?* Her chest constricted with apprehension but, when he reached for her hand

and led her to the sofa, she didn't hesitate to sit next to him.

His head dipped down until his lips brushed ever so gently against hers. He lightly pecked the corners of her mouth. When she closed her eyelids, he kissed her lashes then the tip of her nose.

A small sigh escaped her, involuntarily encouraging him. His arm slid around her back, pulling her snugly against him, while his other hand removed the ribbon from her hair.

"I want you very much, Aster. You understand that, don't you?" Rom breathed the words into her ear between kisses that burned her throat and neck.

Aster squeezed her eyes tightly against the expected assault. His mouth took possession of hers, yet she wasn't at all repulsed. To the contrary, she wanted more. Her fingers snaked their way around his neck to tangle in his hair. An unfamiliar pulsing had begun deep within her and settled between her legs. She arched against him, seeking a satisfaction she was not certain existed for her. Amazingly, she found she *could* quit thinking and just feel.

When his tongue outlined her lips, she parted them and his tongue touched hers. She tensed again but his teasing movements tempted her to return the pleasure. He tasted wonderful. How could she have known such bliss existed?

Abruptly, he pushed her away. In one savage move, he ripped her blouse from her shoulders, leaving shreds hanging from her wrists. He shoved her onto her back and yanked down her bra. The mouth that had been so tender a moment ago, viciously closed over one exposed nipple.

The scream was inside her head but the sound never escaped. Her entire body had frozen and gone numb the second she heard her blouse tear.

He finally noticed the change in her. He stopped his attack to look at her face. Her unblinking eyes were filled with terror, not lust, and her skin was more ashen than her hair.

"Aster? Is something wrong? Didn't I do it properly?" She stared straight ahead, not answering him. When her body started to tremble, he knew he had made some terrible mistake. "Aster! I didn't mean to hurt you. I was trying to please you. I read it in an Outerworld book! It was supposed to be a classic romance. I wanted it to be perfect for you. Do you hear me? Aster!" He took her in his arms and hugged her hard. A minute passed with no response from her. In desperation, he resorted to the only other way he knew how to reach her. He placed his two fingers at her temple.

What he saw when he touched her mind brought tears to his eyes. How could he have known? The heroine in the book fell madly in love with the pirate who had treated her in the same fashion Rom had imitated. He relayed all of this to her and hoped she could forgive him.

Touching her mind was like grabbing hold of a lightning bolt. Never had he experienced anything so powerful. He had to use every bit of his will to break the contact, but before he did, he gave her a gentle suggestion to have a good night's sleep with pleasant dreams. Rom held Aster tightly until he felt her tremors stop and heard her soft whimper. She fell asleep with her head next to his heart.

Aster dreamed the old dream again but this time the handsome man had finally kissed her. And, oh dear god, what a kiss it was.

"Good morning, Aster. It is 0700. Are you awake?"

"Mmm. Not now, Grandmother," she moaned,

irritated by the interruption. What bad timing! Slowly, she became aware that she was on the sofa, not in bed. She'd been covered by a blanket, but beneath that her blouse was torn.

"Good morning, Aster. It is 0715. Are you awake?"

"I heard you the first time. Yes, I'm awake."

"Please remember to respond to your wake-up call if you do not wish me to repeat it."

Aster wondered how a computer managed to sound insulted. She should be able to grumble at a stupid machine without feeling guilty about that too. She wished she had not insisted on starting her new job this morning, but then she never could have anticipated what happened last night. What a fool she had been. She had actually begun to think Romulus was different, that he could awaken something exciting hidden inside her. Instead, he put it deeper to sleep.

In the past, she shut out her fears by staying overly busy. Today would be the same. She just wouldn't think about it.

At the Economics Center her supervisor, a shy, grandfatherly man named Keshu, showed her around then stationed her in the Center's Research Room.

Once she assured him that she had no questions at this time, he left her to her own devices. For hours she poured over volumes of material, purposely not stopping for a lunch break. The possibility of running into Romulus in the dining room effectively killed her hunger pangs.

At the end of the day, the five-minute shuttle ride to her apartment contrasted sharply with ugly memories of driving in traffic to and from the foundation offices every day. She admitted that there were a few things to appreciate in this new world and she could hardly wait to get back to her studies tomorrow. It was a good sign.

Cherry dropped in while she was having dinner and, before she thought about it, Aster told her about the episode with Romulus. "You see what happens when I follow your advice?"

"Whoa, kid. My advice was good. After what you told me the other day, I understand how he would have scared you and that bit about him talking to your mind is really freaky. But he told you what his mistake was. His only crime was reading the wrong book while trying to do the right thing. More than likely, if he had just acted naturally, we'd be having a much more interesting conversation tonight. Aw, c'mon, kid, give him another chance."

"He won't want another chance. He knows. He saw it in my mind." Until she said the words, she had not realized that his reading her thoughts and knowing her secret had upset her almost as much as what he had done.

Cherry twisted her features into an expression of complete exasperation but refrained from giving more advice. "Okay, my turn. Starting this Friday, I'm going to work in the Indulgence Center."

"What?"

"God, what a face! I'll be working in Fantasy World as an actress! I'll play parts in other people's fantasies, bit ones at first, but when they see how good I am, I know I'll be doing lead roles in no time. The best part is, because it's in the entertainment field, even the small roles pay fairly well.

"This is a dream come true for me. When I was a kid, I would pretend I was a star and everyone came to see me, begging for my autograph. My parents swore I'd burn in hell for such thoughts but I never forgot that dream."

Aster managed a genuine smile. "I know you'll be

great too. I always thought you were a big showoff."

Cherry beamed under Aster's encouraging words. She never felt as confident as she acted. "Geez, I only meant to visit for a minute. I assume you got a job working with numbers. Do you think you'll like it?"

"I think so. I'd tell you about it but I know you'd be totally bored by the details."

"You're right there. I've got to go, kid. Keep your chin up. I have a good feeling about this guy. You'll see."

Aster gave her friend one last skeptical look before closing the door behind her. Try as she might, it was impossible to deny that from the first moment she saw Romulus, Aster felt drawn to him. And not simply because he had the power to assist her. She could not forget the unfamiliar longing that had accompanied the touch of his lips on hers, a kiss so sensuous that the memory of it made her sigh.

Rom recalled occasions in the past when he may have made a slight error in judgment. But never had he so grossly miscalculated a situation. It was completely illogical.

The signs had been coming for some time. He had made excuses for the tension that had begun weeks ago and the fierce burning that ignited four days ago when he had first touched her. But now there could be no more denials. Touching Aster's mind only confirmed it. Part of him had fought to remain with her.

His mating time was upon him at a point in his career when it could be ruinous, at a time when Innerworld needed him to be at his levelheaded best. His fever would soon build to an internal inferno until nothing mattered but the antidote. He knew for certain now that the cure was Aster—an unacceptable female.

To possess her completely, to *join* with her, would destroy his career. He already realized how vulnerable he was to her when he had been unable to refute her logic at lunch in a calm manner and when the need to kiss her made him forget to confront her about her interest in the filters.

There was one thing he was not mistaken about. Her initial response to him, though hesitant, had been filled with desire. Would the fever consume her also? He was certain Terrans did not suffer the same symptoms as Noronians. At least she would not be coming to him—not after what he had done. It simply remained for him to stay away from her. Somehow he had to ignore the burning. As far as he knew, he would be the first Noronian to accomplish that feat.

CHAPTER 8

Nick Valentino always believed he would make it. Even when he had to quit school at fourteen to get a job, he had told himself that it was only temporary. His older brother was in jail, his father was a bum, not around half the time and drunk when he was, and his mother had gotten too sick to work. It had been up to Nick to feed them.

He had taken care of his mom until she died and never forgot his promise to her not to end up like his father or brother. He would be somebody, someday.

On his sixteenth birthday he had headed south in search of his fortune. Nick landed in Fort Lauderdale along with the other runaways who slept behind garbage dumpsters, but he never considered himself one of them. His situation was only temporary.

When he couldn't get work, he sold his blood then learned to sell himself. There were plenty of wealthy, older women happy to pay for his company. He became Valentino and learned how to give more pleasure than he received. He taught himself a gimmick to use when he was with an exceptionally old or unattractive customer. While his hands and mouth did what he was being paid for, he concentrated on the money he would have someday, itemizing each expensive thing he would buy. By the time he got to the accessories on his Ferrari, he had a satisfactory erection. Nick knew his mother would not have been proud of what he did, but he slept on clean sheets and ate three meals a day. And it was all temporary.

One woman had seen something more in him than a pleasant diversion. She referred him to a friend who got him his first steward's job. It was a definite step up. Of course there were still bored, lonely women on the cruises he worked and he was not above earning extra tips. The difference was that he could afford to be more choosy. His bank account had been growing but he was years away from keeping his promise to his mother.

Until now. Nick's thoughts jerked back to the present. One day he was scrounging for nickels and the next he had the key to a fortune.

Signing on at a volterrin mining camp was serious business to these people. Leaves of absence were doled out sparingly and a miner agreed to remain in one of the distant provinces for at least two years. Nick laughed at all the points the counselor had considered negative. After the last four years, it sounded like a vacation to him.

So what if mining was boring, manual labor and few human women resided at the camp? He would be rich! If only he could brag to all the assholes who thought he was nothing. If only his mother knew that he had kept his promise.

Thoughts of untold riches produced the usual result for Nick. Rubbing his hand over the bulge in his pants, he knew no woman had ever aroused him as much as a hundred-dollar bill, but he still preferred a woman for sexual relief.

Having received a large bonus for signing up as a miner, he was sure he could afford a night out. His caretaker had told him about the Indulgence Center. He had never paid for sex before. It might be kind of a kick to be on the receiving end for a change.

Wearing his customary skin-tight jeans and muscle-revealing t-shirt, he left to find the Indulgence Center.

Tarla frowned at the unopened correspondence on Rom's desk. For all the work he had done he may as well have stayed out the last two days. One minute he had his head buried in his work and the next he stomped out of the office, only to return a few minutes later and repeat the whole process again. She had tried to talk to him but he insisted nothing was wrong. Well, she thought, whatever it was had better peak soon. He was driving her crazy.

Tarla's intuition told her Aster was his problem and she wondered how it would feel to have a man behave so foolishly over her.

The emptiness she had lived with for so long threatened to take over again and she decided to do something about it. Perhaps she would treat herself to a fantasy, maybe something exotic. Yes, that was the answer. She felt better just thinking of what the IC might offer her tonight.

As Tarla approached the reception desk, she spotted a dark-haired young man wearing a very interesting outfit which blatantly emphasized every muscle in his compact body. He was studying the directory with a puzzled expression. The way he looked, he should be on the menu.

"May I be of some help?" Tarla offered.

Nick had seen the woman approach out of the corner of his eye and was immediately intrigued by her sultry voice. He turned to charm her with one of his sexiest smiles but was halted by the vision in front of him. She was the most beautiful woman he had ever seen. Her long black hair hung straight to her tiny waist and her thick bangs stopped just above her dark, slanted eyes. Her exotic looks made him think of a Tahitian princess.

"Are you, I mean, do you work here?" Nick asked when he finally found his voice.

Tarla smiled, wondering at his discomfort. She could even detect a slight blush under his tanned complexion. "No, but I've been here before and you look confused."

"That's putting it mildly. I've only been here a few days and I've been confused most of the time. I mean, I know why I came but then I started reading this directory and—"

"You just arrived, literally?" Tarla interrupted. "I mean, are you one of the new arrivals?" She made no attempt to hide her interest.

"Yeah, I guess that's what they call us." He was pleased with the way her eyes got bigger when she heard that. "Anyway, I'm not sure what to make of all this stuff."

"Then you should definitely have my help. My name is Tarla. I hope we can be friends," she said sincerely.

"I'm Nick Valentino. Umm, could I buy you dinner?"

"I think that would be a nice start, Nick. Then maybe you'd like a tour to help you decide how to spend the rest of the evening."

Tarla directed him to a cozy, dimly lit restaurant where they were seated at a table next to a fireplace. Nick was completely entranced with the beautiful creature seated across from him. Her hair reflected the dancing colors from the burning logs and her body moved with the swaying sounds of the background lute music. It was a very romantic scenario for two people who had met only ten minutes ago.

When the waiter had taken their order, Nick launched the first and, for him, the most difficult, question. "Look, I really don't know what's expected of me. I mean, if I was in my own world and I was with someone as gorgeous as you, I'd know all the right moves. Here, I'm not sure about anything."

"First of all, nothing is expected of you, except to enjoy yourself. Second, you should always follow your instincts, unless they're harmful." It would have been easier to answer him if she was feeling indifferent but the opposite was true. The nearness of this excellent specimen of masculinity was exhilarating. The fact that he was a Terran as well had her blood sizzling. How could she ever have thought they were an inferior breed? She searched Nick's dark eyes and saw a reflection of her own hunger.

"Relationships are much simpler here. A human's need to couple is a natural physical urge and it's unhealthy to suppress it. On the other hand, love and friendship involve an emotional attachment. When a Noronian couple mate for life, it's called joining. It's a lot more complex than your marriage."

Nick had gathered that people here had a different attitude toward sex the minute he'd started reading the directory in the lobby. He decided to take his cue from the relaxed manner in which Tarla discussed the issue. The conversation continued as each asked technical and hypothetical questions about the other's world, but never straying far from the subject of male/female relationships.

"Tarla, I haven't heard anything you've said for the last ten minutes. I am so turned on that if I stand up

I'm going to embarrass myself. Is that following my instincts?"

Tarla was not embarrassed. Her flush was from sheer pleasure. His unpolished flattery was refreshing and added to her own arousal. She reached across the table, slowly dragging a long fingernail along his muscular forearm.

"I'm very glad to hear that, because I think if I just rubbed my thighs together I could bring my own release. But I won't. Instead, we're going to sit here a while longer and talk about something *un*-stimulating and then I promised you a tour, remember? Now, tell me what career you've selected."

His body's heated reaction to her words astonished him. He couldn't remember that ever happening so easily before. Although she suggested a cooling-off period, her voice and eyes kept the burner on.

She could not have chosen a better subject to sidetrack him though. A discussion of Innerworld mining and his personal future led to his reasons behind his decision. Gradually, she encouraged him to tell her about his past. Of course he couldn't tell her everything, but as he spoke, he felt his heart soften for the first time since his mother had died. Tarla, a complete stranger *and* an actual alien, made him feel whole again and he didn't want to question why.

Tarla remained quiet, holding his hand and letting her eyes speak of her compassion. She had no way of understanding the kind of life he knew in Outerworld but she had the ability to draw the pain from his soul. It wasn't necessary for Nick to know how she was doing it. After all, keeping a secret was not the same as being dishonest.

Nick was not the most intelligent or sophisticated male she had ever encountered but he was sweet and sexy and so very vulnerable. He called to every one of her feminine instincts. Mostly he was begging to be loved, though he seemed unaware of it, and she wanted to be the one to give him that love. Yes, she thought, we could be very good for each other.

"Come, Nick Valentino. You came here for a good time and so did I. If you'll put your trust in me for a few hours, I'm confident we'll both leave here a lot happier."

Hand in hand, Tarla led Nick through the four wings of the complex, purposely leaving the West Wing for last. In each area, she was careful to point out what was offered there and the price ranges, like any competent tour guide.

Nick asked a few questions and paid attention as she spoke, but he was not interested in a haircut or seeing a play and she knew it. "Since you've been such a good boy, I'm going to let you have what you came here for," she teased. "You paid for dinner, dessert will be my treat." She stopped his objection by quickly placing her finger on his lips. She stepped closer to him until their bodies were separated only by the light touch of her hand on his chest. "What is it you came here for, Nick? A quick release or a fantasy come true? You can have either you know." Her words came out breathlessly and she could feel his rapid heartbeat beneath her fingers, keeping pace with her own.

"Why don't I leave it up to you?"

She smiled softly and nodded. "I want you to stay right here for a little while. I'm going to make the arrangements for your special pleasure. Someone will come and tell you when it has been set up and where you should go. Do whatever that person says, okay?"

He had not expected her to leave, just like that. "Wait, uh, what about you? I mean, didn't you come here for something tonight too? I thought, maybe, well, uh, will I see you again?" He knew he was stuttering like an inexperienced boy but he didn't want her to get away.

"Now, now. You said you would leave it up to me. I promise you will see me again. Please, just relax and enjoy yourself."

Nick was totally bewildered as she hurried away but he would not move from that spot for anything short of an earthquake. It felt like hours instead of only the thirty minutes that passed when a short figure, dressed in the trappings of a desert nomad, shuffled up to him. The head, completely covered by a beige muslin scarf, remained bowed.

"You are The Sheik? Valentino?" The voice was a whisper, possibly a woman's.

Nick almost laughed out loud but he did not want to spoil the surprise Tarla had arranged. "Yeah, I guess so."

"Come with me please."

Nick obediently followed the woman into a room decorated for a sultan. Brightly colored silks billowed from the ceiling and white satin pillows were scattered all over the floor. An oversized chaise longue sat in the center. Its gilded framework was embedded with hundreds of glittering gems and a rich burgundy velvet covered its cushions.

While Nick gaped at the sumptuous display, his escort stepped aside and clapped her hands once. Instantly, three robed men came forward, bowing low before him.

One man opened the lid of the box he was holding. Handing it to Nick, he said, "A tribute to The Sheik from his loyal subjects." It was filled with diamonds, rubies and emeralds of all shapes and sizes. They looked very real Nick thought as he tried to keep a straight face.

The second man offered him an ornate silver key which was more than a foot long. "My country would be most honored if you would accept our gift of a palace overlooking the sea."

Entering into the play with all the majesty he could muster, Nick solemnly took the key with a slight nod of his head and handed it to his guide along with the jewel box. With his feet apart and his arms folded across his chest, he took on the stance he imagined a sheik would assume while the third man spoke.

"From my country I bring you four beautiful slave girls to ease the burdens of your days." He snapped his fingers and the women hustled forward with downcast eyes.

Nick coolly inspected these last gifts. The four very different women, one fair and buxom, one dark-skinned and lean, another Oriental and petite and the last was tall and muscular with flaming orange hair, were clad in transparent harem costumes. Was he supposed to make his own selection for the evening?

Nick barely noticed when his guide clapped her hands again and the men backed out of the room. The four women came forward and removed his clothing. Accustomed as he was to having strange women admire his naked body, he had never found himself exposed to so many female eyes at once.

Somewhere a flute began playing and the slave girls gyrated to the rhythm. They circled him, forty fingers stroking with light feathery touches from his neck to his thighs until Nick's flesh was covered with goose bumps.

When he shivered violently from head to toe, his torturers led him to the chaise, propping up his head and back with pillows. They passed a painted vase amongst them from which each poured a golden liquid into their palms.

Each woman stationed herself at the end of one of his limbs, and at precisely the same second their hands returned to his body. Beginning at his toes and fingers and working their way inward, their oiled hands manipulated his rippling muscles. The oil smelled spicy and left his skin feeling warm and tingly. A drum joined the flute and the massage took up the beat until his body pulsed to the music.

Rather than becoming aroused, he was getting drowsy. He closed his eyes and imagined that the wealth around him was truly his and his body reacted accordingly.

Two pairs of hands worked their way across his shoulders and down his chest and stomach at the same time as four other hands reached his hips. Without any effort on his part now, his blood surged into that region. His eyes flew open again when oily fingers curled around his manhood and massaged that as well. Each slave paid him like homage until he was ready to explode.

A loud clap brought him back to his senses and sent the women scrambling out of the room. He had forgotten the heavily shrouded person who had brought him here. The mysterious escort came to the foot of the chaise. Leaving the scarf over her head and face, she methodically bared her slender body. Her hands massaged her small breasts, twisting her pink nipples until they hardened. She then let her hands roam seductively down her body and between her thighs.

Nick was going crazy watching her. Just when he was about to go to the woman, Tarla removed the head covering and shook her long hair free.

With the sleekness of a tigress, she climbed over his body, trapping his thighs between her own. She pressed herself against him, holding him still while she rubbed her core along his oiled length. When she could no longer tolerate her own delaying tactics, she firmly impaled herself on him and rode her stud with wild abandon until she brought about her own climax.

Nick's orgasm burst forth a heartbeat later, forever spoiling him for anything less exciting or satisfying in his future. Only when they had each enjoyed the aftershocks of their passion did Tarla lie beside him and let him return the pleasure she had granted him. Kissing and touching took the place of words between them.

When morning came and they were still together, Nick willingly accepted Tarla's explanation that it was all meant to be.

CHAPTER 9

Victor calculated how many meals he had eaten. Assuming he was being fed on a regular basis, it was the only way he could mark the passing of time. Night and day did not exist for him as his sleep was constantly disrupted so that he could be interrogated, psychoanalyzed and tested physically and mentally in no particular order. Annoying? Fuck, yes. Abusive? *Mielda*! He could teach these clowns a few things about getting a man to talk.

His years spent getting around the legal system had trained him to behave remorsefully in front of law enforcement authorities and to say whatever the shrinks wanted to hear to convince them he was a victim of a terrible childhood. He knew how to make humility eke from his pores.

After the second session under the bright light, he had recognized its tranquilizing effects. During the treatments that followed, Victor had remained outwardly submissive while concentrating on multiplication tables to keep his brain alert.

He was no strung-out doper, like Pete. He liked coke, but he didn't need it. During this past week he had noticed the last traces of craving had disappeared but he remembered the feeling, the incredible high he could reach with the white powder. He didn't want to face the future in a place where such highs did not exist.

Again and again he had asked himself what went wrong with the hijacking and was now convinced that it was not his fault that it had failed.

It was hers. The bitch with the big *basura*. Everything had been planned down to the last detail. Having the two young broads on board had simply thrown off his timing. He had taken care of the little brunette and he should have taken a piece out of the other one right away, gotten her out of his system. Then everything would have been fine. But he hadn't and once he got out of here, he would find her. Then she would make it up to him somehow.

His guard, a seven-foot-tall side of beef, interrupted Victor's plans for revenge with a summons to the chief warden's office. Taking a moment to assume his humble persona, he fell into step behind the giant.

A scrawny, gray-haired man of indeterminate age awaited Victor. His flat expression and piercing black eyes revealed a suspicious nature.

"My name is Zenton and I am Chief Warden of this Rehabilitation Clinic. Your file contains encouraging reports from your counselors. You have convinced them of your desire to improve your behavior to a more socially acceptable standard. This willingness to adapt, along with your obvious remorse, weighed heavily in the decision reached by the Rehabilitation Board this morning."

What Zenton did not say was that the prisoner's superior intelligence was the additional factor that had tipped the scales against further treatments. Due to the Noronians' deep respect for natural genius, every possible avenue for rehabilitation was to be pursued before resorting to reprogramming Victor.

Zenton failed to rid himself of his nagging doubts about this case. It was not a matter of his being prejudiced against the Outerworlder, as the Board implied. A student of the criminal mind and penal systems of other civilizations, Zenton was convinced they were dealing with a sociopathic personality. The Board flatly rejected his recommendation to read the man's thoughts once more before releasing him. In Zenton's opinion, their objection was carrying the right to privacy much too far.

"You watched the orientation the first day you were here, so you know what is expected of you."

Victor bobbed his head. He remembered the show well enough. "I mean no disrespect, sir, but I found that video pretty hard to believe."

"It is not my responsibility to convince you that what you heard is true," the warden answered. "Once you leave this clinic, your own eyes and ears will do that for you. My function today is to explain the terms of your release."

At the suggestion of freedom, Victor's complacency slipped.

"It has been decided to permit you to leave here. Your guard will escort you to Car-Tem Province and remain with you for a time. If you choose not to conduct yourself according to our laws, your case will be reconsidered. We have the power to force your rehabilitation. Therefore, it is to your advantage to take the initiative."

Victor tried to look as meek as possible. "I understand, sir, and believe me, I am very grateful for the opportunity to prove myself. I would like to ask one question though."

Zenton was not deceived by the man's act. "What is

it?"

"What about José? Will he be coming with me?"

"No. He was judged incorrigible and could not be rehabilitated sufficiently as he was."

"Well, what happens to him then? Does he stay locked up?"

"Locked up? Certainly not. That would be unproductive. It is more efficient to alter the individual to fit into society rather than the other way around. Here is your manual. I suggest you study it during the trip to Car-Tem." He picked up a file and swiveled his chair around, presenting his back to Victor. The interview was over.

Victor snorted then covered it with a sneeze. Accepting his unspoken dismissal, he casually sauntered into the hallway where the giant waited.

As they turned down a corridor, Victor spotted a familiar figure walking ahead of him. "José!" He ran to catch up to his friend then grabbed his shoulder. Lifeless eyes in a stranger's face turned mechanically to his.

"I am sorry. Were you calling me?" It was José's voice, but he was speaking perfect English in a halting monotone.

Victor was stunned. He had no idea how it had been accomplished but this man was José. Yet he was not. *Mielda*! He had to get out of this place!

The guard motioned for him to resume their exit from the building. Victor was so shaken by the encounter that he was outside for several seconds before realizing that he truly was a free man.

As he boarded the peculiar wheel-less vehicle, Victor scanned the vast gray desert around them. A bright orange sun was surrounded by a white ring and looked bigger than it should. By the time they reached a glittering city and his caretaker demonstrated the marvels of his temporary apartment, Victor gave up all previous notions that he was still in the United States.

Edward read the file on his next appointment, another new arrival. His curiosity mounted as he absorbed the information regarding Victor's criminal background. To his knowledge, there had never been an attempt to integrate an Outerworlder with such primitive tendencies without reprogramming. He felt a tremor of anticipation.

The counselor understood intimately how someone could be compelled to commit violence, even be excited by it. Since such aggression was unacceptable however, he had to conceal that difference between himself and those who had no such urge, the perfect people…like Chief Administrator Romulus.

Heredity had cursed Edward with an imperfect exterior and average intelligence, and not even head-to-toe cosmetic corrections could make him tall, well-formed and brilliant. So Edward did nothing at all about his deficiencies. Had he been born centuries ago, before genetic experimentation was outlawed, he might have been pleased with himself…like Romulus.

As young men, Edward and Romulus had attended the academy together and Edward remembered well his former classmate's accomplishments and personal charm. Romulus only had to smile and girls fell at his feet. He had achieved the highest scores without opening a book and he had excelled at any game he tried with absolutely no effort. Edward's resentment of his lot in life had always centered around Romulus, since Edward firmly believed that everything the man achieved was merely fate smiling down on one more beautiful person. Now people were talking about making Romulus governor, while Edward envisioned himself floundering indefinitely at his current level.

Hoping to change his lot, Edward had seen the arrival of the Outerworlders as a golden opportunity to discredit Romulus and, at the same time, to prove that the Terrans were too uncivilized to be permitted to live freely among Noronians. If his impromptu plan using Karl had succeeded, he was certain his great-great-great-grandfather would have been impressed and would have given him some recognition. But he was not discouraged. Next time he would plan ahead. Next time he would be more careful.

Victor's appearance broke into his mental grumblings. No wonder the criminal had been released unchanged, Edward thought. He was one of the privileged, an attractive specimen. Then Edward noticed the man's eyes and felt chilled by the beast he sensed was hiding behind the attractive façade.

"Please sit down. My name is Edward. Your file contains insufficient background information for me to assist you in selecting a career. Perhaps we should begin with you telling me at what you excel, aside from breaking the law."

Victor's lip curled up at the ugly, squat man. There was something strange about the way the counselor looked at him, as if he were examining a bug. Yet Victor's instincts told him he was dealing with a nobody, the easiest kind of victim to manipulate. "Would you mind answering a few questions for me first?" Victor inquired in a respectful tone.

"Certainly not. I am here to help you in any way I can."

Victor wondered just how far the little creep could be encouraged to help. "Where am I?"

Edward looked at him curiously. "I understood that you had been briefed before you came to me."

"I watched a video of some guy named Romulus

telling the rest of the people from the ship about how we all got here. At the time, I figured it was a hoax." Edward's grimace at the mention of Romulus did not escape Victor's notice. "Then today I saw things that don't exist where I come from."

"What you heard is true. Falsehoods are not tolerated here."

Now Victor studied the counselor who sounded disgusted by the system. It was an impression worth testing.

"All right, let's say I believe I'm in the center of the Earth, even though I definitely saw a sun out there. And everything here is wonderful and everyone is good and honest. How the hell do I get out of this damned Utopia and back to where people are more, uh, human?"

Edward's pulse quickened. The criminal's attitude was delightful. He often felt the same way but saying it aloud was dangerous. Such ideas could result in being reprogrammed. "I strongly suggest you keep such thoughts to yourself. Most people would not consider your sentiments to be, shall we say, appropriate. You are here to stay. It is in your best interest to accept your situation as soon as possible and try to fit in."

Victor noted that Edward's use of the phrase "most people" clearly did not include himself. "No way. I have to get back."

"Only a few individuals have the power to authorize a departure. The man you referred to earlier, Chief Romulus, would be one of those. I assure you, nothing you could say or do would convince him to agree to your return to Outerworld."

Victor recalled Karl's sloppy attempt to force Romulus's assistance at the end of the orientation. He certainly could do better than that. "Would you care to make a wager on that?"

"Pardon me? I am sorry. I do not follow."

"Naturally, I'm just speaking hypothetically."

"Naturally." Edward was not sure what the man was leading up to. It sounded devious and he wanted to hear every syllable.

"Let's just say the chief has a weakness, a soft spot perhaps. If someone learned what that was, then that someone might use it to force his cooperation." Victor had gone much further with this man than he had intended but the gleam in Edward's eyes told him he had found the inside help he would need. Lady Luck had apparently stayed on his shoulder all the way to this weird-ass world.

"That would certainly prove to be an interesting experiment, hypothetically speaking that is." Such an incident could cost Romulus the governorship, Edward thought, a glimmer of hope beginning to rise inside him.

"Of course, one would need help," Victor continued. "Inside information, so to speak, to pull such a thing off. I'm sure there would be some way to reward such a person."

"It is possible that the success of the experiment might be reward enough. I am certain, though, that the accomplice would want to remain in the background. Let me ask you something now. By a weakness, could you mean a loved one?"

"Exactly!" Victor responded excitedly. He had not expected a plan to formulate itself so soon. The simplicity of the scheme amazed even himself. "Did you have someone in particular in mind?"

"No, not at the moment. I was only curious. It presents an interesting scenario." Edward squirmed in his seat with nervous energy. He only had his suspicions, which would have to be confirmed before passing any information along. But the beauty of such a plan boggled his mind and this criminal would work out so much better than Karl had since he would be acting entirely on his own.

Victor knew he had his pigeon. He did not care what was in this for Edward. Maybe the man needed a little excitement. He really didn't give a fuck why the guy had it out for this Chief Romulus character, just so he could get back before his network of associates forgot about him. "If you do think of something, I'd be glad to discuss the *experiment* further. One other thing." Victor dropped the last pretense of submissiveness with the civil servant. "There was a woman on the ship, a friend, Aster Mackenzie. Would you know how I could find her?"

Edward smirked. Could this be a simple coincidence or did this criminal already suspect that she had wiggled her way to the chief's attention? "Friend you say? I suppose that would be in order." He wrote her address on a piece of paper. "Now, as much as I have enjoyed our hypothetical discussion, I am required to find you immediate employment."

"That shouldn't be too hard. What can you get for me at the Rehab Clinic?"

"The Clinic?" Edward asked incredulously. "But are you not concerned about Zenton? He does not trust you."

Victor was getting a charge out of playing teacher to his attentive, but completely naïve, pupil. "If I work there, the warden will have me watched constantly. If I am under his nose, I will quickly prove what a good citizen I intend to be and he will relax." The real reason for working at the clinic he would keep to himself. "Also, I would prefer to live on the premises, if that's possible. Can I do that?"

Edward had never witnessed such negative use of

intelligence. He would have liked to observe this Terran at closer range but right now he had to complete the man's processing. Edward quickly arranged a low-level job assignment and living quarters at the Clinic, commencing in three days.

As Victor left his office, Edward mulled over the interview. There was no question who had controlled the appointment but he was not in the least disappointed.

CHAPTER 10

By Friday afternoon, Aster realized that the week had sped by in an orgy of studying. At work she had immersed herself in economics and finance and at night she had researched details of Innerworld's technology. She needed to believe that someday, somehow, she would return home and share her findings with her own people. She also knew that eventually she would have to reestablish communication with Romulus. There didn't seem to be any way to leave Innerworld without the approval of a high-ranking official and only in her dreams did she admit that was not the only reason she needed to see him again.

Hearing the door open and close behind her, she turned to say good night to Keshu. The words she meant to say disintegrated at the sight of the imposing figure standing there.

"Hello, Aster," Romulus said quietly.

She opened her mouth but no words came. Instead, all the stored-up emotion of the last week threatened to spill over. She lowered her eyes.

"I behaved abominably, but I swear it was a

mistake. I need you to forgive me." He had spent the last four days berating himself for wandering the halls, hoping to bump into her. Work had piled up until his desk looked like he had gone on holiday. This afternoon he had finally given up his futile struggle to keep his distance from her.

His sincere apology made her look up at him again. She had seen rain-drenched puppies look better and his voice actually cracked when he spoke. This could not possibly be the same confident chief administrator. Always a sucker for the underdog, the last remnants of her uncertainty melted away. Offering him her hand, she took the first step in closing the gap between them. "It's already forgotten. Maybe we could just start over."

Romulus met her halfway and enclosed her hand in both of his. As soon as he touched her, he knew he was lost. During their separation, his fever had worsened to the point where he thought his blood was boiling. He was certain that the only way to reduce the pain was to couple with Aster. Even if violence was not abhorrent to him, he instinctively knew it would do him no good to take what he needed. His only choice was to court her until she was willing to accommodate him.

"I have a surprise for you but you'll have to come to dinner with me to see it," Romulus teased, back in a semblance of control.

The rumbling quality had returned to his voice, tickling her deep inside, and she decided it was worth the risk to be with him again. "All right, let's go." She felt so much better, she didn't even mind his holding her hand as they headed out.

"We can walk to where we're going. It's not far."

Aster would not have believed it possible but, as they walked together along the sidewalk, the city appeared more beautiful than the first time she had seen it.

"Here we are," Romulus announced, coming to a halt in front of a restaurant. The overhead sign read, *Feinstein's Honest-to-Goodness New York Deli.*

As Romulus opened the door for her to enter, the aromas of garlic and dill pickles assailed her senses and she wondered why there were no customers.

"Paul! Paul! Look who's here." Sheila Feinstein bustled from behind the pastry counter, anxiously wiping her hands on her apron. She rushed forward and gave Aster a vigorous hug and a pinch on her cheek. "How wonderful! You'll be our first customers. Come, sit down. First you'll eat then we'll talk. Whatever you want, we've got it. I worked a few miracles and you'll never know you're not eating the best pastrami ever sliced." Sheila's enthusiasm bubbled around them.

"This is absolutely fantastic! I can't wait for Cherry to see it. But how did you manage it in one week?" Aster asked, stunned.

Paul joined the happy reunion. "We owe it all to this young man. He helped us find something we'd enjoy doing now that we've been given a new life." He pulled Sheila close and planted a loud kiss on her forehead before continuing his explanation.

"We remembered our happiest times together were spent working our tails off in the little deli we owned in Brooklyn. We described what we wanted and, poof, here it is."

"That's enough talk, Paul. Go finish what you were making. You two, sit down. I'll get the menus."

Paul stopped Sheila with a light touch on her arm. "I'll get the menus. I want you to go back and taste the sauce for the stuffed cabbage. Make sure it's got enough salt. You always were a better judge."

Sheila gave him a suspicious look but headed for the kitchen anyway.

Immediately, Paul grasped Romulus's hand and pumped it several times. "I want to thank you again for everything you've done. Sheila doesn't like me to talk about it but when the doctors said there was no hope for her, I wanted to die with her. We've been married almost sixty years but I love that woman as much today as the first time I set eyes on her. If I can ever do anything for you, well, just ask." Paul saw Sheila returning and quickly placed two menus on their table.

"You were right. It needed a little salt. Now get back to work and let me take their order," Sheila said. Paul gave them a conspiratorial wink and left.

"Men!" Sheila muttered, shaking her head. "Let me give you some advice, honey. Always let them have their little secrets. Then they'll never need any big ones."

Aster smiled, although she hadn't really heard. She was thinking how wonderful it would be to have someone speak about her the way Paul had spoken about Sheila.

"Aster, would you order for me?" Rom asked. "I have no idea what most of these items are."

"Sure. Let's see. Okay, Sheila, how about two Reuben sandwiches and egg cremes."

When Sheila left, Aster placed her hand over Rom's. "Thank you for being nice to them. They are really good people and so much in love."

"I must admit helping the Feinsteins was not all one-sided. They don't look like my parents but the way they treat each other makes me think of my mother and father. It pleased me to see them happy."

"That's the first time you mentioned your family. I wondered if you were hatched in a test tube. I don't know a single personal thing about you, yet you know my entire life story."

He refrained from embarking on a dissertation about the test-tube's role in reproduction and before he could say anything else, Sheila arrived with their meals. He imitated Aster as she smeared a dark yellow dressing on the inside of the top slice of brown bread and took a bite of the sandwich.

With an exaggerated swallow, he turned to Sheila, who had been hovering expectantly nearby. "My mother never made anything like this. It's, um, different." He tried another bite under her watchful eye and managed an appreciative nod.

"It's perfect, Sheila," added Aster. "If I didn't know better, I'd swear you smuggled that corned beef in from a kosher butcher in Brooklyn."

Sheila happily accepted the lavish praise and returned to her chores.

"Romulus! I thought you never told a lie!" Aster whispered. She could see the taste did not appeal to him.

"I didn't say anything that wasn't true. My mother was never one to experiment with nature's gifts. Everything we ate was grown on our farm and its form didn't change much by the time it got to our table."

"A farm? Everything I've seen so far seems so space age. I hadn't considered where the food came from."

"Most of the food is a by-product of either sea kelp or vegetables. I grew up on a land farm on Norona. My parents are still there. They've had a very satisfying life but I couldn't wait to get away from all the peace and quiet.

"I wanted adventure so I chose the academy in Innerworld. I soon realized the opportunities for advancement in administration were better if I remained here. Back home I may never have reached my current position. So, here I am, end of life story."

Aster looked disappointed. "That's it? No intergalactic odysseys?"

"Not for me but a few of my classmates flew off in search of exotic civilizations. I was an only child living on the outskirts in a rural area for so long that I wanted to be in the middle of a busy city for a change. The closest I came to distant galaxies was in my astrophysics studies. One of my professors got me fascinated with the subject. It would have been my second career choice."

"Do you ever go back? Or do your parents come here?"

"I go back occasionally, sometimes on business. Mother and Father came here once for my graduation. Father hates to travel, even short distances. After one week each way in a starship, he swore he'd never do it again. Besides, he despised our *artificial environment*, as he called it. Speaking of environments…"

"Yes?" Aster immediately straightened her relaxed posture.

Now that he had brought it up, he wasn't certain how to proceed and not anger her again. "Are you enjoying your research?"

She tensed, hoping she had misunderstood him. Perhaps he meant her new job. "Oh, yes. Innerworld's economics are so much less complicated than—"

"I was referring to your other research." He noted her guilty flush. "The research you started at the library and have continued every night in your apartment. It seems a bit intense for leisurely reading."

Aster gasped. "My apartment? How do you know that?" She suddenly imagined hidden cameras behind her walls and was afraid she was going to be ill.

Rom could see he had upset her but there was no way he could avoid this argument, even if it was at cross-purposes with his physical need. He intentionally kept his voice stern so that she would know the difference between his business and personal discussions. "You've been accessing sensitive files so I was automatically alerted. You are free to study our technology in as much depth as you wish so long as you realize it will do you no good. You're not going back, Aster. The sooner you accept that, the better off you'll be."

She slammed her fist on the table. "I'll never accept it!" She noticed Sheila freeze in her tracks and lowered her voice to a hiss. "How dare you spy on me?"

"I was not spying! Your computer is programmed to record your daily activities. Every citizen's usage of time is monitored to assure a well-balanced existence. I was only alerted because of the nature of your reading material and the fact that you're a new arrival. In that regard, you *are* my responsibility. By the way, you're not getting enough exercise."

"And here I was shocked about what goes on at the Indulgence Center. I didn't know how disgusting you people really are!"

Rom was stunned by her outrage. She was angry at the wrong things and he had to steer her back to the real problem. "You're circumventing. I don't like having to repeat myself but I gather you weren't listening all the previous times I've said this. You…can…*not*…go…back." He didn't realize he was squeezing her hand until she winced and tried to pull away. He relaxed his grip but didn't release her. "Drek. I'm sorry. I'm not usually so…" So what? So emotional? So easily rattled? So…*in heat*?

Aster sat rigid, staring at the stranger who had taken over Romulus's body. Or was the stranger the considerate one?

Rom sighed and tried again. "I believe honesty may be the only way to set this straight. I am extremely...attracted to you, and I shouldn't be. It's causing me to act irrationally and I apologize."

She wasn't certain exactly what he was apologizing for, but she was quite sure she didn't want to hear anything more about his *attraction* to her. It was all she could do to adjust to what she had just learned. Not only was she living in a world where sex could be purchased at the same place you could get your hair done, but her every activity was recorded in detail. She decided since he had changed the tone of their conversation, she would take advantage of it. It was time to take the gloves off.

"I'll forgive you, if you'll give me one good reason why one of your emissaries can't pass along how to build your air filters to one of my people. I read that they interfered before when the planet was in danger."

"*Imminent* danger. And how would we choose the recipient of this information? A seemingly innocent hint could have devastating results if it ended up in greedy hands. That good intention could alter the natural progression of Earth's development. Only when we are left with no alternative do we dare to play Supreme Being with your people."

Aster frowned as she found herself conceding his second point. All right, no aliens appearing in public and no passing on free hints unless the world is nearly done for. That left one more possibility. "But what about me? I shouldn't be here. You've interfered with my work, my natural progress. My absence could cause things not to happen that should."

He shook his head. "We prefer to believe the

Outerworlders who are brought here were meant to come, metaphysically speaking." He wondered what the Supreme Being had in mind when he sent Aster. Rom needed her and he shouldn't. He attempted to court her and ended up infuriating her.

Aster pulled her hand away and stood up slowly. "Thank you for dinner. I'll think about what you've said."

He rose and reached for her elbow but she moved away. "I'll drive you home."

"No, thank you. I'd rather you didn't." She wished Paul and Sheila luck and quickly headed for the shuttle.

Aster decided a visit with Cherry was in order but there was no answer when she knocked on her friend's door.

She sensed a movement behind her and turned. "You!" At the sight of the tall, dark man standing inches away from her, the blood rushed from her head, leaving her weak and shaking. Her gaze darted around the lobby and stopped on a huge, black-uniformed man standing by the entrance. Remembering that color put him in the security business, she relaxed slightly. "What are you doing here? They said you were sent away!"

Victor Rodriguez's jeweled tooth sparkled as he smiled broadly at Aster. "Please forgive me, Miss Mackenzie. I had not meant to startle you. You don't look at all well. May I see you to your apartment?"

"No! Just leave me alone." Aster forced the words out through gritted teeth.

"Please calm yourself," Victor said smoothly. "I mean you no harm. I am here to apologize for the wrongs I've done. It's part of my rehabilitation. May I say you look even more ravishing than I remembered." Victor bowed elaborately in front of her and attempted to draw her hand to his lips.

Aster recoiled instantly at his touch. "I don't believe you. You must have escaped. No one in their right mind would have released you."

"My, my, such hostility, Miss Mackenzie. I assure you I have been released. You see, they gave me treatments, took away the bad parts, so to speak. I am not the disturbed man I once was."

Victor looked and sounded sincere and Aster almost fell for it, until she noticed his gaze move to her breasts and linger there. She drew herself back another inch, glaring at him with all the hate he stirred in her.

"I can see you are not yet ready to forgive. Perhaps in time you will find room in your heart for a kind word."

"The kindest thing you could do for me is to get out of my sight and never come near me again. We may be in a strange world but I can still smell garbage when I'm this close to it." Suddenly Aster was afraid she had been too brazen. He looked as though he might tear her apart with his bare hands.

"One day you will regret that this was your choice." Victor turned on his heel and headed out the lobby door. *Bitch!* We'll see who's so high and mighty soon enough, Victor raged inwardly. So, she thought he was not good enough for her. During his stay at the Clinic, he had remembered why her name had sounded familiar and he'd decided that when the time was right, he would let her in on what he knew. Then he would have the upper hand.

Aster stared at Victor's stiff back as he strutted away. No, he hadn't changed. As hard as he tried to be charming, his evilness oozed through.

Once inside her apartment, she collapsed on her couch. It had taken every ounce of energy she had to stand up to that animal and she had the sick feeling he would be back. The only person she could think to turn to was Romulus. She would simply have to set her annoyance with him aside.

Her vidcom held a message from Cherry, bubbling as usual. "Hi, kid! I was hoping to find you at home so I could brag about my life. I met two fabulous, sexy guys and I've got a date with both of them tonight. Well, I'll have to wait to tell you more tomorrow. Bye."

So, Cherry's first date in Innerworld would be with two men. Leave it to her. Despite the unpleasant ending to dinner and the disgust seeing Victor stirred in her, Cherry's message still managed to make her smile.

Aster decided to take a shower and unwind a bit before calling Romulus. Afterward, she wrapped a towel around her and touched her vidcom screen. "Josephine, please put me through to Chief Romulus." As she waited for him to accept her call, she proceeded to fix herself a cup of chamomile tea.

"Hello?"

"Rom? It's Aster."

"Uh, Aster, I think—"

"I didn't know who else to call."

"But, you—"

"Please. It was Victor—from the boat. He came to see me, here at my apartment, pretending to be sorry and polite but I could tell it was an act. He scared me to death and I'm terrified he'll be back. What should I do?"

"I'll request his release report immediately. Stay in your apartment tonight. I'm sure you're safe for the moment. I had something in mind for tomorrow and this cinches it. As long as you're with me, he won't get near you, I promise. But first—"

"If you want my assurance that I'll go somewhere with you tomorrow, you've got it. I would be a nervous wreck sitting here alone."

"Aster, if you'll just hush for a second, I'm trying to tell you that your hologram is pacing back and forth in my bedroom. I love the way you look in that towel but I doubt the transmission is intentional on your part."

"Dear Lord!"

Rom choked on his own breath when the three-dimensional image of Aster rushed toward him, clutching her towel about her. The shocked look on her face confirmed the fact that the enticing picture was an error. When the blur faded in front of him, he discovered he could breathe again with a little effort.

"Oh, Rom, believe me, I had no idea. Cherry had me playing around with it days ago and I guess I never reset it properly. I'm so embarrassed I could crawl inside one of the supply cabinets."

"I can't imagine what you have to be embarrassed about." He could have said much more but he thought better of it. "Well, you've already agreed to go with me tomorrow, so I guess I won't need to use all the convincing reasons I had ready. I hate to think I actually have something to thank Victor for. This way it will be a complete surprise."

"Another surprise? Or another bribe to get me to behave? Never mind. I don't care right now. What should I wear?"

"Wear? Um, how about something you'd put on to take a hike. I'll pick you up at 1000 hours. That's ten a.m. Try to get some sleep. Would you feel better if I sent a security agent over to stay with you?"

"No. I don't think I need another stranger in my home. But maybe you could just have one do a few drive-bys?"

That term was not familiar to him but he caught her

meaning. "I can certainly arrange that."

"Thank you. And thank you for taking my call so quickly. I'll see you in the morning."

Romulus sat staring at his viewing screen long after the call was disconnected. He sincerely hoped the outing would go well. When he saw how intent she was on going home, he was determined not to contact her again for a day or two but that determination had barely lasted a full minute after she left. His fever demanded a remedy.

CHAPTER 11

Aster requested breakfast from Josephine but was too nervous to swallow more than coffee. All night long in her dreams Victor jumped out at her from behind bushes and walls. In one dream Romulus rescued her from Victor's clutches then began to make love to her. When his kisses became insistent, she turned into a fish and he threw her into the ocean, where the sharks were waiting.

A long steamy shower and a second cup of coffee helped her regain a modicum of calm. She was more than ready to get out of her apartment by the time she heard Romulus's knock. She sprang from the chair then hesitated a second before opening the door. She did not want to appear too anxious.

"Good morning. Did you want to come in for coffee or are we heading off right away?"

Rom let his gaze slide over her as he smiled broadly. "If you're ready, let's get going. I've had enough coffee."

Aster mentally congratulated herself on choosing the same kind of apparel he was wearing. The close fit of his short shorts and sleeveless shirt exhibited his muscular contours and made her stomach flutter again.

"Before we go, there's one rule you have to promise to abide by today."

She looked sideways at him. "Tell me what it is first."

"For the entire day, I am not the chief administrator of Car-Tem and you are not a prominent Outerworld environmentalist. We're just two average people out to have some fun."

"And if I agree?"

"Tomorrow you can get your soapbox back out and I promise to listen without arguing."

"You've got a deal." It was easy to agree to something she had already intended to do.

Riding in his red commuter made Aster think of her Prius. "As convenient as airbuses are, I miss having my own car."

Romulus looked surprised. "You like to drive?"

"Yes, except in traffic. I once wanted to be a race car driver when I grew up. Sounds silly, huh?"

"Not to me. I'm one of a very small minority who owns an individual commuter. I'll tell you what, once we're out of the city, I'll turn her over to you."

"What? Oh, I couldn't. I'd be too afraid of crashing."

"I insist. This is one wish I can easily grant. We've got a considerable distance to travel with a lot of unpopulated area in between. You'll see, it's easy."

Aster could not tell which one of them was going to have the fun. He looked absolutely overjoyed at the news that she liked cars. If that's what it took to gain his friendship, she was in luck after all.

Aster was aware that they were heading in a direction she had not yet seen. The city came to an abrupt end and a gray desert stretched out before them. Romulus stopped on the side of the road and got out.

"Okay, switch." He came around to her side and assisted her out of the low seat. "Go on. Get in the driver's seat."

"This is really crazy. If I have an accident, don't forget this was your idea."

"Aster, look around you. There is nothing out here. Even if another car or bus comes by, you'll be fine. The car's computer would avoid a collision before you could react. There's very little you need to know for regular driving. This commuter is designed for computer and voice commands, as well as manual control. I prefer the feeling of driving it myself. I think that would be more familiar to you too.

"Press the button to turn her on and activate the air cushion." He covered her right hand with his and held her index finger over it to demonstrate. "The button on the right side of the steering bar directs the car forward. The harder you push it in, the faster you'll go." His face was so close that his breath warmed her ear. Aster wondered if he had any idea how suggestive his instructions sounded or what his nearness was doing to her.

"To go in reverse, move this switch, then the button." As he pulled her hand down and forward, her arm brushed against the hair on his leg. His right hand remained over hers after he returned it to the bar. "On the left side of the steering bar," he continued while moving his left arm behind her shoulders and reaching for her left hand, "is the brake button." He firmly enveloped that hand as well, showing her how to use her thumbs to operate the two buttons.

Aster could barely hear what he was saying over her own lecherous thoughts. He was simply explaining how to operate a machine. So why did she want to forget the driving lesson and throw herself at him? She was scarcely breathing as she turned her face to his. Her lips parted slightly at the sight of the bright green eyes so close to hers. But something wasn't right. He looked more mischievous than passionate.

"Ahem." Romulus cleared his throat, withdrew his arms and casually leaned back in his own seat. "She's all yours."

Aster had heard him clear his throat like that before. He could not be as relaxed as he pretended. She certainly was trembling inside. Out of the corner of her eye, she saw him suck in his cheeks in an effort to repress a smile. Of all the nerve! He had known what he was doing. She wished she could be more like Cherry for just five minutes. *She* would certainly be able to give him back some of his own medicine.

Taking a slow, deep breath, Aster turned the commuter on and the air cushion raised them above the road.

"What about all these other switches and dials? It looks like there's more to driving this car than the couple of buttons you showed me."

"For the first lesson I strongly recommend you stick with going forward...*slowly*. I'll be glad to give you a full demonstration after you turn the controls back to me."

Aster agreed and applied pressure to the right-hand button. The vehicle jerked forward at a frightening speed and then abruptly stood still as she released the power button and pressed the brake. "I guess it takes a little lighter touch," Aster mumbled, then burst out laughing when she saw the horrified expression on Rom's face.

He was extremely relieved when, after a few more erratic starts, she mastered the sensitive button. Soon she was handling the vehicle as if she'd been doing it for years. Then she came to a stop and got out of the car. "Now show me what she can really do," Aster dared.

As soon as he was back in the driver's seat, Rom rose to the challenge. His fingers moved confidently over the control panel in front of him. The rear of the commuter slid open and a flat square of clear glass emerged. The square consisted of countless thin layers which unfolded in segments, growing larger and larger, until the entire top of the vehicle, including its inhabitants, were enclosed in an elongated bubble. Aster was not only amazed by the speed at which the transformation was accomplished but also, when it was completed, she saw no seam or crease.

"Ready?" Romulus asked with a grin. Without waiting for her answer, he flipped a switch and pulled the steering bar toward him.

Aster's mouth dropped open as the commuter shot straight up then sliced through the air in front of them. This was wilder than the lift at her apartment building. But in spite of the incredible velocity at which they left the ground, there was no gravitational pull inside the cabin.

"You said you wanted to see what she could do. We could go back down and do it the slow way, but it'll take forever to get to where we're going."

"No, no, I'm okay. You could have given me a little warning though. I definitely owe you one now. Go ahead, do your worst."

He was not sure what it was she owed him but he was anxious to give her the ride of her life—so far, that is. He maneuvered his vehicle through spins and turns and the tension left Aster's face as she began to enjoy the flight.

"Look down to your right," Rom directed. "We're back over Car-Tem One. There's your apartment building."

"Is this what you wanted to show me? This is great!"

"As a matter of fact, this is a little unscheduled detour, but I'm glad you're amused."

"An unscheduled event? I got the impression you didn't do such things," she said with a smirk.

Rom could not tell if she was kidding. "I don't, normally. It seems I've been doing a lot of things lately that I don't normally do." He stared at her meaningfully until she turned her head away.

She knew what he meant. She was undergoing some behavioral changes herself. The question was, what were they going to do about it?

Rom made a point of keeping the conversation light for the rest of their journey and about a half hour later landed his commuter in front of a colonial-style house standing alone in a country setting. As they got out of the car, a woman came out of the house and ran into Rom's arms. He lifted her off the ground in an uninhibited bear hug.

"Romulus! You should have called first. What if we weren't home?"

"Hah!" he replied after setting her down. "You never leave this farm. You're just like my parents and you know it. Where is the rest of the clan?"

"Frank is out inspecting the crops and the boys stay at the academy most weekends. I'm afraid they take after you in that. They just aren't interested in being farmers. Frank will be back before lunch, you can bet on that." The older woman smiled at Aster then wrinkled her forehead at Rom. "Well?"

"Marya, this is Aster Mackenzie, recently arrived from Outerworld. Aster, this is my mother's sister, Marya."

"How do you do?" Aster said, smiling politely.

Marya was a tall attractive woman with graying hair. It became apparent that Marya was scrutinizing her and Aster worried that she did not share Rom's liberal attitude toward Terrans.

Obviously coming to a satisfactory conclusion, Marya smiled. "You'll stay for lunch, of course."

"No, but we'll be here for dinner. I'm taking Aster on a picnic. May I borrow two horses?" He stole a glance at Aster to see how she had taken his announcement of their plans and was rewarded by the bright twinkle in her beautiful eyes.

Marya glanced from her nephew to his friend and arched one brow without speaking her question. "You know you don't have to ask. We'll see you back here for dinner. Don't get lost!" She shook her finger at him and returned to the house.

"You do know how to sweep a girl off her feet," Aster said with a smile she felt all through her body.

"Oh, you want to be swept? Let's go!" Rom grabbed her hand and pulled her into a run toward the red-painted stables behind the house. He swung the heavy door open and waved for her to precede him. "Milady, choose your mount."

Aster stopped to catch her breath. "Rom, I've only ridden a couple of times. I mean, I'm a real amateur." A high whinny from the rear of the barn caught her attention.

In the last stall, in all their legendary splendor, were a male and female unicorn, not small as she had imagined they might be, but the size of the other stallions and mares housed with them. Snow-white, with long translucent manes and tails, and enormous aquamarine eyes, the unicorns stopped their play as Aster approached. She wondered if their hooves and spiraled horns were really gold. They glittered so brightly.

Rom came up behind her and handed her a couple of sugar cubes. The unicorns were nuzzling their hands before she had a chance to offer them the treat.

"You've made a good impression on Blizzard and Snowflake. They don't usually stop playing with each other long enough to pay attention to mere humans. If you like, we can take them for our ride."

"Rom, I'm in shock! I thought they were mythical. They're incredible. Please, let's take them."

Rom began saddling the mounts as he explained, "We never found out what happened to the unicorns in Outerworld after the Great Flood. There were plenty of guesses, of course. Some believe that something happened to one of the pair chosen, and the other would never have left alone. You see, unicorns mate for life, like our two. Unfortunately, they're even a bit rare here. Only a small number had been brought in from Outerworld originally, and a mare only gives birth twice in her lifetime, if that."

Aster's eyes were wide in disbelief. "You mean there really was a Noah and an ark?"

"Among others. Okay, they're all set. I just have to get my bag out of the car and we can go."

A few minutes later Aster and Romulus trotted the two unicorns into a wooded area not far from the stables.

"Do you come here often?" Aster asked.

"No, but we won't get lost. My mother and her sister were raised on the farm I grew up on. When Marya and her mate came here, they designed this one as an exact duplicate, including all my favorite hideouts."

The thinly wooded area became a jungle as they rode along a crooked, overgrown path. Suddenly Blizzard nudged his mate's hindquarters and Snowflake rushed headlong into the bushes. As quickly as the unicorns had changed pace, they came to a halt.

They were at the edge of a dark lagoon surrounded by tropical plants and trees. Wild orchids of every color dangled from branches and burst out of cracks in gigantic boulders. Brilliantly colored parrots, toucans and other exotic birds squawked at the intruders. A bush beside Aster rustled and out strutted a magnificent white peacock displaying its grandeur just for her.

So awestruck was she that she didn't realize Rom had dismounted until he touched her arm. Lifting her leg over the saddle and turning to face him, she placed her hands on his solid shoulders and let him help her down. His hands slid under her arms as he pulled her from her saddle.

"It's breathtaking, Rom," Aster said in a hushed voice when her feet touched the ground.

"So are you, Aster." There was no space between their lips when he spoke, yet his need to move even closer was overwhelming. The slightest increase in the pressure of her hands on his shoulders was enough to encourage him. Afraid of frightening his captive bird, his kiss was fleeting. But the captive became the captor as Aster pressed her lips to his, silently demanding more.

She welcomed the feel of his tongue against her own, rushing to reach the plateau she had discovered only once before. Rom's hands moved down her back until his palms covered her bottom. Aster felt his body's response and the old fear instantly crept over her.

He felt the change in her and forced himself to withdraw. Gently untangling her hands from behind his neck, he brought her fingertips to his lips for a tender kiss.

The confusion of desire and distress in her eyes made him wonder if he would ever be able to go through with this. The fever in his brain reminded him he had no choice. He had to have her, had to mate with her at least once, but she had to want him too. And he would *have* to be patient for that to happen.

"There's lots more," Rom said. "Take off your shoes and socks. We'll be walking through the water part of the way."

Aster was glad to have something to do with her hands as she took off her shoes. She left her footwear beside his. For once it was easier for her simply to follow orders.

Rom removed the bundle from Blizzard's saddle and the unicorns disappeared into the forest. With one arm circling Aster's waist, he led her around a large outcropping along the edge of the water. As they came to the other side, Aster heard the sound of rushing water. At the far end of the lagoon, a wall of water gushed off the rocks from high above. Dozens of rainbows danced in the spray from the falling water, captured by streaks of sunlight peeking between the dense overhead foliage.

Aster's concern over her failure was forgotten at once. She walked ahead of Rom toward the waterfall until she thought she could go no farther without getting soaked. The roar of the water was too loud to hear, so Rom directed her with his hands to go behind the falls. There she discovered an uphill ledge wide enough to walk on that led into a cave hidden by the sheet of cascading water.

The farther into the cave, the darker it grew and the more muffled the sound of the water. A few seconds later Aster could see light at the other end of the path they were on. There was no waterfall on this side but the ledge was much larger and about twenty feet above the lagoon.

"It's so magical. I don't think I'd have left home if I had these kinds of hiding places. May I help with anything?"

"Absolutely not, except maybe stand back a little so I can perform a little more magic."

Leaning back against the cave wall, Aster watched him unfold a small package into a sizable mat. It instantly puffed up with air to make a comfortable cushion. The rest of his bag of tricks turned out to be their picnic lunch. One sniff told her Sheila Feinstein had prepared the feast set before them.

"Good heavens, don't tell me you're hooked on deli food after one sandwich."

"No, but I had no idea what else you might like, so Sheila fixed this up and said some of it should be familiar to me."

After clearing away their repast, Rom stretched out on his back. "You know, I actually forgot how relaxing this place can be. I hadn't thought about it in years…until I imagined seeing you here."

"Thank you, Rom, for bringing me and, well, for everything, I guess. Today has been absolutely wonderful. I'm just sorry about, you know, before."

He sat up and took hold of her hands. "Aster, I wouldn't have kissed you earlier except I was sure you wanted it as much as I did."

"I did! That's why I'm sorry. I want you to kiss me and I shouldn't. Not when I—"

Rom touched a finger to her lips. He couldn't bear to let her end her sentence. "I know about your bad experience. I don't care about anything that happened to you before, except how it upsets you. You've got to put it behind you."

She felt she owed him an explanation, and if he was going to reject her, she would rather get it over with while her heart was still intact. She found the courage to talk to him about her past, finally revealing her belief that she would never be a good sexual partner for any man.

Rom was astounded that she could be so naive. "Frigid? I've only kissed you twice but neither time was your response anything I would describe as cold. I don't know how it was with anyone else—"

"Oh, I never had any response like that before, believe me. I just couldn't stand it if I disappointed you too." Aster turned her back to him to hide her embarrassment.

"I think that should be my problem, not yours." He had to keep from laughing out loud at the idea that she could ever disappoint him. Gently, he put his arms around her, pulling her back against his chest and resting his cheek on her head. "I know that wasn't easy for you to tell me but you're wrong." He held her like that for a minute and felt her relax. "Will you let me kiss you again?"

A hundred butterflies took flight in her stomach. She swallowed hard and nodded.

"Come lie down next to me." When she stiffly got into position, he almost gave up. She looked like a child awaiting a deserved punishment. He brushed strands of silver hair away from her face. "Now I want you to close your eyes and relax. If I do anything you don't like, just tell me to stop. Okay?"

Aster nodded. She would risk anything for another of his delicious kisses and this time she would not need to feel guilty about enjoying it. He had been given fair warning. She gave herself up to the tingling sensations caused by his fingers roaming up and down her arms and over her face and throat. When his lips touched hers, she quickly wrapped her arms around him and tried to deepen the kiss but Rom pulled away.

"Not yet. Don't try so hard. In fact, I want you to try to do nothing. Understood?"

She managed a small nod and concentrated on relaxing again. This time when he kissed her mouth, he lingered. His tongue traced her lips and she opened them.

"Do you like that?"

"Mm-hmm."

He left a trail of tiny, hot kisses along her throat and whispered in her ear. "And that? Does that feel nice?"

"Mmmm."

He returned his mouth to hers and nibbled on her lips. His palm brushed over her breast before resting on her arm. Even through her clothing, he felt the response he wanted. When her arms tightened around him now, Rom shifted her to her side and inconspicuously inserted his knee between hers. Tenderly, he cupped her full breast, rubbing his thumb back and forth over the tip.

Without thinking about what her body was doing, she straddled his leg. As his hand continued to lightly arouse her flesh, stroking her bare arm and thigh and her concealed breasts and hip, she noticed the ache building again.

Slowly, he pressed his knee upward and his hand grasped her bottom, encouraging her to move against his muscled thigh.

Aster moaned softly and pressed forward on her own. The more she moved, the greater the need to rub against him became. The hand on her bottom urged her to increase the pace of her grinding. Her kisses became more frantic and her hand searched his face and hair, moving down his back and holding him as he held her. A moment later a tremendous shiver ran through her body and a small whimper escaped her throat.

Romulus rolled with her onto her back. His erection pushed against her sensitive core and absorbed her aftershocks.

Aster's eyes flew open to meet his. Propped on his elbows above her, he gave her a lecherous grin. "Cold, huh? Lady, I never even got you out of your clothes."

"My heavens, Rom. I didn't even realize what I was doing. I didn't think, I mean, I never...and you didn't..."

"I know. It's all right. We have the whole afternoon," he promised and lowered his mouth to hers again.

Soon enough he felt her arch against him. Now awakened to her own passionate nature, she would find it easier to seek her satisfaction. He moved away from her and raised her to her feet in front of him. Bestowing sweet kisses, he peeled away her clothes then stepped back to remove his own. He noticed she avoided looking at him and he decided to put off a lesson on male anatomy for a later time.

Aster stood frozen. She wanted to grab her clothes and run away. Her tormented mind told her that was what she should do. But her trembling body wanted to stay where it was, being touched and coming alive in ways she had not thought possible. She was at his mercy and enjoying every minute of it.

"Aster, look at me," Rom said softly in the deep rumble that vibrated through her being. "You're beautiful, every inch of you. Don't be afraid. It can only get better."

Aster was certain he could see the blush covering her entire body but she didn't turn her gaze away from his. She felt hypnotized by those hazel-brown orbs.

He kept her eyes linked to his while his fingers explored her flesh. Parting the dark curls between her thighs, he stroked the wet bud out of its hiding place. He inserted one, then two fingers inside her, while his thumb continued to stroke her. He heard her gasp as her legs strained from the effort to remain standing. In one smooth movement, he knelt and replaced his thumb with his tongue and teeth.

Aster's hands clutched at his shoulders, not sure if she wanted to push him away or to hold him closer. Her fingers meshed in his hair. There was no more thinking to be done. Her body overruled her reasoning and gave in to the intense ripples of pleasure overtaking her.

Her musky taste and feminine scent drove him on, until he tasted her passion flowing freely and she collapsed into the cradle of his arms. He held her close, listening to her ragged breathing. When he felt her heartbeat return to normal, he urged her to lie down on the mat beside him again.

Aster was amazed that a man could give her such satisfaction and not take his. Her only sexual experiences with men had been the other way around.

Reaching up, she caught his hair with her fingers and pulled his head close to hers. She plundered his mouth, forcing her tongue between his teeth.

This time it was his turn to break away. He had been using every ounce of willpower to keep from pushing himself inside her before she was ready. But another kiss like that would bring on the finale before he had planned.

She saw the look of surprise on his face. "I just wanted to say thank you. I really didn't know."

"You still don't, my shalla, but you will soon." He ran his hand down her stomach and over her mound then nudged her thighs apart. On his knees, he positioned himself between her legs and captured a breast in each hand. Bending forward, he burrowed his face in the deep valley he made. His teeth captured one pink nipple, then the other, teasing it with his lips and tongue until the peaks had hardened again.

Aster could not believe it was possible to feel so sated one minute and yet be starving the next. She could not remember ever wanting anything so badly in her whole life.

Rom had pushed himself to the limit of his restraint when he saw Aster's eyes cloud with desire for a third time. He was certain there would be no gripping fear now. Once more he dragged her under his trance-like spell. Supporting himself on his arms above her, he shifted his hips until the tip of his shaft touched her.

"Aster?" was all he could whisper.

"Yes, Rom, *please*," she cried as her hips moved to welcome him. She was so moist she took in the full length of him with one thrust.

Rom shook from the relief of being within her body. No woman had ever accommodated him completely. When he was sure he had not hurt her, he slowly began the age-old rhythm, wanting to make it last. But he had waited too long, wanted her too desperately. When she locked her legs around him to bury him deeper, his self-imposed control was ripped away. The urgency of the raging inferno inside him carried her along with him every inch of the way, until simultaneous orgasms rocked them both.

Aster felt as if she were soaring through space, diving to the ground and flying up again as she clung to Rom, fearing this ecstasy would never end, then fearing it would.

Rom rolled over, pulling her with him, so that she was now on top. He had his release but he was still hard and throbbing inside her. For the first time in weeks, the incessant boiling of his blood was reduced to a simmer.

But it did not disappear completely and that discovery was so shocking his desire ebbed. It meant he could keep the fever under control by possessing her body, but only joining with her would put the fire out permanently. And *that* was out of the question. It was forbidden. He would be ruined, probably exiled. He also had to consider what joining might do to her. If she survived it at all, she could be driven insane.

Aster had never known such happiness existed and she wanted to run and laugh and play. She squeezed her muscles tightly around him. "What's next, teach?"

His eyebrows shot up in surprise. Such a radical personality change was beyond his understanding. Yes, this was wrong, it couldn't go on, but he decided her smile made him feel too good not to enjoy every minute he had with her. "Do you swim?" he asked as he disengaged himself from her body.

"Of course, why—"

Aster's question turned into a shriek as he jerked her to her feet and yanked her over the ledge with him, plummeting down the twenty feet into the chilly water.

Aster emerged, choking and sputtering. "You rat! I could have had a heart attack." She tried to sound angry but couldn't stop laughing.

He dove back under the dark water and disappeared. Aster tread water while trying to figure out where he had gone. Abruptly, she felt his hands at her ankles and barely had a chance to hold her breath before he pulled her under with him. He kissed her hard on the mouth and held her snugly against him as they bobbed to the surface again.

In spite of the cold water, the satiny texture of her body rekindled the fire in his blood. One look at her smoldering dark blue eyes told him she had not yet had enough either.

With frantic urgency put at bay, they were able to spend the rest of the afternoon in paradise, exploring the tropical area as well as discovering the secret sensitive spots of each other's bodies.

When they returned to the house where dinner had been kept waiting for them. Aster felt as though she were hearing everything from inside a tunnel and she couldn't taste anything but Rom's kisses.

Before they left, Marya called Rom aside. "Young man, since your mother isn't here, I believe it's my place to have a word with you." Rom looked at her quizzically. "You said that woman is an Outerworlder and you know better than most people what that means. She seems like a sweet person and I wouldn't want to see her heart broken."

Rom snorted and kissed her cheek. "Marya, if you only knew what that lady is doing to my heart, you'd take pity on me. Even so, I honestly don't know what I'm going to do about it. What she makes me feel isn't supposed to be happening. But I can't seem to stay away from her."

"Ohhh," Marya said with understanding and sighed. "I'm sorry, son. I know you'll do whatever's best for both of you. Good luck." She stood on her toes to give him one last hug and said goodbye to the handsome couple.

As soon as they settled in the car, Aster snuggled close to Rom.

"Happy?" he asked, lifting her chin to see her face. In answer, she coaxed him into a long wanton kiss. "I think I'll show you another function of this vehicle." He programmed the vehicle's computer to return them to Aster's apartment on automatic. With the touch of another button, the seats reclined. He gave her a mischievous grin and pulled her back into his arms.

"And here I thought my Prius was a smart car. By

the way, what was that word you called me before? *Shalla*?"

Rom didn't even realize he had said the word. It literally meant *soul's mate*, but he doubted she was ready to hear that explanation. Instead, he gave her the looser translation. "It's an old Noronian word meaning special one. For a man, the word is shallar."

"I like that. Thank you." What he had actually called her was "my shalla". It warmed her to have him think of her as his anything, even if it was in the heat of the moment.

Rom was shocked at the ferocity at which the burning had returned, in spite of the countless times they had coupled throughout the day. It seemed to be getting worse instead of better. No one had warned him that it could be this bad—and this good. He had to have her again, immediately.

"Good heavens." Aster sighed when she could breathe again. "I'm afraid you've created a monster! What's going to happen when I'm away from you for more than a few hours?"

Rom groaned. She didn't know the half of it. "Let's not find out yet. We have two days before you go back to work and Tarla can handle the office without me for a day." He saw Aster's sudden crestfallen expression. "What's the matter? What did I say?"

"Nothing. It's okay. Forget it." The mention of Tarla put an instant damper one her warm thoughts.

"It's not okay. Listen, you're an Innerworlder now. It's time you started adhering to our code of honesty. Now, tell me the truth. What upset you?"

Aster paused. He was right. It was best that she face the truth right away before she depended on him to be there and he wasn't. One wonderful day certainly did not constitute a commitment.

"It's about Tarla." She stumbled through the events

that led up to Cherry's investigation.

Rom admired Cherry's ingenuity but felt ill when he saw Aster try to blink away a tear.

"I'm sorry, Rom. I've been trying to understand your freer attitude toward sex. Only, after today, I don't think I could stand knowing you were with other women in the same way. Damn! I sound like a possessive shrew. I'm sorry." She turned her face away but he turned it back to him again.

"First of all, stop apologizing for everything. Second, you've drawn all the wrong conclusions from a little information. I have had exactly two physical releases with Tarla, on two separate occasions, and both were highly forgettable. You are all I've thought about since the moment I saw you. The real reason I want to stay with you tonight is to get some sleep. I figure the only way that's possible is if you're in my arms."

Aster sniffed and laughed with him. "I know what you mean. This hasn't exactly been a restful week for me either. Every time I closed my eyes, you were there in my dreams. Anyway, I'll try to be more understanding."

"Aster Mackenzie!" Rom shook her shoulders. "Aren't you listening to me? There's nothing for you to be understanding about. Maybe I do think of sex differently than you but I have never had to deal with a strong sexual urge. What happened today was because of us, you and me together, not some animal instinct. I have never craved any woman the way I do you, and as long as I have you, I have no need to search for satisfaction elsewhere."

Aster felt her cheeks flush again, only this time it was due to pure happiness. It was ridiculous she knew. He was talking as though they had a long-term future together...after one day. Ridiculous. And yet..."But then, how, umm..." She wasn't sure she had the nerve to ask her question when he guessed what was on her mind.

"How did I know how to please you?"

She nodded.

"The mechanics are taught to every maturing young Noronian adult, but I never had much use for all those lessons. I guess you could say you inspired me." He kissed the tip of her nose.

"There's definitely no doubt you've inspired me," she admitted.

They both chuckled and kissed again.

Later, when they were nestled in her bed, Aster ventured a quiet question. "Will you teach me how to please you as well?"

"Aah, my shalla," he said softly into her hair as he stroked her back. "I can't imagine you pleasing me any more than you do."

"All right then, I'll go to the Indulgence Center and pay for some lessons," she replied saucily.

Rom held her away from him and surveyed her face until he was convinced that she meant it as a joke. The thought of any other man touching her made him sick. He felt...*jealous*. He didn't know he was capable of such an emotion, yet there it was.

"You do and you won't sit down for a week." He playfully patted her backside. "I'll tell you whatever you want to know, only not tonight, okay? I wasn't kidding about being tired."

"Josephine, dim the lights please," Aster called out. "Mmmm, much better," she said, curling herself spoon-fashion against Rom's stomach. "Rom?"

"Yes?"

"I don't usually sleep naked."

"You do now." His fingers tiptoed up her arm and across her breast.

"Rom?"

"Hmm?" His voice was beginning to fade.

"May I get one more thing off my chest?"

"You mean besides my hand?"

"No, I want that right where it is. I just wanted to thank you for helping me find out there was nothing wrong with me."

"That's nice," he said through a muffled yawn.

Minutes later as his steady breathing softened in slumber, Aster realized two astonishing things. First, she hadn't thought of returning to her world all day and second, she knew she would never dream of Dennis again.

CHAPTER 12

The next morning Aster discovered how satisfying a shower could be when shared. She was just beginning to appreciate the sensual art of being towel-dried when she was distracted by someone pounding on her door.

"They'll go away. There's not enough room in here for anybody else." Rom returned to planting urgent kisses all over her face, as his body demanded relief...*again*.

"Well, I can't stand it." She gently pushed him away and donned a robe.

Rom stared dumbfounded after her. Obviously, Aster had a way to go before she learned to relax completely. Suddenly he realized that the visitor could be Victor and he hurriedly wrapped a towel around his waist.

As he entered the main room, Aster opened the front door.

"Hey, kid! Where's the coffee? What took you so— " Cherry stopped dead in her tracks at the sight of Romulus, wet, half-naked and casually leaning against the kitchen wall. She swiftly looked back at her damp friend, to the unmade bed and the mess of clothes on the floor. "Well, I'll be damned! Now I know what caused that earthquake I felt last night."

Aster knew there was no stopping her, so she patiently folded her arms and let Cherry have her fun. The little brunette inspected Rom like a piece of merchandise, running her long fingernails up his arm and down his back.

"Ooh, Aster. He's perfect! Promise you'll let me have him when you get bored. Better yet, let me borrow him for a night."

Cherry sneaked her hand beneath his towel and pinched his buttock. Rom choked. "Oh, yes, this is definitely prime beef y'all got here, gal!"

Rom grasped her wrists and firmly moved her away from him. "Sorry, Cherry. I'm afraid Aster's more than I can handle at the moment." He attempted to look regretful and shrugged his shoulders then gave Aster a wink.

"Oh, pooh! You aren't any fun at all. Just get back to whatever you were doing. You won't even know I'm here."

"Cherry!" Aster burst out but resisted scolding her friend for her crudity when she realized how comical the whole situation really was in Cherry's eyes. "Can we interest you in some breakfast to go with your coffee?"

"That's it? C'mon, I'm not done teasing you yet."

As Rom walked over to the supply station, he said, "Then I'll leave you to it while I get dressed." He retrieved his clothing and disappeared into the bathroom.

Cherry pounced on Aster. "I don't believe my eyes! You finally came to your senses. Quick, tell me how it happened."

"Hush! He'll hear you. I'll tell you every steamy

detail when he's not around."

"From the way he looks at you, I'm not sure that day will ever come."

Rom dragged out the process of getting cleaned up and dressed. He was sure they were talking about him, and if he read Cherry correctly, she was completely on his side. When he figured a reasonable amount of time had passed, he returned to the living room.

Breakfast was laid out on the small table, Aster was dressed and the bed had been put away. It was as if nothing extraordinary had occurred in the room.

Cherry snickered. "Poor Rommy. All his toys got put away while he wasn't looking. I swear the bed will fall back out of the wall as soon as I leave." Cherry burst into giggles when she saw how shocked Rom was that she had guessed his thoughts.

"I think you have the makings of a tracker, Cherry."

"A what?" she asked with real interest.

Rom described Innerworld's version of a detective.

Aster spoke up. "Could a tracker check on Victor?"

"What's this about Victor?" Cherry was genuinely frightened at the mention of his name. Aster briefly told her about the unpleasant encounter, much to Cherry's dismay.

Rom explained, "Unless Victor gives us reason to suspect him of breaking the law, it is against the privacy code for a tracker, or any other person, to invade his mind. We're going to have to wait and see what he's up to."

Anxious to change the subject, Aster asked Cherry how her date went the other night.

"Fabulous. Their names are Thor and Apollo. You know, like the gods. What's amazing is neither one thinks there's anything wrong with sharing my attention. We all work together at the IC." When Rom's eyebrows shot up, Cherry hastened to add, "At

Fantasy World, Rom. I'm an actress now. Anyway, last night I went with them to the big dance you told us about. You were right. I had a blast! Wow, can Apollo dance! Oh, I almost forgot another shocker! Nick was there, and guess who he's gotten chummy with? Tarla—Rom's assistant! The two of them met the other night and, bang, lust at first sight."

She stopped for a breath and noted the eye signals passing between the couple. If she hung around them too long, she might start thinking about love herself. For now, she was looking forward to about fifty more years of fun with the likes of her two new playmates. Unable to sit still any longer, she abruptly stood up. "Well, I'm off for a rousing game of screwball. I came to drag you along, but I guess Rom can keep you occupied now." She gave them both a hug and skipped out the door.

"Drek!" Rom gasped. "I feel like I was scooped up in a tornado and dropped down again. Is she always like that?"

"I'm afraid so. You get used to her."

"She was wrong about one thing."

"What's that?"

"The bed didn't fall back out of the wall when she left." He wore a wicked grin as he stalked her.

"Rom! You just got dressed!"

"But you didn't. And I bet I could get undressed faster than you could order clothes."

Much later, Aster leaned over him and combed her fingers through his hair. "What are we going to do today?" His response was a deep rumble in his chest. "Besides that. It's Sunday. Do you have churches here?"

Rom pulled back his head and gave her a puzzled look. "If you mean the House of Spiritual Renewal, I'll be glad to take you there. I think you'd find it interesting, to say the least. I have one condition though. Afterward, I'm taking you to my house to stay. Mentioning Victor made up my mind and I won't take no for an answer. I doubt if he'd bother you there."

"I can't think of any better excuse to keep sleeping with you." She kissed him quickly. "Just kidding."

"Good. Let's get moving." He knew if he didn't leave the apartment soon they wouldn't be going anywhere for some time. It was uncomfortably obvious that the length of time of relief he felt after each coupling was decreasing. He wondered how much time he had before even that respite was stripped from him.

On the way to his car, he asked, "Do you want to drive?"

"No, thank you. I need a lot more practice before you let me loose on a street full of pedestrians."

Once again Aster found herself soaring above the desert. When the commuter landed, she gasped at the monument before her. She had never been to Egypt but she recognized an enormous stone pyramid when she saw one. "Good heavens. It looks like the Great Pyramid of Giza!"

"Actually, the one you're referring to and this one were both copied from the original—on Norona." He took her hand and led her inside.

Each large stone in the entrance hall was engraved with the identical prayer translated into several hundred languages. Aster easily identified a few, but some of the alphabets were unknown to her. She found the block of English and read it in a hushed voice: "God grant me the Serenity to accept the things I cannot change, Courage to change the things I can, and Wisdom to know the difference." It was the Serenity Prayer. Aster had always felt there was something special about it and now she was certain.

Unlike the pyramids in Egypt, there were no walls inside the Great Room. Tall, thick candles illuminated the edges but the air seemed cool and fresh. The only other objects were square black cushions strewn on the floor.

In spite of the considerable number of people, the room was eerily silent. Some of the worshippers knelt, some sat lotus-fashion and others stood with arms outstretched and heads tipped toward the peak of the pyramid.

Rom kissed her cheek. "I'll wait for you outside. I can't do this today. Take as long as you need." He left her alone.

Aster moved farther into the room and sat on a cushion.

Aster's grandmother had baptized her a Catholic and Aster discovered some peace, practicing the religion. After Dennis's death she had automatically turned to the church for emotional support and she fondly remembered the priest who had helped her deal with her grief and loneliness.

Now, sitting with her feet beneath her, she folded her hands on her lap and closed her eyes. A strange warmth began at her fingertips and toes and slowly crept through her entire body. It felt comfortable and exhilarating at the same time. She quashed her natural tendency to control the feeling and gave in to the elusive sensation of being levitated.

Thoughts and images flowed freely into her mind— her grandmother, Cherry, her coworkers, Dennis. Bits and pieces of her life flickered by. Blank spaces of her past were remembered. She saw herself as a child in the commune and knew it had not been the totally carefree, happy life she chose to recall.

Her grandmother's face appeared, soft and tender

for a brief moment, before the usual harsh demeanor took over. The woman had not known how to share her love with her granddaughter any more than she had with her own son. But she had done her best.

Dennis's face drifted in the distance. It was different somehow, not quite right. His hands moved to his ears and removed a mask that had been his face. Beneath was an ugly distortion of his pleasant features.

The mental journey ended with a glimpse of the shipwreck and her arrival in a foreign land. The original feelings of panic and frustration were replaced by comfortable acceptance and the certain knowledge that it was all meant to be. Her future was with Romulus.

Gradually, the warmth dissipated and Aster was again aware of her surroundings. She said a small prayer of thanksgiving for surviving it all. *Lord, I know I should have trusted you when you brought me to this place. Thank you for Romulus. He has given me the first deep happiness I have ever known.*

When she exited, Rom took her hand. He could tell something had happened and waited for her to talk.

"You could have warned me," she said simply.

"I've never heard of a Terran making the bridge. You did, didn't you?"

Aster looked at him with sparkling eyes. "It was strange and wonderful but I don't understand how it happened."

He put his arm around her shoulders and walked her to the car. "I think it might have something to do with me, or rather with us. I want you to tell me if anything else unusual happens to you."

Aster automatically began to worry. He sounded so serious. Apparently, the good feeling from the pyramid was not meant to withstand any stress.

Rom turned the commuter's controls over to the

computer. "You're special, Aster. And I don't just mean how I feel about you. Your soul took flight in there. Any Noronian can make that separation, but you should not have been able to. I don't understand that any more than I understand what's happening between us. Two weeks ago I didn't want anything in my life but my work. If you left me now, well, I don't know what I'd do."

"Oh, Rom, what a lovely thing to say. I feel exactly the same way." She curled up next to him and put her head on his shoulder. "Will you tell me about joining?"

"Yes, when you're ready."

"Ready for what?"

"Never mind. I'll know."

"I think there's something else we should talk about."

"What's that, shalla?"

Aster felt a definite glow when he called her that. "I realize it's a little late, but we didn't use any protection yesterday. I'm really not ready to deal with pregnancy on top of everything else."

Rom arched an eyebrow at her. "What did you do, avoid the notebook section on reproduction?" When she lowered her lashes, he knew he guessed right. "Okay, here goes. When a Noronian boy becomes a man, a quantity of his sperm is frozen for future use. His tubes are closed off at that time.

"When a couple wants a baby, the mother's egg is removed, fertilized with the father's sperm, and reinserted in the mother's womb. There's nothing left to chance that way and it ensures a controlled growth of the population."

"I understand. That's already been done in my world."

"A long time ago, doctors experimented with raising

the fetus outside the mother's body. Unfortunately, the children were unhealthy mentally. There's simply no way to replace the biological mother completely. I'm sure childbirth itself is considerably easier here than in Outerworld though."

"Do the parents get to pick what the child's sex will be or what the baby will look like?"

"Genetic planning, you mean. No, not anymore. It was outlawed centuries before I was born, except for the control of hereditary diseases and handicaps."

Shortly, they entered a single-family residential area. Rom continued through the neighborhood until they came to a high stone archway leading off the main road. He pressed a button in the car before driving under the arch. "No one, including Victor, can pass through here without the proper access."

The paved street was now covered with cobblestones. Instead of sidewalks, hard dirt paths wound their way through neatly manicured lawns and flower gardens. Aster's gaze flew from house to house, from right to left. They looked like country cottages, complete with thatched roofs.

"It's like an old English village! Which one is yours?"

He pulled into a driveway at the end of the street. Magnificent rose bushes of every size and color bordered a two-story house.

"English Tudor—my absolute favorite!"

Her reaction was better than Rom had hoped for. As he opened the front door for her, he explained, "The woman who designed this neighborhood said she got the idea out of an Outerworld picture book."

Aster loved the masculine decor on the first floor. There were no dividing walls, only comfortable-looking furniture to define area uses.

Rom led her out the back door and onto a brick

patio. Three terraced steps lined with more of the brilliant roses led down to a small pond.

"I'm all out of descriptive adjectives. Would a kiss be as good as a compliment?" She placed her arms around his neck.

"Even better," he murmured in his huskiest voice. When all she received was a peck, she pouted. "I want to show you the upstairs." Rom gave her a hug and they went back inside.

A bedroom and bath comprised the entire second floor. Unlike the downstairs with its dark woods and earth tones, this area was a striking contrast of ebony and ivory. Beneath her feet was plush cream-colored carpeting. The furniture looked like it had been intricately carved out of teak and inlaid mother of pearl. On one side of the room was an enormous bed covered in thick black velvet. The same material was draped above and behind the bed and over the windows.

Opposite the bed an oriental screen divided the room in half. Aster stepped around it and sighed. The bathroom was done with black marble fixtures and a white marble floor.

Rom touched a panel on the wall and water rushed into a circular whirlpool tub. He removed his shirt then his pants. Aster stood mesmerized by his striptease.

His eyes turned brown as they raked over her. Aster swiftly discarded her clothes, amazed at how quickly her body responded to a simple look.

By the time Rom was helping her up the steps, the water reached the proper level, shut itself off and the jets activated. The hot bubbling water soothed their muscles without cooling their ardor.

Rom reached for Aster but she gave him a tiny buss on the mouth and pulled away.

"What do you call that?" he asked in disbelief.

"I'm just giving back what I got from you outside."

"Yes, but I knew what I had waiting inside." He splashed a handful of water into her face. Playfully, she pushed both palms through the water to drench him, only to get a thorough dunking in return.

"Uncle!" she cried.

Rom looked at her curiously. "Uncle?"

"It's a saying, like, you win or I give."

"Well, since I won, what will you give me?"

Aster tapped her index finger against her chin. "Gee, I don't have anything with me at the moment."

"That's not quite true. You have the only thing I do want at the moment." His mouth claimed hers before another word could be exchanged.

The next week hurried by in a rose-colored haze. During the day, Aster plunged into her on-the-job training at the Economics Center. At night she reveled in their lovers' games, eager to become all Rom would ever hunger for.

Rom returned to his usual unexcelled efficiency with one major change. His recent impatience and intolerance for errors had been miraculously moderated.

Everyone in the Administration Building had heard about their chief holding hands with the new Terran female in the cafeteria at lunch by five o'clock on Tuesday. By Wednesday, Aster became the recipient of knowing smiles or curious stares wherever she went.

Although no one would say anything to his face, Rom knew there was malicious gossip as well. He hoped to postpone the day when Aster would become aware of it too.

Much to Rom's relief, Victor reported to work at the Rehabilitation Clinic where he could be observed and remain far from Aster.

On Friday afternoon Rom had a meeting with Outerworld Monitor Control regarding the lack of progress on Operation Palomar. Although a backup team had been sent out to assist the tracker, Emissary K66 had not yet been located. Also, nothing had been picked up to indicate that Outerworld's scientists were aware of any impending danger. In four weeks, the situation would reach the critical stage.

When Rom let her know he expected to be late, Aster went home ahead of him.

Several hours later Aster heard his car door shut and put down the book she was reading. As she got out of her chair, the front door flew open, crashing against the wall. Rom hesitated in the doorway until he located her then entered, slamming the door shut behind him.

He looked awful. His hair was a mess, perspiration stained his shirt, three long bloody gashes marred his left forearm. But the worst was his eyes. The whites were blood-red and the pupils were so dilated no color could be seen.

"Good Lord, Rom! What—"

He came at her, grabbing a handful of her hair to yank her head back. His mouth crushed hers in a bruising kiss. He smelled like a beast and the sound that came out of his throat was more animal than human.

"I must...have you...*now!*"

The tremendous heat radiating from his body made her feel like she was trapped in an oven. She could barely breathe, he held her so tightly. With much more calm than she felt, she said, "All right, but let's go upstairs and clean you up first."

"No...can't...wait." His words were barely intelligible.

He was sick, that much was obvious. Aster didn't struggle as he pushed her down on the floor and flipped up her skirt. She flinched once when he ripped her panties and tore open his slacks. Other than that, she lay still as he plunged savagely into her. A primal scream filled the room then he collapsed.

Immediately, his skin cooled against hers. He hadn't hurt her, nor had he actually raped her, since she was always willing to make love to him, but this was something else entirely. Aster felt his chest shake and realized he was sobbing.

"I'm so sorry," he choked out. "I know that was the worst thing I could do to you. I had no idea how bad it could get. I'll get help. Tomorrow. I promise." He rolled away from her onto his back with his arm covering his eyes.

"Rom? What happened? What do you mean you'll get help? What's wrong?" Aster sat up and pulled his arm away from his face. His eyes were damp but back to normal.

Quietly, he said, "I thought I could control it. I swear that won't happen again." Straightening his clothes, he sat up and brought her fingers to his lips. "Please forgive me. I never meant to frighten you again." His gaze remained on her hands.

"Rom, I don't know what you're talking about. What frightens me is knowing you aren't well and I don't understand." She turned his hands over in hers. "There's blood under your fingernails. You scratched yourself, didn't you?" He looked away from her. "Don't deny it. I've seen you scratching your skin all week. You said it was nothing. But there is something very wrong." Aster pressed her palms to his cheeks and forced him to face her. "Talk to me, damn it!"

Rom groaned. "Something happens to Noronians' bodies when our mating time comes. It's been building up in me for weeks before you arrived. When I touched you that first time, it was like throwing a match on dry kindling. It feels like my blood is boiling and biting insects are crawling all over my flesh. I didn't even realize I'd cut myself tonight.

"The only time the fever cools is when I'm inside you, but it doesn't last for long. I had a very stressful couple of hours tonight, trying to deal with a critical situation. I guess I gave so much concentration to that problem that I lost what control I had over my body." He paused and inhaled deeply. "Only a Noronian female should have triggered my mating time. Shalla literally means soul's mate. It doesn't make sense, but that's what you are to me and I can't do anything about it."

Aster considered what he was telling her. "If I were Noronian, what would you do?"

"We would have already joined, long before the fever progressed this far."

"Then we should join," Aster concluded without hesitation.

"We can't. It's prohibited for a Noronian and Terran to join. No one has ever had any reason to dispute that law. Aside from that though, I have no idea what it would do to you. You could go insane, maybe even die. What good would it do for me to get rid of the fever and lose you in the process?

"You see, joining is the mating of the body, the soul and the mind. After the joining ceremony, two people are two bodies sharing one mind and their spiritual energies combine to form an unbreakable bond. Even if the bodies separate, their minds are permanently linked and the souls are mated for eternity. I have no doubt you are my soul's mate but you aren't suffering the same symptoms. I will not risk your physical or mental stability to satisfy my need."

"But maybe I'd be okay. Remember the pyramid? You said I was special, that a Terran usually can't make the separation. Is there any way around the law?"

"No. Even if there was, I won't take the chance of hurting you."

"So, does that mean we have to spend the rest of our lives in bed to keep Dr. Jekyll from turning into Mr. Hyde? Not that I would object to that mind you." Aster smiled at him reassuringly.

Rom leaned over and kissed her softly. "Thank you. I needed to see your smile again. At any rate, I'm afraid even that won't be enough soon. I'll go to Medical tomorrow. There must be something they can do for me." He had not gone before this because he had imagined the reaction he would get. A Noronian getting his fever over a Terran would be shocking enough. But his position would almost assure it becoming big news. After tonight, however, he had to get help regardless of the repercussions or next time he might really harm Aster.

"Shallar," Aster said, trying out the masculine form of the word. "Why don't we go upstairs? I think my temperature is beginning to rise."

CHAPTER 13

"I have some information I thought might be of interest to you." Edward's shrill voice identified the caller.

"Yes?" Victor replied cautiously.

"A friend of yours filed a change of address form."

"Why should that be of interest to me?"

"Because the new address belongs to someone with, shall we say, special privileges," Edward answered.

"Let's have it."

"Not over the phone. Come into the city tonight—to the dance. I will see you there."

This was it, the last piece of the plan. Each day Victor had behaved like a model employee. By night, however, he roamed the vacant rooms and offices scouring for bits of information that could be of use to him in escaping this hellhole. He studied very closely the laboratory where José had been reprogrammed. His genius appreciated the technology involved and his cunning considered how he could employ it to his benefit. He had also gleaned everything he needed to learn about how the various security measures were managed...and circumvented. The naiveté and open-book policies of the Innerworlders was definitely going to be to his advantage.

The only information he could not find was the route back to Outerworld. He only knew that Romulus had his ticket.

"I have no idea what to wear. Help me."

Rom stepped behind Aster and wound his arms under her breasts. "Always glad to be of service," he murmured, nosing her hair away from her neck.

"You know if you start that again we'll never get to this dance of yours." Her words lacked conviction as she hugged his arms more tightly around her. "As much as I'd like to stay home with you, you already convinced me of how important it is that we go tonight. The last thing I want is to be so late that everyone thinks I'm trying to make a grand entrance. I feel conspicuous enough as it is."

"All right, as you say, Uncle." He moved a chair in front of the vidcom viewer and pulled her down onto his lap. "Let's pick something out that will make all the men wonder what I see in such a frumpy woman."

"I'd rather pick something out that will leave all my competition crying in their beer…or whatever the beverage of choice is there."

Aster finally chose a dark purple dress with a flared skirt and a modest bodice with spaghetti straps. Rom whistled as she twirled around and he caught her in his embrace.

"This is going to be a very long night!"

The Dance Hall was already crowded by the time they arrived. Rom made his way past friends and acquaintances with Aster on his arm. His pride was obvious as he introduced her, taking time to tell her a little about each person as they moved along.

Aster smiled and shook hands, savoring every

envious glance and ignoring the disapproving stares. Her happiness could not be ruined by a few narrow-minded people.

To Aster's delight, there was a live band playing a vaguely familiar American song from the forties. Three women singers decked out in the costume and hairdos of the period and a bandleader, who could have been Tommy Dorsey, completed the picture.

The band broke into "Boogie-Woogie Bugle Boy" and several couples ran onto the dance floor. Aster clapped her hands excitedly when she saw the wildly acrobatic contortions of the young people in the center of the room. "They're doing the jitterbug!" She raised her voice. "I love this music!"

"Some time ago a musician got interested in the sound when he was watching an Outerworld video transmission. He found a group of other musicians who were also interested in recreating the songs and dances. The Dance Hall opened up as a big party for their friends and then became popular. Look, there's Cherry." Rom guided Aster around the edge of the dance floor.

Cherry beamed at them as they approached. "It's about time you found your way over here. I observed the entrance of the *royal couple* and decided to wait until the rest of your lowly subjects kissed your ring." Rom's scowl could not discourage her teasing. "I hear you're up for king or something."

Aster looked at Rom for an explanation. He shrugged his shoulders then murmured, "Later."

Cherry reached for a man's hand behind her and brought him forward. "Aster, Rom, this is Thor. Say hello, darlin'." Thor was powerfully built, of medium height, with unruly black hair and a thick moustache. His brooding eyes made Aster think he was not at all the type to be content sharing Cherry's affections. He nodded to each of them without speaking.

"Thor doesn't say much. Then again," she said, stroking his well-developed biceps, "he doesn't need to. Out there on the floor, the tall, blond hunk swinging the girl between his legs is Apollo. He said he could teach me to do that stuff."

Aster caught the narrowing of Thor's dark brows and turned to Rom. "Would you excuse me for a minute? I'd like Cherry to show me the lady's room."

Inside the lavatory, Aster voiced her concern. "Thor looks like he wants to make a change in your relationship."

"Yeah, I know, but it's not the kind of change you'd expect. Truth is, I like them both. It's sort of like salt and pepper…food tastes better with a little of each."

"Hmm. Have you, I mean, have any of you, you know, been intimate?"

Cherry burst out laughing. "You're too much, kid. Here you are, probably having sex day and night, and you still can't bring yourself to say the words. Well, the answer is no. There's been plenty of heat with both of them, but the clothes stayed on and all hands remained above the waist. Gawd, I wish I had a picture of your face. I'm just fitting in with the natives. Anyway, Thor wants more and that would change everything. He and Apollo are best friends, like us, only for much longer. I'm afraid this is one triangle that would eventually hurt their friendship and I'd lose them both. I haven't decided what to do yet. But enough of that. You are absolutely glowing. Hell, even your little worry lines have disappeared."

"Why, thank you, dear." Aster made a quick check of her appearance in the mirror. "Of course, that's because I've died and gone to heaven, so I have nothing more to worry about."

"Well, kid, you know I've waited years to see you

this happy but there's something you better worry about, and I'd rather you hear it from me than some stranger." When she was certain Aster realized she was serious, Cherry continued, "I heard more than a few comments this week, some of which were downright ugly, about the beloved chief administrator losing his marbles over a lowly Terran. Somebody's even started a rumor that you aren't even from Earth, but some other planet where the women are witches and you've cast an evil spell over Rom. He's getting a pretty bad rap and the insinuation is it's bound to hurt his career. He really is up for the governorship."

"I heard that too, but I thought it was something in the distant future. He hasn't said one word about it. He *has* told me there are some restrictions about relationships but I didn't think we were breaking any of their laws by being together unofficially."

"Apparently, only a handful of people really care about who someone like Thor or Tarla spends time with. It's different for Rom. He's a politician for goodness sake. Doesn't he know anything about being discreet?"

Aster felt as if she had been kicked in the stomach. "He, um, hasn't been himself lately." She gave Cherry's hand a squeeze. "Thanks for telling me."

Forcing a smile back on her face, Aster followed Cherry back to the dance floor, where Johnny and Betty Basiglio were chatting with Rom.

"Hi, Aster, Cherry. It's good to see you," Betty said in a cheerful voice. "Nick and his lady friend are here too."

It took several minutes to catch up on each other's news but Johnny saved his and Betty's surprise for last. "We wanted to do something where we could still be near the water. You know you can't teach an old dog new tricks. With the chief's help, we were able to set ourselves up as kelp farmers."

Betty took over the conversation. "The business is only the beginning. All our married life there was one thing we wanted terribly, but couldn't have. We both went through some thorough exams this week and we've been given the most wonderful news. By this time next year, we should be parents!"

Everyone was hugging and congratulating them when Cherry excused herself with a frustrated sigh. Aster's gaze followed her as she headed for the two men in her life. They were clearly having a heated conversation. Aster could not imagine how that story could have a happy ending.

The band struck up "Deep Purple" and Rom held out his hand to her. "I believe they're playing your song."

It was a dreamy slow song and Aster melted against him as he led her around the floor. The other dancers made room for them and eventually stopped dancing completely.

When the music came to an end, Rom dipped Aster dramatically, and the room filled with applause. Aster hoped the lights were sufficiently dim to hide her pink cheeks.

The next song was pure swing and, before Aster could object, Rom curled her into the crook of his arm and whipped her out again. She had never learned all the intricacies of the jitterbug but she knew enough to keep up with the basics. Soon the other dancers crowded back onto the floor again. Rom and Aster had had their moment in the spotlight.

The fast-paced dance was fun but Aster was even more delighted when the next song began and Rom held her close again.

Someone tapped Rom's shoulder and he turned his head to see a moustached stranger, almost as tall as he, with a smile that revealed a diamond in his tooth. The urgent pressure of Aster's fingers on his hand and neck and the alarm in her eyes told him who the man was.

Victor looked directly at Rom then greeted Aster. "You make a most attractive couple. I was hoping you might permit me to dance with the lovely lady."

Rom did not return his smile nor bother to exchange introductions. He felt Aster trembling in his arms and saw no need to be cordial.

"The *lovely lady* has reserved all her dances this evening for me. The room is filled with available partners. You should be able to find someone else to your liking." With two sweeping steps, Rom whirled Aster away from the offensive man.

Over Rom's shoulder, Aster watched Victor storm away. At the edge of the dance floor, she recognized the counselor, Edward, glaring at her. Edward spoke to Victor as he pushed by then they both disappeared into the crowd.

"Are you all right?" Rom searched her troubled face.

"That was Victor."

"I gathered that. I think your intuition is on target. There's something very wrong with that man, no matter what his file says. You're still shaking. Let's go sit out in the garden and cool off for a few minutes."

She gave him a slight nod and linked her arm through his. Casually, they promenaded out the back door, as if nothing were out of the ordinary.

Rom found a secluded bench hidden from the shimmering lanterns hanging along the main path. Aster gave herself up to his protective arms, and for the first time, talked about the hijacking. "He thought nothing of killing those people or shooting Cherry.

During the entire trip, he snorted cocaine and played with his knife. He as much as told me he didn't care if I was dead when he got around to raping me. A man that sick cannot be made healthy again in a couple weeks."

Rom rocked her slowly. "I'll take care of you, shalla. You believe that, don't you?"

She lifted her face to give him a soft kiss. "Yes, of course, I do. I guess it was the way he walked up to us, as normal as can be. I'll be okay now, really."

"Good. Sit still for a minute and look at me." He pulled out the tail of his shirt and used the underside to wipe the makeup streaks from her face. "I have no idea why you wear that stuff. You're beautiful without it."

"And you're a sweet liar. Aha! I caught you telling an untruth!"

"Wrong. I was being honest, as I see it."

"I understand now. There's variations to this honesty code of yours."

"I refuse to answer such a leading question. Now hush and kiss me again…like you mean it this time."

Aster needed no further incentive. "Oh, Rom, I love you so much," she breathed into his mouth.

Slowly, he pushed her away from him and tried to read her eyes in the dark. "What did you say?"

"I said I love you. I'm not sure if those words mean anything to you. They're the most important words in my world to tell someone how deeply you care for them. I know we've only known each other a short time but a lifetime wouldn't make any difference in the way I feel about you."

"Aster, I—" Rom tried to interrupt.

"I understand with you this is a biological obsession and I don't want you to feel obligated because I'm telling you this. I just had to let you know that I love you with all my heart and soul, no matter how you feel."

Rom drew her to him and his voice shook when he spoke. "How could you not know how I feel? I fell in love with you the moment I saw you and you weren't even conscious. The fever is only a symptom. If it ever goes away, I'll still love you just as much. It's been torture not telling you how much I love you. I was afraid of frightening you away if you knew the depth of my feelings. I love you, my shalla, and I want you to be a part of me...forever." He dotted little kisses on her nose, her cheeks, her eyes.

Aster felt her heart racing. Was it knowing he loved her that made her feel so lightheaded? She was suddenly so hot! Wherever his lips touched her, a tiny spark ignited and spread, until her entire body seemed engulfed in flames.

She became aware of the center of the heat. The pulse between her thighs increased, harder, stronger, uncontrollable. She had never experienced such desire without Rom being inside her. She urgently needed him this instant. He had to stop this ache before she exploded.

"*Rom!* Something's...it's so strong...*I need you now!*"

Rom stared at her in shock. Her voice was a ragged imitation of itself, her pupils dilated, her skin hot and clammy. Aster knelt between his legs, pulling at the opening in his slacks. As his manhood sprang out at her, she caught it, taking him deeply into her mouth. He could not catch his breath, as she devoured him.

The next moment she stood up and kicked away her panties. Without a pause, she straddled him, pulling him into her depths. Now as frantic as she, Rom tugged at her bodice. Driven to madness, he ravaged her breasts. When their mutual release came seconds later, they muffled their groans into each other's mouths.

"I love you," they both gushed at once.

Then Aster gasped. "Good Lord, what have I done? What if someone had come along?"

"To tell the truth, I didn't care at the moment. This particular moment is a different story, however." He gently kissed her, and lifted her off him so they could make themselves presentable again. "Let's go home. We have to talk."

A lone figure stepped out from behind a tree and watched the lovers' departure.

"How sweet," Victor hissed aloud in the dark. "So, you love the little nympho, eh, big shot? We'll have to find out how much you'll do for her."

Aster stretched her sated body in Rom's big bed. "Now, will you please tell me about this governor business?"

"Let's see, the head of each province is a chief administrator. Over the seven provincial administrators is the governor of Innerworld."

She punched his arm. "Don't be a smart aleck. You know what I mean."

"I'm getting there. The governors of Innerworld and other colonies report to the Ruling Tribunal on Norona. All top government positions are achieved by Tribunal appointment, but popular support influences their decisions.

"The current governor, Elissa, is retiring and one of the seven chiefs will be appointed to replace her. I'm one of the nominees. There's a strong possibility that I'll get it."

Aster remained quiet as she wrestled with her emotions. She edged away from him and reached for her robe. "This is what you've worked all your life toward, isn't it?"

"Except for the last couple weeks, I'd say I hadn't thought of anything else for forty years."

Keeping her back to him, she donned her robe and rose. "I'm moving back to my apartment tomorrow." It only hurt a little, like a small dagger piercing her heart. "In fact, the best thing for everyone would be if you just sent me back to California. Then you wouldn't be tempted anymore."

Rom couldn't believe what he was hearing. He was out of the bed and forcing her to look at him in a heartbeat. "Why would you say such a thing? You can't leave me. No one hates politics that much."

Aster felt her resolve crumbling beneath his crushed expression. "I have to, Rom. You've been protecting me all week. I found out tonight what's being said about us. They think you've gone crazy or I've bewitched you. You'll lose the appointment if I stay here with you. I won't be responsible for ruining your career."

"Aster, I'll repeat what I said. You can't leave. Look at what happened to me last night. But it's not only me now. What do you think happened to you tonight in the garden? That was hardly normal Aster behavior. I can only assume the stress Victor caused and your admitting how you feel about me triggered it. I don't know all the answers or how it's possible, but it's happening to you too, even though you're a Terran. I can assure you that the fever won't stop building now that it's begun.

"Medical could treat you as well by desensitizing your skin and reducing the pain. But they can't end the burning. I've discussed our situation with the doctor. He assured me there's no biological reason a Terran couldn't survive the joining ceremony. He's positive it's a Noronian myth created to keep the race pure. As far as your sanity, I told him about your intelligence and what happened in the pyramid. He thought there's an excellent chance you could adapt to the mental union in time. Now that you've begun to burn, I'm sure we were meant to join. There are no more reasons to put it off."

"You're confusing me." Aster knew she had to fight him, no matter how logical he made it sound, for his own good.

"The first time you spoke, when you arrived in Innerworld, and I held you in my arms, you said, 'I know you. You've been in my dreams before.' I remember your exact words."

"I had dreamt about you or someone who looked like you. It was why you made me so nervous."

"Don't you see? It was me. Our souls hung in limbo until we found each other."

Rom hugged Aster closely, running his hand along her spine. He supposed her hesitation could be due to fear. He had to convince her she had no more choice in the matter than he did. "You don't need to be frightened, shalla. I believe what the doctor said. You can talk to him if you want. And I even thought of a way for you to practice mental control to prepare for the joining."

"I'd know your every thought?" Aster asked.

"At the same time I do. And feel whatever I feel. It will be easier for me at first because I've been trained to control my mind. I would be able to close off your thoughts when I needed to concentrate on something else. Eventually, I'm sure you would be able to do the same," Rom said hopefully.

"And, in the meantime," she deduced, "I'd also know the exact moment you stopped loving me. The precise second you began to resent what I'd done to you and your career. You're not thinking clearly, Rom. There's no way you'll get that appointment if you're joined with me. In my country, a politician's wife can ruin him if the press uncovers some dark secret about her. She influences her husband's thinking and they aren't even sharing a brain. Take the blinders off, Rom. They will never allow someone they consider an inferior being to share the most important position in this colony."

"I've considered that. We'll present our case to the Tribunal. They know what happens to a Noronian during his mating time. It's not something we choose and they should take that into consideration. If we guaranteed not to produce offspring, that might satisfy them.

"If that fails, I'll give it up. The only ambition I have now is to be joined with you. If they want me for governor, fine. If they want me for supply station collector, that's fine too. However, if they want me to forget about you, they'd have to reprogram me. If we have to, we'll find another world to live in where they can't rule us. We could go to your world. I'm familiar with the political situation there."

"My world?" Aster asked in disbelief. "Where you could be the first alien to run for city council? Where you might live to the ripe old age of eighty instead of one hundred fifty? Now you're being ridiculous as well as naive."

"You think so?" Rom was getting angry with her rational answers. "Go ahead and move back to your apartment. What are you going to do when the burning starts again and I'm on the other side of town? Attack a passing stranger?"

Aster gasped.

"It won't help you know. No one will put out the fire for you but me."

"Stop it! We're not the only two people involved here. I've accepted the fact that I'm helpless to do anything more for my world as long as I'm here. But you're still an integral member of your world. You've achieved so much for the Terrans in Innerworld and I know in my heart that one day you'll accomplish wonderful things for the people on Earth too. I would love to be at your side when that happens but my being with you now will eliminate that possibility. All the things we've both worked for—"

"Don't you dare use this conversation to start in on your precious environmental issues again. In less than a year, there may not even be a planet Earth for you to crusade for!"

Aster froze. "What did you say?"

Rom heard his own words echoing in his head. How could he have let that slip?

"Oh, my God," Aster whispered as she backed away from him. "It hasn't just been this mating fever or your concerns about your career. There's more, isn't there? You've kept something horrible from me, haven't you?"

"I couldn't tell you."

"Don't tell me—it's forbidden! Well, damn it, I'm forbidden too, but that didn't stop you from having me!"

He touched her shoulder but she jerked away. "Aster—"

"No, don't touch me. Don't look at me with those eyes. Don't…love me." She took a deep breath. "Rom, you just proved yourself wrong. Your career is still the most important thing to you."

"That's not true." He let out a sigh and sat on the edge of the bed, his face in his hands.

The slump of his shoulders told Aster all she needed to know. He had been fighting a battle all alone and he was sick to death of it. She sat down next to him and touched his cheek. "I'm sorry. That was unfair. I don't even know what I'm saying anymore."

"It was never a matter of not trusting you. I just didn't want you to worry when there was probably no reason."

"And now there is?"

"I don't know." Without any consideration as to whether he was betraying his position, Rom shared the facts and his concerns about the approaching planetoid. "If the emissary is not found within the next week, drastic measures will have to be taken. It will be up to the governor to make the final decision but it looks like we'll have no choice but aggressive interference."

"Imminent danger—that was what you called it before. I promise not to worry until you tell me to, if you'll promise not to keep anything else from me. I don't want you to bear the burdens of our relationship along with the problems of the world. At least let me share the load."

Rom pulled her into his arms. "Agreed. But your talk of leaving isn't helping my state of mind. I'll make you a deal. I won't pressure you about our joining, if you'll stay with me one more week. If tonight was a false alarm and you don't feel anything like that again, you can go. I won't stop you."

An idea had occurred to him that would bring her around without any more words. All he had to do was not make love to her until she reached a feverish pitch again. He had gotten his first treatment this morning and would go back for another tomorrow. Meanwhile, he was absolutely certain she would not last more than a couple days without his help.

Aster couldn't imagine what had changed his attitude so drastically but she agreed to his terms. She felt better knowing she had another week before she had to give him up.

As it turned out, Rom's estimate was excessive. Less than twenty-four hours later, the distress in her eyes was so terrible, he took pity on her and did not make her beg for him to make love to her as he had planned.

The separation was not mentioned again.

CHAPTER 14

Aster had the next day off but convinced Rom to go into the office, telling him that Cherry was coming to visit. She regretted lying to him but knew he would forgive her when he got the surprise she had planned for him. As soon as his car pulled out of the driveway, she headed for the Arena.

The only person in the lobby of the castle was a man dressed in black, with his back to her. He had the most gorgeous hair she had ever seen—honey-blond with streaks of light brown and gold, flowing to his shoulders in thick waves. She would have thought it was a woman if not for his body. A few inches shorter than Rom, he was still tall and muscular in a lean, sinewy way.

"Excuse me," Aster said as she approached him. "Do you work here?"

"Among other things," the man answered cryptically in a resonant voice that seemed to stroke her physically. When he turned to face her, she was momentarily speechless. He was more than simply an attractive man. The sensuous quality of his luminous, gold-topaz eyes would have been intriguing enough but the black pupils within were marquis-shaped and reflected her own face like twin mirrors. His incredible hair and strange cat's eyes made Aster think of a beautiful tamed lion.

"Might I be of service?" When he spoke this time, she picked up an accent similar to a Scottish brogue. She explained what she was looking for.

The leonine man pondered her request for a moment before answering. "A gift for Chief Romulus…an item he would treasure. I believe I can help you with that. Follow me."

He took her to a room behind one of the playing fields and removed a sword from a leather case. Aster held out both hands to accept the long weapon. The hilt was of ornately carved black pearl and the steel gleamed from attentive polishing. The only evidence that it was not new was a small nick in one side of the blade.

"It's magnificent," Aster said, honestly impressed.

The man was blatantly enamored with the piece himself as his fingers caressed the metal. "A few weeks back, the chief was victorious in a difficult match with the Black Knight. This is his opponent's sword. Here you see the damage Romulus inflicted. He would recognize it, I am sure."

"Would the Black Knight be willing to sell it to me?"

"It would be impossible to price. The Black Knight has great admiration for Chief Romulus. He would gladly offer this sword as a gift for the Blue Knight."

Aster could hardly believe her ears. Nothing could have been more perfect. "I can't thank you enough. He'll love it. You didn't tell me your name. Would Romulus know you?"

"My name is Falcon. He is acquainted with me, in a way. Enjoy the giving." He replaced the sword in its case and handed it to Aster.

She had assured Rom she would not go to the Indulgence Center for lessons on how to please him but she had not made any such promise about doing some research at home.

An hour later, with flushed cheeks and an insistent pulsing between her thighs, she turned the viewer off. She was anxious to try every technique she had learned on Romulus. But since she had to wait, she got her private party started with a call to his personal vidcom.

"Chief Romulus here."

"Aster Mackenzie here," she said, imitating his deep voice. "Are you alone?"

"What?"

"Is anyone in your office, like Tarla?"

"No, why?"

"Go close your door."

"Aster! What's this about?"

"I won't tell you until you close your office door. And lock it if you can."

"This is crazy. All right, I'm locking my door." Rom got up from his chair and closed the door. He turned around to find himself facing Aster, or rather her holographic image, wearing only a black lace teddy. His jaw dropped in both shock and admiration.

"Hello, shallar," Aster teased in a breathy voice. "I have a surprise for you." Slowly, she lowered the straps until her pointed nipples peeked over the top of the teddy up. "You'll have to come home to get the rest of it," she whispered then vanished.

Romulus leaned heavily against the door. Was that the same woman who once believed she was frigid? He had practically climaxed just watching her. No treatment could hold back the fever after a teaser like that.

Aster smiled after she turned off her transmission. She could imagine Rom's reaction. Tonight she would return some of the pleasure he had given her.

No more than five minutes passed when she heard his car door thud. How in the world had he gotten there so fast?

Anxious to continue his seduction, she hurried to open the door. "Welcome—"

Victor! Aster quickly pushed the door back but Victor moved faster. His fingers clamped on the door's edge and prevented her from getting it fully closed.

He applied his greater strength and put an end to the skirmish by relaxing his pressure then slamming his full weight against the wood.

The blow knocked Aster backward. On her knees, she scurried toward escape. The door crashed shut in her face, just as the heel of his boot collided with her jaw. Aster's neck snapped back and her body followed like a marionette's.

She opened and closed her eyes several times in an attempt to reorient herself. Her mouth tasted of blood and her jaw throbbed painfully. As she raised her hand to assess the damage, Victor pressed the point of a long, razor-thin knife into her cheekbone.

"Freeze, bitch," he snarled, "unless you want to lose one of those pretty eyes."

"What do you want?" Aster murmured through clenched teeth.

"Come now, Miss Mackenzie, I didn't take you for a stupid woman. However, since you just let me know you were expecting the big shot at the door, I guess we don't have time for any fun before we go. Your alien freak will be slightly delayed I'm afraid. I borrowed his car for our convenience."

Aster had been clinging to the fact that Rom would

be bursting through the door any second to rescue her.

"I need your assistance with a small matter. I thought you might not do so willingly, so I took an added precaution. Your friend, Cherry, is in my protective custody. You will come along quietly or I will kill her...*again*."

He lowered the blade to slash one of her straps. Aster whimpered as a trickle of blood ran down from her shoulder. She tried to cover herself and watched the knife bite the back of her hand.

"I told you not to move. The next time you disobey me you will be half-blind. I'll take you either way but your *protector* might not appreciate my artwork."

She would not cry. If she could keep her wits, she might come out of this alive—again. "Where is Cherry? I'll do whatever you want. Just let her go."

"You don't need to know where she is. You will have to accept my word that she will be released if you behave. Now stand up slowly and get a piece of paper to write a note. He'll be coming along to fetch you soon enough. I only want to delay the meeting a bit longer.

"I am a very lucky man, you know. I thought it might be weeks before I'd catch you alone. I could hardly believe it when I got the call this morning. What's the matter, bitch? Somebody at his office a better lay than you?"

It took a moment for his words to sink in. He had an accomplice. Someone who had been watching her and Romulus was reporting to Victor. It had not mattered at all that he was far away at the Clinic.

"What do you want me to write?"

"Tell him you went out to run an errand."

"Can I tell him I borrowed his car? He loves that car more than me. He'll be very upset when he discovers it's gone."

"Yeah, that's a good idea. I knew you could be cooperative, with the right incentive." He twisted the knife in front of her face.

Aster tried to ignore the bloody cuts and the fierce pain in her jaw. As she composed the note, she told herself Rom would know something was very wrong.

R—Sorry I left you stranded. I needed the car to run an errand. You know how I love to drive it every chance I get.—A

"Okay?"

"Yeah. Let's go."

"Can't I get dressed first?"

"No more time. Move."

Just then the vidcom began to beep. Aster turned toward it but was brought up short as Victor grabbed her wrist and twisted it up her back. Shooting pain tore into her shoulder.

"Let it go," he ordered, giving her arm a yank and shoving her out the door. The insistent beeping continued behind them.

Victor again credited his good luck when no one noticed him pushing the half-naked bitch into the car. He snapped handcuff-like clamps on her wrists behind her back and stuck a piece of wide adhesive tape across her mouth. Another longer strip bound her ankles.

"Can't stand a broad talking while I'm driving," he said with a snicker at his own joke.

Aster closed her eyes against the reality of what was happening to her. *Rom! Hear me. I need you.*

Victor leered at her breasts straining against the see-through material. The side with the severed strap barely covered her nipple. He pulled the sheer material the rest of the way down and cruelly pinched her flesh.

She couldn't stop the painful moan that escaped her throat. But as he proceeded to grope the naked breast, the taste of bile was worse than the pain.

"I've seen your big tits before, bitch, so you don't need to be shy with me." In answer to her furrowed brow, he replied, "I caught your act in the garden the other night. Interesting dialogue, although a bit corny for my taste. I have plans to thank you for the entertainment later." He stopped kneading her exposed breast to squeeze the growing bulge between his legs.

Rom! Find me!

"Thanks for the lift, Falcon. I really appreciate it. Let me know if you have any luck tracking my commuter." Rom was bewildered by the missing car. He was more upset by how it may have interfered with Aster's surprise. He had called to let her know about the inconvenience but she hadn't answered, which seemed very odd also.

"Chief Romulus. Stop." Falcon's raspy voice halted him before he reached the front door. "Your car was here a little over an hour ago." The tracker climbed out of his sleek speeder.

"That's impossible. I drove it to work this morning."

"Would you stand aside for a moment, please? There is a great darkness here." The man with the special abilities placed his hand on the door and closed his eyes. A violent shiver ran through him. "A struggle occurred. Let me go in first, before you disturb anything."

Rom stood tensed in the open doorway. Falcon moved slowly through the room, randomly stopping to touch objects. When he picked up Aster's note, he called for Romulus to enter.

"Tell me about this."

Rom took the paper and recognized Aster's handwriting. "This isn't right. I offered her the car this morning and she refused. She's afraid to drive it herself. What is it, Falcon? What's happened here?" A steel vise closed around Rom's heart.

"Do you know a man, very thin, almost your height and coloring, with a gem in his tooth?"

"Victor." Rom's voice turned to ice.

"He was here and took your female away. He is the one who stole your commuter."

"Let me see what happened."

"No. You do not want to do that. It is uncomfortable for me and I am not involved with her."

"I said show me! That's an order."

Falcon nodded and positioned himself in front of Rom. "What you will see and hear are the events as they happened and the words spoken aloud. I do not have the ability to discern thoughts of someone not physically present. You will not experience the emotions I am picking up. If you are certain you wish to do this, you may touch my mind."

Each man placed two fingers on the other's temple and closed their eyes. Like a video with poor sight and sound, the scene replayed in Falcon's head for Romulus.

"I'll destroy him," Rom growled as he broke contact.

"He did not say where he was taking her but I can follow their brain waves. I should be able to overtake him with my speeder. I will contact you when she is safe."

"Like drek you will. I'm going with you." Romulus's powerful grip closed over the other man's forearm.

"Romulus, you will be in my way. You are so full

of anger that it is interfering with my reading. Besides that, you are burning for her. I felt it the second I touched you. I would be distracted by your emotion. Let me go so I can help her."

"I'll get it under control. I have to go." Romulus was out the door and in the speeder ahead of the tracker.

They were beyond the city for several minutes before they both realized precisely where Victor had taken Aster. Falcon shifted his speeder and they soared into the air toward the Rehabilitation Clinic.

Victor's timing was perfect. The daytime employees of the Clinic were gone for the day. The skeleton evening crew never came to this end of the building. He had spent enough nights in the laboratory to know he had complete privacy.

He removed the wrist cuffs and gave Aster a shove. "Lie down on that table, bitch. And don't try anything cute or you'll watch me when I slice that little Cherry into bite-size pieces."

She obeyed as slowly as she dared. If only he would remove the tape on her mouth, she could try to talk to him.

Victor snorted loudly at her grunting and expressive eyes. "No, I will not remove the tape. You have nothing to say that I want to hear. I, on the other hand, have several things to say to you." He painfully secured her wrists and ankles in the restraints at the table's four corners.

"Oh, my. I forgot to take that thing off you before I got you ready. Well, we can fix that."

Aster shrieked with terror as he brought the blade down to the hollow between her breasts. Dragging the razor-sharp edge down the center of her body, he split the teddy in half, leaving a thin bloody trail behind.

With a flick of his wrist, the material fell to her sides, exposing her helpless body to his greedy eyes.

"My, my, how pretty you look in red. I think a touch more color would make it even better. We want to make sure the chief knows we mean business, now don't we? Let's see. We have this nice spot here by your eye." He touched the point to her cheekbone and fresh blood crisscrossed over the dried blood dripping into her hair. "Then we have an attractive decoration on the right shoulder."

Aster held her breath as the steel passed across her chest to prick the other side. "There. That's an interesting addition. I think one more line right here should complete the look." The knife sliced across her ribs, more deeply than the other cuts. Aster could feel her taut skin pop open like a zipper as her blood seeped down her sides and under her back.

This is not happening! It's another nightmare and it's going to end in a minute and I'll wake up in Rom's arms and I won't cry because this isn't real. Lord, tell him where I am, Aster's mind screamed as she tried to block out the pain.

"You think you're too good for a Julio like me, huh? It didn't need to be like this you know. When I came to your apartment house, you could have been pleasant. You could have offered to help me, simply as a kindness, but, no, you had to be a smart-ass, some kind of ice queen. And all the while sleeping with some creature from outer space like he's normal and I'm not. I don't think he'll be so hot for you after I get through."

Aster tried to follow him with her eyes as he strolled around the table then stopped near her face.

"I know. I'll brand you, like the cow you are."

Aster gagged on the acid that rose in her throat as he carved a deep V in her forehead. The bubbling red liquid gushed into her eyes, burning and blinding her.

Victor's demonic laughter echoed in Aster's ears and she slammed her eyes shut against his insanity and her own pain. Why am I still conscious? she thought, surprised at her ability to stand the agony wracking her body.

"Are you praying, bitch? You should be. Pray that that freak boyfriend of yours cares enough about you to give me what I want. Otherwise, what I've done so far is nothing but foreplay for the big finish!" Victor snickered at his metaphor. "I almost forgot about that character flaw of yours—being so very religious. He used to laugh at you. Little Miss Innocent praying in church for salvation every Sunday, especially after she had done that dirty awful thing with him on Saturday nights."

Aster blinked open her bleary eyes and warily listened to his cruel words. He swaggered up several steps behind a raised counter. Suddenly an enormous light glared down on her. It was so bright it made her squint, even with her eyelids closed.

"You never had any idea, did you? That was the funniest part. You, so righteous, engaged to one of the crookedest pigs on the Frisco police force."

Certainly her hearing was being affected by the searing pain coursing through her. The only person she was ever engaged to was Dennis. Victor could not be talking about him.

"I see I have your full attention again. Your name was familiar to me when I heard it on the yacht but it wasn't until a few days later that I put two and two together.

"He talked about you a lot, especially when he was high. So beautiful yet so cold. If it wasn't for the fortune you inherited, he would have kissed you off after he had you the first time. He said you lay there like a dead fish. He didn't know you were only turned on by aliens."

Aster blinked against the verbal assault. This had to be another part of Victor's perverted torture. Dennis had been a good police officer. He had hated drugs. He had loved her, not her money.

The light burned through her eyelids. What was he talking about now? She could not remember. Was it important? She was so tired. Maybe Victor would let her take a short nap.

Victor! Her mind snapped to attention again. She recalled the healing light from when she first arrived in Innerworld. It was similar to this one but not so bright. Victor was operating this light. Perhaps if she concentrated very hard on what he was saying, she would stay awake.

"Are you still with me, bitch?"

Aster blinked.

"Are you relaxed yet? No? You will be soon enough. Then I'll sample what you never gave easily to good old Dennis. I don't like women who move around too much when I take them.

"He said you only did it one night a week and even then you were stiff as a board underneath him. I heard you cried sometimes after he came, no matter how easy he tried to go. Do you think you could do that little trick for me? Unlike some men, I don't mind a woman's tears. As you might have guessed, I find inflicting pain somewhat exciting." Victor laughed aloud as though he'd just heard a very funny joke.

He knew! No one knew exactly how their love-making had been except her and Dennis. Could he have guessed? Could he be telling the truth? Why would Dennis have confided such a private thing to this beast? Unless...

"We had a good thing going, your Dennis and me.

An associate of mine turned me on to him. I bought all the product he could confiscate on his little drug busts. Then he had to get greedy. He wanted double his prices or he'd turn me in, as if everything he had done was part of some undercover operation."

Aster's confusion mounted. She didn't understand why this man was so angry with her. Had she done something and forgotten what it was? He didn't seem to like Dennis very much either. It was all very strange.

"Do you know what José and I did to him then, bitch? We tied him up and blindfolded him in his own apartment and while he was on his knees begging for forgiveness, I blew his fucking head off. It made such a mess I had to burn the clothes I was wearing. Splattered brains don't wash off very easily." His voice crept higher and his laugh mutated into a shrill giggle.

Aster's mind crawled through a field of muck. It was all around her. The man was stark raving mad. She screamed in her silent world. Victor murdered...somebody. Or was it that terrible nightmare again of Cherry's blood gushing uncontrollably?

Victor watched her gradually stop straining against the clamps. When her face muscles relaxed, he knew it was time. First he would take his payment from her then he would call her lover and let him know just what the ransom would be for the bitch's release.

As he came down from the platform, he admired his handiwork on Aster's devastated body. Her battered condition exhilarated him. Sweat oozed beneath his moustache as he urgently pulled at the closure of his pants.

CHAPTER 15

The laboratory door slammed against the wall, exploding its glass window on impact. Falcon pounced into the doorway, pointing his weapon directly at Victor.

Victor hurled himself to the ground, rolling toward the platform as a lightning bolt shot across the room and burst in the spot where he had been standing. Falcon fired again as Victor scrambled up behind the platform.

It took only a moment for Victor to recover from the shock of being found. "Drop the gun or she's gone!" he shouted menacingly.

Falcon glanced sideward at the grotesque sight on the operating table then stared into the panel sheltering Victor. He saw the man's hand resting on a control, read the violent emotions cowering there and lowered his paralyzer to the floor with a clatter. Victor stood up and nodded at the meddler.

"Why don't you come in too, Chief Romulus? I should have guessed you might not need an invitation."

Romulus stepped cautiously into the room. His eyes

took in the bloody mess Victor had made of his love. A growl thundered out of him as he moved toward Victor. Instantly, the intensity of the light increased and at the same moment Rom heard Falcon shout inside his mind.

Stop, Romulus. Stop the anger. Do not look at her. She is alive, but we cannot help her until you regain your self-control.

When Victor saw Romulus halt in his tracks, he lowered the light to a less harmful level.

Romulus hammered down his rage and kept his eyes riveted on Victor.

Victor leaned nonchalantly against the control panel. "You might have noticed I've had some fun with her before you got here," he taunted.

Fight it, Romulus. Use your control.

"I didn't ruin her, but I may have spoiled her for lesser men...or aliens." Realizing that he could not provoke Romulus further, Victor changed his tack. "I'm sure you're familiar with that light over her head. My hand is on the control dial and is going to stay there while we have a very short conversation. Right now, she's just very relaxed, slipping layer by layer into deeper states of unconsciousness. She can be brought out of that eventually without any permanent damage.

"But if my hand should slip and accidentally knock this dial to full power, like it did a moment ago, I'm afraid the sexy lady's brain gets fried. Poof! She's a vegetable with no memory. Personally, I would keep her that way. As long as she's a good fuck, who needs her brain? Then again, you could have her reprogrammed, like they did my friend, and just fill in the blanks any way you like."

Rom lowered his eyes for a moment. *Falcon, does he know how to do that?*

He believes he can. It is a possibility.

Victor instinctively sensed something was going on and raised the light to its full beam once again.

"Hold it!" Romulus clenched and unclenched his fists. "Get to the point. What do you want?"

Victor turned the beam down again. "It's simple really, at least for you. I want out of this stinkin' place and back to the United States. I don't know how it's done but I know you're the man who can make it happen. I also know all about your foolish codes of honesty and nonviolence. Give me your promise that you will send me back, alive and in one piece, *tonight*, and I'll walk away from this control panel."

Rom was momentarily stunned by Victor's extraordinary demand. "If you know so much about us, then you also know we cannot allow anyone to return to Outerworld once they learn of our existence. We have unlimited resources. There must be something else that would satisfy you."

The light flared again.

"*No!*" Rom shouted and the intensity of the light softened. "This isn't something I can do on my own. There are details that have to be worked out."

Victor recognized the stall and flipped the dial again.

"All right! Whatever you want. I'll figure out a way. Now shut that damn thing off and get down here."

"Sorry, Chief, but I'd like to hear you say exactly what it is you're agreeing to before I move one inch."

Rom's heart pounded in his chest as he ground out the words. "If you will leave Aster alone and come down here, I promise to send you back to the United States, tonight, alive and in one piece. I believe that was your precise request."

Victor looked disgustingly triumphant as he turned off the overhead light, stepped down and strode across the room.

At the last possible second Rom lurched forward. Powered by his unleashed fury, his fist smashed into Victor's face.

Victor's shocked expression registered the deception as he stumbled backward. Blood streaming from his broken nose, he bent forward and charged Rom. In one continuous move, Rom connected his bent knee with Victor's chin, followed instantly by a powerful kick to his groin.

Victor staggered but didn't fall. In desperation, he unsheathed his knife from inside his boot and swiped at the air in front of Rom's chest.

The appearance of the deadly weapon in Victor's blood-encrusted hand raised Romulus's temperature to the boiling point. With an ear-splitting cry, he attacked and grappled Victor to the floor, prepared to kill or to be killed.

Falcon struggled to shut out the violent emotions bombarding him. Finally regaining control, he retrieved his paralyzer and shot Victor whose body collapsed on top of Romulus.

Flinging Victor aside as if he were weightless, Rom turned on Falcon with all his pent-up anger. "Why did you do that?" he shouted.

"Because you would have killed him and I could not let you face the consequences of that action. He is only stunned. You will have to decide what to do with him rather quickly." Falcon glanced toward Aster. "I will call for a medical team."

As Falcon walked away, Rom went to Aster's side. He stared at her blood-streaked beautiful face. He had to know what she had been through. His fingers moved to her temple.

Warden Zenton and two guards accompanied Falcon when he returned and the guards hauled

Victor's body away.

Falcon placed a comforting hand on Rom's shoulder. *I know.*

"I told her I would protect her from him." Romulus spoke quietly as he pulled himself together. "Reading about such evil existing outside our world was one thing. Having it here, touching us...Drek, Falcon, what he did to her. I can't stop this ache in my gut. I know it's against everything I ever believed but I could have strangled him with my bare hands even before I saw everything he'd done. Now...maybe if I could take that knife of his and cut out his heart I could repair the hole in my own. What am I going to do?"

Falcon did not need to be told how Romulus felt. His anguish made itself known to the sensitive man. "I can help you. I have some arrangements to make and then I will wait for you to come with me when you are ready."

Romulus removed the restraints and tape from Aster's mouth then covered her abused body with a sheet. Holding her lifeless hand in his, he found no pulse. He had never felt so helpless in his life. The sickness inside him threatened to drown out the last remnants of reasonable thought.

When Doctor Xerpa arrived, she recognized the chief standing next to the patient but he did not respond to her greeting. Gently, she drew down the sheet to examine her patient. An unprofessional gasp escaped her and she cringed at the malicious destruction before her. She had been told something awful had occurred but no words could have prepared her for this. As a woman, she was nauseated. As a doctor, she was repulsed but challenged.

Romulus did not move a muscle as Doctor Xerpa went to the control panel then returned to her patient.

"The light was on a low-medium setting and, as such, she should sustain no permanent brain damage, but she is in a deep coma. We will run some tests and repair her body. My prescription for you is a long, brisk walk—away from here. You look wretched. She won't be conscious for at least another twelve hours."

Rom's lungs burned in his chest as they filled with air again. He firmly clasped the doctor's hand then asked Warden Zenton to take that walk with him as he quickly presented his suggestion for handling Victor.

Within an hour, the Rehabilitation Board convened by vidcom and an urgent call was put through to Governor Elissa. Rom's suggestion was unanimously approved.

After checking with the doctor once more, he followed Falcon out to his speeder. His need to avenge Aster was a bitter pill lodged in his throat.

When they pulled up to the Arena, Rom sighed. "Falcon, I know you mean well, but I'm not up to a game."

"Trust me, Romulus. Something unusual is awaiting you."

They took a tram to a small playing area where a rack of medieval weapons stood on each side.

Falcon explained, "Tonight you will have no games of skill. There will be no play or audience to cheer you on. Whatever happens will go no further than this room. My healing gift to you is a fight to the death— no armor, no protective tips. Your opponent is entering the field."

Rom turned in the direction Falcon indicated. His mind reeled. Coming toward him was his diamond-toothed nemesis. Now they could finish the battle begun at the Clinic. Rom's gaze was drawn to a glint of steel. The moment Rom saw Aster's dried blood on the man's knife and hand, he bolted into action.

In a heartbeat, Rom grabbed a sword. He swung and caught the hilt of Victor's smaller weapon with his own. Nose to nose, hand to hand, the weapons were only an accessory to the brute strength of the two men. With a violent jerk, Rom twisted Victor's wrist and the knife flipped out of his grasp. When he dove to retrieve it, Rom's sword arced down on the rolling body, slashing Victor's arm. Blood gushed through his sleeve.

Victor's disadvantage was short-lived as he rolled in the opposite direction and leapt up fast enough to reach his own rack of weapons. He grabbed the mace. With a bloodcurdling scream, he swung the deadly ball over his head and ran toward Rom. Rom's sword caught in the circling chain and as it was yanked from his grip, the iron ball grazed his forehead. Victor quickly untangled the chain and prepared for another attack.

Rom took up his battle axe, hoisting it in the air just in time to halt the oncoming mace with a horrendous clang. Immediately, he closed in on Victor, eliminating the space required to swing the mace. Victor retreated, trying to reach another weapon. Rom locked his eyes onto Victor's, his axe poised in mid-air. He was not thinking strategy now. All that mattered was putting out the savage fever in his brain.

Vibrating with hatred, Rom swung the great axe down on his victim, slicing through the jugular vein, the spinal cord, and out the other side. For one obscene moment, Victor's head teetered on its severed neck then tumbled to the ground. A red fountain bubbled from the body as it collapsed.

Rom dropped the axe and fell to his knees. His emotional floodgates burst open and the thirst for vengeance poured out. But at what cost? He had taken the life of another human being. His bloodlust now satisfied, he could think more rationally. Regardless of how wicked that life had been, he would have to face charges, in spite of Falcon's promise of secrecy.

As Rom pulled himself to his feet, Falcon appeared at his side. "I know what you said but you'll have to take me into custody. I couldn't live with the knowledge of this crime."

"You have committed no crime, Romulus. Look." Falcon picked up Victor's knife and swiftly slashed the beheaded man's chest open. Oblivious to the blood, Falcon pulled the skin aside to reveal the computerized equipment inside. It was an android.

"But I thought...The blood...How?"

"I will admit to a slight deception. As I am not full Noronian, I do not always adhere to a code of honesty but rather to a vow to help others. I relied on your anger to cloud your perception. I had to risk the possibility that you could have been severely injured as well. I hope you will forgive me for that. I was relatively certain you would be the victor. I have seen you fight when it was only a game."

"Falcon, you've done me a great service this night. Perhaps someday you'll come to me for a favor."

"Perhaps. Now, get cleaned up and let someone repair your head. I will return you in time to see your lady awaken."

"How do you feel?" Romulus tenderly stroked Aster's face with trembling fingers. He knew the light had dulled her memory somewhat, but at least her mind had not suffered serious damage.

Aster's sleep-dazed eyes focused then squinted shut. She remembered what had happened to her and sat up and pressed her cheek to his chest. He held her as tightly as she needed.

"You're safe now. He can't hurt you anymore.

Nobody can, because I'm never letting you out of my sight again."

Aster slowly relaxed in his arms. "What about Cherry? Is she all right?"

"That was a lie to lure you here. Cherry was at work the whole time. She'll come to see you tomorrow."

"I still don't understand what he wanted."

Rom described the events precisely as they occurred, purposely stopping at the point when Falcon stunned Victor.

"Well, I'm sorry you broke your law about violence but I'd be lying if I said I wasn't happy that you got in one good kick for me. Speaking of lies, I hope that's what it was when you agreed to send him back to the United States. You wouldn't really do that, would you?"

"I kept my word. He's already been sent back."

"No!" she cried, falling back onto her pillow and covering her face with her hands. "It's all my fault. If it wasn't for me, he wouldn't have been able to coerce you into anything."

Rom pulled her hands away from her face. "There's nothing for you to feel guilty about. With the governor's permission, I worked out a way to keep my promise, punish Victor and render him harmless. It came to me when I remembered your comment about variations to the honesty code. Before he was transported, the medical team assisted my plan with their special talents.

"Victor is now John Smith, a balding and plainly unattractive, traveling salesman, walking along a country road in Nebraska. He's been provided with a memory of his reconstructed life as a lower middle-class family man, with one missing piece of information. He has no idea what city his beloved wife and two children are living in, awaiting his return. He will be compelled to spend the rest of his life searching for them. I thought it was rather ingenious, although my first plan was to beat him to a pulp."

"Ingenious? It's brilliant. At least he won't hurt anyone now but himself. By the way, did you say the name of the tracker who helped you was Falcon?"

"Yes, why?"

"Good-looking man with great hair and cat's eyes?" she asked.

Rom arched an eyebrow.

"Did he tell you we'd met?" she pressed, looking very worried.

"No, he didn't mention it. You have ten seconds to explain before my jealousy detonates. I'd never met him before yesterday."

The expression on his face let her know he wasn't joking about the green monster. She caressed his jaw with her thumb. "Let me rephrase my description of him—a man, not nearly as tall or as handsome as you, with hair like a woman's and really weird eyes. I hardly noticed him. I met him during my excursion yesterday. He said you were an acquaintance."

"Did meeting him have anything to do with my surprise? From what I saw of it, the answer had better be no."

Aster laughed at this new side of him. "As a matter of fact, it did." She hurried on when his mouth dropped open. "But not the part you got a preview of."

"You know, none of this would have happened if we were joined. I would have known what was going on immediately. This should convince you. Be my mate, Aster. Please."

Aster felt a ripple cross her stomach. "The whole time Victor had me, I talked to you in my head, knowing you really couldn't hear me. There is nothing I want more than to be your mate. I would be the happiest woman in both our worlds if we were joined."

Rom crushed her to his chest and sighed with relief.

"But," Aster continued as she pushed him away, "I won't do it."

"What?" Rom said, shocked. "How can you say that after this? I almost lost you forever." His joy transformed into angry frustration.

"Because nothing's changed, Rom. True, I can't and don't want to leave you. Both of our worlds need you as governor, now more than ever. I'm praying the Tribunal will overlook your infatuation with an inferior being. That definitely won't happen if I'm inside your head. I don't believe you could shove our joining down their throats with a toilet plunger!"

"And I told you I no longer care about the governorship or the Tribunal. Another competent administrator will be chosen." Rom paused. This was not the time to have another argument. He would give her time to recover before insisting she give up her stubborn attitude on the subject of their joining.

CHAPTER 16

Cherry came to visit on Wednesday as she had promised. Rom would not go into his office but did let the women have some privacy. He refused, however, to allow Aster to get out of bed and was taking great pleasure in waiting on her.

After Aster brought Cherry up to date, she asked, "What about the problem you were having in your love life? You all looked a little stressed at the dance."

Cherry giggled then grew serious. "You know, I don't want to get tied down to one man. Maybe it was growing up in such a large family, I don't know. I was always just one of the flock. Half the time my own mother forgot which one I was. I love being the center of so much attention for a change. Besides that, I always felt I had to keep a tight rein on my sexual desires. Suddenly I find myself in a world where nobody sees anything wrong with an active, diversified sex life."

"Cherry, you don't have to make any excuses with me. I'm not the same old prude I used to be."

"Well, the point is, Thor and Apollo each have qualities that I adore. If it was either one separately, there's no question I'd have already been to bed with him. Thor's the problem, as you guessed. He's fine when it's the three of us together, but he can't stand it if Apollo and I do anything without him. And Apollo hates it when Thor's upset.

"Their solution is to make it a threesome, in every way, rather than break up any part of the triangle. Although I'll admit to fantasizing about it, acting it out for real is a little much, even for me. I can't keep holding them both off though and they've agreed to leave it up to me. I have to make a decision of some sort."

The old Aster was shocked. The new improved Aster tried to be helpful rather than critical. "There's an educational video about it, if more information would help."

"Hah! That's my Aster! When in doubt, study!"

"You wouldn't laugh like that if you saw the triple X-rated instructional videos I watched!"

Cherry shrugged her shoulders and jumped into her next topic. "I do have some good news to share. I was selected to play a fair size part in someone's fantasy and everyone said I was wonderful! My manager actually told me he believes I'm headed for stardom! Do you believe that?"

Aster just smiled.

Cherry was pensive during her ride to work that night. Unlike dear Aster, she did not need a book or video to show her what it might be like to have two men at the same time. Hell, it was her favorite fantasy to masturbate to. How often had she joked about needing two men, so that the second could jump in when the first pooped out? But actually doing something about it was another thing entirely.

The more she thought about it, the more certain she

was that her strict moral upbringing still influenced her life. Perhaps, some years from now, she would be as uninhibited as the average Innerworlder but for now, a *ménage à trois* would remain relegated to her private fantasies. Assuming she could convince Apollo and Thor to agree to her choosing only one of them to be her lover, the question was, which man would she prefer?

Thor, so dark and intense, would come to her with barely controlled hunger. His mouth would plunder hers as his large hands would arouse her body, demanding she be as wild and as desperate as he. She could easily imagine his strong, muscular body taking possession of her smaller one with just enough roughness to add a dangerous edge to their lovemaking. She knew, without needing to see him naked, that he would be larger than the average man and that he might take her to levels of excitement she had never before experienced. And he would want her again and again.

Then there was Apollo, so beautiful and free-spirited, who would come to her smiling. He would tease her with his delicious kisses and soft caresses until she was weak from wanting him, yet he would make her wait for her fulfillment. Just looking at his gorgeous face and perfectly formed body was enough to turn her on. She would try to play his game of self-restraint, but he would insist on pleasuring her at least once before gratifying himself. And when he finally entered her, he would know ways to make the climb to the top last longer than she had ever thought possible.

Thor would love her deeply and want to keep her at his side, promising stability and security.

Apollo would love her lightly and avoid a commitment of any kind, promising fun and laughter.

After reporting backstage, she sought out both men to tell them she wished to take only one of them as a lover or keep both as friends. "The truth is," she said, holding a hand of each man. "I'm crazy about the both of you and I love the fun we have all together. I am sorry, but I'm just really confused."

Apollo squeezed her hand and gave her a peck on the forehead. "We understand. And we're flattered that you can't decide which of us to choose." He stared into Thor's eyes and, after a few seconds, his best friend nodded. "So, you don't need to make such a difficult decision. We'll do it for you. But we'll have to discuss this between ourselves."

Much later that night, she was wondering just how long they planned to discuss the matter, when her vidcom announced that she had a visitor. A moment after her vidcom monitor showed her who it was, she opened her door to greet her guest. "Hey, Apollo, I had a feeling you're the kind to keep a girl waiting."

She had the door half closed when a large hand grasped the edge.

"And I'm the kind who knows what you really want." Thor stepped inside and pulled her hard against him.

As his mouth took demanding possession of hers and his hands clutched her bottom, he thrust his thick erection against her, confirming everything Cherry had imagined about the dark man.

Apollo leaned down behind her and whispered in her ear. "We decided we wouldn't be very good friends if we didn't stop you from making a terrible mistake. And that's where we think you're headed. Besides, it's unfair of you to push one of us away without knowing exactly what you'd be giving up," Moving Thor's hands from Cherry's hips to his own, Apollo eased his rigid shaft into the valley of Cherry's bottom. "C'mon, Cher," he murmured, shifting himself from side to side against her. "We're too good together. Just give us a try. And if you still want to send one of us away after we've done our best to change your mind, we'll go along without an argument. But *you* are the one who will have to decide which it will be."

Cherry's desire shot into high gear as much from Thor's eating kisses as Apollo's words. But what was making her panties damp was the thought of being sandwiched between the two of them without the obstacle of so many clothes.

"Ah hell," she muttered. "What good is it to be in an alien world and not take advantage of *everything* it has to offer?" She slid one hand between her and Thor's bodies and the other between her and Apollo. Her fingers closed over the two cocks teasing her into anticipation.

"Okay boys, I'm ready for you to teach me how to be a real Innerworlder."

PART II

Outerworld

CHAPTER 17

Early Friday morning, Aster and Rom were awakened by a call from Tarla. When Rom disconnected, he was frowning. "I promised not to leave you alone but Governor Elissa needs to meet with me as soon as possible."

"The governor?" Aster sat up straighter and spoke sternly. "Romulus Locke, that was a silly promise you made about never leaving my side, so it doesn't count. I love you more than I dreamed possible but if you don't stop hovering over me, I am going to scream. You have responsibilities that are not going to disappear because you want to play doctor. Please go to work."

Rom laughed and gave her a soft kiss. "Okay, I can take a hint. You know, shalla, if we were joined, I could leave you and take you with me at the same time." He never missed an opportunity to chip away at her resistance.

"If we were joined, you wouldn't have a job at all."

Relieved to have a day to herself again, Aster began making preparations to put an end to Rom's over-solicitous behavior. She was feeling better. Even the fever had gone away for days due to the effects of the light. But the symptoms had returned this morning. She hoped Rom would relieve her but she was concerned he might resist. His new medication worked too well. He had not made love to her all week.

"Governor Elissa, Professor Schontivian, sorry you had to wait. I gather Operation Palomar is at a head."

"I'm afraid so," the governor said. "Before we commence, however, I apologize for calling you in from your leave but I was assured your friend was doing quite well after her tragic ordeal. I am looking forward to meeting the young woman who captured the heart of one of Innerworld's finest."

"Aster's looking forward to meeting you, also, Governor."

Elissa smiled briefly then became serious. "As you recommended, Warden Zenton received a commendation for his insight and has been given the power of veto over any of the Rehabilitation Board's decisions in the future. It seems we were not prepared to deal with such a devious personality. Mind you, I still have great faith in the Terran people as a race.

"As to today's business, Emissary K66 and his mate were found. They were killed in an automobile accident. It is believed their identification was stolen after the accident and none of the Outerworld officials could determine who they were. Yesterday our tracker finally found them stored in a morgue. There was nothing that could be done for them after so much time had elapsed. It has been confirmed that K66's assignment was never begun.

"We are now three weeks to the situation becoming critical. We no longer have the option of subterfuge. The most expedient course would be to approach a reputable Outerworld scientist and offer the information the Terrans need to prevent the planetoid's collision with Earth and to increase the speed of their ships.

"We do not have another emissary already in place where he or she could be effective without destroying his or her cover and there is no time for a new infiltration. Evacuation of our entire population is out of the question. I don't need to tell you how much Norona depends on this planet's volterrin. We must prevent its destruction.

"The person needed for this mission would have to have a considerable scientific background to be accepted as credible and able to answer any questions that might arise. Because of the delicacy of the situation, this person would also need to be an accomplished diplomat. I have chosen the United States as the most logical destination for our emissary.

"Romulus, I cannot order you to accept this assignment but you are the most qualified person I know of for this job. No other individual with the right background is as familiar with Outerworld."

Without hesitation, Romulus accepted. "Any ideas on how I convince this Outerworld scientist that I'm on the level?"

"This was a difficult decision for me to make. Unless you have a better idea, I suggest you take Aster with you to attest to our existence. She has an outstanding reputation in certain scientific communities. And by now, the Terrans have probably verified the mysterious circumstances surrounding her disappearance. She might also be able to help smooth over any difficulties you encounter while there. You may have studied Outerworld but she truly knows it. Because of your relationship, I have assumed there is no other Terran you would prefer to take. I will trust your judgment where she is concerned. Could she do this, or more to the point, would she do this, for us?"

Rom did not like the idea of being separated from Aster but had agreed to the mission because of his sense of duty. Taking her with him on a possibly dangerous assignment concerned him even more. He realized part of his worry stemmed from the remote possibility that she might not want to return with him once she was home. His emotional side argued that she loved him and her new life enough to return, and yet…

"Elissa, I should tell you, Aster and I are burning for each other. I have no idea how or why it happened but she is my shalla. I know it is prohibited but if you would grant us special permission, we could be joined before we leave. The mind link could be helpful if we had any problems."

"And it would also ensure that she would come back with you, wouldn't it? No, Romulus, even if I was willing, the Tribunal would have to approve such a unique joining and I seriously doubt they would, even under the circumstances. We can't wait to find out either. Also, you have no idea what the mind link would do to Aster. She would be of no help at all if she was spending all her time trying to sort out your thoughts, hers and outside voices. There's too much at stake to take such a chance. As to her returning to us, depend on her fever. It affects women as strongly as men, although I never heard of it happening to a Terran."

"You're right, of course. I'll speak to her tonight. I'm sure she'll agree. When do we leave?"

"Tomorrow." Elissa placed her hand over Rom's. "I realize the timing could not be worse for the two of you."

"I understand. Perhaps the professor and I should

begin working on what information I'm to present and to whom."

Although a shy, awkward man in social circumstances, when discussing his chosen field, Professor Schontivian's expressionless face and squinty eyes became relatively animated. He unrolled a large chart of the Earth's solar system and pointed to the various planets and areas as he spoke.

Except for one short break to let Aster know how late he would be, the cramming session went on for most of the day. By the time Schontivian departed, Rom's eyes ached and his neck was stiff with tension. Usually, he thrived on stress but since Aster came into his life, it did not give him the same thrill of accomplishment. He just wanted to go home.

He was clearing his desk when he spotted a letter from his father. It was not very long, but long enough.

Son,

A very uncomplimentary report was received by the Tribunal regarding your relationship with a Terran female, implying that her influence has severely impaired your judgment and competency. My "informant" said you should expect a summons to return to Norona in the near future. The governorship could be at stake.

Also, your mother has insisted that I add, if there is someone in your life, you must bring her home as well. Do not do anything rash. You know how she gets when she's worried about you.

Love,
Father

Rom put the note in his pocket and headed home. He found Aster sitting by the pond in the back yard and sat down beside her. Without saying a word, he pulled her into his arms. Aster instinctively sensed his tension.

"Please don't be angry with me for being up. I could not stand another minute in that bed," she said as she sat up and looked into his eyes, trying to see the source of his anxiety. "You look so tired, shallar. Can you tell me about it? Or maybe you would like something to eat and then relax in the whirlpool." It was her turn to worry about him.

"Yes, to all of the above. I have a lot to tell you and I can't eat or relax until that's out of the way." He summarized the morning's meeting and the governor's request for Aster's participation.

"It doesn't surprise me in the least that you would be called upon to save the world. If the governor hadn't suggested I accompany you, I would have stowed away in your luggage. You may be book smart about Earth but I'm familiar with the real thing. I might be of some help." Suddenly her eyes opened wide with awareness. "My heavens. I'm really going back."

Rom could see the light bulbs flashing on in her head. "I know you're not going to like this but I don't want you to misunderstand. You still can't reveal anything you've learned here. There is a specific amount of information we are to pass on and that's it."

"You're right, I don't like it." She carefully worded her next sentence. "But I swear I will not give away any of your secrets." Her own secrets were another matter entirely.

"You are so incredible," Rom murmured, holding her tightly and stroking her hair before moving away from her. "As if that weren't enough, I got a letter from my father today. You may as well read it yourself, if you promise not to say *I told you so*." Rom handed her the paper.

Sadness took possession of her as she read it. Perhaps now Rom would realize they could never join.

He rubbed his tired eyes. "I had assumed that if I wanted you, they would accept you. How could anyone not love you once they met you?"

Aster gave Rom a quick kiss. "I still love you, if that helps any. Now, unless you have some other bomb to drop on me, we have a lot to do tonight." All her organizational skills surged to life. "Outerworld doesn't have supply stations with disposable clothing, so we'll have to pack a few things. Also, we'll need money, just in case something goes wrong."

"Whoa! You sound like a little general heading into battle. Everything we need will be provided before we leave. I'm afraid you're going to be disappointed if this turns out to be as simple as I expect. I intend to be out and back in one day, so there's no need to pack anything."

"Who are you kidding? There is absolutely no way that you and I are going to pop in, out of the blue, talking about Innerworld and a coming disaster, and have it turn out to be *simple*. C'mon." She pulled his arm to get him up. "Let's get you some food while you tell me how we're going to do this."

While she ordered a meal for him, he started preparing her. "I wrote down some basic information that you'll need to memorize, as you said, just in case. We'll be going to the Palomar Observatory outside of Escondido, California. Apparently, it's the most likely place where someone might have sighted the planetoid, but that doesn't ensure that they picked up the planetoid's shift. I understand the air and light pollution in the area occasionally cause distorted or incorrect readings. Have you been there?"

"A long time ago," Aster replied. "I shouldn't have any problem getting us around the area though."

"Good. We'll be contacting a scientist named Doctor Katherine Houston. Her specialty is tracking the asteroid belt and we've been told she's very trustworthy.

"A lot is depending on the reports we have received from our emissary stationed at the Rand Corporation in Santa Monica. We've been assured that Doctor Houston always works in her lab at the observatory on Saturday.

"I don't expect it to happen, but if we get separated, you will contact that emissary. He's been notified that two people will be coming out."

"Wait a minute. You have an agent working at the Rand Corporation? That's a think tank. Why doesn't he just say he thought up this new formula for fuel and give it to Doctor Houston himself?"

"Because our emissary is a night janitor there. A lowly position, but a trusted one, with keys to every door and access afterhours. No one would believe he became a genius overnight."

"How would I contact this person?"

"This man has provided us with information of untold value for many years and we must avoid jeopardizing his position in any way. It would take years to establish another emissary in such a sensitive area. We are only to contact him in an extreme emergency. Your portable vidcoms must be left in Innerworld. If necessary, call this number on a public phone. When someone answers, don't speak. Punch this code into the phone instead. That will advise our contact that there is an emergency and you need to meet.

"Before we leave tomorrow, a homing device will be implanted in our ears. I will be able to find you if we are separated and the emissary will be able to locate either one of us using the device."

"Ouch. Do I have to?"

"You'll never know it's there. Also," Rom said, reaching into his pocket, "we each wear one of these rings. The emissary wears one too. That's how you would identify him."

Aster picked up the smaller gold ring and tried it on her third finger. There were markings and raised bumps of gold on both sides of the band. A large fire opal winked at her from the center setting. When the light hit the stone, she could make out a geometric design deep in the center of the gem.

"That's the insignia for Innerworld," Rom explained. "Be careful with the stone and nodes. The opal can be turned in either direction or opened like a door, but each movement has a purpose which may generate a message or action. These nodes on the sides gives access to a microcomputer and the transmigrator. Don't worry about it. You have enough to remember without learning how to operate the ring."

"Wow! I get my very own secret decoder ring. How very cloak and dagger. I'm sorry. This isn't funny. I must be getting hysterical. How do we get there? I refuse to go through what I did to come here."

Rom laughed. "It will take less than a minute and you'll feel a bit like you're on a roller-coaster ride. One second we'll be here then we'll be there. That's all there is to it."

"You mean our bodies dematerialize here and rematerialize in another location."

Rom was impressed with her comprehension. "Basically, that's correct. I could get more technical if you'd like."

"No, thank you. You are talking to someone who

can barely stand to get on an airplane, so I think the less I know, the better. Just guarantee me I won't end up with my feet on backward or anything like that."

"Guaranteed." Rom chucked her under her chin. "Are you really afraid to fly?" He was going to have a time convincing her to go to Norona with him as it was.

"I'm better than I used to be. Just hold onto my hand."

Rom pulled her onto his lap with a wicked laugh. "I intend to be holding on to a lot more than that." He nibbled her ear as his hand crept up her thigh.

Aster felt the heat rising and quickly got off his lap before her evening's plans were ruined. "Is there anything else we need to go over?"

Rom was totally confused. Her body was hot when he held her. He knew that she must need him now. He hoped she was not still thinking about Victor's abuse. But, if necessary, he would seduce her all over again. He walked up behind her and slid his arms around her waist.

"Whatever it is can wait until later. How about that whirlpool now?" His husky voice breathed into her ear. "Will you share it with me?"

Although dizzy from wanting him so badly, she was determined to give him his whole surprise or nothing. "No, I can't. I...have something to do. Would you like me to get it ready for you?" she asked nervously as she pulled away.

"Never mind. I'll just take a shower." He sounded so disappointed Aster almost gave in as he turned away and slowly climbed the stairs.

As soon as she heard the water turn on, she ran to the bedroom, tearing her clothes off along the way. She moved at breakneck speed to get ready before he got out of the shower.

With tousled wet hair and a towel wrapped around his waist, Rom stepped out from behind the bathroom screen. He was so devilishly appealing that it took Aster a moment to remember the lines she had carefully rehearsed.

"Stop!" she commanded.

The order was unnecessary. Rom froze at the shocking sight of the Amazon waiting for him at the foot of their bed. She had tossed her hair so that it was in wild disarray around her beautiful, but stern, face. She stood akimbo, over six feet tall in her spike-heeled shoes and dressed in a revealing red lace bustier. Black fishnet stockings attached to a black lace garter belt completed the outfit.

Holding a riding crop, Aster slinked toward him and inserted the end of the quirt into the top of the towel, easily flipping his only protection into a corner of the room. She slowly circled his nude form as if inspecting her property, finally giving his rump a light taste of her whip.

"Acceptable. Get on the bed, on your back. Now!"

Rom had gotten over his initial surprise and was struggling to hold back a full-fledged horse laugh. He quickly did as she bade. Whatever she had in mind was fine with him.

Coming around to one side of the bed, she dropped her prop and brought his one arm up, swiftly tying a red velvet cord around his wrist. The other end was secured to the bed frame. She moved to his ankles then his other wrist until each of his limbs was prettily bound to a corner of the bed. He was no longer sure this was funny.

He watched her kneel at one of his feet and sighed when she began massaging the arches. The relaxing moment ended when her tongue came into play, tracing each of his toes with special attention to the sensitive flesh between. As she got to his smallest appendage she drew it between her lips and sucked gently. When each toe of that foot had been properly loved, she repeated the treatment on his other foot.

Crawling onto the bed between his legs, she let her stomach caress his burning flesh as her mouth closed over one of his nipples. Aster's tongue played with him as he had done so often with her. When she felt the small pebble harden, she moved to the other.

Rom moaned and pulled at the cords keeping him in place. His desire was too great to hold back much longer.

"Oh, no, you don't. You're my love slave tonight and you can only be rewarded if you're a very obedient boy."

Aster backed off the bed and stood straight before him. She untied the bustier and let the material fall to the floor. Her hands cupped her breasts and lifted them to him. "My breasts ache for you, my shallar. Can't you see how much they want you to touch them?" Her fingertips rolled her aroused nipples then slid down her abdomen to lightly brush the dark curls between her legs. "My body has missed you terribly. But then, you know I have an emptiness only you can fill."

Her words were like warm honey pouring over his body. His limbs felt numb. All his blood rushed to the center of his being, forming the eye of a storm within him.

Leaving the garter belt and stockings on, she came back to him and enveloped his shaft between her full breasts. Using her hands to press herself tightly around him, she manipulated his flesh. Her lush embrace ripped away the last of his self-control. A tormented groan escaped and he came against his will. As he gasped for breath, she sat back on her feet.

Staring into his eyes, she leaned over and nibbled his chest and stomach.

Within minutes, he was ready for her again and she untied his restraints. She lay down beside him, wordlessly urging him on top of her. Slick with desire, Aster's body easily absorbed his without further guidance. Her hands trickled down his back and massaged his buttocks as he began his rhythmic probing.

Bringing her hands back to her own waist, palms up, she eased them between their bodies. Rom lifted his head and looked at her curiously just before her fingertips applied pressure to the two nerve bundles above his groin. His head catapulted forward into the pillow and he involuntarily plunged deeper inside her.

He was totally unprepared for the explosion that rocked him with his second release. When he regained a semblance of his strength, he rolled onto his back, bringing her with him. Aster propped her head on her fist and gazed at him with a Cheshire Cat grin. He drew her lips to his in a long, sensual kiss.

"Don't ever do that again," Rom whispered breathlessly, "at least not for another week."

The spell broke and they both gave in to a fit of laughter as she described how she had done her research.

"Oh, I almost forgot. That wasn't the whole surprise."

Rom looked horrified. "Aster, please, I don't think I'd survive any more right now!"

"No, silly. I don't mean that kind of surprise. Wait a minute." She got off the bed and brought up a long package wrapped in shiny red paper. She placed it on his lap as she sat up. "This is to thank you for loving me no matter how inappropriate. Go ahead, open it." She could barely contain her own anticipation.

He couldn't imagine what it could be but his curiosity didn't make him remove the wrapping any less carefully. When the splendorous sword was revealed, he was speechless for several seconds. Touching the gleaming steel, he murmured, "It's the Black Knight's sword. How did you get it?"

"Remember I told you I had met Falcon? Well, I went to the Arena to look for a souvenir for you. Falcon works there and he gave me this. He said the Black Knight admired you very much and would want you to have it. He told me you put that nick in the blade when you defeated the knight. Do you like it?"

"Oh, Shalla. It's the most wonderful gift I ever received—next to you. Thank you." He started to pull her to him when he had another thought. "I can't believe I didn't realize it before. He has the same build, the same catlike walk, even the same gravelly voice. Of course! Falcon *is* the Black Knight."

CHAPTER 18

Nervous energy made up for lack of sleep as Aster and Rom headed for Medical the next morning. A nice-looking man in a white uniform introduced himself as Doctor Gemina. He instructed them to lie down on two separate examining tables and relax. Aster mentally laughed at the suggestion that she would be capable of relaxing.

The doctor worked a set of controls and studied the viewer at Aster's head. A foot-wide chrome arch hovering over her head crept down and back up the length of her body. When the arch stopped where it had begun, the overhead light beam came on, radiating warmly down on her. She automatically closed her eyes but soon realized the intensity was much gentler than she had previously experienced.

When their exams were completed, the doctor reported, "You are both in excellent condition. The beam has projected a temporary sanitizing shield around you to protect you from any harmful bacteria you may encounter on your journey."

Aster started to sit up when Doctor Gemina placed his hand over her wrist. "You can't escape quite yet.

Aster. I need another few minutes." His hand stayed on her for a moment as he gazed into her eyes with masculine interest. She lay back down wondering why, with all this sophisticated equipment, would he take her pulse the old-fashioned way?

"Ahem!" Rom loudly cleared his throat.

Aster turned her face to him and saw that he was propped up on one elbow, scowling fiercely at the handsome doctor. Gemina removed his hand and a hint of pink appeared on the man's fair cheekbones.

"Yes, uh, as I said, uh, a few more minutes, for the homing device." The doctor was flustered at his momentary lapse in front of the chief administrator. As he pulled open the underbed drawer of implements, he caught the fearful grimace that distorted her features.

"I'll tell you what," Gemina offered. "I'll do Romulus first and you can watch." Her face softened a little but she was still frowning at the items in the drawer. The doctor thought an explanation might help calm her.

Gemina held up a small glass plate for her to see. "Do you see that black speck?"

She nodded.

"That's the homing device. It's only necessary to insert it under the top layer of skin inside the ear canal. I won't even draw blood, I promise." He turned to Romulus and received an uncharacteristic dark glare. With a lopsided grin, the doctor looked him straight in the eye then shrugged his shoulders.

Rom reclined on the table and attempted to smooth his smoldering temper but he kept his eyes on the doctor. Drek! He was doing it again. Getting jealous. If she would just give in and join with him…

Aster watched the two men in fascination, recognizing their little dance for exactly what it was.

When she caught Rom's attention, she shook her head at him in mock disapproval and made him laugh at himself.

Gemina placed the device in Rom's ear, using an implement resembling tweezers made of two extremely thin strands of stiff wire. Rom didn't even blink. Aster resigned herself to the necessity of the implant and clenched the sides of the table when Doctor Gemina turned his attention to her.

"The homing device has several uses," Gemina explained. First, you each have your own frequency which can be picked up within five hundred miles by anyone with one of these rings and the knowledge to use it. Homing in on your frequency would bring someone within three hundred feet of you.

"At this closer range, the device's second function as a communicator can be activated." When Aster narrowed her eyes, he gave her an example. "Once you both have the implant, Romulus could use his ring to tune into your frequency and relay his thoughts directly to you."

"Oh, I like the sound of that. Will I be able to talk back?" Aster could imagine all sorts of interesting possibilities arising but Rom squelched them immediately.

"Probably not. It takes innate ability and a lot of mental discipline. There are some Noronians who have never mastered it."

A second later as Doctor Gemina stood near her, Aster felt a tiny prick in her ear and the doctor announced that it was over.

Governor Elissa, Professor Schontivian and a technician were the only ones to see them off from the transmigration station. The governor handed Rom and Aster each an envelope, saying, "We had typical United States identification made up for both of you—driver's licenses, credit cards, and so on—and there's two thousand American dollars in case you need cash. However, I've been assured that the credit cards will be accepted as payment in most places."

Rom gave Aster his envelope to put in her bag with her own. "Thank you, Elissa but, as I told Aster, I don't expect this to take that long."

"I hope you're right," the governor answered with a smile then clasped Aster's hand. "I would like to visit again with you, Aster, after this is over. I wish you both success. The professor and I well be available the moment you return."

Rom took Aster's hand and led her into a glass-enclosed chamber. He pulled her close to him, enveloping her in his comforting embrace then nodded to the technician on duty at the control panel.

Aster experienced a tingling sensation that began in her extremities and crept up to her scalp. Then her stomach dove into a bottomless pit. She clamped her eyes shut and pressed her face against Rom's chest, at least she thought she did. She knew she was still in his arms and yet the physical contact itself was missing. She wanted to open her eyes but her body no longer responded to her mind. She remembered what Rom said about the detachment but she had not expected this horrible feeling of total isolation.

To Aster, a lifetime passed before her feet again touched solid ground and Rom's hands pressed reassuringly against her back. At the same instant they arrived, a mother and her young son crashed headlong into them.

"Oh my! Excuse us." The woman quickly pulled her child away from Aster and Rom.

"Mommy, did you see that? They just appeared out of nowhere. Wow! I bet they beamed in from outer space!"

The woman smiled apologetically at them. "Young man, I'm going to have to stop you from watching so much television. Your imagination is getting out of hand." She gave him a sharp yank to get him to stop staring at the couple. Before the little boy turned his head away, Rom gave him a conspiratorial wink and the child happily winked back.

"Are you okay?" Rom asked, squeezing Aster's hand.

"I think so." She looked down at her feet then counted her fingers. "That was definitely weird. I can see that we made it but it's still hard to believe."

"Next time, try to relax. It'll be much easier." He quickly surveyed their location. They had arrived in the Palomar Observatory's photographic museum. A handful of tourists were making their way up to the Visitors' Gallery in the dome. "Do you see a directory anywhere?"

"No. There's a gift shop. Maybe someone in there can direct us."

Romulus approached a young girl sitting behind the cash register. "I wonder if you could give us some assistance?"

She dropped the book she was reading and gaped at him.

"We're looking for one of the scientists who works here, Doctor Catherine Houston. Would you be able to direct us to her?" Rom smiled warmly at the girl.

As if she had not heard any question, the salesgirl sat forward, supporting her chin on her hand. "Like, are you a movie star or something? You look so-o-o familiar, like, really."

"No, I'm no one you would know but I would like to find Doctor Houston. Do you know her?"

"Oh, for sure! Everyone knows Kate. But visitors are supposed to, like, stay in this part of the observatory, okay?"

Rom held the girl's eyes with his as he spoke in his deepest voice. "We're not visitors. We're friends and we want to surprise her. I would really appreciate your help." A minute later he had the directions he needed and was leading Aster away from the gift shop.

"I don't think I will ever get used to that," Aster commented jealously as they walked away.

"What?"

"You'll get *what*." Aster nudged his ribs. "Her tongue was hanging out exactly like Cherry's when she's ogling you."

"No kidding. I didn't notice." He said the words very seriously but Aster saw the bright green glint in his eyes and jabbed him again. Rom tucked the annoying elbow firmly under his arm and kissed the back of her hand. "Just so you keep ogling me, that's all that matters. Anyway, I figure that makes us about even after I had to watch that adolescent doctor drool all over you this morning."

Following the numbers over the doorways, they entered a small room with a neat desk that looked like it might belong to an assistant. There was no one around, however, and Rom tried the door behind the desk.

"Walter, did you find that—" A heavy-set, gray-haired woman was writing on a chalkboard and glared over her bifocals. "You're not Walter. I'm sorry, but the tour does not include my workroom. If you go back down the hall the way you came, I'm sure you'll have no trouble finding the Visitor's Gallery." She turned back to her calculations.

"We're looking for Doctor Katherine Houston," Rom said to her back.

The woman angled her head without shifting

position. "And why would you be looking for her?"

"We have vital information concerning the safety of this planet."

She turned slowly around to face them, her expression clearly revealing her annoyance. "I am Doctor Houston and I am extremely busy with a very real problem at this moment. Perhaps you could find someone else who has a bit more time to listen to your story."

Rom fed her the bait. "Does this problem you're working on have something to do with a shift in Jupiter's gravitational pull resulting in the change of a certain planetoid's orbit?"

The scientist was obviously stunned. "How could you know about that? I only discovered it myself yesterday when I was reviewing the computer analysis. I haven't mentioned it to anyone yet and we have the most advanced technology on this planet. Have you hacked our server? Is that it?" Her panic was controlled but evident.

Before Rom could answer, a slender, middle-aged man entered the workroom. "I have the file you asked for, Kate. Oh, I didn't know you were expecting anyone this morning." He nervously pushed his glasses up on his nose with his finger and ran his hand over his crewcut.

"I wasn't, but it's all right, Walter. They are…acquaintances."

Walter wondered at the fretful expression on Kate's face. She had been so insistent on not being disturbed earlier. Since she did not seem inclined to introduce him to her guests, he placed the file on her cluttered desk. At that moment it occurred to him that something might be amiss. Not wanting anything to happen to Kate, he surreptitiously slid his hand over her intercom and opened the channel to his outer office. He would eavesdrop only long enough to assure himself that the visitors were not upsetting his boss.

"Please close the door on your way out, Walter and please, see to it we're not disturbed."

As soon as her assistant was gone, Doctor Houston turned back to Romulus. "You were about to tell me how you could be in possession of such information."

"If I may?" Romulus nodded to the chalk board and Doctor Houston shrugged noncommittally. He picked up the piece of chalk he had seen her using but when he applied it to the board it only made a terrible screeching sound. Promptly dropping the offensive implement, he frowned at the white residue on his fingers. "What is this stuff? Never mind. Could I have a pencil and paper please?"

A half-hour later, he handed the scientist a sheet of paper covered with numbers and symbols. She studied the calculations for some time before frowning up at Rom and Aster over her glasses.

Before she could ask any questions, Rom confirmed her worst fears. "Impact will occur in eleven months, thirteen days, unless proper action is taken. Have you charted the planetoid's new orbit yet?"

"I...I started but...who are you?" Kate was bewildered. She pointed to the chart of the solar system she was working on and Rom quickly completed her work for her.

He decided he had her undivided attention now and began his explanations. "My name is Romulus Locke and this is Aster Mackenzie. We are friends who have come to help you and your people avoid this disaster. We will gladly answer all your questions—who we are and how to solve your problem. First, however, I must ask that you agree to complete confidentiality. Can we count on your cooperation, Doctor Houston?"

The older woman looked from Rom to Aster and back, trying to judge them without having all the facts about them. She looked back at the calculations and chart that might have taken her several more days to complete by herself. Without confirming all the information, it appeared to be valid based on what she had already ascertained about the asteroid. It did not take her long to realize the hopelessness of the situation. Earth was doomed to destruction unless someone came up with a miracle. She was certain no country in the world possessed the technology needed to prevent the collision.

Her mind reeled in several directions at once. Could this man truly have some knowledge that none of the world's scientists had? Was this some sort of international blackmail or terrorism? Like most of her colleagues, she avoided getting involved in politics and believed science should not be hindered by its restraints.

In the end, her scientific curiosity got the best of her. "All right, if you're legitimate, I'll be happy to agree to your stipulations. You must realize I'm open to any suggestions. If this all turns out to be an elaborate hoax or something illegal, or you're trying to get me involved in some complicated spy game, then I rescind my agreement."

"Let me begin my explanations with Aster. She's from San Francisco. About a month ago she was on a pleasure yacht in the Atlantic Ocean when it disappeared without a trace. If it would help you believe our story, I'm sure you could verify the circumstances and her identity. Since that time she and the others have been living in my world, in the inner core of the Earth." Rom paused when he saw the scientist's look of utter disbelief.

"You must realize how preposterous this sounds. I

have an open mind but I am a scientist first," Kate sputtered. "However, the name Aster Mackenzie is very familiar." She turned to her computer, typed in the name and quickly confirmed who one of her visitors was and that she had, indeed, disappeared at sea. "All right, you have my attention."

"One of the reasons I brought Aster with me was to allow you to question one of your own people about what happened to her, what she has seen and to let her tell you about our culture, which you will soon see is advanced far beyond your own."

Kate sat back and crossed her arms, continuing to look at him doubtfully. "And your world is inside this planet?"

"I am originally from the planet, Norona, in a galaxy you would not be able to locate with any of your charts. We have an interest in the survival of the planet Earth and wish to help you save it from destruction."

"My vanity insists I ask, why me?"

"We maintain a regular vigilance over your world. You are situated in the one observatory in the world that was most likely to have spotted the planetoid. We were assured you are an honorable person, one we could trust with our secret. The only question we have is, will you be able to cut through the bureaucracy and see to it that appropriate action is taken within the time available? As you must realize already, that's going to be a major problem."

"I hardly think that will be the only problem. Redirecting the planetoid is beyond our capability." Kate shook her head as she pondered the enormity of the situation.

Romulus unraveled the facts and solutions he had come to present. "As you can see, the planetoid enters the rendezvous area in three weeks. There is only about a two-week leeway and then you will have lost your advantage."

"But our ships couldn't possibly make it to that location in that short a time. Maybe where you're from you travel beyond the speed of light, but here we've barely conquered hypersonic speed during the space shuttle liftoffs." Kate's voice became more confident as she quit wondering whether he was legitimate and began anticipating the information he offered.

"My people prefer not to interfere with your culture or development. In this case, however, we have decided to assist you by giving you information which you would eventually discover yourselves, but not in time to save this planet now." Romulus then explained the mechanics, formulas and information needed to increase the speed of Earth's ships sufficiently to reach the asteroid in the time available.

Katherine Houston was a brilliant scientist and a leader in her field. But her expertise was not in rocketry, nuclear physics or engineering. Rom had to go over the data several times before she began to grasp the concept. She made volumes of notes as he spoke but it was still not enough.

Finally Aster had a suggestion. "Rom, if you touched her mind, would she be able to understand better?"

He thought it might be the best way and described to Kate what he wanted to do. Although she hesitated, Kate had heard too much to stop now and agreed to submit to his touch.

With his fingers gently contacting her temple, they communicated on the deepest level. When he took his hand away, Kate sat staring at him with widely dilated eyes. "Good Lord, you've been telling me the truth. I actually felt your honesty. And the fuel, the speed…Why, I understand it perfectly now. Was that your world I saw?" She could barely control her excitement over the experience he had given her. To Aster, she asked, "You've actually been there? Is it really that beautiful?"

Aster smiled broadly. "Whatever you saw could not possibly be as incredible as his world really is. You would have to go there to understand."

"You're going back with him, aren't you?"

Aster smiled and gazed at Rom. "Yes, I'm going back."

Several hours of questions and answers flew by as Rom filled in as many blanks as possible to help the scientist with the job that lay ahead of her and Aster satisfied Kate's curiosity about Innerworld.

Her aging face lined with tension, Kate admitted, "I have always believed in the existence of life on other planets. We may have a tougher time convincing the powers that be."

"We? Our intention was to give you the information and return to Innerworld. We want you to take full credit for the discovery." Rom saw Aster stiffen in her seat.

Kate attempted to reason with him. "I would be more than content to accept the Nobel Prize for the most stupendous discovery of the century and never tell a soul about you. The problem is, even if I understand the theory, it is highly improbable that I would ever have come up with it on my own. Some people would be so suspicious that they would become sidetracked from what had to be done to find out how I did it.

"Also, it's obvious to me that our country cannot do this alone. Off the top of my head, I'd say we'll have to bring in China. Although I've met many scientists from all over the world at various symposiums, I don't carry enough weight in our government, let alone any of theirs, to ensure everyone's immediate cooperation."

Aster watched the woman's expression change several times from dismay to deep thought, to consideration and finally to a very feminine smile, with just a touch of pink on her plump cheeks.

"There is someone, a man I was once…very close to. It's been a long time since we worked together but I'm sure he'd help. He's Professor David Ingram, a nuclear physicist and professor emeritus at Harvard. He helped develop one of the earlier rocket fuels. The Central Bureau for Astronomical Telegrams is at Harvard, also. He'd know better than I who could be trusted in the Bureau and together I'm sure we could present a solid case. But to whom? The Secretary of State? The President? Possibly both, but it would eventually have to go to the United Nations Security Council. Between David and the Bureau, they could probably force an emergency meeting without having to explain where the information originated."

"The two of you would be sharing that Nobel Prize, Doctor Houston." Aster imagined there was a sad love story involved and wished for a happy ending for the kindly scientist. Kate blushed fully this time and Aster knew she had guessed accurately.

"It would undoubtedly save a lot of time, though, if you would appear at the Council meeting and do that mind link," Kate added.

"No way!" Aster interrupted. "Romulus cannot be exposed to so many people. You know his world would never remain a secret after that."

"Aster's right," Rom said. "I can imagine people searching for the doorways to my world and disrupting our normal course of business."

"I understand," Kate said as her worried look

returned. "But I'm afraid you're going to have to at least meet with David personally. I comprehend the theories better now but I'm not certain I could explain them to him. And what if he has questions? I assure you he's as trustworthy as I am."

Rom considered her words carefully before he finally agreed. "All right. It's against my better judgment but I'll meet with him. What do you suggest?"

"He's in Cambridge, Massachusetts and the United Nations is in New York. The most logical thing would be for us to go to Cambridge on the first available flight."

Aster groaned at the thought of another cross-country airplane trek.

Rom touched her hand. "We have our own means of transportation. How soon could he meet with us?"

Kate squelched her curiosity. "Let me call David and set everything up."

Aster noticed the woman did not have to look up the phone number. How many times had she almost called that number over the years? Aster's sense of romance was having a field day.

Fifteen minutes later Kate had made two phone calls and still hadn't reached David. His housekeeper had informed her he was in London. When she called his hotel there, he was out. She left messages in both places.

"I'm sorry. I don't know what to tell you. He could call in ten minutes or ten hours. It wouldn't make much sense to fly to Massachusetts until I hear from him. You could wait here or at my house, or I could call you wherever you're staying."

Aster glanced at Rom. "Can we stay?"

"It doesn't appear we have much choice."

"Could your assistant make some arrangements for

us for tonight?"

"Certainly." Kate walked to her desk to call Walter in and noticed the open channel. She could not remember the last time she used it and assumed she had left it on without thinking. After all, Walter had been her right hand for ten years. He would never intentionally eavesdrop on her.

"Walter, are you still there?"

"Yes," his slightly high-pitched voice answered her.

"Please come in. We need a favor."

Walter appeared with pad and pen in hand almost instantly.

"Walter, this is Miss Mackenzie and Mr. Locke. They need a place to stay tonight. Please assist them with whatever they would like."

Again Aster spoke up, her voice bristling with authority. "I remember there was an excellent resort on the outskirts of Escondido. If they have a suite, I'd prefer that. Otherwise, I'd like a large, non-smoking room with a king-sized bed. Also, we'll need to rent a car when we get there. If you can reserve us a Prius, please do so, if not, another hybrid will do." She reached into her purse and pulled out the "corporate" credit card the governor had given her. "Here. I'm sure you'll need this to make the arrangements. Also, if you would please get us a cab to take us there that should do it." She gave the man an appreciative smile.

Walter rapidly wrote down her instructions and practically clicked his heels as he whirled to perform his tasks.

Rom raised an eyebrow at the woman he had once thought of as a nervous colt. Aster was on her own turf and very accustomed to doling out orders and being obeyed. She would do just fine as Co-Governor of Innerworld.

Kate held out her hand to Aster then to Rom. "I'll

call you at the resort if any problem arises. Thank you hardly expresses how much I appreciate your visit."

"It was a pleasure, Doctor," Rom said seriously.

When they exited Kate's office, Walter had everything in order. "I will drive you to the resort. It would take forever to get a taxi up here," he offered with a nervous giggle.

The threesome remained quiet on the long, slow drive down the winding mountain road. Rom didn't appear overly impressed with the unpopulated countryside and its occasional pine tree. Aster could see most of his concentration was centered on popping his ears during the descent from the mountain. Eventually, they were out of the Cleveland National Forest surrounding the observatory and made their way through the rural Indian reservations.

Suddenly Rom bolted forward, darting his head from side to side in alarm. He quickly recovered his composure for Walter's benefit but Aster could see by his eye movements that he was not relaxed by a long shot. Walter did not seem to notice Rom's concern as he blended in with the bumper-to-bumper traffic on Interstate 15, heading for Escondido and San Diego.

It tickled her to think that the proverbial shoe was now on the other foot. Rom's first experience in Outerworld would include a traffic jam. Rom gripped the dashboard as Walter alternately rushed forward and slammed on his brakes inches from the car in front of him.

Several cars had radios blasting so loudly that the noise vibrated through their closed windows. Horns blared every few seconds whenever one car cut in front of another. They also passed drivers casually reading their newspapers or talking on their cell phones, unwilling to lose their precious time in unproductive activity.

Rom now had a much better understanding of how the emissary could have been killed. When he got back, he was going to recommend hazardous duty credit for everyone forced to cope with traffic in Outerworld.

A stressful half-hour later, they arrived at the resort. Walter insisted on ushering them to the registration desk to make sure all his requests had been complied with.

As soon as they were in their room, Aster took Rom's hand. He had not uttered a sound since they left Palomar. "Are you all right?"

"I guess so. I understand why descending a mile-high mountain would affect the pressure in my ears. I was even expecting the automobiles to look and move the way they do. What I cannot fathom is what all those people were doing on that road? I was beginning to think we were facing a threat greater than the planetoid. And what is that horrible smell outside? And the noise! How can you stand it?"

Giving him a quick kiss, she smiled and said, "That, darling, was a freeway. You should see L.A. if you think that was bad. Smog, automobile exhaust and some other factors, account for the smell. I couldn't have thought up a better example to initiate you to air pollution. Now you see why I was so fascinated with your filters. There's still time for you to reconsider."

"Aster…" His deep voice warned her to give it up.

She shrugged her shoulders. "One other little thing," she said as she walked to the door, turned the lock and fastened the chain, "we double-lock everything here. Is there anything you'd like to see while we're in my world? The Pacific Ocean? The San Diego Zoo? You know what you probably would have liked if we had time? A football game! I wonder if the Chargers are playing at home tomorrow."

"I saw a football game on our monitors many years ago. Interesting game but it never caught on in Innerworld. As for points of interest, if it means getting back on that freeway, I think I'll stay right here. A sign downstairs said this place has a restaurant, shops, a theater, a pool and..." Rom paused as he pulled her down onto the bed with him, "I have you."

Aster gave herself up to the sweetness of his kisses until her stomach made an angry rumbling sound. "I haven't eaten all day," she said with a laugh. "At least let's go to the mall. We really do need a change of clothes. It's not far and we can eat there." She refrained from reminding him who had wanted to pack something. "Besides, I have to get Cherry some of her favorite perfume. I promise I'll only take side streets and I'll drive very carefully. Okay?"

"Do you think I could deny you anything you really wanted? I'd like to ask you a question first. What was your impression of Doctor Houston and Walter?"

"I'm sure she'll do the job and keep your secret, if at all possible. Her assistant is another matter. Aside from the fact that he is very high-strung and decidedly effeminate, he was gawking at you as if you were peculiar, not as though he was attracted to you. Another thing that I thought was strange was how quiet he was on the drive here. Every devoted admin I've ever known would have pumped us until he knew our connection with his boss. But it's probably nothing. I'm probably just being overly suspicious."

"I don't think so. Remember your intuition about Victor. We can definitely trust Doctor Houston though. I'm glad you suggested I touch her mind. She doesn't have a deceitful bone in her body. I have no doubt about her abilities, either."

Rom helped Aster to her feet and kissed her

forehead. "I can hardly wait to see this *mall* of yours," he remarked, and rolled his eyes.

CHAPTER 19

"Mr. Underwood, this is Walter Adams from Palomar Observatory. You may not remember me…"

"Nonsense, Walter," a booming voice returned. "We spoke at last year's Christmas party. It's almost that time again, eh? How's your mother doing? Alzheimer's wasn't it?"

"Uh, yes, sir, uh, she's doing as well as can be expected. Thank you for asking." Walter was thrilled that the corporate magnate would remember someone as insignificant as him. His pleasure faded when he recalled reading how the man kept extensive notes on everyone he met. "Uh, two years ago you asked me to keep my ears open, and, well, I know I've never had anything extraordinary to report—"

"You are getting your pay supplements, aren't you? I wouldn't want one of my key people having problems."

Walter was astonished to hear that he was considered a key anything and Mr. Underwood sounded genuinely concerned. "Oh yes, sir, every month, just like clockwork, and believe me, I've always appreciated the extra money, especially with the way the medical bills keep piling up for my mother's care."

"What is the problem, Walter?" Underwood cut in.

"I'm calling because I have something I think would be of great interest to you. You see, uh, Doctor Houston had a very unusual visitor today."

"Not over the phone, Walter. Are you at home?"

"No, sir. My instructions were to call this number from a public telephone."

"Good. Give me the address where you are."

Walter complied.

"Stay there. I'll pick you up in my limousine in precisely one hour. Fortunately, I'm in my L.A. office at the moment. We'll talk in the car."

"Yes, sir. I'll be waiting and I promise it will be worth your—" Walter stopped talking when he realized the line had disconnected. His heart pounded erratically in his chest and his sweat dripped from the telephone receiver when he hung it up.

He stood very still until the pain in his left shoulder subsided somewhat. It seemed to be getting worse all the time. He had to keep going though. There was no one else to take care of Mama. Oh, God, he thought for the thousandth time, why doesn't she just die? Immediately, guilt pangs overtook him. He spent most of his time these days feeling guilty about one thing or another.

When his father died of a heart attack twenty years ago, Walter had felt guilty that he had never been the man he was expected to be. Now he felt guilty because he was sick and tired of caring for an old woman who rarely remembered who he was.

Recently, he had also been feeling the burden of accepting the extra monthly payments from The Underwood Institute without giving anything in return. He was certain they were getting ready to take him off their special payroll and his debts were too great to allow that to happen.

Walter might have been relieved to finally have something to offer to secure his position with them, except for the magnitude of what he was about to disclose. This was no tidbit of information he had heard. What would a powerful man like Gordon Underwood do with it? And what about Kate?

When Mama's health started declining, he had transferred much of his affection to his elderly boss. During the ten years he worked for Doctor Houston, he had never given her cause to distrust him. He prayed she would never find out about his betrayal and tried to think of some way to shield her from Underwood.

He went over all he heard one more time since he had not dared take notes. Perhaps if he only revealed part of what he heard, he could repay his obligation to Underwood and still protect Kate.

With that idea in mind, he mentally outlined what he would report. One, a huge asteroid was heading toward Earth which could destroy the planet. Two, an extraterrestrial named Romulus Locke came to help Earth's scientists redirect the asteroid. Three, Doctor Houston and her two visitors would be meeting with a rocket scientist tomorrow. Romulus would give them all the details at that time, including a formula for increasing the speed of Earth's ships. If he lied about that part, that should cover Kate temporarily. Four, the alien brought an Earth woman with him, who had previously disappeared under mysterious circumstances. Perhaps if he didn't reveal her name, he could protect her as well. Five, they were now both living in an advanced civilization located in the inner core of the Earth. And sixth, they would be returning to that world, but tonight they were staying at the

Village Resort.

As he waited, Walter considered the man he'd met only twice before. The man's wealth was overwhelming on its own but Underwood was physically impressive as well. Tall and built like a defensive linebacker, his features were sharp and intelligent. What Walter remembered most was his massive shaven head. He'd found it strangely erotic. After he agreed to accept the Institute's secret assignment, Walter read any article written about the billionaire.

One of the few remaining self-made men in his tax bracket, one writer described him as brilliant, intuitive, generous and a fair employer. Another wrote that he was scheming, ruthless, power hungry and heartless. Walter had heard that Underwood was asexual, desiring money and power more than a relationship with another human—woman or man. Then there was the private hospital he had built for himself in the Nevada desert. It was rumored to have the most advanced medical technology in the world. And Underwood was its only patient.

The long black car came to a stop in front of him interrupting his thoughts. Walter tried to rub the pain out of his left arm as he approached the car. It was too late to change his mind and go home.

The mall was beautifully decorated for the upcoming holidays, including an elaborate North Pole display with a jovial Santa posing for photos with the children.

"Do you celebrate Christmas, Rom?"

"No, but it sounds like fun. I certainly like exchanging gifts with you." He gave her a hug as they continued past the colorful shops.

Aster hustled him from store to store, picking out

clothes for each of them, plus a supply of Cherry's expensive scent.

"Okay! We did it with minutes to spare!"

"Minutes to spare for what? Aster, I see these other people rushing around but why are we in such a terrible hurry?"

"Closing time. Let's beat the rush to our car."

Rom shook his head. "I can see Cherry enjoying herself in a place like this but in the future I will be extremely grateful every time I sit in front of my vidcom at home and order my supplies, calmly and at any hour I choose."

Gordon Underwood smiled smugly as the weak little man walked away from the limo. Once again his personal network had panned out and he thought back to the days when he had set it up.

At the age of twenty, he had acquired his first patent in Silicon Valley, and possessed a cunning and genius to excel in many other areas as easily. Once his bank account boasted six figures, he had diversified into real estate and stocks. A taste of wealth only served to increase his hunger for money and the power attached to it. He had a voracious appetite for knowledge and read in depth about any topic that triggered his interest. The general consensus was that Gordon Underwood was an expert in a great many fields.

His investments had prospered. When he foresaw the beginnings of the energy crisis in the late nineteen-sixties, he had bought vast amounts of oil stock before the prices soared. In his search for the ultimate tax shelter, he had created The Underwood Institute, with the altruistic purpose of endowing nonprofit organizations and college grants with special emphasis on scientific achievements and more particularly on astrophysical research. Underwood knew the future was not earthbound and was prepared to do whatever was necessary to keep ahead of the pack.

After being recognized as a benefactor to an institution, such as Palomar Observatory, he was able to meet, and subsequently investigate, its employees. He would usually find one with a weakness or need and lure that person onto his special payroll, like he had with Walter Adams. The result of this plan was an international network of eyes and ears in every corner of the scientific and astrophysical communities.

Sometimes he was given valuable data, more often the information was worthless, but occasionally, years of unrewarded patience paid off with one enormous score, like tonight.

He made it a practice to listen personally to an agent's initial report and, depending on its worth, future reports might be delegated to one of Underwood's assistants. He was greatly relieved he had been the first to hear Adams' news. Goose flesh rose on his large bald head as he considered the possibilities presented by the appearance of an extraterrestrial, right here in California, exposing himself for the good of the planet. It was a dream come true for the billionaire.

He refused to consider the asteroid as a serious threat. A magnificent future awaited. The power he knew that would one day be his had not yet come to him. It was not his destiny to build an empire only to have it wantonly destroyed by a freak act of nature.

Adams had not even finished his report before Underwood's mind clicked off the conclusion. The person who could tap the alien's mind would have access to the information he had come to offer, before it could be presented to the scientists. The bargaining power achieved by such a move staggered the imagination. There would be those who would accuse him of extortion at the risk of global destruction, but Underwood considered it taking advantage of an opportunity.

The woman with Romulus sounded like insignificant decoration and was an earthling besides. She was probably just glad to be back in her own world. As a man who covered every angle, however, Underwood decided to have her followed to see where she went when she discovered her companion missing.

By the time he was back in his office, Underwood had written a detailed list of people to call, arrangements to be made and questions to be answered by the alien...for the good of The Underwood Institute. He had not felt so exhilarated in years.

Two men in waiter uniforms pushed a long, tablecloth-covered cart along the third floor hallway.

"Where the hell you been, Wink?" the shorter man complained in a hushed voice. "I was wondering if you were ever going to show up."

"One of the kids was throwin' up and the old lady was bitchin' about my goin' out tonight. She just don't understand business. Is it ready?" Wink asked, blinking several times.

"Yeah, and I almost didn't make it. Geez, I hate these last-minute rush jobs. I barely finished drilling the hole when the two of them walked up to the door."

"The hell you say! Did they see you?"

"Naw. They were too busy making goo-goo eyes at each other. Hold it. This is the room." Cooper glanced up and down the corridor in his usual cautious manner, despite the fact that it was the middle of the night and the floor was barely occupied. Reassured, he placed his listening device against the door.

"Well? Are they asleep or what?" Wink blinked more rapidly as the time for action drew closer.

"It's quiet. Go ahead insert the hose."

Wink lifted the cloth and unwound a thin hose, carefully feeding one end through the tiny hole in the bottom of the door. He attached the other end to a small tank on the bottom shelf of the cart. When Cooper nodded at him, Wink opened the valve. The gauge indicator dropped as the colorless, odorless gas escaped from its container through the connecting tube. As soon as it read empty, Wink retrieved the hose and plugged the hole.

Five minutes later, Cooper efficiently picked the lock. His lanky partner pulled out the bolt cutters and the chain was split in two. They both donned gas masks and sped the cart into the room, closing the door behind them.

These men were professionals, accustomed to performing their assignments unemotionally and competently. The sensuous scene on the bed momentarily delayed them both. On their sides, the man was cradled in the woman's arms. Cooper and Wink pulled the naked man out of the woman's embrace.

While Wink securely tied the man into a fetal position, Cooper pulled out a huge laundry bag. Spying the clothes on a chair, he stuffed a man's outfit into the bottom of the bag.

"What the hell you doin' now?"

"The orders were to treat this guy like royalty. I don't think he'd appreciate our leaving him without any clothes."

Their victim weighed considerably more than either of them and it took some time to stuff the unconscious body into the bag and hide him on the shelf under the tablecloth.

"What about her?" Wink's eyes twitched rapidly.

"We ain't getting paid to do anything with her."

"Damn, nobody'd have to pay me to do anything with her."

"You're a sick bastard, ya know that? The damn broad's unconscious in case you didn't notice. You been married too long. Let's go! We're already behind schedule."

Reluctantly, Wink helped Cooper push the cart on its way.

CHAPTER 20

The loud trill of the class dismissal bell vibrated through Aster's head. After four rings, she realized it was not a raucous dream about school but the telephone next to her bed. She clumsily grabbed for the receiver to stop the noise.

"He-hello?" Her raw throat impeded her speech.

"Miss Mackenzie? Aster, is that you? This is Kate Houston."

"Yes," Aster pressed her palm against her other ear in an effort to hear better. She had not yet dared to raise her eyelids to let in the piercing morning light.

"I finally heard from David. He's leaving London immediately. I've reserved a room at Le Parker Meridien in New York and I'm taking the ten o'clock flight out of San Diego. We should both be at the hotel by seven tonight. You will be able to make it, won't you?"

"Of course," Aster managed to whisper a second before her stomach lurched involuntarily. "Please hold on a moment," she pleaded urgently. She dropped the phone on the bed and ran for the bathroom. Although she instantly noticed Rom's absence, it was secondary to her desperate need to reach the toilet.

The contractions in her stomach convulsed into a fist and the remains of last night's dinner shot forcefully up her throat. This was worse than the one hangover she had had when she was a teenager. Even the inside of her nose hurt. Back in Outerworld one day and she'd picked up a virus! So much for the protective beam. She hoped Rom was okay, but realized if he felt as bad as she did, he would still be in bed or at least here in the bathroom with her.

Aster struggled to make her brain function through the pain in her head. Perhaps he went out to get breakfast while she slept in. That didn't sound right. Even in her debilitated mental condition, she did not believe he would have left the room without waking her. If only she could get some aspirin, she was certain she could think clearly again.

Suddenly she remembered the telephone and staggered back to the bed. "Kate? Are you still there?"

"Yes. Is everything all right?"

"I seem to have picked up the flu. I'm horribly sick and Rom's, um, gone out for breakfast. Could I call you back?"

"I'm sorry to hear that. Don't call back. I'll be gone in five minutes. Are you sure you'll be okay?"

"Don't worry. We'll be there if I have to bring an airsick bag along with me."

Aster said good-bye and laid her head back on the pillow. She would rest a few minutes until Rom got back.

It was mid-morning when she forced her eyes open again. She felt no better and Rom had not returned. An internal alarm was clanging in her brain. *He would never have left without her!* Her stomach threatened to revolt again if she moved, but panic began to worm its way into her disoriented mind.

Fighting against her nausea and headache, she dragged herself out of bed to get dressed. Waiting for Rom to return made no sense. Unfortunately, she couldn't think past how awful she felt. She decided that if she made herself feel better first, she would then figure out where he had gone and why.

She found the desired medication in the gift shop and went to the dining room to look for Rom. When she did not see him, she ordered plain toast and black tea to go, and headed for the front desk. Aster realized her condition improved steadily while she walked around.

As she had in the restaurant, she asked the front-desk clerk if he had seen a man matching Rom's description and was soon convinced he had not come by there either. Next she went out to the parking lot on the remote chance he had taken the car. The Prius was where she had left it. Growing increasingly agitated, she hurried to the pool area, hoping he had been drawn there but Romulus was nowhere to be found.

Something was very wrong. Sitting on a lounge chair, she gulped half a bottle of thick pink liquid. She then forced herself to swallow the dry toast and washed down four aspirins with the strong black tea. The cool crisp air and warm sunshine seemed to help. Aster tried to let her intuition control her thinking. She must not panic. She had to think. Where could he be? She returned to their room, praying they had crossed paths.

This time she noticed his new slacks and shirt were missing but his sweater, shoes and socks were still there. Confusion blended with anxiety and she was aware that the throbbing in her skull was rapidly returning full strength. On impulse, she went back outside and soon felt better again. She recalled stories about poisoned houses and wondered if she might be having a reaction to something in the room. Concerned about drawing too much attention to herself, she decided against reporting the problem in her room.

She returned and stood outside the door. Her watch told her an hour had passed since she started her search. Drawing a deep breath, she held it while she reentered the room. Quickly, she snatched up a shopping bag, filled it with their belongings and escaped the deadly chamber.

Aster's mind ran amok. What if he went back to Innerworld without her, leaving her behind? Maybe he never loved her at all and this was the ultimate goodbye. *No!* He does love you and need you as much as you need him. Besides, he certainly would not have left his shoes.

She analyzed and rejected every possible excuse for his disappearance and knew she was wasting time. She should be doing something. Terror threatened her sanity. Had they not rehearsed what she should do if they ran into trouble? Aster worried if sufficient time had elapsed to warrant pushing the panic button. Suddenly she was afraid she had waited too long.

Hurriedly at the cashier's desk, she exchanged several bills for a handful of change and found a pay phone. Her shaking fingers missed their mark and her coin clinked to the floor. Ignoring, it she shoved another then several more into the slot. Punching in the Santa Monica telephone number she had memorized, she tapped her foot impatiently as she waited for a response. On the fifth ring, a woman's voice said, "Yes?" Aster then carefully pressed the series of numbers that would tell the party she needed help.

"Hold on," the abrupt voice ordered.

Aster paced back and forth in front of the telephone. Her heart ached from pounding so hard and she had to keep wiping the perspiration from her upper lip. It seemed forever before a man's voice came on the line.

"The Chargers are playing the Raiders at Qualcomm Stadium in San Diego this afternoon. Enjoy the game." Then she heard a click.

Aster stared at the telephone in shock. He wanted her to go to a football game? He had not been specific about who would meet her or where. Then she remembered that her ring would act like a GPS for the emissary to find her.

After checking out of the hotel, she got a map of San Diego and vague directions to the stadium from the front-desk clerk, along with a warning to expect heavy traffic getting there. Although she did not believe he would ever read it, she left a message for Rom at the front desk.

As she made her way onto the freeway, awareness exploded within her. One blatant clue had eluded her. The chain on the door had not been taken off. It had been cut! She had seen it, but hadn't *seen* it, until now.

Think, Aster, she prodded herself. They had not eaten or drunk anything in the room, so they probably had not been drugged. Yet she was positive that she had blacked out after they had—

Her foot hit the brake and she swerved off the edge of the highway. She ignored the screeching brakes and honking horns of the cars behind her.

Someone had rendered them unconscious, had entered their room and abducted Romulus. That someone had looked at them, had handled Rom's naked body. Her stomach roiled and she pushed the door open just in time to vomit on the ground. It must have been some kind of gas. That would explain her illness this morning and her burned nasal membranes.

But what had happened to Rom? Only Doctor Houston knew what they were doing there and she felt sure the woman would not have betrayed them. Walter? A definite possibility considering his behavior. Was someone watching her? She had not paid the slightest attention to anyone looking at her, since she was so busy searching for Rom.

She needed the emissary's help, but Rom had impressed on her the importance of keeping that man's identity a secret. She would have to be extremely careful for all their sakes. Pulling back into the traffic, Aster stayed alert for any sign of a car following her.

She soon suspected a gray Audi two cars back. It had been on the side of the road about a mile ahead of where she pulled off, and when she passed it, it reentered the slow-moving traffic behind her. When she exited the interstate and drove toward the stadium, the gray car followed. As she searched for a vacant parking place at the stadium, several tours around the same blocks later, she knew for certain the Audi was tailing her and appeared to have only a single occupant.

Now she understood the wisdom of choosing a meeting place as enormous and congested as the stadium during a game. Even if the person in the Audi was an expert, he would have trouble keeping an eye on her once she was inside. That is, if he ever found a parking space after she did. Finally locating an available parking spot, Aster ran as fast as she could to buy her ticket at the front gate, hoping to take advantage of her tail's predicament.

She hurried to her seat, confident that she had lost him for the moment and pretended to watch the game. After halftime, she began to panic. What would she do if the emissary did not show up by the time the game was over?

She was brought out of her gloomy thoughts by the wildly cheering crowd. The Raiders fumbled on their first down in the third quarter and the Chargers recovered, bringing them within yards of scoring.

I'm here. What do you need?

Aster turned her head from side to side to see who had asked the question. The people around her were jumping out of their seats to get a better view of the exciting play. None of them showed any interest in her nor had they spoken to her.

What's the matter? Am I not coming in clearly? Is your device not functioning properly?

Her device? Aster whirled around again in every direction. Someone was using the homing device in her ear. The problem was she had no idea how to respond.

If you can hear me clearly but can't answer, wave at the hot-dog vendor with your ring hand.

A few rows behind her, Aster caught sight of the vendor coming slowly down the stairs. He was an elderly black man stopping occasionally to sell his food. Aster raised her hand to get his attention, flashing the Innerworld ring in the process.

Put your hand down. Will you please concentrate? I'm not reading anything but a muddle. Holy stars! You're a Terran!

With agonizing slowness, the vendor worked his way closer to her. "You be wantin' a hot dog, missy?" His voice was subservient, but the deep wrinkles in his dark brown face were tense and his black eyes bore into hers. Aster recognized the opal ring on his finger and let out a sigh.

Buy a hot dog. When I hand you your change, drop it. I will help you pick it up. You must let me touch you. It's the safest way. Try to concentrate on the problem.

Aster ordered her food and dropped the change. The man sitting on the aisle next to her did his best to assist her, his clumsy efforts helping to cover what was transpiring. Swiftly, the emissary's calloused fingers grazed her temple. When he pulled his hand back, she had an idea and blurted it out.

"Can you get Falcon for me?" She realized her mistake as he rolled his dark eyes heavenward and turned his back on her.

The man next to her looked at her quizzically. She shook her head at him and glanced at the vendor's back before returning her attention once more to the game.

The emissary was beyond frustration. The woman's mind was as crowded as the stadium. Through her highly charged emotional state, he gleaned something about Romulus being taken. Her verbal request could have jeopardized both of them if she was being closely watched. He tried another tack.

Do not turn around. I am going to ask you questions. If the answer is yes, tap your ear with the homing device once, twice for no. Do you understand?

One tap.

Has Romulus been abducted?

One tap.

Do you know by whom?

Two taps.

Is Falcon an Innerworld tracker?

One tap.

Do you believe he can help you find Romulus?

One tap.

The emissary relaxed a little. At least he would not

have to get involved personally in the hunt. He quickly calculated how long it would take to get Falcon out to her.

Aster was perspiring again, in spite of the cool weather. It was more than nerves. The fever was building inside her and only one thing cooled it. But she couldn't think about that now. She wondered if the emissary had abandoned her when she heard his voice again.

I will bring Falcon here for you. Stay until the game ends. He will find you on your way out. You will not hear from me again unless I cannot reach him. Understand?

One tap. Aster sat stiffly for a few seconds then slumped back in her seat when she was certain he was gone. She stared at the cooling hot dog in her hand. Her stomach rebelled at the thought of the greasy food and she quickly shoved it under her seat and out of sight.

"Yes?" Gordon Underwood drummed his fingers on his desk. He had been anticipating this report being called in by his personal physician, Doctor Quinn.

"You didn't tell me what I'm supposed to be looking for but I've run a full battery of tests on this man, everything short of an autopsy." The doctor glanced at the pale man strapped to the bed with a hose in his nose and tubes running fluids in and out of his body. "He's in perfect health."

"Perfect, huh? Would you say he's...human?"

"What?" asked Dr. Quinn in surprise. "Of course he's human. What else would he be?"

"What else indeed? Describe the physical makeup of this man, particularly anything unusual about him."

"He looks like a young Tom Selleck. Six foot three, two hundred twenty pounds, excellent muscle tone. I would estimate him to be between thirty and thirty-five years old. He has all his own teeth, no fillings. From the lack of scar tissue anywhere on his body, I'd also say he's never had an operation. Although that was odd. Among other things, he has no appendix, must have been born without it."

Underwood interrupted. "What other things?"

"It's almost as if he was from some future time on our evolutionary scale. He has no tonsils, no coccyx and no nails on his little toes, all the things we assume will eventually disappear from our bodies.

"Also, he has practically no antibodies in his blood and no sperm count. His vasa deferentia are severed, as if he had a vasectomy, although there is no evidence of surgery or scar tissue.

"Your boys overdosed him on the flight here. They insisted they injected him only once with the standard amount. It was touch and go for a while there. I spent most of the morning trying to keep him alive. They might be telling the truth though. He definitely has a very low tolerance to the drugs I've given him. In spite of his unconscious state, he has a higher level of brain activity than most alert adults. To be perfectly blunt, I can't explain any of these peculiarities."

"Watch the anesthetic levels carefully and continue to monitor his life signs. I want him kept unconscious until I get there but it's imperative you keep him alive. I'm leaving for the airport as soon as I hang up. Be prepared to give him something to encourage his cooperation in answering my questions as soon as I arrive. Did he have any weapons or tools on him?"

"Mr. Underwood, the man was delivered to me stark naked in a bag." Quinn did not attempt to veil his sarcasm. "The only thing on him was a rather gaudy opal ring."

"Lock up the ring. I'll be there shortly."

Gordon Underwood had heard enough to convince him the man was truly from another planet. With the help of Doctor Quinn and his mind-altering concoctions, he would soon learn what was in the alien's head.

Quinn had been one of the easier people he had ever bought. When Underwood decided to build himself a research hospital, he needed a very special man to head it. Quinn was rewarded for his loyalty and obedience with the freedom and funds to perform his experiments with drugs and surgery which had been banned in the United States. In return, he was on call to Underwood twenty-four hours a day and questions about his assignments were not permitted. Having more to lose by exposure than Underwood, Quinn's discretion could be depended upon.

But Quinn was only a small part of Underwood's master plan. Already having acquired more wealth than he would ever need, he had switched his efforts to accumulating power. To achieve that goal, he had needed a secure and secluded headquarters.

Underwood had come up with the original idea for a subterranean community during the nuclear-war scare of the fifties but construction did not begin until many years later.

He had selected an uninhabited stretch of desert in central Nevada as his refuge and had built the entire compound underground, with the exception of a small run-down shack and the airstrip adjacent to it. The shack was the entranceway to his haven from the world. A small city in itself, the compound was totally self-sufficient, the hospital taking up only one section.

All of the Underwood Institute was now headquartered there and the number of people who lived and worked under the desert topped five hundred. Carefully selected, each employee had a reason to be loyal to Gordon Underwood whose grandest wish was to discover the secret to immortality. But he would settle for ruling his own country.

CHAPTER 21

The football game was over. It had been a struggle from start to finish but San Diego squeaked ahead by one point at the end. Focusing on the game had helped Aster stay somewhat calm. Just as she stood up, she heard a throaty, male voice in her head. There could not possibly be two men with that same purring quality to their voice.

Do not turn around. It is Falcon, as you requested. I am very close to you but you are being observed. We will have to correct that before we can leave. Go into the ladies room and trade or buy yourself a disguise. When you come out, we will walk off together.

Aster did as he suggested, ordering herself not to turn around to see where Falcon was. Fortunately, it only took Aster about five minutes to find a woman willing to part with an old trench coat, cowboy hat, sunglasses and a fifteen-minute head start, in exchange for her sweater and two hundred dollars.

As she stepped out of the lavatory, Falcon appeared at her arm. He was dressed all in black and his unique eyes were shielded by black, wrap-around sunglasses. "Do not rush. The man is still watching for you to exit." Falcon gave Aster a look of approval that took in how her hair was completely hidden under the wide-brimmed hat and turned-up collar of the baggy, unattractive coat. The big glasses covered half her face.

As briefly as possible Aster updated Falcon. "You were the only one I could think of to help." Her desperation came through loud and clear.

"We will find him."

"I have a car outside. Have you picked up Rom's signal yet?" Aster asked hopefully.

"He is not within range of the homing device. You must take me back to the last place you were with him. From there, I can pick up images of what occurred and, if necessary, I will follow his brain waves, like I did to find you."

"Oh, Falcon, I've been nothing but trouble to you."

"On the contrary, Aster. I rarely get to use my gifts. You and Romulus are sharpening my skills."

As they left the stadium, Falcon scanned the people they passed on the lookout for a threat. "Aster, are we getting close to your car?"

"Yes, it's down this street."

"There is a man up ahead carrying a transmission unit. His aura is dark. Follow me but remain silent."

"Excuse me, sir," Falcon said as they approached. The man with the cell phone next to his ear made it obvious he did not want to be disturbed. Falcon reached into his pocket and pulled out a piece of paper. "Could you tell me where this address is?"

As soon as the man's eyes shifted to the paper, Falcon's fingertips contacted the stranger's temple. A second later the man crumpled to the ground, curled up in a peaceful sleep. He would not remember seeing Falcon or Aster when he awoke.

"That man was a drone. He knew nothing of

Romulus. Only that he was to follow you. Let us return to where it began."

Aster drove back to the resort and led Falcon to the room. "I turned in the key this morning. Is this good enough?"

Falcon nodded, placing his hand on the door and concentrating on the images playing out before his eyes. A few minutes later he turned to Aster. "Are you feeling better now?"

"Yes. Oh, you could see that, couldn't you?" Her complexion colored as she realized what he might have seen.

Instead of answering her question, he said, "Come with me."

Aster would have willingly followed him off a skyscraper, if he told her that was how she would find Romulus.

In the parking lot Falcon stopped her. "Two men piped a gas into that room, carried Romulus out in a bag on a big cart and drove off in a boxlike vehicle in that direction."

"I'm so frightened, Falcon. It's been so long, maybe eighteen hours. What if we find him and he's already—I mean, could someone in Innerworld bring him back, like they did with the captain of the ship I was on?"

"I am sure he will be fine, once we get him back." Again Falcon was relieved he was not bound by a code of honesty. The time limit to reverse the death process was only twelve hours. "I will need you to drive."

When they got in the car, Falcon placed the back of his hand on Aster's cheek. "Romulus is alive, Aster. If he were not, you would not be feeling what you are. It is not only this morning's illness that is bothering you, is it? I know of Romulus's fever. I was unaware that a

Terran would suffer from it also."

"Believe me it's a surprise to me too—an extremely unwelcome surprise at the moment," Aster said sarcastically as she wiped away the beads of perspiration on her upper lip. "Let's just find Romulus quickly."

"There is something we have to do first. I am an empath, Aster. Your emotional and physical distress are interfering with my reading. You must let me help you."

Aster's eyes narrowed suspiciously. "How do you mean?"

"Let me touch your mind. I will draw away your pain and give you the relief you need."

"I'm not sure you—"

"There is no other way. Romulus would understand," Falcon cut in.

That's what you think, she thought, remembering Rom's jealous reaction to her merely describing Falcon. On the other hand, she would never find Rom if Falcon's abilities were being hampered. "All right. I give you my permission."

Aster closed her eyes when Falcon's fingertips gently touched her temple. For a moment there was nothing.

Romulus appeared before her, his eyes seducing her as he moved closer. He was naked and fully aroused. In invitation, she opened her legs and felt his hard body bear down on her fevered flesh. Smoothly, he slid inside her and she cried out in relief. It was wonderful. She needed him so badly and he was there, big, hard and deep inside her. The ache built as he pumped faster and faster, harder and harder, until finally, with one extraordinarily deep thrust, she shuddered her release.

Warm lips pressed against hers. A rough tongue

licked at the inside of her mouth. Aster's eyelids fluttered open to discover gold topaz cat's eyes watching her.

"You were so very beautiful in your passion, I could not resist a kiss." Falcon stroked her cheek again before leaning back.

Aster's fever had subsided, but her face was burning in shame. "You...we...but I really felt..." She hid her face in her hands. They were still in the car, fully clothed. She had just experienced one of the most powerful climaxes she had ever known...and a virtual stranger had brought it about.

"Aster." Falcon said her name in his low voice which vibrated like a cat's purr. "You were with Romulus, not me. I only assisted. I did not know it would embarrass you so. You are better now though. Even the illness has left your body. We can leave whenever you are ready."

Aster uncovered her face and sat up straight. She supposed she was being foolish, as far as Falcon was concerned. Apparently, he had not been affected by what had happened to her. Taking a cue from his behavior, she determined to act as if it had been a perfectly normal occurrence. She buckled her seat-belt and started the car.

Falcon kept his expression impassive but he was very shaken by the episode. He often felt the emotions of others, but not his own. He had never tried to do that for anyone before and had not been certain it would work. He had felt no desire for Romulus's female. He was only trying to help. Once he had planted the image in her mind, it was she who had supplied the details and had carried the fantasy to its satisfying conclusion, satisfying for her, that is. To help her hold the image, he had shared her emotions but not her physical orgasm. He never would be able to experience that part of being human. But he had been unable to resist a small taste of what it would be like. That was really why he had kissed her.

An hour later they arrived at a small airfield outside San Diego. "The two men brought Romulus here," Falcon explained. "A small plane and pilot were waiting. I cannot tell you where they went and I am still not picking up his signal."

"What about the log? They should have logged in at the office over there before they could take off." Aster flushed with the excitement of being able to help. In the office they were bluntly informed the log was confidential. When Aster began to protest, Falcon pulled her outside.

"I already have the destination, Aster. The man's eyes moved to the log as he spoke."

"You mean you can see through things also?" Aster's voice was a mix of awe and fear. She stopped herself from asking if he was originally from the planet Krypton.

"It depends on the depth and material. That book was simple. Now that I know the coordinates I can take us directly there. I have no way of knowing what we might encounter. You should stay here."

"Not on your life, Falcon. I'll stay out of your way and I'll do whatever I can about my...*emotions*, but don't make me stay behind. I'll die of worry. *Please.*"

"Romulus refused to stay behind when you were in trouble also. The two of you had better join as soon as you get together again. I saw your reason for objecting, Aster. You are wrong. Romulus would never resent a part of himself and that is what you are. You cannot deny both your souls' desire to mate. The fever will only get worse. If for no other reason, you should join just to keep track of each other. I may not be available next time." For the first time since Aster had met him, he smiled at her, then his usual serious expression returned. "Go to Norona. Your answer is there."

Aster laughed at his joke and accepted his advice. "You're right. I know that now." Romulus had warned her the day might come when she would attack a delivery man to get relief. What had happened with Falcon was proof of that.

"Let us return the car to that crowded restaurant down the road. It will be much less conspicuous there."

Once the car was safely parked, Aster watched in fascination as Falcon worked the pattern of nodes on his opal ring and turned the stone. Then she shouted, "Wait!" She opened the car trunk and grabbed the shopping bag. "I'm ready now." Falcon finished programming the ring and gripped her shoulders in his strong hands.

The migration took much less time and was less frightening than the first trip. Aster looked around. They were standing on another airstrip, only now they were in the desert. The only objects visible for miles were a small jet and a dilapidated house.

"Is Rom in there?" Aster asked excitedly.

"No, but he is here, very close. Wait."

Aster held her breath.

"He does not answer. Either the device has been removed or he is unconscious somewhere below us. I cannot see it, but I can feel life forms under the ground. His brain waves are among them but they are very weak. He was carried into that structure, so I think it is safe to say that is the usual way in and well-guarded. We are going to have to migrate in as close to Romulus as I can get and pray we do not wind up part of a wall or piece of furniture." Aster's horror-stricken expression made Falcon laugh aloud. "That was a joke, Aster."

Aster stood perfectly still, feeling useless as Falcon walked back and forth over the ground, searching for Romulus's brain waves. It was a painfully slow process. He moved to one side a few feet, turned and took two more steps. If anyone else saw him, they would assume he was drunk or doing an Indian dance of some kind. Finally he stopped and waved her toward him.

"His brain waves are strongest here. Ready?"

Aster shook her head vigorously until she saw him pull a black box out from his jacket. She had seen the weapon at orientation.

"It will only put someone to sleep."

Aster held herself stiffly in his tight embrace as they passed through the earth to whatever lay below. Instantly, they rematerialized in what appeared to be a hospital room.

Z-z-z-t! Z-z-z-t! Falcon's lightning bolt struck a man in a white lab coat. His body went rigid and thumped to the floor. Keeping one eye on the door, Falcon balanced the man back on his chair. He touched his mind, replacing the reality of what he had seen with a less astounding memory.

Aster hovered over Rom's still form. "Oh, my Lord! Rom, can you hear me?" Aster whispered through the tears choking her throat. She touched his ashen face and clasped his cool hand tightly. "Falcon, please, is he all right?"

The tracker touched Rom's temple, nodded to Aster, then placed his finger to his lips and pointed to the door. Someone was out there.

Aster, a very black presence is moving this way. We must hurry! Falcon reprogrammed his ring for their destination then quickly ripped all the tubes, hoses and wires from Romulus's body. Suddenly one of the

machines started making a continuous beeping sound.
By the fourth beep, he pulled Romulus into a sitting
position between him and Aster. A millisecond later,
they were back on the surface.

"What is the meaning of this?" Gordon Underwood
bellowed as he stood in the doorway, absorbing the
scene before him. Dr. Quinn sat in a chair, slack-
mouthed, with his eyes fixed on the empty bed. Hoses
swung freely from the bottles they were attached to,
tubes and wires dangled over the edge of the bed and
machines beeped out an insane cacophony. "I repeat,
what the hell is going on here?"

Frowning, Doctor Quinn stood up but looked back
at the bed one more time before speaking. "It was the
damnedest thing, Mr. Underwood. I was sitting here
monitoring the man's life signs and then, I don't
know, I seem to have passed out. And when I opened
my eyes, he was gone."

Underwood turned to Wink and Cooper who had
followed him into the room. "You two, did anyone,
other than Quinn, enter or leave this room today?"

"No, sir. We took our breaks separately so one of us
was outside of the door at all times since we brought
him in," Cooper answered somewhat defensively.

"We heard the machines start beeping at the same
time you walked up." Wink's eyelids fluttered
nervously.

"Okay, you two may as well go."

As soon as Wink and Cooper left, Underwood's big
fist latched onto a glass bottle beside the bed and
hurled it against the wall. Clear fluid streaked down
the wall to join the broken glass on the floor.

"Damn! They got him. Right from under my nose. I
should have come straight here and had you examine
him later but, no, I wanted to be sure he was the real

thing. Damn it all to hell!"

The doctor was not sure if he was expected to respond. "They who? You heard your men. No one's been in or out of here but me."

"His people, you idiot. What do you think this was, some sort of locked-room mystery? We're underground, Quinn. There is only one way out. They *beamed* him out, just like in a movie. Thank god I had the woman followed. Maybe I'll discover something about her. Damn! You said there was a ring. I want to see it. Now!"

Doctor Quinn fetched the ring as quickly as his feet would carry him and placed it in Underwood's palm. Underwood felt its considerable weight and held it to the light. The design in the center caught his eye and when he touched the stone, he found it could be moved.

"This is not merely a gaudy ring, Quinn. It's bait. They will send someone back for it, I'm positive. And when they do, I'll be ready. Yes, next time, I'll be ready for them."

Falcon gave Aster's hand a gentle squeeze as Doctor Gemina walked toward them.

The doctor nodded briefly to Falcon, who stood beside Aster like a lion guarding his cub.

"Romulus will be fine in a few hours. He was heavily drugged but we're cleansing his system now. They used some rather primitive chemicals on him. While he's recuperating, we can do both of your post-journey physicals."

"No, I can't." Aster shook her head. "At least not yet. I have a job to finish."

Falcon placed his hand on her shoulder. "Let someone else do it, Aster. You have had enough adventure."

"I'm afraid that's irrelevant, Falcon. Romulus promised Doctor Houston we would meet her and another scientist in New York tonight. We're past due but I'm sure they'd wait all night if necessary. If someone else went to meet them, he'd have to waste precious time convincing them he was legitimate. Doctor Houston already trusts me."

Falcon nodded once. "Shall we go?"

Aster smiled broadly at her new friend. "Thank you, Falcon. I knew you'd understand. There's only one other problem. We have to take someone else with us. Do you know Professor Schontivian?"

The elderly professor was not at all pleased with the turn of events but once they arrived in the lobby of Le Parker Meridien, he relaxed. Using a house phone, Aster informed Doctor Houston they had arrived and got directions to her suite.

Kate opened the door then narrowed her brows at the two men who accompanied Aster inside. "Where is Romulus?"

"He was abducted during the night." Kate gaped at her in shock. "Apparently someone learned that he was special. He's being cared for right now in Innerworld. So, I've brought you another expert. This is Professor Schontivian." She gestured to him then to Falcon. "And this is Falcon, my guardian angel."

The black-garbed man with the dark glasses looked the opposite of angelic but Kate smiled and shook both men's hands. "I'm Kate Houston. This is Professor David Ingram."

As Aster shook his hand and introduced herself, it occurred to her that his electrified crop of white hair made him look a bit like Albert Einstein.

David was anxious to get started. "It's incredible—the asteroid, alien communication. Kate started spouting formulas for a fuel unlike anything we have on the drawing boards. I'm sorry that Romulus had such a bad experience during his visit. Do you know who was responsible?"

"Are you familiar with a man named Gordon Underwood?" Falcon questioned in return.

Kate, Professor Ingram and Aster showed their surprise. Kate answered, "Of course. His institute is one of the benefactors of this observatory. The man's a famous philanthropist."

Aster quickly added, "He's a financial genius with a rather loose code of ethics. Why do you ask?"

"When I touched the physician's mind before we took Romulus out, I learned he was working for Gordon Underwood and the facility we were in was owned by the Underwood Institute. The doctor had no idea why he had been ordered to examine Romulus. From the perversions I saw in that man's mind, Romulus was lucky we reached him before the doctor was given permission to use him for one of his private experiments."

"It wouldn't take much imagination to suppose what Underwood might want with Romulus," Aster reflected, "but how did he know we were here?"

Kate's eyes became very sad. "I didn't think anything of it at the time." She sighed aloud. "After you left, I discovered my intercom had been open while Romulus gave me his information. It is possible my assistant, Walter, overheard our conversation and relayed it. That would mean he had a connection to the Underwood Institute. It's hard for me to believe Walter would do such a terrible thing. He was a very devoted employee and as close to a son as I ever had. I'm afraid we'll never know for certain now."

"Why do you say that?" Aster asked.

"Walter died of a heart attack last night on his way home. His neighbor called before I left this morning."

Kate wiped the dampness from her eyes. "Walter had a lot of stress in his personal life. Now it appears he was spying too."

"There doesn't seem to be much we can do about it," David concluded. "Even if Walter was alive, we couldn't bring any charges against Underwood without bringing up Romulus and his world. Who would believe us?"

Kate thought for a moment. "You're right about that. But perhaps there's a way I could stir up an investigation about Walter's death. For all we know, Underwood precipitated Walter's death to keep him from talking to anyone about what he knew."

Aster wanted to see Underwood punished too but she knew it would never happen—not with his clout. Although she had never met him, she knew of him. Their foundations were often at cross-purposes. "At this point I just want to be able to assure Romulus that his mission was a success when he awakens."

"Of course," Kate said. "We've contacted the Central Bureau for Astronomical Telegrams and they are already working on the special meeting we discussed. As soon as we get confirmation that it's been set, David and I will start putting in calls to our colleagues around the world. We'll ask them to put the pressure on their governments to cooperate."

Aster relaxed. "It sounds good so far." She turned to David. "I'm glad Kate started filling you in. Professor Schontivian can answer any questions you have. Meanwhile, I'd like to discuss something with Kate." Like a true guardian angel, Falcon remained at her side.

She recalled her exact promise to Rom and what she was about to do would not involve passing on any of Innerworld's advanced technology.

"I realize you have more than enough to do in the

next few days, but I'm going to burden you a little further. As Rom told you yesterday, the Noronians have a law against aggressively interfering with Outerworld's culture. He convinced me there are good reasons for that and I would never do anything to jeopardize him or his world. But there is something you can do for them."

Kate smiled. "After what his people have done for us, no request would be too great."

"I'm sure I don't have to tell you that Planet Earth is dying. What I learned from Rom, though, is that his world could eventually be sealed off because of Outerworld's neglect. It's already affecting their tunnels and creating havoc with their monitoring systems. In spite of their need to continue to trade with their home planet, they are under orders not to help Outerworlders solve the problem. It's hoped the people on the surface will grow up and learn to treat their world with respect on their own.

"There are efforts being made throughout the world, but it's not enough. Preserving our environment needs to become mandatory, not just a token effort by a few countries.

"Soon you'll be meeting with the Security Council of the United Nations. While you have the attention of some of the most powerful people on this planet, I'm hoping you might make a connection with one or two who would be receptive to receiving suggestions from the Mackenzie Foundation—for the future of Outerworld and Innerworld."

"Honestly, I'm not sure if anything short of an alien visit would make any difference but I promise to do my best. I'll also give you my promise to stir up more support among my colleagues." Kate got a pad and pen to jot down notes as Aster hit the highlights of various projects the Foundation had in the works.

When they were finished, Aster had something of her own to write. She could not let The Mackenzie Foundation turn into something like The Underwood Institute. She wrote a letter to her attorney, explaining that she had not in fact disappeared at sea and thus, was not to be declared dead. But for health reasons she had been forced to take an immediate and lengthy sabbatical. She named a trustee who had always backed her completely to act as director in her absence and gave that trustee her proxy for all votes until she returned. That would keep the wolves at bay for a while at least.

The letter went on to say that if she did not return to San Francisco within one year, her entire estate was to be donated to The Mackenzie Foundation, with the stipulation that all monies be used toward rehabilitating and protecting the environment.

She borrowed Kate's cell phone and had Falcon do a video recording of her reading the letter and sitting with Kate and David as they witnessed the document. Aster instructed Kate to email the video to her attorney and the trustee. Then she asked her to make three copies of the letter, one for herself and one for Kate to hold...just in case any question of authenticity ever arose. The original was to go to the attorney and the other copy was to be sent to the trustee, along with a personal note introducing Doctor Houston as his new best friend on the international stage. A huge weight was now lifted from her mind.

As if perfectly timed with the completion of their duties, the phone rang. David listened to someone intently for several minutes. When he hung up, he was grinning. "An emergency session of the Security Council is set for eight o'clock tomorrow morning. I told them we'd be there with bells on."

"I wish I could be there too," Aster replied with a

wink at Kate, "but I'm sure we'll hear all about it."

David shook his head. "I doubt it. Even with the threat minimized, news of an oncoming asteroid could cause global panic so I'm betting the entire operation will be kept under wraps."

As they said their good-byes and extended good wishes, Aster saw David fold Kate's hand into his. She would have her happy ending after all.

The first thing Rom's eyes focused on was the sleeping beauty curled up in the chair next to his bed. Slowly, his mind came awake. The last thing he could recall clearly was holding Aster in a bed in Outerworld. This room resembled one in Medical in Car-Tem. How had they gotten here?

Aster murmured in her sleep and Rom decided to wake her up through her homing device and moved his fingers to program his ring to her signal. But it was gone. He sat up just as Falcon entered the room.

"So, you decided to rejoin the living. Stay in bed. I will let the doctor know you are awake." Falcon turned and left but his voice had awakened Aster.

She rushed to Rom, propelling him flat on the bed with her weight. Smothering his face with urgent kisses, her hands reacquainted themselves with the feel of him.

Rom lay still for her mad caresses. When he felt her calm down, he pulled her the rest of the way onto the bed.

"Aster? Shalla? What happened?"

She was still holding him as if her life depended on it. "I was so afraid I'd lost you." Piece by piece, Aster relayed what had occurred, with the exception of her private moment with Falcon and what she had asked Kate to do for her. He would find it out eventually, but not today.

As she was winding up her tale, Falcon and the doctor reentered. "Feeling better I see," Doctor Gemina teased when he saw the lovers on the narrow bed.

Aster's face flamed and she squirmed to get away. Rom allowed her to sit upright but refused to loosen his hold. "Aster caught me up somewhat already. Did any of you remove my ring?" They looked at each other and shook their heads.

Aster voiced her immediate concern. "That means it's still out there. If Underwood has it, could he do anything with it?"

Rom shrugged. "It's hard to say. He'd have to figure out how to activate it first, but even if he did, the odds against his being able to analyze its programming are astronomical."

"Rom, the man's a genius, with time and money on his side. I would not assume the ring is harmless in his hands," Aster offered.

Falcon added, "He radiates a totally black presence. I suggest you inform Governor Elissa when you speak to her that Underwood has the ring. If she agrees someone should go out for it, let me know. I should be able to track him easily enough."

"Speaking of the governor," Aster said, "she asked us to meet with her as soon as you're up to it."

"Fine. Falcon, I wonder if you could get me a uniform to wear. Then I'd appreciate your accompanying Aster and me to the debriefing."

Governor Elissa sat spellbound throughout the recounting. Falcon made it sound as if he had done very little compared to Aster's contributions and the governor was impressed.

"Aster, your courage is to be commended. On behalf of Innerworld, I thank you. And, Falcon, I am relieved Aster knew you well enough to call for you.

No one could have done a better job for us. Now, about the ring."

Romulus cleared his throat. "Since I am the one responsible for its loss, I should—"

"No!" Aster exclaimed, effectively cutting him off.

Elissa held up her hand to quiet them both. "I certainly do not hold you responsible, Romulus. But, even if I did, I would not permit you to return. You are too valuable to this colony to risk your life again. Besides, you do not possess Falcon's skills as a tracker. He is the one I am assigning.

"I don't believe it is wise to go after the ring immediately. From your assessments of Gordon Underwood, he might have a trap ready for just such a move. We will postpone the recovery mission for a while. Let him think no one is interested in retrieving the ring. Falcon, I will advise you when the time has come for you to return to Outerworld."

Falcon nodded his head in acceptance of the future assignment.

The governor then handed a folded paper to Romulus. "This came for you. Tarla forwarded it to me in case it was urgent."

It was a formal summons to appear before the Ruling Tribunal on Norona. He was to leave on the first outgoing ship. Rom passed it to Aster.

"The summons is vague but I've heard the rumors," Elissa said. "I intend to write a lengthy report, including Aster's loyal service to us in this crisis and the ordeal she went through with that criminal due to our shortsightedness. You'll take it with you. It might help."

"We'll take it with us," interrupted Aster. "I'm going too. Romulus and I are going to be joined, with or without their approval, but we'll present our case to them first." She gazed into Rom's surprised eyes and mouthed, "I love you."

Elissa failed to hide her dismay. "Aster, Romulus, do you realize what you're saying? They are completely against such a joining and one member of the Tribunal has never been convinced of my stand on Terran rights. Your whole future hangs in the balance."

Romulus took Aster's hand. "We know...and it doesn't matter. We have to do this. I've said it before. If they don't want us to join and live here, we'll find somewhere to live where their dictates can't control us."

"I only felt it needed to be said," Elissa said with a nod of understanding. "Be careful, though. They want you very badly for governor, and I don't know what they would resort to if you balk. Use your head, not your emotions. I'll have to draw up a special permission visa for Aster to travel. The ship leaves in two days."

A short time later, Rom sat down on the bed next to his sleeping mate-to-be. The fact that he had been close to death was worth it, if it had changed Aster's mind about their joining. She would never be sorry. He would make sure of that.

He lightly kissed her parted lips and felt her shallow breath touch his cheek. His love for her was a living thing that had grown from the first moment he saw her until it had become his only reason for living. If that was not enough, she was now responsible for his being alive and safely home. What she had done was so much more than his rescuing her from Victor.

But once again they would have to prove that nothing could keep them apart. This time, the most powerful authority in the universe had to be convinced.

PART III

The Joining

CHAPTER 22

Aster gazed at the magnificent ships housed in the transportation hangar. They varied drastically in size and shape and Rom pointed out a few, describing their uses and different capabilities.

"The passenger ship is not in Innerworld right now. It's as large as this entire hangar and is built for comfortable travel. The carrier we'll be traveling in is built for speed with minimal attention to comfort. We won't want for anything but it's not very elegant. Here it is." The ship bore a strong resemblance to a gigantic silver pterodactyl in flight. It was about twice the size of a DC-10 jet and appeared to be molded from one solid sheet of stainless steel.

"She's beautiful, Rom," Aster said, honestly impressed.

"Are you ready to board?"

"Oh, yes. I can't wait to see inside."

"Hello, Chief Romulus. Welcome aboard," a maroon-uniformed man said as they stepped inside the ship. About the same age as Rom, the man was thin, blond and of average height and features, except for his smile. That feature was dazzling and hinted of a mischievous personality.

"Captain Kertus, good to see you again," Rom said. "This is Aster. We're going back to Norona with you this trip."

"I was forewarned. Hello, Aster." Kertus took her hand in his. "I'm glad to see that the jealous rumors about you bewitching the chief were ugly distortions. It was probably the other way around." The captain laughed heartily at his own joke. "Aster, would you like to sit on the bridge for take-off?"

Aster's eyes lit up as she turned to Rom and he winked at her. "We would both enjoy that, Kertus, if you're sure we won't be in the way."

"There's plenty of room on this trip. Follow me and I'll give you a brief tour on the way." The captain escorted them, pointing out rooms and areas as they passed. "This section houses the crew's quarters and the dining room. I'll be staying with the crew for this trip. I think you'll find my cabin satisfactory."

Aster objected immediately. "Captain, we can't possibly allow you to give up your own comfort for us."

"It's already done." He went on to explain the layout of the ship. "The business end of this craft is all housed on the deck below this one, with the exception of the bridge, which is above. Over here are the recreation facilities. There's a complete exercise room with sauna and whirlpool, games, movies and a fair library. You'll be staying here." Kertus placed his hand over the door frame and it disappeared into the wall with a whoosh. Before entering, they reprogrammed it to open to Rom's or Aster's hand.

"It's very handsome, Captain. Thank you." The cabin was larger than the stateroom she had had on the yacht and as nicely appointed, in a decidedly masculine way.

"You have your own supply station in the cabin but you're welcome to eat in the dining room whenever you like. Now, if you're ready, it's time to take off."

Captain Kertus led them to the bridge and directed them to the two seats in the observation area to the side. Rom was relieved to see Aster enjoying herself. Not even a trace of fear lingered in her midnight-blue eyes.

"Don't we need to be belted in or wear special spacesuits or helmets?" Aster inquired.

Rom smiled at her naive question. "Unnecessary. Air pressure, oxygen levels and gravity are all regulated within the ship. There will be a slight pull as we leave the Earth but if you sit still you'll barely notice it."

"Aren't there any windows? I was hoping I'd be able to see out." She was genuinely disappointed.

"The entire bridge is surrounded by protective shields. After we leave Earth's atmosphere, Kertus will transform their molecular structure and they will become transparent. Until then, you can watch that viewer if you want to see what we're passing."

Aster glanced at the screen and was shocked to discover they were leaving the hangar. She had not even realized they were moving. She automatically gripped the arm of her chair and Rom quickly took her hand in his.

The ship smoothly entered the tunnel that would lead them to the planet's surface. Aster intently observed the captain and his crew as they performed their customary routines. Anticipation bubbled up inside her until her fingertips tingled.

Aster detected a subtle change within the craft. The viewer showed only a blur of blacks and grays as the ship shot upward out of the inner core of the Earth. She only felt a sensation of being lifted in a fast elevator, similar to the lift at her apartment.

Some time passed before they broke out of the tunnel and began tearing through the ocean. Aster remembered the wall of water she had witnessed from the deck of The Baronette. Hopefully, there was no Earth ship or plane hovering there today.

Their carrier burst through the frothy surface and Aster felt the slight gravitational pull Rom had spoken of. Suddenly she could see the green of the Sargasso Sea surrounded by the bluer Atlantic Ocean. "Rom, look! There's the Florida coast and the Bahamas." As quickly as she pointed it out, the image encompassed more and more of the Eastern seaboard, large parts of which were hidden by cloud cover.

"How long before they change the shields?" Aster asked, making no attempt to mask her childish delight.

"Soon now. The slowest part of the trip is coming through the tunnel and breaking away from Earth's gravity. By tomorrow you should be able to see Saturn."

"My heavens!"

"I'm sure the captain will be happy to point out anything along our course once he gets us on our way. The asteroid belt is one of the most interesting things you're going to see. Compared to the openness of deep space, it's fairly cluttered. The captain actually earns his credits then."

"I heard that, Romulus," Kertus grumbled. "You're welcome to take over the bridge at any time if you need to impress the lady."

"No, thank you. I'm strictly a passenger this trip."

Aster turned to Rom in surprise and he answered her unspoken question. "Kertus has let me *play* at being captain on previous trips. He was teasing, believe me."

When the captain transformed the shields, Rom took Aster to a window. Gradually shrinking before her eyes was the planet Aster knew as home. In spite of the cloudy atmosphere, she had no trouble making out the United States and South America and the bodies of water on their borders. She had seen pictures taken by American astronauts but those had not prepared her for this breathtaking view.

"This is unbelievable! Never in my wildest dreams would I have come up with this fantasy. Thank you, Rom." She kissed him despite their audience.

"Aster, do you want to stay here awhile longer or start your lessons and come back later?" Rom asked when the Earth was far behind them.

"My lessons? What lessons?" she asked hesitantly.

Rom's words held a combination of mystery and sensuality. "Come with me and find out."

Her curiosity was aroused enough to follow him anywhere. As soon as they were in their cabin, she asked, "Well? What does my teacher have for me today?" Her arms snaked around his neck to bring his face closer to hers.

Instead of returning her passionate embrace, he kissed her nose, unwrapped her arms and directed her to sit down in a chair. She watched him rummage through the small bag they had carried aboard. When he handed her a thin, leather-bound book, she tilted her head at him.

Rom dragged another chair to a spot directly in front of her and sat down. "It's time for you to start preparing for our joining. This book will explain how you must prepare yourself, what will occur during the ceremony and how it will affect your life afterward. Not only must you read it, you must understand and accept all of what it says before we can be joined. It's necessary for you to memorize the words and actions of the ritual in the proper sequence. We can't practice it ahead of time. There's really not much to learn, but it must be done perfectly. You won't have any trouble. We have a week of solitude ahead of us."

Aster's heart thumped as her fingers opened the cover. Rom placed his hand over hers and reclosed the book. "Before you begin, there's something else we're going to work on together. I came up with an idea to practice your mental control. Hopefully, by the time we're joined, you'll have the basics mastered and sharing my thoughts won't be so confusing."

Setting the book aside, Aster perched on the edge of her chair. "I'm all yours, teach." She wasn't sure if she was anxious to hear his idea or glad for a temporary reprieve from discovering the secrets of the book.

Rom removed two Innerworld rings from his pocket, slid one on her finger and the other on his.

"I thought you didn't have yours."

"This is another one. I've already programmed yours for my signal and mine for yours. This is why I didn't want the homing devices removed yet."

"Oh, dear. I told you what happened when the emissary tried to talk to me. He said my brain was muddled!"

Rom laughed at the funny face she made. "Well, I know it's not. You only need some guidance." *Can you hear me?*

"Of course I can. Oh! You didn't say that out loud, did you?"

"No, and don't answer me aloud, either. Don't try to give me any lengthy answers. Try for a word or two first." *What's your name?*

Aster thought she had answered him very easily, but the way his eyebrows bunched together told her she had not accomplished even that simple task.

"What did I do wrong?" she asked, upset with her failure.

"It wasn't completely wrong. I definitely heard you think your name somewhere in there. The problem was all the other thoughts and images thrown in. This room seems very quiet but you picked up a sound and wondered what it was. Your eyes moved to that picture on the wall and it reminded you of one you'd seen before. Besides that, you're hungry. I'd like to try one thing then we'll get you some food."

"I didn't realize I was thinking all those things at the same time."

Rom ordered something from the supply station and carried it to a table behind her. "Close your eyes," he said as he tied a blindfold on her. "Perhaps if I shut out two of your senses, you'll find it easier to concentrate. After I put these plugs in your ears, I'm going to think a word. All I want you to do is picture the item and try as hard as you can to hold that image, without letting anything else break in. Remember, no talking, okay?"

When Aster nodded, he placed the plugs in her ears.

House.

Aster focused on the outside of their home then bits and pieces of the yard and the interior.

One image, Aster. Pick one and hold it.

She bit her lower lip, determined to send him a single isolated thought. She conjured up the front of the house.

Good. I can see it. You're still wandering, though. Let's try a couple more.

Aster succeeded in sending him a blurred picture of a tree and part of her wristwatch, but after that cheeseburgers and french fries kept interrupting her thoughts. She tore the blindfold off in frustration and threw it down.

I'm never going to be able to do this! I'm hopeless.

Aster! I heard you! It wasn't perfect but I could make it out.

Aster looked as shocked as Rom and tried to tell him something else. Her concentration was lost again however, and Rom decided it was time for a break. He removed her earplugs and deactivated their rings.

"Why don't you have that cheeseburger then I'll leave you alone for a while to start your studies. We'll work some more on that muddled brain of yours later. Maybe we can figure out what you did to block everything else out."

Aster frowned at him then laughed. "Just make sure my stomach's full when we start!"

The second day of their journey passed much like the first. They spent some time on the bridge with Captain Kertus, a few hours working on mental telepathy and a time apart while Aster read and memorized parts of the book for the joining ritual. Their nights were peaceful times for loving and resting.

By the third day Aster had witnessed the dangers in the asteroid belt, spied the rings of Saturn and the oblivion of a black hole.

During their practice that day, she was finally able to remove the blindfold and earplugs and still think clear pictures of Rom's words. Her study of the ritual of joining progressed, although every sentence raised another question since she wasn't familiar with a lot of the terminology. When their trip began, she thought a week was a very long time. Now she worried that it was not long enough.

Aster sat staring at the pages without seeing the words. She knew Rom left her alone to study so he would not distract her but she missed his presence.

He had been gone longer than usual when she

decided to try calling him back. She had been getting better at concentrating and had learned how to activate the ring and home in on his signal. She arranged her thoughts and closed her eyes.

Romulus sat in the recreation room, chatting with two of the crew members. In mid-sentence, he was surprised at the vivid image that broke into his thoughts. It was the lagoon, complete with colorful birds and tropical flowers. He opened his mouth to finish his sentence when a second picture popped into his head. He saw himself standing in front of Aster on the ledge where they had had their picnic lunch.

"Romulus? Hello? What happened to the Black Knight?"

"What? Oh, I'm sorry. I suddenly remembered something. I'll finish the story another time." Romulus ignored their puzzled expressions as he hurried from the room.

As Romulus headed toward the cabin, the love scene continued to unfold in his mind, step by passionate step, exactly as it had first occurred the day he introduced Aster to the joys of love. He took his time, knowing where the thoughts were coming from and, rather than shut them out, he chose to see how far she could go with them.

He watched himself kneel at her feet and taste her flesh. His body was on fire but he waited outside their room until he saw the moment in their encounter when he was poised above her, asking permission to enter heaven for the first time.

The whoosh of the door broke her concentration. Aster sat cross-legged in the middle of the bed with a sly grin.

"I received your invitation," he rumbled as he removed their rings and then his clothes. "Why are you so overdressed?"

"I wasn't sure you'd know what I wanted," she murmured innocently. She openly admired him as he dropped his pants to display the proof that he knew precisely what she wanted.

Two days later Aster closed the book and set it aside for the last time. Parts of the joining tradition were simple to follow and she could easily understand the symbolism. Other sections were purposely vague and bordered on the occult. He had only explained that those parts would be clear when the time came.

As if he sensed the completion of her task, Rom returned to the cabin. "I sent a message to my parents. They'll be meeting us. We'll be expected to spend the first day with them and then I'm to appear before the Tribunal the next day."

"Have you thought of how you're going to get me in there with you?"

"We're going to be defending ourselves, not just presenting a request for a waiver of the law. You have every right to be present. I'll insist on it."

"Can you prepare me for that?"

"Unfortunately, I'm not sure what they're going to throw at us. You just keep in mind how I feel. We will be joined the following night regardless."

"I've already accepted that, Rom. All right, tell me about your parents. I want to make a good impression."

Rom turned her around and pulled her down onto his lap in a chair. "You can't help but do that. Just be yourself. Their names are Marcus and Yulan. They are uncomplicated, friendly people, who love each other and their only son without question. And they're going to love you too, you'll see."

"I only pray I can get through this next week without having a nervous breakdown."

"After what you've been through recently, this'll be

child's play. Now, what do you say we work a little more today? You were so close this morning. Let's work on words without images this time. If you have to, try concentrating on seeing the word spelled out."
What's your name?

A-S-T-E-R, she thought, slowly picturing each letter.

Very good. I especially like the red heart at the end. What's your favorite color?

B-L-U-E.

Where did you live before you came to Innerworld? S-A-N...San Francisco...California.

What do you want to do when this lesson is over?

Make love to you. Aster's eyes opened wide. The way to send a whole thought at once suddenly came to her. It was so easy she didn't understand why she hadn't figured it out before. She finally knew the difference between regular thinking and directing a specific thought outward. Her attempt had been shaky but she had conquered the concept.

Rom gave her knee a squeeze. "You felt it this time, didn't you?"

Aster hugged him so hard he choked. "I did! I—"

Rom placed his finger on her lips. *You're not finished with your lesson yet. Don't get cocky just because you managed to think one sentence. Although I definitely approve of the thought.* Rom brought her face close to his and kissed the corners of her mouth. As his tongue traced the outline of her lips and snuck between her teeth, he prodded her to continue her practice. *Well? Tell me something else.*

When he kissed her like that, Aster could barely think at all, let alone sharpen her new-found skill. The only thing in her head was how he made her feel. It was easier to stick to the subject at hand. *I love the way you kiss.*

Thank you. Go on. Rom found her tongue and

sucked it into his mouth. His hand crept under her shirt to fondle her breast, causing Aster to shift uncomfortably on his lap.

You're not playing fair. I don't want to do this anymore.

No? What do you want to do? he asked, deepening his kiss.

Rather than answer his foolish question, Aster sent him an explicit depiction that spoke louder than words. Rom deactivated their rings and wasted no time before switching from mental to physical pursuits.

CHAPTER 23

"Aster, wake up! I want you to see something. Hurry up!"

"Good grief, Rom. How do you manage to wake up so damn chipper? What is it?" She stretched and struggled to wake up for him.

"I was just on the bridge. I could see Norona!" Rom sounded like a little boy on Christmas morning. "I want you to see it before Kertus transforms the shields."

"Are we that close? I need time to make myself presentable before I face your parents."

"We've still got about an hour but I want you to see this first, then you can come back here and fuss all you want."

She donned yesterday's clothes and he hustled her to the bridge. At the window, he pulled her into the circle of his arms with her back snug against his wildly beating heart. Resting his chin on her head, Rom sighed quietly.

"There it is, love. That's Norona."

The planet did not look so different from Earth, except for a complete lack of cloud cover. The greens and browns of the land and blues of the water sparkled in the early-morning sunshine. There seemed to be much more land mass than Earth possessed.

Soon the captain had to reactivate the shields in preparation of their entry into Norona's atmosphere. Rom remained on deck while Aster returned to the cabin. An hour later, Rom showed up to hurry her along. His pacing in the close quarters did not help her building case of nerves.

The landing was no less interesting than their takeoff had been, but Aster was too worried about how Rom's parents would receive her to pay close attention. As they exited the craft, Rom kissed Aster's icy fingers and whispered, "They'll love you." Aster straightened her shoulders and gathered her courage as they approached the man and woman waiting at the bottom of the ramp.

"Rom!" his mother exclaimed and walked into his open arms.

Aster fixed a smile on her face as Rom returned the maternal kisses and hugged his father. Rom's mother was attractive, in a mature way, and as tall as Aster, with brown hair and eyes. The man at her side was an older version of Romulus. The two men were clearly father and son.

Rom stepped back beside Aster and put his arm around her waist. "Mother, Father, this is Aster Mackenzie. Aster, Yulan and Marcus."

Yulan stepped forward first and embraced Aster, kissing her lightly on her cheek. "I'm so happy to meet you. Welcome to Norona. I've heard a lot of good things about you."

Aster raised her eyebrows and glanced at Rom, who looked equally bewildered by his mother's comment.

Yulan laughed. "After Marcus sent you his letter, we received a rather lengthy missive from Marya and

Frank. You pleased her very much by visiting her that day, though you should do so more often. At any rate, they were both very impressed with Aster. Marya passed along the latest Innerworld gossip, so you've been spared a lot of time bringing us up to date."

Rom's father stepped toward Aster and took her hand. "We're very glad you came to visit us, even if it took my practically having to order it to get you here." He smiled warmly at Aster then gave his son a look that blended fatherly approval with pure male admiration. "Let's go home."

As they glided along, Marcus said, "We'll go straight to the farm. You've seen Car-Tem, Aster, so you already know what our city looks like. There it is on the horizon to your left."

Aster leaned toward the window and saw the crystal prisms of the taller buildings reaching toward the lavender-blue sky with its large, ringed sun.

"The air is cooler, though isn't it?" Aster asked.

"That's because we have real seasons here, not prefabricated like that artificial environment in Innerworld," Marcus answered emotionally.

Rom chuckled. "I told you he wasn't very fond of my adopted home."

Yulan quickly changed the subject. "I thought you might prefer to stay in your sanctuary, so I had it cleaned up and installed a supply station for you."

"That's terrific. Thank you. We'll appreciate the privacy." Rom pulled Aster toward him and kissed her softly.

She blushed instantly. She was proud that he did not hesitate to be affectionate in front of Yulan and Marcus but, after all, they were his parents and it didn't seem right even to suggest that they needed privacy. "Did you say sanctuary?" Aster asked to hide her momentary embarrassment.

Yulan smiled. "That's what we always called it. When Rom was a boy, he had one place on the farm where he went to be alone. He built himself a shelter there. He wasn't like other little boys. Little Romulus tended to be a bit stuffy and introverted. At least we always knew where to find him."

"I was not stuffy! And I'd rather you didn't spend the rest of the day reminiscing about my childhood," Rom warned.

"Well, now that I see that it bothers you, I'll make a point of remembering all the worst things you ever did, so that Aster knows all about you. Tell me the truth, Aster, didn't you think he was stuffy when you first met him?"

Aster muffled a laugh. She already liked Rom's mother. "Very stuffy, and egotistical, and overbearing...and absolutely irresistible." She winked at her love.

Marcus shook his head. "I can see you two are going to get along great. Here we are. Welcome home!"

When Aster stepped out of the hauler, she gasped. "It's an exact duplicate of Marya and Frank's farm."

"You're wrong there, Aster. My sister copied ours!" Yulan tucked her hand under Rom's free arm as they walked to the house. "My parents used to live here. They spend all their time traveling now. I doubt if there's a habitable planet in all the universe they haven't visited at least once."

The day sped by as Yulan wanted details of the gossip Marya had written about and Rom and Aster filled them in on the events of the past weeks. His parents rode an emotional roller coaster while they alternated between laughter and sadness.

Yulan prepared their meal from home-grown foods. She rarely used their supply station, she explained to

Aster, since she liked to cook and Marcus preferred his food being prepared that way.

"Everything's delicious," Aster complimented seriously. "I agree with Marcus about this homemade bread. The computer can't match it."

"I'm glad to see that you're such an astute young woman," Marcus said, smiling at Aster. "Now, son, it seems to me that we've covered every subject except the reasons you're here. Are the two of you intending to join?"

Yulan sent her mate a look of disapproval for his bluntness. Aster knew they did not have to speak to communicate but Yulan's face gave her thoughts away.

Rom laughed. "I wondered how long you could wait." He reached over to take Aster's hand. "I never completely understood about finding one's soulmate...until Aster came into my life. She may not be Noronian by birth but that didn't prevent her from getting the mating fever. That alone is unheard of for a Terran. She also experienced the separation during her first visit to the pyramid. Long before she entered Innerworld, she had dreams of me. I felt her soul call to mine the first time I saw her and she wasn't even conscious. It seems impossible that I have lived all my life without her." His adoring gaze spoke even better than his words.

Marcus and Yulan became serious as they pondered their next questions. Yulan looked to Aster. "Dear, you may be exceptional but you are still not of our race. Joining is not simply a legal bonding, like your marriage in Outerworld. Has Rom explained what is involved?"

Marcus interrupted his mate. "Besides challenging the law, which is no small matter, there are possible complications, dangers to your sanity. Have you read the book?"

Rom's impatience began to show as he opened his mouth to answer. Aster squeezed his hand firmly and replied confidently, "I have read the book. I understand the ritual and the consequences and I accept it. We've discussed the risks. At this point I believe the only threat to my sanity will be if we are not joined. We have almost lost each other twice and I thought I would lose my mind without him."

"Aster's extremely intelligent, Father," Rom said more calmly than he felt. "On the way here, we started working on her mind control, using the homing devices. She's already able to receive and send clear thoughts. That part had me worried at first but not anymore. I'll bet by the time we get back she'll even be blocking out my thoughts." Rom stroked her cheek.

Again Aster sensed the silent communication between Rom's parents and could see they harbored doubts.

Rom was already feeling defensive and their extended silence provoked him to speak again. "I can assure you nothing you say will change our minds."

Yulan looked surprised. "You've jumped to the wrong conclusion, Romulus. We are very pleased you have found your true mate. We don't doubt your sincerity or your love for one another. Any fool can see it. We want you to be as happy as we've been, to know the wonderful completeness of joining. It's only that—"

"What your mother is slowly getting around to," interrupted Marcus, "is that in your particular case there is more involved than whether Aster will have difficulty with the mental union. Romulus, you are not one of the millions of people who go about their business with their personal affairs unnoticed. You are one of the selected. Up until now that knowledge fed your ambition. The governorship was the goal you've worked toward your whole adult life."

The storm clouds gathered in Rom's eyes as he responded through tightly clenched jaws. "*Was* is the operative word. Not anymore. Aster and I will present our case tomorrow and—"

"You can't take Aster!" Marcus burst out. "No alien has ever been permitted in the Tribunal's chambers."

"Then this will be a first. How can she defend herself from whatever charges they've trumped up if she can't be present?" Rom pushed his chair back and got up from the table. His hands balled into fists as he paced back and forth across the room. "I don't even know why we're bothering. They've probably already made up their minds against us."

"Sit down!" Marcus barked. "You don't know what they intend. You'll have to answer their summons to find out. Your attitude is not going to sit favorably with them, I can tell you that much. You want them to accept Aster *and* grant you the governorship? You won't get it by shouting and telling them their opinion doesn't mean drek to you.

"Where's the cool, efficient diplomat, son? Dig him out from this emotional avalanche you're buried under." Rom waved his arm at Marcus. "And don't give me that *you-don't-understand-what-I'm-going-through* look. You may only think of me as your aging father but I am no less a man than you. I am a Noronian. I burned with the same fires torturing you now. I know precisely how it feels to need a particular woman, to possess her and to give yourself to her completely. The difference is, I didn't have an entire colony depending on me to keep my head."

Rom stopped his pacing but kept his back to the others.

Yulan stopped Marcus so that she could continue in a quieter tone. "If the Tribunal decides you are the best choice to govern their most treasured colony, they will not accept a refusal from you. Your personal desires mean nothing compared to the good of Norona."

"And when it comes to the good of Norona," Marcus cut in again, "the Tribunal is above the laws they've made. It sounds as though you've conveniently forgotten that they each possess powers far beyond the average Noronian and there is no one to stop them from using those powers to achieve what is necessary. If you try to tell them you'll give up the governorship before you'll give up joining with Aster, they could exile or even reprogram her and make you forget you ever knew her! I'm sorry, Aster. I'm not trying to frighten you. I just want to make sure this hotheaded son of mine realizes what he's up against."

Aster stared at Marcus in stunned silence. It had not occurred to her that the peace-loving, honorable people of Norona would force their will upon her and Rom. Nothing she had learned in Innerworld had suggested such aggressive, unethical behavior.

"Thank you very much, Father," Rom said sarcastically, when he noted Aster's sudden pale complexion. "For someone who is not trying to frighten her, I'd say you've done a great job. Now, I think we will retire. It doesn't sound like we're going to have a normal conversation in this house until the confrontation is over tomorrow." He held his hand out to Aster to leave.

Like a sleepwalker, she moved through the departure amenities and went with Rom to the barn. Aster shook herself slightly when she saw Rom saddling two horses. "Is it far?" She glanced up at the darkening sky.

"Far enough. Come here, love." He held his hands out to her. The moment their fingertips touched a spark kindled and a tiny charge ran up her arms. Rom pulled her closer, trapping her hands against his chest. His eyes were warm and brown and drew her into their depths. "You feel that, don't you, shalla? Nothing anyone says or does can change that between us. You must believe that above all else and we'll get through this just fine. I love you. It won't be long now." His head bent slowly down to hers for a light caress. He helped her into the saddle then mounted his own horse.

Aster set aside her worries when her horse delivered her to the edge of their lagoon. "Oh, Rom! I should have known this is where you'd have built your sanctuary. What a wonderful surprise."

Rom grinned from ear to ear, glad to have been able to keep this a surprise until the last minute. "This part you haven't seen." They dismounted and he led her along a narrow path to a clearing amidst the jungle foliage.

There she saw a miniature stone castle, about twenty feet long on each side and ten feet high, with turrets at the corners. Ladders of light angled down from small square windows around the top. Rom stepped forward and yanked on a rope. The drawbridge creaked and yawned open for them to enter.

"You made this yourself? It's fantastic! I guess your interest in medieval times goes back a ways."

"I've often wondered if I was a knight in some previous life." He nudged her inside and let out a whistle. "Mother said she cleaned up. But it's more like she did a complete overhaul. Believe me, it did not look like this when I was a boy."

On one wall was a modern supply station, a small table and two chairs. A partition in one corner concealed the bathroom facilities. Filling most of what was left of the room was a bed completely surrounded by rainbow sherbet-colored drapes hung from a point in the ceiling above the bed's center. Thick rugs and big, pastel pillows were scattered over the stone floor.

"It's lovely, but I can't imagine you playing here as a little boy the way it's decorated tonight." Aster stroked the silky material at the foot of the bed.

Rom moved behind her, nuzzling her neck. "Maybe not but the big boy can imagine it just fine."

There was no more talk of fears or appearances before powerful people that night. Their loving was gentle and reassuring, making Aster recall the proverb about the calm before the storm.

"Step forward, please."

Aster heard the voice in her ears and her mind *almost* simultaneously. She glanced around the small, vacant vestibule but could not identify where the voice had come from. Rom directed her to stand with him in the center of a black triangle embedded in the cold, gray stone floor. She was certain that, any second, her knees would give out and she would dissolve into a puddle at his feet. All of Marcus's warnings of the night before came flooding back to her. What was she doing here? How could she, a mere Terran female, hope to get through to the almighty Tribunal of Norona?

A beam of light poured down, forming a bright three-sided wall encasing them. "State your business," the voice demanded in the same near-echo quality.

Aster's nerves jangled uncontrollably but hearing Rom's voice, so strong and confident helped enormously.

"I am Chief Administrator Romulus Locke, of the

Innerworld Colony. She is Aster Mackenzie. We have been summoned."

"That is incorrect. You, Chief Romulus, have been summoned. You may enter."

"I beg the Tribunal's indulgence in this matter. We are as one. I do not wish to appear without her."

Neither Aster nor Romulus took a breath as they waited in the silent moment that followed his defiance.

"You, Chief Romulus, have been summoned. Only you may enter. She will wait."

Rom gathered every ounce of self-control he possessed. He would use his logic not his roiling emotions to win this round. "I have a letter from Governor Elissa which is self-explanatory. I humbly request that the Tribunal read it before turning us away."

Rom pulled the folded letter from his pocket and held it in front of him. One second it was in his hand. The next it was gone.

Then they waited.

Aster couldn't tell if an hour had passed or only a minute when their prison of light evaporated into the ceiling and two huge doors slid open in front of them. Aster was grateful for the courage, passing from Rom's hand to hers. Her shoulders back, her chin high, she walked proudly at his side and prayed the Tribunal would not read her cowardly thoughts.

The chamber they entered was dimly lit and much too warm. Aster's eyes slowly adjusted to the light and focused on a raised triangular dais, approximately five feet long on each side. At each angle, a figure sat in a high, straight-backed chair. Rom and Aster stopped before the base of the triangle.

The figures to their left and right were draped in dark purple robes and only their heads were visible.

Aster assumed they were heads perched atop the yards of flowing fabric. The withered flesh of each figure looked like lizard skin pulled tautly over its skull, with two small holes for nostrils and a slash of a mouth. A snow-white beard hung straight and smooth until it curled into the figure's lap. Similar hair covered their scalps and disappeared below the shoulders in the back. But their round eyes were alive, dark and piercing from deep within sunken caverns as they examined their subjects. The figure at the third point, directly in front of them, could only be differentiated by a white robe and no beard. Perhaps it was female.

"Out of respect for Governor Elissa…"

"We will permit this breach of tradition."

"Her letter is very complimentary. You may introduce us."

Aster's gaze darted from one figure to the other. She had heard three voices, one definitely more feminine than the other two, but no mouths had moved. There was no way to tell who had said what or whether they had actually spoken aloud.

Though it seemed impossible, Rom drew himself even taller as his deep voice rumbled throughout the chamber. "Members of the Tribunal, Lamed, Mem and Nun," he said, nodding to each in turn, "it is with great pleasure that I introduce Aster Mackenzie, of whom Governor Elissa has only written the truth. We are well aware of the rare privilege you grant us today and thank you for your consideration."

Aster wished they could sit down. The room was claustrophic and she could not stop shaking. Please, Lord, don't let me faint and embarrass the both of us. As if sensing her discomfort, Rom squeezed her hand until it actually hurt. The pain stabilized her and she concentrated on his physical contact with her.

The voices began their interview.

"Romulus Locke, we summoned you here today…"

"to announce our decision that you have been chosen…"

"as the next Governor of Innerworld."

"We received a communication…"

"from Innerworld…"

"warning us about this female's influence impairing your judgment."

"We had intended to prohibit you…"

"from further contact…"

"with this alien."

"In light of Elissa's report, we now believe…"

"she has proven herself worthy of our consideration."

"You may keep her by your side…"

"for as long as you wish…"

"but we cannot approve of her as a mate for you, our chosen, or as Co-Governor of Innerworld."

Rom took a deep, controlling breath before speaking. "And I will not accept the governorship if it means that Aster and I cannot be joined. You will have to choose someone else." Rom's interruption was highly irregular but his refusal was unheard of. The three pair of eyes glared down at him.

"Our second choice for governor does not have the assured support of the people as you do."

"We will have you at any cost."

"We can help you forget her. She is only a Terran. You will find another, more suitable mate."

"*No!*" Rom shouted then regained his calm façade. "Our souls have been waiting in limbo for our joining. Mem, I speak to you now. You came to me when I was a boy. You know me as I know myself. Do you not feel the burning within us?"

"I do, but it may not be enough." It was the woman's voice.

"She is not one of us."

"If she were Noronian, she would understand why she must give you up. The people need you more than she."

"It is for the greater good."

Rom tried to keep his voice level as he reasoned with them. "It's not only for ourselves that we ask this, but for Innerworld, my adopted home, as well. Outerworld is becoming more complex every year. You are aware of the problems we are experiencing because of Earth's pollution. Aster's career involved solving those problems. I've learned how different studying the culture can be from living there. If we were joined, I would share Aster's knowledge and judgments concerning her world.

"Last week we made ourselves known to two Terran scientists to prevent Earth's destruction by a planetoid. It was the first time in centuries we have openly communicated with them but it will undoubtedly be necessary again.

"One day in the near future the two cultures will inevitably blend together. There must be a reason why a Terran and a Noronian never heard the mating cry of their souls before, but we have, and it cannot be denied. Perhaps it's because it is time to begin the joining of the two races. Wasn't that the original intention when the rebels were exiled there?"

"May I speak?" Aster's voice cracked with strain.

"She dares to speak..."

"to us?"

The voices actually sounded emotional, which frightened Aster that much more.

"I wish to hear what she has to say," the feminine voice declared.

Aster squeezed Rom's hand as hard as she could then ventured bravely into the enemy's territory. "I *do* understand that the people of Norona and Innerworld need this man. And I would give him up if I truly believed that was best for him. When I first arrived in Innerworld, I learned that being productive and enjoying what you do were mandatory. Wouldn't you want the same for your chosen? You've offered him no chance for happiness. He's prepared himself for this appointment and if he passes it up, sooner or later it will cause him distress and resentment. If he accepts it but cannot be joined with me, he will never feel whole again. You can't simply tell him to find another."

When she received no response, she continued, no longer trying to appear submissive. "I am meant to be his mate, his shalla. If he is so special to you, how can you treat him with so little compassion? Have you never known a love so deep you would rather die than be separated from that person?" Aster stopped when Rom's fingers bit into her palm. She had gone too far.

A deadly silence filled the room. Seconds tiptoed by as Aster fought back the tears in her eyes.

"It has been a very long time…"

"since anyone dared remind us…"

"of our humanity…"

"or our youth. This is a difficult decision."

"She is not bound by our code of honesty. What if she is not what she appears?"

"We should touch her mind to be certain."

"No, you will not," Rom stated firmly. "She has as much right to her privacy as anyone else. She has proven her loyalty to Norona at the risk of her own life. Without her help, I would not be here today. She completed my assignment in Outerworld when I was unable to and could have stayed there and betrayed us if that was her intent. She returned to Innerworld because that is her home now, and she returned to me because we belong to each other."

Aster stared at him. His tone of voice suggested there was a good reason for his refusing to allow them to touch her mind. She would trust his judgment.

"Aster Mackenzie…"

"it is your decision."

"Will you give us permission to touch your mind?"

Aster hesitated and looked to Rom for confirmation. "No."

"Then we will base our judgment…"

"on what we have read and heard today."

"You will receive word tomorrow."

There were no words of dismissal. The doors behind them reopened and the Tribunal's heads bowed. A moment later Rom and Aster were inhaling the fresh air outside as though it were a precious gift. Aster turned and looked at the building they had just escaped. Made of the same crystal-prism construction as the other buildings in the area, there was nothing about it to hint of the power housed within.

"That was really spooky," Aster finally muttered.

"Spooky? I never thought about them like that. I suppose they are." Rom smiled as they walked to the commuter.

"How old are they?"

"I'm not sure. They've been here forever…at least three or four hundred years. There's always speculation about who will replace them when they die though no one's really sure they will."

"Why didn't you want them to touch my mind? I have nothing to hide and it might have helped."

"I don't know. Too many people have been warning us about the Tribunal. I didn't know what to expect. It sounds terrible but I didn't trust them to get inside your head and leave it alone. Hey, don't look so sad. We got a lot further than we had any reason to hope for. At least they're considering the possibility of us as a team."

"I don't know how you can sound so casual about this. I'm still shaking."

"Then let's stop talking about it. You know my parents are waiting for us to return and to report everything to them but afterward, what do you say to a replay of our first picnic?"

Aster raised an eyebrow and snuggled closer. "If you want, I could pretend I'm still innocent."

"Hold that thought."

Late that night, comfortably settled in the big bed in the sanctuary, Aster thought about Rom's parents' reaction to the interview. It was their belief that the Tribunal's allowing her to speak was akin to their planet suddenly revolving in the opposite direction. But their picnic and afternoon at the lagoon had dispelled most of her gloomy thoughts.

Rom's eyes closed and his voice dragged sleepily. "I think I liked this afternoon even better than the first time. I don't know if I'm sorry it flew by so fast or glad because we're that much closer to tomorrow."

"We can always have a repeat performance tomorrow, after we hear the decision." When Rom didn't answer, Aster leaned over and kissed his slightly open mouth. He was already asleep. She nestled beside him and drifted off soon after.

Aster Mackenzie. Aster Mackenzie. You cannot deny me now. Come to me and give me the proof I must have.

Aster moved the drapes aside and rose from the bed. The drawbridge opened before she reached it. A great gust of warm wind stroked her naked flesh as she stepped outside. The wind lifted her within its tentacles, encircling her and covering her like a cloud.

She floated inside the cloud above and beyond the lagoon.

When her feet touched the ground once again, the cloud and the wind abandoned her in front of a doorway. The door opened and she walked inside.

"You have come, as I knew you would. My powers are as strong as they ever were," the ancient one stated proudly. "Ah, you are a beauty, Aster Mackenzie," he said, as his black eyes surveyed the gifts nature had given her.

Aster remained standing before him, oddly unashamed of her nudity.

"Even one as old as I could be distracted by one who looks like you." The old man removed his purple robe and wrapped it around her. Without it, his shrunken body and hunched back were harshly displayed.

Aster felt his cold, claw-like fingers touch her cheek.

"I am Lamed." His voice was weak and sounded much older than it had earlier that day. "Mem and Nun have agreed that you and Romulus should be given permission to join and govern Innerworld together. However, the final decision must be unanimous. Therefore, your fate is up to me. I am swayed by them but not convinced. An alien in a position of power is not acceptable to me and yet, I sense a quality about you that is not alien at all. It has occurred to me that you could be a descendant of a Noronian sent to Earth many millennia ago. Do you know our history?"

"Yes."

"Your ancestry would not be difficult to discern and

a genetic connection between you and the Noronian people would be reason enough for me to have a change of heart. My mind was already made up against you in this matter. Then you spoke your young, passionate words. You awakened a memory I had believed dead. You spoke of *love* as though it were a living entity. It has been too many years since I held a female's body, soft and warm beneath my own. I had forgotten the deep feelings and emotions of youth. I do not want to die without knowing them again."

His breathing became labored and it took him a moment to continue. "I am not accustomed to talking so much. Even that small act has become very tiring. My purpose in bringing you to me tonight is twofold. The first, as you must realize, is to ascertain your fitness to be Co-Governor of Innerworld. The second is personal. For both, I must touch your mind. In doing so, I will also be able to trace your ancestry.

"I am not a villain, Aster Mackenzie, despite what Romulus fears. Yes, if I were in his position, I would have thought the same thing. I am an honorable man and I assure you, you will remain unchanged. I would like to offer you a compromise. If you agree to let me touch your mind, you may join with Romulus and govern Innerworld together." He paused to catch his breath and Aster held hers.

"I want to be young again, Aster Mackenzie, for one night, and you can do that for me."

"I don't understand."

"Let me possess you this night and you will have all you wish for in the morning."

Aster's eyes widened and she took a backward step to the door. It was as if, up until this moment it had all been a very peculiar dream, but his outrageous request shocked her into wakefulness.

"Ah, you need not be so horrified. Our language is alike but not identical I see. I do not refer to possession in a physical sense. I am afraid even your merest hug would crumble these brittle bones. What I desire is to enter your mind, your private world of hopes and dreams, fears and sorrows, to live anew through your thoughts and feelings. It would not harm you and it would give me new, fond memories to cling to in my final days as a mortal. I want more than to touch your mind and learn the facts of your past and your suitability for Romulus. I want to dwell there and relive your experiences with you. I considered forcing you, but that would not do. You might hold back from me and I need it all. Will you agree?"

Aster opened and closed her mouth several times without being able to form a response. This shriveled, white-haired skeleton was asking permission to crawl around inside her head, vicariously experiencing her memories and feasting on her emotions. It was almost as bad as what she first thought he meant. An image of her afternoon at the lagoon with Romulus flashed before her and she knew he meant to indulge himself with those feelings as well. If she denied him, he would probably cast a negative vote tomorrow. If she agreed...

"Romulus does not want me to allow this. He would surely find out, if not now, then after we're joined."

"If you approve, I can ensure you will have no recollection of our night together. There will be nothing for him to learn."

"Will you tell me one thing and allow me to remember it?"

He nodded.

"Who sent you the communication about Romulus and me?"

Lamed looked at her curiously. He had expected a

deeper question, more philosophical perhaps, but that was the difference about being young and, of course, she was only a Terran after all. "His name is Edward, a career counselor in Car-Tem One. It appears that he expected a commendation and promotion for his loyalty. We have learned of his guilt in other crimes aimed at disparaging Romulus. We do not reward criminals whose jealousy overrules their common sense."

Edward? Jealous? Aster remembered his snide comments about Romulus. Suddenly she pictured him passing a paper to Victor at the dance and knew he had been involved in her kidnapping as well. "I will remember this?"

"Yes, but not how you came by the knowledge. By the time you return to Earth, he will have been exiled to another colony, a cold, remote place, where everything he sees will be ugliness. Only the fact that he is a direct descendant of mine will save him from reprogramming. It grieves me to say he is my great-great-great-grandson and I am somewhat to blame for his crimes. He thought he could impress me by showing that his distaste for Terrans was as great as mine. I was grossly mistaken in my attitude."

Aster believed him and her intuition told her she was safe in Lamed's care. He held no threat for her or Romulus. In fact, she felt very sorry for him. She could not imagine how horrible it would be not to remember any of the emotions that were so familiar to her. She looked into the large dark eyes waiting for her answer.

"Promise me you will not hurt me, nor will you take any existing memory away, nor leave any new thoughts, other than about Edward."

"I so promise."

"And Romulus will never know what has transpired

here?"

"He will not awaken until you are again at his side. I will be the only one with this memory and I will horde it."

"Then I agree."

The slash in his masklike face opened a little wider but it could hardly be called a smile. He sat in a comfortable low chair and directed her to kneel at his feet. His crooked fingers shook as he brought them to her temples and made contact. She forced herself to relax when she heard him sigh and realized she would not be seeing where his journey would take him.

Young Lamed emerged in the playground of Aster's mind. For the remainder of the night he frolicked in green meadows, cried tears of desperation, felt terror and helplessness and the joy of personal achievement. He fell in love and rediscovered depths of passion long forgotten, all while Aster slept dreamlessly.

CHAPTER 24

One sweet bird chirping at dawn could be a very pleasant way to be awakened. However, hundreds of exotic winged creatures screeching and squawking their good mornings was a different matter entirely. Aster and Rom turned their heads toward each other at the same moment and laughed at their mutual reaction to nature's alarm clock.

"Good morning, shallar," Aster said softly. "Apparently, our neighbors think it's time to be up and about."

"Hmmm." Rom shifted to his side and propped himself up on his elbow. "Awake, maybe, but there's no reason to be up and about." He gently kissed her eyelids, her nose, her lips, while his hand crept under the sheet to caress her hip.

Aster returned his touch and warmed to his kisses. Just as he moved against her, the vidcom beeped.

Rom felt Aster stiffen beneath him. "Ignore it," he commanded.

The whole purpose of being in his sanctuary was to be left alone and he returned his attention to his love. But she was distracted by the consistent beeping.

When the vidcom finally switched over to its message mode, Rom's father's voice filled the room.

"Romulus. This is important. I know you can't be asleep. The sun is up and so are the birds, so get out of that bed."

Rom groaned. He would not easily recover his passionate mood with his father talking in the background so he got up and went to the desk.

"And good morning to you too, Father. What's so important?" Rom grumbled in a barely civilized tone. When he saw Aster frown at him, he switched to a more polite tack. "Were you expecting us for breakfast? I didn't realize…"

"No, no, nothing so trivial, son. Turn on your video. Your mother wants to see your face when I tell you the news. I'd have you both come over but we can't wait."

Rom did as requested and instantly his parents appeared on his screen. He unconsciously gripped the arm of his chair as he waited for his father to speak again. There could only be one subject worthy of such prelude. "Well?"

"We can't see Aster. Can she hear me?"

Rom smiled at Aster. Clutching the sheet over her nakedness, shaking her head and waving her hand all at the same time, there was no doubt she preferred not to be seen in her present state. "She can hear you fine. Now will you please get on with it?"

Marcus blurted out his announcement. "The Tribunal sent us a courtesy copy of a message to you. I guess they really wanted to make sure you saw it first thing this morning." An instant later, the message appeared on the screen.

Romulus Locke:

The Ruling Tribunal of Norona is pleased to

confirm the unanimous approval of your appointment as the next Governor of Innerworld, the term of which will commence in ninety days.

Investigation of Aster Mackenzie is completed. It has been verified that she is a descendant of one of the Noronian rebels originally exiled on Outerworld Terra. Her Noronian ancestry was awakened upon contact with her own race. The citizens of Innerworld will be informed.

Felicitations on your upcoming joining.

You will both reappear before the Tribunal three days hence for the swearing-in ceremony.

Lamed/Mem/Nun

Aster let out a cry. Regardless of her lack of attire, she needed to be next to Rom. Hurriedly wrapping the sheet around her, she ran to his arms. On the screen, Marcus and Yulan hugged each other also.

Brushing a happy tear off her cheek, Aster said, "You did it, shallar. You beat the system, as they say in my country."

"You mean, *we* did it, shalla. But I'm stunned. I had such a strong feeling that at least one of them was going to hold to tradition and deny us." He kissed her hard. "We'll be joined tonight. Mother? Father? Do you approve now?"

Yulan turned toward them again. "It was never a question of us approving, Romulus, only one of concern for you both. Let's see, I'll help Marcus rearrange his schedule and you bring Aster to me when you're ready."

"Fine. See you shortly." Rom touched the screen and the picture vanished.

Aster let go of the sheet and threw her arms around Rom's neck, pulling his head down to receive her excited kisses. "I don't know whether to be thrilled or scared. It seems like we've been talking about joining forever." Aster kissed him again then pulled back as she recalled the full message. "What do you think about that business of my having a Noronian ancestor?"

"It helps to explain everything that's happened to you. And since it was a factor in the Tribunal's decision, I'm certainly not going to question it. I hate to admit it but that pronouncement is going to make a difference in how easily some Innerworlders will accept you as Co-Governor. Maybe it won't matter anymore when our children grow up. Let's just be grateful whether it's true or not."

"I will be very grateful, if you will finish what you started, *Governor* Romulus," Aster murmured, her body brushing against his.

As he carried her back to the bed, she considered his casual comment. Yes, there would be children. And like those American immigrants he had once compared her to, the reasons for prejudice against Terrans would begin to dissipate with the mixed blood of the next generation.

Romulus made a concerted effort to love her slowly. It would be the last time they would share their bodies as separate individuals. He wanted it to be as memorable as everything else that would occur that day. Also, he wanted her to be as relaxed and receptive as possible as the events of the day and night unfolded.

The sun was well above the horizon when Aster reminded Rom that Yulan was expecting them. "Shouldn't we be going soon? Where will the ceremony take place? I remember the book said it had to begin at midnight and we are each to spend the day in preparation with one of our own parents. Is that why your mother said to bring me to her? Will she be able to stand in as my mother?"

"Slow down," Rom said with a laugh. "Yes, it will be tonight at midnight. My father and I will erect the necessary structure near here and my mother will bring you to us when it is time. She will provide your joining robe and will spend the day with you reviewing the ritual. It will be a good opportunity for the both of you to get to know each other better. We will have to be on our way soon but I'm not anxious to leave you, even if it is the last separation we will experience."

Aster wondered at the serious expression on his face as he stroked her jaw with his thumb. "What's wrong?"

"I love you so much. I don't know what I would have done if you had continued to refuse me. You know that, don't you?"

"Of course I do, but I didn't, did I? So why are you looking at me like that?" Aster felt the tension growing between them and pulled back to look at him better as he spoke.

"Something very strange and powerful will occur tonight. You're going to experience feelings and sensations unlike anything you've ever felt. You mustn't be frightened of any of it. I'll be feeling the same way but we'll be together through it all."

"What if I can't overcome my fear? Will we be unable to join?"

"No, once the ritual begins, there is no way to stop it. Perhaps I'm worrying over nothing. You see, the drink we will consume at the beginning of the ceremony contains an ingredient that will heighten our senses and our awareness of each other. It also tends to make you feel removed from your physical surroundings. If you accept that as what is supposed to happen, you should have no reason to be afraid."

"An ingredient? It sounds like a drug. I thought Noronians prohibited that sort of thing." Aster pulled slightly away from him. Drugs were one subject that could take precedence over her anxieties.

"It is an *ingredient*, one vital to the ceremony. That's really all I can tell you about it. Since it is only used in the joining ritual, I have never tried it. I do know that without it we would never reach the spiritual level where we must go. I wouldn't agree to anything that would harm you, shalla. Keep in mind, this is my first time too. For all I know, there are things my father will tell me today that are new to me. I have to bide my time as well."

Aster moved close to him again and sighed when his arms encircled her. "You're right, of course. I can do anything as long as you're with me. Whatever it takes, I want you right here." She tapped her temple with her index finger. "Then I won't be frightened of anything ever again."

Rom lifted her face to his and stared for a very long time into her eyes. Although she couldn't read his actual thoughts, she felt his strength and love injecting itself into her mind. She could do it. She had to.

Aster's nerves began to calm within minutes of being left alone with Yulan. The two women exchanged past experiences and plans and hopes for the future. The one common bond between them was their love of Locke men. Aster could not help but compare her life with what it might have been like if this intelligent, caring woman had been her mother. She could not change the past but she could look forward to the pleasure of having Yulan as a mother-in-law in the years ahead. By the time they sat down to dinner, Aster felt as though she had known Yulan her entire life.

"Yulan, how does it feel to have Marcus in your head all the time? On the one hand, I feel that's how it should be. On the other, it's such an alien concept, literally, I have no way of imagining it."

Yulan smiled. "It takes some getting used to, even for a Noronian. Eventually the advantages and mental companionship far outweigh any disadvantages. Aster, what you are doing tonight cannot be reversed in this lifetime. You will still be everything you were before but you will also be reborn as the creation of a new entity that is made up of the both of you. Do you understand that?"

"Yes." There was nothing more for Aster to say.

"Good. Then let's go over the ritual and start getting you ready."

The midnight hour approached. What Aster had expected to be the longest day in her life had sped by.

The scented soap Yulan gave her to bathe with left Aster's skin unusually sensitive. When she slipped the hooded, white caftan over her naked body, she swore she could feel every one of the silken threads in the robe. Aster stared at her reflection in the mirror. A beautiful stranger stood there, with shining silver hair and a soft glow radiating from her face. Only her eyes betrayed the fact that she was scared to death.

If Yulan had not led her by the hand out the door and onto a horse, Aster was positive she would not have made it. Just before they reached the lagoon, they dismounted. Yulan pulled the hood over Aster's hair and took her hand again. With a firm squeeze and a kiss on the cheek, Yulan let Aster know she would be fine.

When they stepped into the clearing, they halted again. Clearly visible in the moonlight was a large tent shaped like a pyramid. Four crystal poles joined at the top. The triangular, white chiffon sides gently billowed in and out from a subtle breeze, while shadows flickered behind the material.

Yulan raised the front flap and motioned for Aster to enter. Her bare feet welcomed the thick woven rug inside as her eyes adjusted to the firelight offered by candles in hurricane-style lamps.

Knowing she was not permitted to look directly at Romulus at this time, Aster kept her head bent. But it was easy enough to recognize his toes peeking out from beneath the hem of a white robe like hers. A glimpse of shoes and pant legs told her Marcus was positioned to Rom's right.

Marcus's voice penetrated the quiet of the shadowy tent. "I, Marcus Locke, mate of Yulan, have come to this place to witness the joining of the son of my body with his chosen mate. Romulus Locke, have you read and understood the sacred words and are you prepared to abide by them for all time, to become one with this woman?"

"I have and I am." Rom's answer was strong and sure and Aster drew courage from the sound.

"I, Yulan, mate of Marcus Locke, stand in the place of a blood relation to Aster Mackenzie. From this moment on, I will call her my daughter and she shall think of me as her mother. I have come to this place to witness the joining of my new daughter with her chosen mate. Aster Mackenzie, have you read and understood the sacred words and are you prepared to abide by them for all time, to become one with this man?"

Aster parted her lips, intending to speak as confidently as Rom had, but the words were a mere whisper. "I have and I am."

"Let it begin," Marcus declared.

Yulan continued to hold Aster's hand as she led her the few steps to a low table. When she felt a slight pressure on her shoulder, Aster sat down cross-legged on one side. With her head still lowered, she saw Rom being seated opposite her. His parents moved to a corner of the structure.

On the table in front of her was a silver chalice filled with a deep burgundy liquid. Aster's hands shook so badly she wondered how she would ever get it to her mouth without spilling any.

When Rom began speaking his vows, Aster flinched involuntarily.

"Aster Mackenzie, only you can satisfy my thirst and my desire. You are all the nourishment I shall ever need." His hand reached out and lifted the chalice, then replaced it, minus half the liquid.

It would only be a few more minutes before she could look up at his face. It had not seemed like it would take this long when she read the words in the book. "Romulus Locke, only you can provide my wants and needs. You are the only solace I shall ever need." Aster swallowed the first half of the drink. In spite of its color, it tasted like peppermint tea.

"Your happiness and comfort is my greatest desire. I choose to spend all my days and nights with you in my life, my heart and my mind." Romulus drained his chalice.

Aster repeated the vow back to him then finished her drink.

A moment later, a cool draft touched her cheek as Marcus and Yulan silently departed through the flap in the pyramid tent. Aster knew it was now time to close her eyes for the period of solitude, the last she would ever know. For the first time in many hours, a feeling of calm settled over her. A swarm of bees buzzed in the distance...or were they in her head? The humming sound seemed to move closer and louder, then dwindle back to near silence before increasing once again. Her body swayed to its rhythm. No, she was not moving at all. It was her blood, pumping, pulsing through her veins and arteries, like the ebb and flow of the ocean's tide. She became intensely aware of the pounding of her heart, of her lungs filling with air and slowly expelling what they did not need. She not only felt it, she began to see it—all the separate parts of her body, working together to create this wondrous thing known as life. She suddenly knew the essence and source of her being and it was incredible.

"Aster?" Rom's voice came to her in an echo reverberating through her head.

He stood beside her with his hands outstretched. Aster placed her hands in his and tilted her head back to gaze with wonder into his love-filled eyes as she rose. He entered her private world and hovered there. They were no longer in the tent or even on Norona. They floated together in space, where time hung suspended until they decided to make it move again.

"That entity which is the soul within Romulus Locke has been searching for its eternal mate. It calls now to the soul within Aster Mackenzie to fulfill their destiny. Are you ready to be joined with us now, Aster?"

"That entity which is the soul within Aster Mackenzie has also been searching and now recognizes its eternal mate. We are here and ready to join with you, Romulus." Her own voice sounded far away, as though it belonged to someone else.

Together their voices harmonized, "We call to the Supreme Being to be the spiritual witness to our joining."

With steady movements, Aster slowly pushed back

Rom's hood, undid the drawstring at his neck and slid the caftan off his shoulders. Without resistance, it fell to his feet. Likewise, Romulus disrobed Aster. They stood two feet apart, their gazes held hypnotically together.

"There can be nothing between us ever again. Your flesh will be my flesh," Rom said.

"Your blood will be my blood," Aster responded.

"Our minds will be as one," they voiced together.

Rom held up his hands, palms facing Aster. She raised her hands to meet his, palms to palms, fingers to fingers. A tremor shook the ground beneath their feet. The vibration moved upward like an electrical current from their toes to their ankles to their knees, through their bodies and into their heads.

The electrical sensation traveled down their arms and settled in their fingertips, where a golden glow appeared and flared. The light spread over their hands and retraced the path the tremor had taken, coiling snakelike, round and round their arms, spinning around their heads then down their bodies until they were bathed in the burning, golden iridescence.

The hum that had subsided suddenly became a deafening crescendo making any specific thought impossible.

Each moved their hands along the other's arms, fingertips straining forward of their own accord until they located the other's temples and pressed there.

The mundane limitations of time and space were suspended as their individualities were transformed and reborn as a brilliant, blended union of their souls.

Without breaking contact, Rom eased Aster onto the carpeted earth and hovered above her. She could not have broken their eye contact had she wanted to.

He thrust.

She absorbed.

Their hips melded and parted and came together again and again. Aster felt him inside her, all around her. Her body altered. She was larger, harder, pushing into the soft, moist cushion of...herself. It was Rom's sensations she was feeling now, not her own. No, that wasn't quite right. *I feel the both of us together, at the same time.*

Magnificent!

Oh...oh yes...now!

Tumbling, swirling, falling through a starlit sky, Aster and Rom raced together through their lives. They were the child, Rom, playing knights and dragons. They were the young girl, Aster, running barefoot in a field of daisies. They relived the years they were individuals and the hours since they met, the good and the bad.

The hum gradually faded then disappeared altogether. A gust of wind entered, whirled over them and departed, taking the candlelight with it.

I love you, Aster.

I love you, Romulus.

You're all right. I was so worried.

I know. It was wonderful. It is wonderful. Aster glanced quickly around the pyramid tent, half surprised to realize they were still there. *I thought it was good before, but now, well, all I can think is, we'd better try it again, to make sure we're doing it right.*

Rom laughed deeply as he nuzzled her ear. Aster instantly felt her anticipation turn to need inside his body, which in turn fed her own building desire. She wondered if they would be able to control their passion for one another as time went by.

I hope not, shalla. But we may have to work on controlling our baser thoughts when we're out in public or I'm afraid we may both be embarrassed with the results. Rom proceeded to show her exactly what results he had in mind.

EPILOGUE

"Congratulations, Aster. He's a very good man," Tarla said sincerely as she shook Aster's hand then laughed when she added, "almost as perfect as my Nick." Now that Romulus and Aster had forced a change of attitude from the Tribunal, Tarla felt completely free to follow her heart's desire as well. She would be moving to the mining camp next week to be with Nick, openly and without fear of reprisal.

Aster scanned the faces of the friends and acquaintances gathered in the reception room of the Dance Hall. The Feinsteins were like two teenagers again as their restaurant gained popularity. The Basiglios had barely said hello before sharing their happy news that their first attempt at conception had been a success. Yes, there was certainly an abundance of happiness in this room tonight.

Then again, wasn't that what Rom had promised all the Outerworlders that first day?

You will not only accept, you will enjoy what we have to offer, Rom thought to her with a chuckle.

You were listening.

Of course. And that should remind you to behave

when you're with other men, especially well-meaning trackers.

Aster met his gaze across the crowded room. He knew about her interlude with Falcon and it was all right. *You're just jealous because Tarla only shook your hand when she greeted you tonight and Falcon hugged me.*

Aha! So you were paying attention. You're getting better. I couldn't even tell. By the way, did you see Frank and Marya yet?

No, I...

"Hey, kid!" Cherry tugged insistently on Aster's forearm. "Wasn't three weeks in outer space enough for you two? You've got to make eyes at each other at your own party!"

Aster turned away from Rom quickly and hugged Cherry as hard as she could. "You! How in the world did you put this together so fast? We only arrived this morning!"

"You know me. Where there's a will and so on. To tell the truth though, the entire colony knew you were on your way back with shocking news a week ago. Plus, I had plenty of help from Apollo and Thor."

"Speaking of which, I never did hear the outcome of your dilemma."

"Oh, that's right. Well, if you hadn't flitted off to a faraway galaxy—"

"Cherry! What happened?"

"Let's just say they convinced me to give the Innerworld attitude toward intimate relationships a try."

Aster's eyebrows shot up then she gave a shrug and smiled. "I'm not surprised. You're nowhere near ready to settle down. But I have a really strong feeling that one of these days, someone will come along to change that. By the way, have you seen Falcon?"

"He's right over there. Talk about one delicious alien. Too bad he's not interested in anything I have to offer. By the way, he was a big help pulling this off too."

Aster looked in the direction Cherry pointed. Falcon's luminous eyes touched her like a blessing. He would always be her friend.

Governor Elissa too. As soon as they had disembarked, the governor had filled Aster and Rom in on all the reports that had been transmitted from Outerworld during their absence. A monumental discovery had been made by Professor David Ingram that would greatly increase the speed of Earth's spaceships. It was decided in a special session of the United Nations Security Council that its permanent members would conduct a joint exercise into space to test his discovery within the month. As David had predicted, there was no public mention of the planetoid.

Aster hoped that someday in the near future, she would receive a confirmation that the personal favors she had requested of Kate had been taken care of just as successfully. Romulus had acknowledged that Aster hadn't actually broken her promise to him. That, however, did not keep him from grumbling about devious women for several long minutes after he realized what she had done to salvage The Mackenzie Foundation.

At that moment the background music was cut off and the silence brought her out of her reverie. There was a clinking of glass and Aster turned toward the sound.

"May I please have everyone's attention?" Governor Elissa's voice rang out clearly. All heads turned her way. "Romulus, Aster, would you step forward? I would like to make a toast to our two guests of honor. A joining is always cause for celebration but this one is unusually special. Not only have they saved our world at the risk of their own lives but their joining, a Noronian and a Terran, marks the beginning of a new age for Innerworld.

"Ladies and gentlemen, it is my great pleasure to introduce to you the next Co-Governors of Innerworld." Grasping each of their hands, Elissa raised their arms high above her head then joined Rom's and Aster's hands and stepped back.

Amidst a roomful of applause, Rom and Aster kissed briefly but passionately then Romulus spoke to the small crowd. "Thank you all for sharing our joy tonight. Now, I'd like to ask you all to raise your glasses one more time."

He and Aster raised their own glasses and spoke their toast together. "Here's to all our friends, old and new. May your lives always be filled with love, light and adventure!"

Turn the page for an

excerpt from

FALCON

Innerworld Affairs Series
Book Two

Marilyn Campbell

Ring! Steve's hand lashed out for the receiver before the telephone had another chance to sound its alarm.

"G'mornin'," she mumbled through what felt like a mouth full of alcohol-dried cotton.

"Don't tell me you're just waking up! In case you've forgotten, today is Thursday, not Saturday or Sunday." Dokes was teasing, of course. He knew very well that with her two young children she was always up with the sun.

Steve forced one eye open to look at her watch. Eight o'clock already. "Oh, gawd! Let me call you right back, Lou. Ten minutes, okay?"

She hung up, glancing briefly at the other bed where Falcon began to stir. Quickly, she headed for the bathroom, deciding to put off facing him for a few more minutes. As she splashed cold water on her face, she assessed her physical condition. Her head pounded ferociously but some aspirin would take care of that. Stomach queasy but not rebellious. Juice, coffee and toast should help. She had not had so much to drink since the night her divorce was finalized and now she remembered why not. Hopefully, Falcon was the understanding sort. He had told her at dinner he never drank alcoholic beverages. So now he had proven he was faster, stronger, more professional *and* smarter.

Slowly, she opened the door, preparing her apology as she did so, but the words never left her mouth. Falcon stood by the bed with his back to her—his perfectly sculpted, very naked back.

Steve knew the polite thing would be for her to turn away or to clear her throat so he would be aware of her presence in the room, but that would be like one of her children giving back a lollipop after taking the first lick.

She was totally awed by how magnificent his body was, from his wide, solid shoulders, down his muscled back, to his toned thighs and calves. Perfectly molded buttocks flexed as he bent over to slide one long leg into his slacks. No wonder she had felt every intimate inch of him so clearly. He wore no underwear.

The back of Falcon's body was flawlessly smooth, like his chest and arms. If he had any body hair, it was so blond and fine it was unnoticeable. Steve understood American Indians had little or no body hair but Falcon said he was from Wales. She could not help wonder if he turned around—

Then he did...just as his fingers closed the waistband on his designer-quality fitted trousers. Steve instantly felt her whole body warm under his shockingly hungry gaze that swept from her head to her bare toes. An image of the white tiger in the garden flashed in her mind.

Steve's heart picked up its pace as she realized her cotton nightshirt hid very little and her nipples instantly puckered in response. She had the distinct impression he had been aware of her appreciative scrutiny and was returning the compliment. Unlike her, however, he didn't appear to be the least bit embarrassed.

"Good morning, Steve," he said in the resonant voice that stroked her like a velvet glove. "That shirt looks familiar. I believe I like the way you wear it better." He gave her a crooked grin and turned around again as he donned his black shirt.

Steve couldn't be positive, but it sounded like he was actually making a joke. Damn! His lack of a sense of humor was the one thing she thought she could find fault with him. As she rooted through her bag for clean clothes and a toothbrush, she decided to get the worst of her discomfort out of the way.

"Uh, Falcon, I want to apologize for last night. I know getting drunk was stupid and it's hardly an excuse for behaving so badly. I mean, it was very unprofessional of me and I assure you nothing like that will happen again. I was just really excited about the money and—"

"It is quite all right," he cut in. "Please do not upset yourself further about it. Was the call important?"

"It was Lou. I told him I'll call him back." Steve headed for the bathroom then turned back to him. "Wait a minute. Why should I be the one apologizing here? After all I'm not the one who started it. You did! In the desert. You kissed me twice without my invitation." Hell, she had enough to feel guilty about without feeling bad about something that was not *all* her fault.

"I did not start the fight, Steve. You did."

"There's a hell of a lot of difference between fighting and kissing!"

"Yes. And I have decided I like kissing much better."

"I don't give a damn what you like better. You owe

me an apology."

"No."

She blinked in surprise. "And why not?"

"I am not sorry. As I said before, you taste very interesting. I do believe, however, that we should refrain from such activity during our search as it does tend to be distracting."

"We should *refrain*? Of all the cocky, macho..." Steve was across the room in four big strides and, with a frustrated grunt, she shoved him onto his bed. "You just keep your hands and your mouth to yourself and we'll do fine, because I have no intention of touching you again, even for a much-deserved punch in the nose." In a huff she disappeared into the bathroom, slamming the door behind her.

Falcon sat staring at the closed door and could not help but chuckle. Steve was upset with him but she still felt attracted to him. What a fascinating contradiction. In spite of the fact that he had spent most of the night reminding himself why he had to keep his distance from her, he had to admit being around Stephanie Barbanell was too much fun for him to keep his distance from her. He had never considered that this journey to Outerworld would be as entertaining as it was educational.

FALCON

available in print and ebook

THE
INNERWORLD AFFAIRS
SERIES

Romulus
Falcon
Gallant
Gabriel
Logan
Roman

MARILYN CAMPBELL has been published in the genres of suspense, erotic thrillers, futuristic, time-travel, paranormal, erotic and lighthearted contemporary romances, non-fiction metaphysical works and has had a screenplay produced. A true thrill-junkie, she has jumped out of an airplane, raced around the Indy 500 track, driven solo throughout the United States and believes a great roller coaster ride can cure whatever ails her. She currently resides in Massachusetts with her daughter and their four-legged companions, Milk-Dud and Sweetie.

www.ingramcontent.com/pod-product-compliance
Lightning Source LLC
Chambersburg PA
CBHW020638030726
47498CB00002B/266